A VIRTUOUS LIE

A VIRTUOUS LIE

Sam Halpern

BookLocker

St. Petersburg, Florida

DEDICATION

To my mother, and my sisters, Debby and Naomi, who always believed in me when I sometimes failed to believe in myself.

ACKNOWLEDGMENTS

My thanks to the members of The Monday Morning Club, Louise Goodman, Pat Maxwell, Annette Winter, Bess Tittle and Elsie Zala, without whose literary criticism this book would not have been published.

Special thanks to Tah'jai Sullivan for his definition of forgiveness.

CHAPTER 1

Devon Emmanuel was lost. The rental car's GPS had failed shortly after he left the rental agency, and he was navigating by a brochure given him at the counter. The hand-sized map showed a maze of large and small streets, some names printed at angles, the type nearly unreadable. An eighteen-wheeler blocked his frontal vision, and cars flashed past in adjoining lanes, allowing him only seconds to check the off-ramp signs. He clutched the steering wheel, feeling sweat on his palms and physical discomfort as the subcompact he was driving scrunched his six-foot-two-inch body. Occasionally amid the multitude of vehicles, concrete overpasses, and July smog, he could see distant mountains.

Where is the city? How can people build a city without a downtown?

Downtowns made Devon feel secure. He loved his Manhattan. To him, Manhattan was a concrete security blanket. Los Angeles was a recipe for insanity.

A car cut him off. He hit the brakes hard, bringing a screech and a horn blast from the car behind. He steadied the wheel and tried to remain calm.

It seemed like hours since he had left his hotel, a journey of frustrating mistakes. Then just as he made the decision to get off the freeway for the third time and ask directions, he saw the exit sign he had been looking for. He needed to get in the right-hand lane. He moved timidly, irritating a driver who shot past and made an obscene gesture. Leaving the freeway madness, Devon pulled against a curb and parked. Sleepless hours on the red-eye had sucked his energy. He found the seat-adjustment lever, pressed it, closed his eyes, and felt his body morph into a semi-recumbent position. He took a deep breath, exhaled slowly, and relaxed.

Alessandra Gittleman, Alessandra Gittleman, Alessandra Gittleman… a whole night flying at 35,000 feet, trying to learn something about Alessandra Gittleman with the plane's Wi-Fi going down frequently. Court cases by the dozens were associated with her name, constant battles with people and institutions, but almost zero personal information. Famous, and yet, as unknown and mysterious as a jungle-hidden Mayan temple.

God, I'm tired. Four hours' notice. Four hours!

The argument with his wife before leaving New York suddenly emerged from his fatigued mind. He visualized ten-year-old David and fourteen-year-old Sarah peeking around the edge of the living room as their parents yelled at one another.

"How could you! How could you consent to leave tonight? We agreed I would always have a week's notice before you left town so I could arrange for help with the children! How many times have you done this, Devon? My work is important to me. Everything is about you! You and your precious *Walden!*"

"Sonja, they didn't give me any choice. I suggested other writers. They said this was a critical assignment and insisted I had to be the one who did the interview. I told them this would play havoc with my family and – "

"– immediately caved. If courage is a lion, Devon, you're a gerbil. How many days?"

"I have to make the goddam living! Do you expect us to live on what you make?"

"How many days?"

"Eight – nine – ten – I'm not sure. If everything goes right, I might be able to cut – "

"I don't want to hear it! Go! Do your interview. Nine days, Devon! Nine days, and I expect you back here. Furthermore, while you're gone, I'm going to work whatever hours the museum needs me!"

Devon's eyes snapped open as anger flooded his body. He brought the driver's seat into the upright position. He needed to get back on the road, but it was hard to push Sonja out of his mind.

Sonja! He couldn't stand the woman, yet every time he considered dissolving the marriage, he discovered reasons why he shouldn't. He could no longer remember all the reasons.

"There's no way out until the kids graduate high school," he muttered under his breath, as if reminding himself. He began adding up the years before escape was possible; then he erupted in a burst of body movement.

The appointment! Christ, I'm late!

CHAPTER 2

Devon began driving again, looking about anxiously as his car moved farther away from the freeway and deeper into a hodgepodge of small businesses and modest homes. From the short briefing he had received, he knew the interview was to take place in East L.A., an area his editor had warned him was a drug-infested neighborhood he was to make certain he left before dark. The surroundings looked seedy enough to be violent, but he had seen worse in New York. He glanced at the map and recognized the name of a street. Only a few miles from his destination! Rejuvenated, he began driving faster, taking care to avoid the occasional grocery-basket-pushing, rag-clad man or woman.

Proximity to his objective forced him to consider his assignment again – an in-depth feature story on a seventy-four-year-old lawyer named Alessandra Gittleman. A legal friend of his editor had described her as having been very beautiful in her younger years, adding that she always dressed fashionably for court appearances. It was said of her by opposing attorneys, the friend offered, that she looked like Aphrodite and fought like Attila. Devon had heard of Gittleman, actually knew a little of her reputation, but the editor's briefing had intrigued him.

In Alessandra Gittleman's demands for justice for poor women, she had offended most of America's power structure. The objects of her wrath were usually California district attorneys, judges, mayors, governors, and the legislature. However, federal officials, both houses of Congress, and a variety of federal administrators were also victims of her venom. She had once referred to a sitting American President as a "greedy, mindless, war-mongering piece of Texas cow shit." That particular evaluation had been captured and aired on NPR, the station gallantly blocking the offending noun but leaving the "Texas cow" antecedent to vest the bleep with excremental clarity.

Alessandra was also egalitarian. Along with individuals both rich and poor, a variety of institutions, especially those she considered guilty of hypocrisy, were sometimes her targets. This had brought outraged rhetoric from the local rabbinate who accused her of being a self-loathing Jew. She had responded to the latter accusation in a letter to the editor of a major newspaper, stating she had been born and reared Italian Catholic and had later married a Jew, hence the name Gittleman, and that further, the Jews of Los Angeles had turned into a group of wealthy insular heretics whom the prophet Samuel would have urged God to strike dead.

The Los Angeles Christian community, she asserted in the same letter, would have been disowned by Christ. She ended her comments by saying that the Bishop of the Los Angeles Diocese had used and abandoned the Hispanic community, and that the Catholic Church was an uncaring, self-serving, corporate evil.

Retaliation by the offended parties became the order of the day in Alessandra's early years; then her opponents learned the true meaning of the boxing phrase "low blow." What invariably followed a hostile response to a Gittleman attack was publication of embarrassing information she had gathered and held in wait for the purpose of maximizing her critics' pain if rhetoric escalated to action.

Regardless of the consequences, many attempts to retaliate had been made by the powers that ruled California and the nation. Alessandra Gittleman had been investigated by the Los Angeles Police Department, California Attorney General's Office, United States Secret Service, and, of course, the FBI, the last attempting to follow her funding to a source of disrepute. The hunt for malfeasance had been unsuccessful. Her nonprofit organization received no public funds, and she refused donations from all corporations, existing on her own funds, court-ordered settlements and contributions from the occasional true believer.

Amid this turmoil, Alessandra Gittleman, a woman considered by some a saint, by others the devil incarnate, lived and worked in near-monastic isolation. She was reputed to sleep on a cot in her headquarters, a building situated in the heart of what was perceived to be one of the most dangerous areas of Los Angeles. She rarely left the building except to go to court or occasionally to a restaurant she especially enjoyed where a table was kept in perpetual reserve for her, a perk conveyed as a grateful gesture by the restaurant's owner.

Of all California citizens and some non-citizens who loved Alessandra Gittleman, no group was as devoted to her as the Hispanic women of Los Angeles. She had served them faithfully for thirty-eight years. It was thought by many of the women (even though Gittleman was a professed atheist) that she had been touched by the Lady of Guadalupe. Gittleman's services, however, were rendered to all women in need of her assistance, regardless of race, religion or citizenship.

To anyone's knowledge, she had never granted an in-depth interview. Never in thirty-eight years. Until now.

CHAPTER 3

Devon's initial impression of the neighborhood was inexorably reinforced with each grungy mile. Many buildings had bars on the windows and doors. Had it not been for indecipherable spray-painted graffiti, the environs would have been devoid of color. Even the vegetation was drought-ravaged brown. Adding to the effect of this stark world on Devon's psyche was his urgent need for a bathroom.

Suddenly, a white two-story building appeared. The structure had the architectural elegance of a cardboard box, yet the chain-link fence surrounding it was covered with beautifully kept bougainvillea, and the yard beyond was filled with playground equipment and happy, squealing children. An island of vibrant civilization in a barren, dangerous world.

Devon checked the street address. He had arrived. He began looking for a place to park along a street that was lined with rusty automobiles, some extending two feet from the curb. The first available space was nearly a half-mile down the road.

A hot, smoggy walk later, Devon approached the building, the heavy valise containing his equipment causing him occasionally to switch carrying arms. The wooden entrance door was arched at the top and would have been recognized by the inhabitants of a Tolkien novel.

Architect had the imagination of a gnat...sense of humor though.

Devon lowered his head to enter the building. The interior momentarily stunned him. He had expected law offices. What he found was...he didn't know. Fifteen feet inside the door of a huge white-walled room stood a four-by-six-foot desk. The front of the desk bore an impressionistic painting of an American eagle flying through a blue cloudless sky. Far below the eagle were mountains and rivers. An engraved placard on top of the desk read:

CASE
Center for American Social Equality

A middle-aged Hispanic woman sat hunched over the desktop doing needlework. Her hands moved swiftly, the long sleeves of her colorful dress rippling as the muscles of her arms contracted beneath them. As Devon approached, the woman looked up and scanned his face.

"May I help you, sir?" she asked, with a slight Hispanic accent.

"I'm looking for CASE headquarters. From the sign on your desk, I assume I've found it."

The woman smiled. "You have, *Señor*. I am Anita Salazar. How may I help you?"

Devon felt the switch from "sir" to "*señor*" probably had significance, but ignored the nuance. "My name is Devon Emmanuel. I have an appointment with Mrs. Gittleman. I'm late."

The receptionist picked up the telephone receiver and hit a button. "He's here, *Señora*...Okay." She hung up and smiled at Devon. "She is expecting you. Go to the top of the stairs at the back of the room, and she will meet you."

Devon studied the room as he walked. The huge open space extended well beyond the reception desk. Four support columns, each altered to look as if they had been imported from ancient Greece, split the room.

To his left, over-filled bookcases lined much of the wall. Devon recognized a Dr. Seuss protruding beyond the other volumes. A bulletin board and a large toy bin were positioned at the end of the bookcases. In most of the bare white plaster areas between the bookcases were floor-to-ceiling murals of children playing in wildly colorful costumes frequently associated with Latin America. Tables, some seating four, others larger, were surrounded by folding chairs filled with kids reading or writing or talking quietly with young adults, most of whom looked Hispanic and appeared to be functioning as combination babysitters and tutors. Between the tables, small children played with toys. Other than a murmur of voices, the room was remarkably quiet. The left half of the room ended in a small, red-white-and-blue striped bathroom. Devon's urgent need for a urinal increased.

The right half of the room was so different from the left that it presented as non-musical counterpoint. It was populated entirely by adult women. In keeping with the children's side of the room, the white plaster walls here also bore murals, one a vast panorama of the Grand Canyon, and a few feet beyond it, Greek islands rising above a spectacular Aegean sea. The effect was peaceful. Two large bookcases, filled to capacity, stood near the center of the space. Small tables, each with a laptop computer, were scattered about and occupied by individuals working intensely, occasionally beckoning help from wandering adults. All but two of the wanderers – one black, the other white – appeared to be Hispanic and middle-aged.

At the back of the room, in the center, loomed the staircase. It was not elegant, but the polished hardwood was pleasant to the eye. To the right of the staircase was a small open kitchen, and in the corner of the room, another bathroom with a sign on the door saying "*Adultos.*" Devon eyed it longingly.

Suddenly the hum of activity stopped. Chair movements caused Devon to turn. Every adult and child in the room was standing and staring. He followed their gaze. Above him, at the top of the staircase, stood a woman in a simple purple shift buttoned high at the neck and extending to her knees. She was perhaps five-foot-eight, thin, with an attractive figure and light olive complexion. Black hair with a hint of gray, a bit unkempt, was parted on the left with gentle waves caught on the right in a long slender clip as they tumbled nearly to her shoulders. Her wide oval hairline gave fullness to her forehead, framing a face Devon could only describe as beautiful – perfectly angled cheekbones; a straight, but not sharp nose; full lips that looked as if they were toying with a smile, and brown eyes crowned by brows a Hollywood make-up artist might have admired. The only jewelry she wore was a heavy gold chain, at the end of which was a large gold medallion that rested atop her breast.

The woman fixed Devon with eyes that made him feel as if she could see the back of his skull.

"Are you from *Walden*?" she asked quietly.

"Yes, I'm sorry I'm – "

"– late," she said, finishing his sentence. "Go use the bathroom and come up."

Embarrassed, Devon headed for the bathroom, locking the door once inside. The facility was immaculate. A large mirror sparkled above two white sinks. Several small framed pictures, most of them desert or mountain scenes, dotted the white walls.

Devon relieved himself, cleaned a careless drop of urine from the porcelain toilet edge, washed his hands, then stood in front of the mirror drying them on a paper towel. He tried, with modest success, to smooth the travel-induced wrinkles in his dark tan sport coat, then straightened his blue, thin-striped tie.

The image of the person on the stairs revisited his mind. If that woman was Gittleman, she was not what he had expected, even though the persona fit her history. Her manner offended him, and his anger began to grow.

She could have suggested I use the bathroom if needed, instead of ordering me in front of women and kids.

Devon swept back his dark, barely graying hair and inspected his face. He hadn't had time to shave after checking into the hotel, but the slight stubble was acceptable. What he also saw was a long, angular face he had discovered women admired for its cragginess. It matched his tall, lean frame. He had used those features to charm many female interviewees into revealing information they might otherwise have kept secret. This old woman, he thought as he straightened his tie again, would be as susceptible to his good looks as the rest of them.

This is my interview and it's going to be done my way. I'm not going to put up with bullshit!

CHAPTER 4

Devon rapped on the door at the top of the stairs, feeling physically relieved, but still humiliated. The woman's eyes, their seeming x-ray quality, and the fact that people behind him had stood in silence in her presence, burned in his brain.

"Jesus sweet Christ," he whispered to himself, uncomfortably aware that he was being watched. "You'd think this was Buckingham Palace and the Queen of England was granting me an audience."

Indeed, the woman who had stood at the top of the stairs had seemed regal. It wasn't just the way she looked; it was the feeling she engendered – as though somehow she were obliging the world with the right to accept her arrogance – a God-given permission to guide the purpose of humans.

Things – are – going – to – change!

There was no response to Devon's initial knock, so he rapped harder. Footsteps, then the door opened.

She stood in his imagination like a female power figure in a Brontë novel. Her eyes, large, dark, and swimming in a white sea, continued to exhibit the peculiar penetrating quality he had felt earlier. He opened his mouth to speak. He couldn't. He willed his body to move. It wouldn't. Rage welled in him that he could be denied these fundamental properties of life by another human. Yet he remained frozen at the door.

His tormentor smiled slightly, took a drag off a cigarette, then exhaled while extending her hand. "Come in, Mr. Emmanuel," she said. "I'm Alessandra Gittleman."

The voice was soft, but it empowered him to move. This further enraged him. He shook the proffered hand and entered past her without introducing himself. The slight wasn't intentional; he forgot to speak.

"Take the seat at the far end of the coffee table," she called as he walked into the interior. "The recliner on this side of the table is mine."

Devon moved toward the center of a spacious apartment that had been constructed without partitions. Subdued lighting gave him the feeling of having entered a cavern or the interior of a medieval castle, the effect further enhanced by bare off-white walls and a high ceiling supported by large open beams. Part of the room held pieces of dark, elegant furniture set amid abundant clutter. Cardboard boxes predominated, with names written on their sides in large block letters. Some boxes were stacked atop one another; others were open with the contents arranged in piles. Behind Devon's assigned chair was an unremarkable dining room set and three doors he assumed hid a bathroom, kitchen, and perhaps a closet.

Before taking his seat in a brown, frumpy, coffee-stained, overstuffed armchair, Devon set down his equipment valise and scanned the old, somewhat battered table. He eased into the chair. The cushions slowly mushed downward, carrying his body with them. His head was little more than three feet above the floor when his descent ended.

He searched the cluttered side of the room for the cot on which the owner reportedly slept. It wasn't in view. Neither was there evidence of a bedroom. Floor-to-ceiling bookcases, mostly of dark wood, lined the walls. Two other bookcases were about four feet high. On top of one of them was a large framed photograph of a middle-aged man and an extraordinarily beautiful young woman. The man was tall and dressed in a white t-shirt, jeans, sneakers and a blue baseball cap. The woman was similarly dressed, except for a long-sleeved turtleneck top. The couple's arms were around each other's waists. In the background was the Grand Canyon.

While Devon reconnoitered, his hostess sat on the edge of her recliner and silently observed him. Finally, she spoke.

"Mr. Emmanuel, do you have a problem with speech?"

Devon, who hadn't said anything since the door opened, was startled.

"Ahh... no! I apologize for not introducing myself," he said, laughing nervously. "I'm Devon Emmanuel – the journalist *Walden Magazine* sent to interview you. If I'm acting strange, it's because I'm jet-lagged and tired. I spent over an hour trying to find CASE."

Alessandra nodded, and Devon watched the recliner begin to morph as the occupant pushed herself further into it and fingered the controls. When the recliner stopped, it had assumed a gentle "S" shape, and Alessandra's eyes were slightly above his own eye level.

The failure of his hostess to respond to his comment bothered Devon. He attempted to clarify, his voice betraying his pique.

"I'm a New Yorker; we're not used to driving, especially in the type of traffic one encounters on a Los Angeles freeway." He paused and waited for acknowledgment. None was forthcoming. "I was given this assignment late yesterday and haven't had time to do a lot of background research on CASE or you. Hopefully, you'll fill me in as we go."

Still without comment, his subject absently re-arranged her recliner, bringing it into a near chair-like position. When the recliner stopped, she slipped off one of her black pumps by pressing down on the heel of one shoe with the toe of the other shoe. Then, with stocking-covered toes, she freed the other foot. This accomplished, she wiggled her feet up and down, crossed her legs at the ankles and asked in a casual tone, "What exactly do you know about me and my work?"

The question was delivered coldly, yet Devon was grateful for the opening.

"I know of your efforts on behalf of disadvantaged women in Los Angeles, and your battles with authority figures. I know nothing about you personally, or about how CASE functions, although I have heard of it."

Alessandra inhaled, then breathed away the last puff of her cigarette, dubbing it out in a small, half-filled amber ashtray that sat on a wooden end table beside her recliner. A *Mona Lisa* smile spread slyly across her lips.

"Got you out here fast, did they?"

Ahh! She smiled. Thank you, God.

"On the red-eye. I think the pilot flew New York to Los Angeles by way of Bangkok."

She laughed. It was a laugh Devon imagined an actress might use if she were playing the part of a strong woman in a male-dominated movie. Hearty, yet feminine. He liked it. His subject was only a few feet from him now and he could see details he had missed earlier. Her skin was smooth, almost young, with only a smattering of fine wrinkles. Indeed, the appearance of youth embraced her entire face. Yet for all her physical attributes, there was a kind of nonchalance about her personal appearance. She wore little makeup. Devon's mother would have called her purple dress a *shmatteh*. Yet on Alessandra, it was attractive.

While Devon assessed, Alessandra was content to calmly sit. She removed a cigarette from a pack on the table and muttered, "Got you out here before the old broad could change her mind."

"Maybe," Devon answered, not quite sure if he had been asked a question. Then he immediately worried he'd agreed with her assertion that she was an "old broad."

Alessandra laughed again, picked up a cigarette lighter from the table, and held it out to him. Devon lifted his body to the edge of the marshmallow-pillowed chair, leaned across the coffee table and lit her cigarette. In the process, he caught sight of liquor bottles in a cabinet. He had missed those in his original survey of the cluttered side of the room. The glass doors of the cabinet were closed, and he was too far away to read the liquor labels. The bottles were of unusual shape, however, the kind high-end distilleries sometimes used for their signature products.

Wonder if she's a chain-smoking lush. But if she's an alcoholic, how can she look like this? Seventy-four-year-old drunks do not look like forty-something movie stars.

He breathed deeply through his nose and detected a faint scent that penetrated the tobacco smoke. He was about to ascribe it to alcohol when he recognized the aroma as one he had smelled before, bath soap or bath gel. The kind that evokes a feminine essence. Vanity! Something he could deal with! It comforted him. He slid back in the marshmallow chair and let his body sag into the cushions. The sounds of children at play wafted musically through the room.

Must be recess.

The thought startled him. He had to get the interview underway.

CHAPTER 5

Alessandra puffed her cigarette and spoke as she exhaled. "You seemed very tense when you arrived, Mr. Emmanuel. I sense your apprehension goes beyond Los Angeles traffic. Perhaps your editor at *Walden* described me as a fire-breathing dragon?"

Devon shook his head and smiled.

Try Dracula.

"I was made to understand you were a – plain-spoken woman."

Alessandra's laugh – loud, head back, mouth open – was pure Betty Davis. "I can imagine. Who did you offend to merit this assignment?"

Devon was a little shaken by his subject's assumption that he was pressured into taking the assignment, especially since she was right. His editor's instructions ran through his mind: "Gittleman's work is familiar to the majority of people who read *Walden*, but nobody knows shit about her personally. She never gives interviews, much less requests one. She's difficult, so let her talk about whatever she wants. But remember, it's her life story we're after. Above all else, get her life story! When we edit, we'll cut whatever bullshit she wants to a couple of pages."

Devon had agreed to let Alessandra lead the interview as long as he thought it was reasonable to do so.

"This assignment was considered a plum," Devon lied, wriggling about in the marshmallow chair in an attempt to get comfortable. "I'm curious. Something my editor told me before I left New York."

"What?"

"That you never gave any in-depth interviews until now, and this one you requested."

Alessandra glanced down and re-arranged the top of her dress, speaking as she made the adjustments. "Twenty years ago…perhaps twenty…I requested an interview with a college newspaper to discuss the state's increase in university fees and its effect on minority students.'

'Did you like the article?"

"I never read it."

"Why not?"

A Virtuous Lie

Alessandra shook her head. "When was the last time you heard of a college newspaper making a difference in public policy? The interview was a waste of time."

"Will you read this one?"

Alessandra dubbed out her cigarette and spoke in a quick, business-like manner. "Probably not, unless you get going on this interview. Now, as to how we're going to proceed. I'm behind in my work, so we'll be sandwiching this interview between my other demands. Are you prepared to deal with that?"

Devon struggled free of the marshmallow chair and reached for his valise.

"I can stay as long as nine days. I've been a print journalist for seventeen years; I know how to pace myself. Just keep me posted on your schedule."

His answer brought raised eyebrows from Alessandra.

Time to impress the lady.

Devon removed multiple items from the valise and placed them on the table.

"This module," he said, picking up a rectangular piece of equipment, "is more than an ordinary recording device. It allows for high-quality sound, simultaneously converts the audio into text and transfers both to my own and my editor's computer in New York. In real time. Is that acceptable to you?"

Alessandra tilted her head to the side. "Will your editor be interrupting us, and will anyone other than you and your editor be privy to the information as it's being recorded?"

"No."

Shrug. "We've got that confidentiality agreement your editor signed, anyway, so I suppose it's a moot point."

Devon tested the microphone that projected from a headset to the corner of his mouth. His words appeared on a small screen on the module and he could hear the playback. He tested Alessandra's microphone while having her move about the room. Again perfect, and the computer in New York signaled that everything was functioning properly at *Walden*.

"Ready?"

Alessandra nodded and sighed. "Is there any more junk I have to wear?"

"No more junk."

Not exactly impressed by cutting-edge technology.

"Before we start, Mrs. Gittleman, you need to know that your mike will record your voice far better than any ambient sound. That means if we want to engage another person in the interview, we'll have to fit them with their own microphone. I have enough for eight people."

Alessandra hesitated, then said, "One more thing: only information on the recording is to appear in the article. You can use what you see and hear at CASE for background, but no specifics that would identify people by their stories or names. Understood?"

"Of course. Let's get started. The following is an interview with Ms.–"

"Mrs."

"Mrs...Alessandra Gittleman, which is taking place in Mrs. Gittleman's residence at CASE headquarters in Los Angeles on the date and time recorded."

"Mrs. Gittleman, I'd like to begin with some basic information about CASE, rather than starting with the usual personal items."

"All right."

"Did you establish CASE, or was it already a functioning entity when you took over?"

Alessandra fingered the controls of her recliner and shifted her body into a new position.

"I started CASE thirty-eight years ago this summer."

Clock chimes rang and Devon looked about, trying to find the source.

"It's nothing," Alessandra said. "That clock chimes whenever it chooses and rarely on the hour."

Devon had lost his train of thought and struggled to recover. When he felt comfortable, he continued. "How did you start CASE? Was it something you envisioned when you were going to law school?"

"You mean nonprofit law for indigent women?"

"If that's the kind of law you practice."

Alessandra scanned Devon's face. When she answered, she sounded edgy.

"When I got out of law school, my interest was criminal law. When I came to California, I switched to what I do now and started CASE."

Seventeen years' experience told Devon his subject was getting tense. She had drawn back from him, pushing herself into the recliner. Her arms were folded and legs crossed. He decided to put her at ease and pressed the mute button on the microphone.

"Mrs. Gittleman, every worthwhile interview starts with background. What I'm after now is how and why you started CASE. Readers will want to know its origins."

Alessandra gave Devon a questioning look. "I'm not sure what you want me to say. I've answered what you asked."

She's right. Maybe both of us need to relax.

Devon motioned with his head in the direction he thought led to a kitchen. "Happen to have any coffee back there? I didn't get much sleep on the red-eye."

"Black, or with cream?"

"Black."

A short while later, the two people were in their seats sipping coffee, and the atmosphere had lightened. They chatted about the building, laughing when the Hobbit door was mentioned. Alessandra now sat toward the edge of her recliner, legs crossed at the knees, holding her cup in both hands and occasionally smiling.

Devon wondered what the smile meant as he switched on the microphone.

"We were talking about the origins of CASE. Where did you practice before coming to California, and what brought about the change from criminal law to what you do now?"

The ringing phone on the coffee table broke Devon's momentum.

Damn it! This is probably going to happen throughout the interview.

"Turn off the recorder."

Devon pushed the mute button as Alessandra lifted the receiver of the land line on her end table.

"Gaby, I'm in the middle of this interview. I...who?...That's ridiculous...the D.A.'s office and I worked out a settlement in that case two weeks ago. Why can't it wait?...So important I can't call her back in a few hours?...All right, I'll take the call."

Alessandra looked at Devon. "This involves a legal case. You'll have to keep your microphone off and you can't use any part of what I say, even though you won't hear the other end of the conversation."

Devon retreated to the apartment's entrance and waited. The clutter of boxes was close to him now, and he began reading what was written on the sides of the containers. One bore the date July 6, 2010.

That was just a few days before I got here. Probably a case she's currently working on.

His mind was redirected by Alessandra's voice.

"Good morning, Ms. Ellis. Gabriela tells me you're having problems with the Martinez case; I thought we had negotiated a fair...Why won't Judge Brighton accept it? Dead! I saw Judge Brighton three days...She wasn't more than fifty and looked well to me...Huh. Who's taking over the Martinez case? Oh God, not him. No! Ms. Ellis, I'm sorry Judge Brighton is dead, but the fact remains we negotiated a settlement. Brighton was in favor of it, and I expect the prosecutor's office and Judge Wexler to honor...no, you go back to him and get him to understand that the case has been settled...No, I won't agree to that...All right, I'll talk to the District Attorney's office today, but this deal stays. Good day, Ms. Ellis."

Alessandra broke the connection and immediately hit another button on the land line.

"Gaby, I need to talk with the Chief Deputy District Attorney this afternoon. Make it at three or any time after that, but it has to happen today. And try not to let any other calls through…I'm not upset; you did the right thing, but no more phone calls!"

CHAPTER 6

Alessandra ended the call and sat fuming. "Wexler," she muttered. "Of all the judges that could be assigned to the Martinez case, I get that ignorant, bigoted, cretin!"

Devon was intrigued by the call and the outburst. What he had thought was an interruption, he now considered a gift. He was seeing the tigress in action, something he hadn't expected.

"Troubles?" he asked nonchalantly.

"When aren't there? This is going to chew up some of our time together, Mr. Emmanuel."

Alessandra pointed at the recorder. He pressed the button, and she returned to the question he had asked before the phone interruption, her voice still carrying an edge from the call.

"I began my law practice in New York City. When I got to Los Angeles, I was horrified by how poor women – especially women of color – were treated in the California justice system. I began working with some of them *pro bono*. The more I saw, the more I became involved. Within a year of coming to L.A., I quit my criminal law practice and founded CASE."

"When was that?"

Alessandra thought for a moment. "Early '70's...not certain which year."

Devon shifted his body in the marshmallow chair. "Why did you leave New York for California?"

Alessandra's eyes widened. She pointed at the recording device and made a sweeping "X" in the air.

Devon stopped recording.

"My past is my past. One of my reasons for putting up with this interview is to tell the world what's happening to poor women in the California justice system and their problems living in this society. My own life is none of your readers' business!"

Devon spoke softly, almost apologetically. "Mrs. Gittleman, I'm here to record your views on anything you'd like to discuss. But the readers have to feel they know you, or your answers will have little impact. Why you left New York for California will help people understand you as a person."

Alessandra rose from her recliner and began walking about in an aimless manner, moving noiselessly in stocking feet, clenched fists pulled against her sides. Her face could have been that of an enraged voyager lost in wild, uncharted waters. She was turning away from Devon when she suddenly whipped about.

"I knew this was going to happen! I don't give a damn what your readers want to know about me. That's irrelevant! I need them to understand what I know!"

Devon had never interviewed a person who had uttered a comment more contemptuous of the public. He worried she might decide to ask him to leave. Then, insight!

She requested this interview. She's not going to blow it off just because she's miffed. Call her bluff.

Devon slowly moved his hands over the rolled arms of the chair. "You evidently cared enough about my readers, Mrs. Gittleman, to request this interview."

Alessandra glared, then turned away and began pacing, a caged tigress who detested both captor and captivity. Again she whirled. "My personal life is none of your readers' goddamn business!"

More pacing. More silence. Then, the woman who had stood regally at the top of the stairs stopped moving and stared so deeply into Devon's eyes he felt his brain was being churned. Her dark brown irises and huge pupils set in porcelain white gave her face the look of a wild animal about to make a kill.

"Part of the reason I'm doing this interview is because your readers are not seeing what I see daily. That ignorance is allowing California to destroy the people I serve. It's not my past that's important, Mr. Emmanuel, it's my constituents' present."

Devon relaxed somewhat. The message was harsh, but her tone of voice had softened. He decided to push and see what happened.

"Mrs. Gittleman, the public is saturated with that kind of information. Television bathes them in suffering women. I'm concerned that an article detailing the suffering of indigent women will accomplish nothing."

Alessandra sniffed her disagreement. When she spoke again, her tone was more informative than angry.

"Statistics and TV coverage are important, but they're cold. The written word, based on an interview by a good journalist, adds warmth. Feeling. Individual stories about women and children being ground up in the system can be presented in print in a way no other media can match. Americans have to see these people through my eyes, feel them, hear them, smell them, touch them and even by-god taste them! They need to experience the agony of the moment when children are taken from mothers for ridiculous reasons. They need to feel a woman's frustration as public and private slugs use creative ways to deny help – even help that is rightfully a woman's under the law!" Alessandra paused for a few seconds, then continued in a rasp. "I need people to get that gut-deep anger that comes from knowing that these crap artists do this purely for monetary or political gain!"

"Mrs. Gittleman," Devon began in a pleading tone, his hands open, palms up. "My readers will not be interested in the law's disregard for poor women unless, as you've made clear to me, they identify with them. You've got to show what led you to these women, then let readers see your clients through your educated and experienced eyes."

The tigress began pacing again, moving aimlessly and muttering, her body emanating turmoil. "...humiliated...treated like something that should be flushed down the toilet!"

When she bumped into the recliner, she stopped. Her fingers stroked the heavy upholstery as she stared ahead, seemingly lost in thought.

She was directly in front of Devon. He could see the outline of her entire body – neck, back, waist, and through the rumpled linen skirt, a hint of hips and thighs; then, beneath the skirt hem, beautiful legs and shapely ankles. Her hands were smooth, and there was no sag in the skin of her upper arms. He had never seen a seventy-four-year-old woman look so young.

Suddenly, Alessandra's shoulders slumped. She turned toward him and sat on the edge of her recliner. When she spoke, her voice was soft and quiet and carried the sound of despair.

"Why are we doing this interview? My clients are detested for being poor. Americans love dogs. You should do a dog story."

Devon wasn't prepared for the sudden change. "We're doing this interview because it's important, Mrs. Gittleman. You've spent thirty-eight years working as an advocate for disadvantaged women. Who better than you to convey their angst? This story is one of destitute human beings living in rich, well-fed, America. You're the perfect person to tell it!"

Alessandra was silent, but her demeanor remained unchanged. Devon wondered if she had even heard him.

"Mrs. Gittleman, we'll draw all those who read what you have to say through an odyssey of your mind, a story that includes the journey of a remarkable woman no one knows, a unique individual who wields the sword of justice on behalf of the unfortunate. Give me that, Mrs. Gittleman, and I'll take what you see, hear, feel, taste, and smell and convey it with such intimacy that it will touch the very souls of our readers."

Alessandra Gittleman met his gaze. Her face softened and vacant eyes brightened slightly. Devon felt triumphant. She was about to open up! Suddenly, Alessandra's face turned hard, her jaw jutted forward, and her eyes turned cold. When she spoke, her voice was calm and deliberate, the note of despair gone.

"This interview was a mistake."

Devon couldn't believe the turn of events. Had he passed this point only to have everything unravel? All that came to mind was flattery. He spoke in an almost obsequious tone.

"I can only imagine what you've gone through in your battles to help our most needy citizens, Mrs. Gittleman. Your selfless commitment to the cause of justice deserves to be remembered and emulated by each succeeding generation of Americans. There has to have been a lot of pain involved in working so hard and seeing so little change."

Alessandra looked Devon up and down. "Cut the bullshit! If you think there's value in this interview other than turning it into a mindless story of my life, let's hear it!"

Devon felt his control of the interview completely collapse. He pulled his body forward onto the edge of the chair and clasped his hands together, elbows on his knees, eyes on the floor. He was devoid of new strategies and began saying whatever came into his mind.

"Mrs. Gittleman – why does this article have to be about absolutes? You have an agenda. You want to jar the American public from its lethargy and get them to address the terrible things that are happening to poor American women. To do that, we need to tell the story of CASE and what it does to aid your mistreated clients."

"So?"

"You're against having your personal life invaded. Which is understandable. But totally evading your life story works to your disadvantage, because that's what our readers want. They'll put the magazine down after a few paragraphs if I don't give it to them."

"I told– "

"–and finally, to make my argument honest, I want a story that will fascinate my readers who are curious about Alessandra Gittleman, the woman. And I want to be the conveyor of your message."

Devon paused, then looked up into the face of the woman who had stood so regally at the top of the stairs. "Let's both get something of what we want. The reader wins too, because while substantive information is conveyed, it's not being done in a manner in which they're being pounded to death. You, my protagonist, become hope."

Alessandra Gittleman said nothing in response to his argument. Time passed in a silence so deep that Devon could hear a clock ticking somewhere in the apartment.

Then…sudden fury. "My life is my own! This isn't a magazine story at a grocery checkout counter! Do you want this story or not?"

Her ferocity again startled Devon, who thought he had been making progress. He found himself almost desperately wanting this interview. Despite her vicious attacks, the woman intrigued him. Her looks, the mystery of her life, even her acid tongue – all fascinated him. Yet he resented her condescension and obvious belief that she had the right to speak to him any way she chose. He felt his own anger growing, but choked it back and decided to try and maneuver around her personal life. For the moment.

CHAPTER 7

Devon sighed inwardly and stiffly began to address the very areas he had hoped to minimize. "Let's talk about your organization," he said dryly. "What is the CASE mission?"

Alessandra's hostile demeanor eased somewhat, although her body language suggested she was less than pleased with his tone. Without taking her eyes from him, she moved to the edge of her recliner, crossed her legs, lit another cigarette, then sat motionless, her cigarette burning till it formed a tiny, precariously bending cylinder of ash. Finally, she took a last puff, knocked the ashes into the small ashtray, and answered icily, smoke tumbling from her nose.

"CASE does whatever it takes to help poor women get out of society-inflicted misery."

Devon thought he would gag. She wanted total control, and the result was going to be a constant harangue about America's failures, along with far-left bullshit. He considered making a graceful exit, then remembered Clark Andrews' instructions: "Let her talk." He had agreed to do that to the extent it "seemed reasonable."

"An example of how you accomplish this escape from misery would be?"

A malevolent glare and hostile voice accompanied Alessandra's response. "Have you ever been desperate and living in a dirty, violent, slum?"

An exasperated Devon Emmanuel mumbled his answer, his face a mask of disinterest. "New York."

Alessandra's laughter was so loud it was almost bawdy. "So you have a sense of humor!" she said as she eased back into the recliner. "I was beginning to think you'd bore me to death – if I didn't kill you first."

Devon smiled as he contemplated his nemesis. She could change her persona in an instant.

"The Emmanuel family has been poor but never slum dwellers," he said, then added, "In my lifetime."

Alessandra dubbed out her cigarette in the burgeoning ashtray. "I ask about your living in a slum, because it will answer many of your questions. Have you ever considered the possibility that the effects of poverty could become incorporated into an individual's brain?"

Devon thought the question ridiculous. To him, poverty was in large part the product of dysfunctional families, poor education, bad choices, or bad genes.

"You mean, did I ever consider poverty as something that alters the brain's structure? Physically changes it?"

"Yes."

Devon's head wagged slightly, and his voice was negative. "I've read about such studies. They were more or less theoretical."

Alessandra gave her head a tilt. "At least you've heard the theory. If you're raised in poverty, you have to cope with all the immediate social ills. What you don't need while trying to escape poverty is a repressive force that scars your mind forever. That force is the subject of this interview."

The last part of her comment angered the journalist in the now-fuming Devon. His subject persisted in defining the interview content. If he stuck to his editor's instructions to just let her talk, the resulting story would be tedious to the point of pain. He wasn't about to write that kind of article; he wasn't a journalistic hack. It was time to make some changes.

"Have *you* ever lived in a dirty, violent slum?" he asked, his voice tinged with veiled anger.

The surprise that registered on Alessandra's face quickly became a frown. She removed another cigarette from the pack, snapped the lighter hard when she lit it, and answered as she exhaled. "Desperate to write for *The National Enquirer*, are we?"

Devon struck back. "And you've progressed to academic treatise?"

Alessandra's eyes flashed. She moved again to the edge of the recliner, sat erect, then pointed toward him with her cigarette-bearing hand. "The reason we're so far apart, Mr. Emmanuel, is you don't listen! I try to address issues; you trivialize my efforts. I don't think you understand– "

A knock at the door interrupted her, and she glanced over her shoulder. Then she continued. "You think– "

The knock came again, this time as multiple raps. Alessandra angrily twisted her body until she was nearly facing the door, calling loudly, "I have a visitor; I'll be down in an hour!"

More knocks, faster, harder.

Alessandra whirled and shouted at the door behind her. "I just told you–"

A thick, desperate-sounding, Hispanic accent interrupted. "*Señora*, I have great need. Please. I have great need. Five minutes; I take no more."

Another excited female voice joined the first, both women speaking rapid Spanish in what sounded to Devon like an escalating argument. The expression on Alessandra's face changed from anger to futility as the argument outside the door got louder. She lifted her hands, then let them fall to her thighs.

"I need to take care of some business...I'm coming, damn it! Stop yelling!" she called as she rose.

Devon watched as she walked toward the door. Nothing about her movements resembled those of an old woman. She walked with her chin held high, and her body swayed with a sense of grace and music. As she neared the door, he left the marshmallow chair and slipped into the interior of the room to avoid being conspicuous. When the door opened, he glimpsed two Hispanic women, one heavy-set, about forty; the other shorter, slightly plump, and younger.

There were angry whispers for a moment, then, "I'll handle it, Gabriela."

The heavy-set woman left, and Alessandra addressed the intruder in English. "I'm sorry I yelled at you; I meant no disrespect. What is your name?"

"Isabel, *Señora* Gittleman. It is okay you yell. I break the rules. I do not want to break the rules, but my son, Armando, he is in trouble."

Alessandra's hand moved to her hip, and she shifted her weight to one side. "What kind of trouble?"

The words rushed out as the woman spoke. "The school call to me and say they are send Armando home because he is a ganger. Armando, he is no a ganger, he– "

Alessandra interrupted. "Was he arrested?"

"No, but I– "

"Good. Tell me what happened."

The conversation switched to Spanish, and Devon stopped eavesdropping. He reconnoitered, taking care to avoid being seen, meandering slowly among boxes and piles of paper lying on or near the heavy furniture. The most interesting piece of furniture was a strange round table made of rich, dark wood, perhaps seven feet in diameter. In the center of it was a clock supported on the shoulders of four naked Greek athletes, each holding a golden tray. The clock ticked loudly. To Devon's surprise, the time was correct. The centerpiece was mounted on a round base, which he gently nudged. It rotated flawlessly, clock and all.

A definitely unique lazy susan. Who in God's name buys something this hideous?

Against the wall was the liquor cabinet. As he passed it, he could see the spirits he had only glimpsed earlier – high-end bourbon, scotch, vodka, and liqueurs – all in bottles that were nearly full.

The conversation at the door returned to English. He strained to listen. "Go back to Gabriela. She will give you papers to fill out. Gabriela and I will read what you say and speak with you again."

"You will help me?"

"We'll try. Now I must go."

Before the door closed, Devon had turned to the bookcase and begun perusing titles. He pulled one to view the dust jacket. Soon he heard footsteps.

"That book is over twenty years old. *The Politics of Rich and Poor.* The author was a Republican. I have all his books and the works of many other sociologists and economists. Their conclusions are similar. If you're born into poverty in America and not extraordinarily gifted, your chances of getting out without help are near zero. Since the book you're holding was published, the situation has only worsened."

Alessandra pulled a paperback from a shelf and leafed through it as though hunting for a particular passage, then returned the book to its slot. "The fate of the destitute is, to a large extent, fixed in America today. That's especially true for women. America needs poor women to scrub floors, clean bathrooms, bear kids to fight wars, then have the good taste to die before collecting too much Social Security. When these women ask for justice, the system stomps on them – and the rest of our society doesn't give a good goddamn."

Devon returned his own selection to the shelf. He felt as if he were listening to a broken record. He tried, but was unable to mask the irritation in his voice. "Pretty harsh critique."

Alessandra's reply was colder than Devon's accusation. "I was being kind."

Devon's hostility was growing exponentially. He hated comments that painted the country negatively. Proponents of both extremes were idiots as far as he was concerned. America had given him everything, asking only that he work for a living and obey the law.

"Mrs. Gittleman, *Walden* isn't a public policy journal. We're mostly about people and what they do. If I wanted an interview with a policy wonk, I could get one. What I want – what *Walden Magazine* wants – is Alessandra Gittleman, the person."

Alessandra looked Devon up and down. "You don't give a damn about the people I'm talking about, do you? That's the same mindset as the rest of America down through the lower middle class. Most of the human beings I work with are brown or black, although lately, quite a few are white. America says they're all damaged goods, so just trash them. Congratulations, Emmanuel, you're in the majority."

The comment infuriated Devon. Before he could speak, Alessandra pivoted and walked toward her chair. "Most Americans think these women are destitute because they're inferior," she said. *You don't get away with that. We're resetting this interview, and if it ends here, so be it.*

"Americans think there is only so much that can be done for the poor," he answered, speaking to Alessandra's back as he followed behind her to the marshmallow chair.

Alessandra raised her eyebrows as she sat on her recliner, a wry smile playing on her lips. "Christ said 'The poor will always be with us.' Too bad for him he didn't live today. He could have run for the House of Representatives on that platform, made a fortune as a lobbyist after leaving Congress, bought a house in the Hamptons, and escaped the entire crucifixion mess."

Frustration mixed with gnawing fatigue churned inside Devon. He was failing miserably in his effort to launch the kind of interview his magazine wanted. The woman's incessant harping infuriated him. This, along with fatigue from the long trip and the domestic turmoil he had left behind, made him unable to shake his increasingly combative tone.

"Why blame America? It's the same everywhere in the world."

Alessandra glared at him. "I blame America, because this is America. Huddled masses? Golden door? The downtrodden are our shtick, remember?"

Devon's retort was quick and delivered with condescension. "Nonsense! There's nothing in the Constitution about taking care of poor people."

Alessandra laughed and looked at him as though he were a mischievous child. "I never said anything about the Constitution. If you're trying to get a deeper rise out of me, Mr. Emmanuel, be a bit more clever. That was pretty lame."

Devon felt his face flush. Anything he tried, she either finessed or turned back on him. It was going to be her agenda, and if he didn't like it, tough. The photograph on the bookcase caught his eye again.

All right, we're not accomplishing anything I want with the current approach. Let's see how you like playing dirty pool.

"Is that you and your husband in the photograph on the bookcase?"

Alessandra's eyes widened, and she attacked. "We decided personal things were off limits. I've offered *Walden* an exclusive interview. I could have given this interview to a dozen top magazines and they would have taken it without reservation. This interview is important, and you're obsessed with minutiae!"

The insult finally exhausted what little patience Devon had left. "Mrs. Gittleman, since I've entered the building, you've been personally abusive to me and laid down rules that make it impossible for me to write a worthwhile article. I was sent here to do a story important to *Walden* readers. If I continue the way we're going, a week or ten days from now, the best I'll be able to give them is a screaming rant about what they've heard a thousand times. I've been a journalist for a long time and I know how to do my job. I don't need you to tell me how to do it."

As Devon spoke, he reached into his coat pocket, removed a card with his cell phone number on it, then extricated himself from the marshmallow chair. "You want to continue this interview with the kind of latitude I need to make it worthwhile, Mrs. Gittleman, I'll be in town tonight and happy to take your call. If not, I'll catch a flight back to New York tomorrow."

With that, Devon collected his equipment, awkwardly fumbling to remove the mike from his subject, and walked toward the door.

Just as he reached for the knob, he heard a snicker, then, "Don't hold your breath waiting for the phone to ring, Bubby."

CHAPTER 8

As Devon drove, his mind was a jumble, but by the time he reached his hotel, he was certain of two things. First, his boss, feature editor Jesse Moscowitz (whom he detested, and by whom he was equally despised), was going to raise a gigantic stink over losing the Gittleman piece. Moscowitz would then run gleefully to Clark Andrews, *Walden's* managing editor, and demand that Andrews join him in taking the issue to the owner-publisher, Halden-Tennsley, better known as H-T.

Andrews, who was also Devon's long-time (and only) close friend, would refuse to go to H-T, but would resent having been placed in the awkward position of backing a writer whom most of the executives would accuse of having lost an important story due to his own arrogance. If he failed to enlist Andrews' help, Moscowitz would bypass the managing editor and go to the top himself. The result would be the second blow, Devon's loss of *Walden's* miserable two-percent yearly bonus along with a soft-voiced reprimand from the geriatric H-T: "Devon, *Walden* is above this sort of thing."

Screw Moscowitz, screw H-T, and screw Alessandra Gittleman! I'm a journalist, goddamn it! When I do an interview, it's the real thing, not something designed to serve a subject's personal agenda.

Entering his hotel room, Devon flung his valise onto one of the queen-sized beds and flopped down on the second. A half-hour of fuming later, he called Moscowitz. What followed was a five-minute lecture on professionalism. When Moscowitz finished his diatribe, Devon reclaimed his cell phone, which he had placed on the pillow far enough from his ear that Moscowitz' words were barely audible.

"Jesse, the woman was impossible. If I had presented you with an interview developed under Gittleman's restrictions, I would have spent *Walden's* time and money, and we would have published crap. I did what I thought was right."

Devon could hear the loud nasal breathing of Moscowitz. It was, he reasoned, Moscowitz' turn to dish back pain for all the real and imagined slights Devon had inflicted on the little jerk's ego over the years. Jesse's sweet revenge!

Devon hated indulging him but thought it might be politically expedient. "You're probably right, Jesse, I should have talked to you before breaking off with Gittleman, but my actions were in the best of *Walden's* literary tradition. *Walden* is about excellence. That's why I've spent seventeen years being paid less than most of my contemporaries at other literary journals – so I could look at my kids and say, 'Your old man is true to his profession, true to himself, and true to his employer. He's a *mensch.*'"

Moscowitz remained untouched by the attempt at indulgence. The only thing Devon heard on the other end of the line was breathing.

The son of a bitch is going to milk this. He's going to get his pound of flesh.

Devon was certain Moscowitz despised him. One of the few members of middle management with whom Devon occasionally associated had told him of Moscowitz' comment that Devon was the most condescending of all of the condescending *Walden* writers who had gone to fancy schools and looked down their noses at people who had attended less prestigious colleges. Moscowitz, the source had said, especially hated Devon because of his comments about Coston College, Moscowitz' alma mater, and blamed him (correctly) for the graffiti inside the door of the first floor bathroom stall that read "The President of Coston College buys three-ply underwear."

What Devon couldn't see, but could imagine at this moment, was the smile on Moscowitz' angular face as he sat in his small, windowless New York office. Moscowitz would have his hands locked behind his balding head, the phone cradled against his left ear, his favorite managerial pose. He would puff out his skinny chest, then wiggle his behind in the expensive swivel chair he had bought with his own money in an effort to appear more important in the organization than he could legitimately claim to be. The mental image grated on Devon.

"For Christ's sake, didn't you realize the importance of this piece, Devon? What a coup it would be for *Walden*? It would have scooped every other intellectual magazine in the country. This article would have been the benchmark against which every journal in our field would be measured for this entire year. And you blew it. You knew she was difficult. You were told that. But she called *Walden Magazine* and asked for this interview, which meant she had a big story in mind. A story you didn't get, Devon – and could have gotten if you had parked your ego at the door to her building! You just don't get it, do you, Devon? As long as I've been here, I can't remember your giving real consideration to anything that wasn't initiated by you. Now, I want this story, and I expect you to return to Mrs. Gittleman, apologize, and get it."

Moscowitz' words hurt, even though Devon considered him an idiot. Ordinarily, Devon wouldn't have given a rat's ass what Moscowitz thought. In fact, he was certain Moscowitz wouldn't even be working at *Walden* if he hadn't been the son of H-T's close friend. What hurt Devon was that this time, Moscowitz was right. A good journalist should have eaten more shit, used his experience and command of the interview process, and gotten as much information as he could coax out of Gittleman to write the best story possible. Then again, this miserable assignment had been crammed down his throat without an adequate chance to prepare. Suddenly it seemed all things rotten in his life had accumulated, congealed, and at this one awful, disgusting, putrid moment were being heaped upon his head and sent oozing slowly toward his feet. The result provoked an impulsive reaction.

"Well, Jesse, if you want the article, you'll have to send someone else to do the job, because I'm not going back to Alessandra Gittleman and beg for the interview." Devon delivered his insubordinate comment in a seething monotone, one that implied, "Go sweep the floors."

Moscowitz' voice rose in rage. "Obviously, I'm going to get someone else and try to talk Mrs. Gittleman into going ahead with the interview. I'm also going to talk to your editor about your attitude. I'm fed up with it! I'm your boss. You think I'm some kind of joke, but I'm your– "

"–Tell you what, Jesse," he seethed. "You're not the only one fed up. I'm going to get a night's sleep, then catch a flight back to New York tomorrow. It shouldn't take me more than a couple of hours to clean out my desk. Go get yourself another fucking writer. I quit!"

Before Moscowitz could respond, Devon pressed the end-call icon. What he felt at that moment was incredible satisfaction. The sense of having been immaculately cleansed, brilliant white and pure to the center of his existence. He went to the bathroom, got a glass, selected two miniature bottles of bourbon from the small refrigerator, opened both, poured them, then slowly, using both hands, raised the drink above his head as though offering it to God.

"Here's to integrity!" Then he took a deep breath and whispered, "Here's to you, Emmanuel," and gulped down the whisky without taking the glass from his lips. Seconds later, he gasped as the burning in his throat grew in intensity, then subsided. He stood for a while enjoying the moment, then returned to the bed and waited for the alcohol to relax his tired, overwrought mind and body.

Moments after lying down, Devon was struck with all the ramifications of his actions. Leaving *Walden* meant life without a paycheck! And little chance of getting another job at an intellectual journal after Moscowitz, and perhaps even H-T himself, spread the word of Devon's insubordination. He became terrified.

Life had been without serious financial worries since he had been hired by *Walden* only a few years out of college. True, his salary was now comparatively low for his experience and accomplishments, but he had never been without a paycheck, health insurance or the matching retirement package *Walden* provided. Except for his 401(k), that was it! His family health insurance would be gone! His only friend, Clark Andrews, with whom he shared experiences, would be gone! Access to important people that being a *Walden* writer afforded him – gone! He was forty-seven! He would be an aging freelance writer unless someone picked him up! Freelance writers starved!

Thoughts frittered through his brain, crackling from one dendritic complex to another. Nausea wormed a circuitous, writhing path through his gut. How would he and his family live? Sonja worked three days a week at the museum. She grossed forty thousand dollars a year without benefits. It took their combined income to keep the family living a middle-class life in a three-bedroom apartment in New York. He had just thrown away most of their household income and almost all of their benefits! He had blown up his life because he was miffed!

"Sweet Jesus," he whispered. "Sweet Jesus, what have you done? You're an idiot, Emmanuel, a total, mindless, fucking idiot!"

He needed another job and he needed it quickly! The biggest hindrance would be Jesse Moscowitz. He couldn't hope to get a recommendation from Moscowitz. Still, Devon had seventeen years under his belt at *Walden* and was well-known in intellectual journalism. But it was 2010 and intellectual magazines were in trouble. Electronic media was killing them. Print journalism everywhere had cut staff. The entire print industry was in a tumult! He knew writers who had been out of work for two years. One of them was free-lancing for a porn publisher; his wife had turned their home into a daycare center. The fellow's life was miserable, and he had once been considered a *wunderkind*!

And what about Sonja? Thoughts of Sonja nearly sent him into a panic attack. Sonja came from a wealthy intellectual family. They had lost their money, but not before sending her to an elite college. To her, nothing mattered but her job at the museum. When anyone asked what she did for the museum, her answer was always something like, "I search for new artists…exciting young people breaking through the boundaries of the stultifying sameness of today's America." That was quintessential Sonja.

When he and Sonja were first married, her wide-open-for-new-social-ideas attitude had been exciting to him. He remembered baiting her with outrageous proposals and watching as she took the bait. The two of them would sometimes turn a ridiculous idea into an interesting and possibly workable concept. He had loved her enthusiasm, her spontaneous laughter, the fact that she had knowledge of the world far beyond his – knowledge of lands, cultures, history, languages (she was fluent in English, Spanish, and French). She had traveled the world from Europe to China. When Sonja spoke of Tibetan Sherpas, it was because she had spent time climbing in the Himalayas with Sherpa guides. She read voluminously, knew music from Rachmaninoff to rock 'n roll. And she was beautiful – so beautiful. He was flattered she thought that he, a young man at the time unsure of his looks, worldliness, manhood, and so many other things, was worth dating. He would spend hours looking up something she mentioned in the hope of impressing her. Sonja was the kind of woman he had often fantasized as his wife. A woman he would always love, with whom he would enjoy life, have children, and eventually grow old. Time would prove him wrong.

Now love was gone, and Sonja's words and bitterness were a constant source of anguish to him. Sonja, born wealthy, had actually lived a middle class life since they had married. Although the loss of her family's wealth had been a shock to her at first, she had never really seen hard times. How was she going to handle their living on her meager income while he searched for a job?

"I was out of my mind quitting," he muttered, then said loudly, "Out of my fucking mind!"

The whisky began to take effect, and his anxiety eased a little.

Should I call Sonja now and tell her, or wait until morning?

They were three thousand miles apart, and it was almost evening in New York. Sonja might go into one of her freak-out modes, spend the night awake, and he would find himself explaining the disaster a second time twelve hours hence to a stressed-out, sleep-deprived woman with whom he already had major issues.

Devon picked up his glass and looked at the remaining drops of whisky at the bottom. Golden brown. The color always reminded him of the trout he and his father had caught in upstate New York streams on family vacations. The vacations had occurred once a year, but he had lived for those two weeks. They were times when his parents didn't worry about the store, when the air smelled sweet, when he laughed and threw a baseball around with his dad. It was wonderful being an only child and having his parents all to himself. He was protected. He was loved! He remembered all the night games he and his dad has gone to at Shea stadium, even though his dad abhorred the Mets and constantly compared them to his lost Dodgers. In his youth, Devon had been able to quote all the Mets' batting averages and ERAs of the pitchers. He smiled as he remembered the time he had offered to switch allegiance to the Yankees, if it would make his father happy.

My God, that was the loudest scream I ever heard come out of him. My parents were wonderful...and both of them died before I turned thirty.

A pang of loneliness swept over him. "Dad...Mom...I miss you so much," he whispered.

Devon emptied his glass and turned out the light. His initial sensation of being alone in a strange hotel, in a strange city, locked in a strange, lonely, deserted life slowly ebbed as the alcohol did its job.

CHAPTER 9

The ringing hotel phone jolted Devon awake. He looked at his watch. Ten-thirty. He had slept thirteen hours. The phone continued its brain-jangling ring, then suddenly, he felt as if he had touched bare electrical wires.

Sonja! Somebody told her!

He was about to hear a hysterical woman with a high-pitched, nerve-shattering Bronx accent rip his suffering neurons. He considered not answering, then decided it was better to deal with the issue from a distance of three thousand miles.

"Hello?"

"Devon...?"

Jesse Moscowitz!

"YeahJessewhadayawant?"

There was a gulping sound on the other end of the line.

Something's bothering Moscowitz.

Devon could visualize the little man nervously wiggling in his chair. He had used Moscowitz' wiggle as a gauge of where he stood in any disagreement with him. When the wiggling increased, Devon knew he had Jesse worried.

"I'm glad I got hold of you, Devon. We've had a management meeting, and there was a lot of discussion about what happened yesterday. As you pointed out, you've been seventeen years with *Walden*. You're a great writer. We know you weren't given enough time to prepare for the interview. And you were exhausted after taking an overnight flight. Everybody wants to forget what happened yesterday."

Devon felt an enormous rush of relief. His had his job, his benefits, his friend, and his apartment back. He could afford to feed and educate his kids. He didn't have to call Sonja! He breathed deeply and rolled into a comfortable position on the bed, arranging the phone against his ear.

"I'm glad *Walden* is willing to consider the circumstances, Jesse, but I have to share the blame. I'm a veteran journalist, and I should have handled the problem in a more professional way."

Immediately after his *mea culpa*, Devon regretted it and quickly engaged in damage control. "But, Jesse, I really believe what I said yesterday. I'm sorry we're going to miss this interview, because I think Gittleman has something worthwhile to tell the world. We won't be publishing it, but we kept our integrity. I'll catch the red-eye tonight and see you tomorrow. Thanks for calling, Jesse. Goodb – "

"Don't hang up, Devon! We had a second meeting later. We still want the Gittleman interview. We're moving ahead with it."

The corpulent hand of Clark Andrews is mixing this bowl.

"Well, Jesse, it's a brave new world. Better tell whoever's doing the interview to bring a razor-proof jockstrap, or he's going to leave Los Angeles a soprano."

Devon waited for a reply, but none was forthcoming. After several seconds, he decided the connection had broken.

Then Moscowitz spoke. "We want you to do it."

In an action more reflexive than willed, Devon's legs swung over the side of the bed and he stood up. His fast-rising head caused the phone to bounce off the pillow and bang against the end table. He grabbed the receiver and screamed into it. "That's ridiculous! The old bag hates me! She won't let me in the goddamn door! Whose idiotic idea was this anyway?"

When Moscowitz answered, his voice carried an audible quake. "It was…our collective opinion."

Devon sat on the bed again.

They're idiots!

The voice on the phone developed a whine. "It's because you're the best we've got, Devon. That's why it has to be you. Nobody else is going to do this article as well as you. You're the man, Devon. We believe in you. You're the *gantser k'nacker* at *Walden*, Devon. But – you're still going to have to apologize to Mrs. Gittleman."

Devon had gone untouched by the obsequious blather until the last sentence, after which he exploded. "That's bullshit! Besides, Gittleman will never let me near her!"

Moscowitz's whine intensified. "Devon, there are a lot of things involved here. At this point, I'm going to step out of it. Call your managing editor. Keep me apprised. You have a good day."

Moscowitz hung up.

Devon sat for a moment, slammed the receiver onto the phone, reached for his cell phone and pressed Clark Andrews' name in the registry. He began talking the instant he recognized the editor's voice.

"What the fuck is going on, Clark? In the last twenty-four hours, I've been tormented by the super-bitch of modern history, walked out on my assignment rather than be used as a flack, quit *Walden* because Moscowitz-the-Idiot didn't give me any choice, only to be awakened this morning with the good news from Jesse that *Walden* considers me a literary genius and wants me to return to the fold!"

Devon waited for a response. When none came, he continued. "After I agreed to return to *Walden*, I was told I had to go back to this – this – female Attila and apologize! Apologize! And get her fucking story! When I pushed Moscowitz, he referred me to you."

Silence.

Whatever was going on, Devon now felt certain Andrews was deeply involved, because the editor generally came back at him in a heated argument before he could guard his throat.

"What's going on that I don't know about, Clark? I'm asking you as a friend – a pain in the ass but someone who, over the years, has earned my grudging respect."

In the background, Devon heard a squeak and knew Andrews was swiveling his two-hundred-forty-pound, five-foot-eight-inch body back and forth in his swivel roller chair that had needed oiling for years. The silence continued. Why wasn't Andrews responding? They had always worked well together, shared a frankness and honesty, and enjoyed trading acid comments.

Once, in their cups, the fat man had offered what, for him, had been a great compliment, "Emmanuel, you got a real talent for squeezing the exquisite essence out of an interviewee and putting it into the fewest words possible. No other writer at *Walden* can be such a prick and still deliver work of your quality."

Devon now heard a click and knew Andrews had turned on his speaker phone. He imagined the editor's overweight body sagging into the old leather chair, his fingers interlocked on his abdomen.

"If you have any other hostile things to say about me or *Walden*, Devon, this would be a good time."

Devon took the phone from his ear, glared at it, then yelled, "Give me a goddam answer!"

The response was immediate. "During a meeting yesterday in which you were being baked over hot coals, we got a call from Alessandra Gittleman. I took the call right in the conference room. The little lady asked if we still wanted her story. I said yes. Her response was – and I quote: 'Then get Emmanuel's ass back to CASE.'"

Devon was shocked. He could not imagine Alessandra Gittleman requesting his presence in any establishment other than a morgue.

"Didn't you tell her I no longer worked at *Walden* – that I'd quit?"

"I did."

Devon waited for something further. The only sound was the squeaking of Andrews' chair.

"Well?"

"She said – again, her exact words: 'That's too fucking bad. Come up with Emmanuel before close of business tomorrow, or I'm going elsewhere.'"

"What did you tell her?"

"I told her you would be at CASE tomorrow ... uh, that would be today."

Devon leaped from the bed. "You committed me to a story after I quit!"

The squeak of Andrews' chair increased in volume.

He's moved closer to the speaker phone. He only does that if something is really important.

There was a pause, then, "Devon, there are things happening back here you don't know about. I didn't know myself until just before the meeting where all this shit came down. It's hush-hush, okay?"

"Yeah. What?"

"*Walden Magazine* is about nine months from closing its doors unless it can entice a wealthy patron to acquire part of it. Further, if *Walden* is to continue publishing, the angel will have to be willing to let it operate at a very small profit margin."

Devon flopped backward onto the bed, grasped the phone with both hands, and barked in rage. "Clark, no such benefactor exists! You're all living in Oz!"

Another pause, then, "Oddly enough, there might be such a benefactor. That brings me to two truths. The first truth – the wildly theoretical one – envisions a story of magnificent importance, presently buried in the head of Alessandra Gittleman, that would make *Walden* irresistible to our angel."

"And?"

"The second truth is anything but theoretical. In my unerring opinion, the only writer at *Walden* who can dig such a story out of Gittleman and achieve the quality that will warm the heart of our angel is you, and you're being demanded by Alessandra Gittleman, the possible instrument of our salvation."

Andrews sounded as if he were repressing laughter. Devon suddenly sensed what the editor was unsuccessfully trying to mask.

He's terrified.

At fifty-three, Clark Andrews had survived one heart attack, a triple bypass, and had recently re-acquired angina. He still smoked two packs of cigarettes and drank half a fifth of vodka daily, except on weekends, when he smoked an extra half-pack and drank three-quarters of a fifth. If *Walden* folded, Andrews would be out of a job. His kids, who were all he valued in life, would be unable to continue at Princeton. He would lose his benefits and be hard-pressed to pay for health insurance, let alone a place to eat and sleep.

"So! You committed me to do this story even though you know it has almost no chance of saving *Walden.* That it?"

"Yeah," Andrews said nonchalantly. "In case you're wondering if I feel guilty, I don't. I'd do the same thing again, Devon. This is 2010, remember? Print journals are being squeezed out of existence by technology. *Walden* has got to be acquired or it's going bankrupt. To be acquired, we need bait. The only bait you and I can offer is a spectacular story, and Alessandra Gittleman's past could be that story. I want you to get me the personal details of this L.A. mystery woman's life beyond what God knew of Joan of Arc. Maybe it will work. Now you have the straight skinny."

There was silence. The only sound from the phone was the squeaking of Andrews' chair. The void continued for several seconds. Andrews often used silence when working with recalcitrant writers. The ploy unnerved them and made them vulnerable. Devon suddenly wanted some revenge; he remained silent, chuckling noiselessly, grinning into the phone.

Eventually Andrews gave up the battle and spoke. "You going to help me, or are you going to let *Walden* go down the tubes and put all us poor schmucks on the street? That includes you too, Devon. You're pushing fifty, man. Nobody wants you when you're fifty unless you're famous. Or a business maven. You're a fine writer, but you're not famous, and you couldn't find the business office at gun point."

This Devon knew as fact. He suddenly felt as if he were floating in the ocean after two consecutive shipwrecks, seeing nothing but water in every direction. He was about to rip into the editor when he remembered the horror he had felt when he thought he had lost the very job Andrews was now indirectly trying to save.

"Clark, let me think about this, OK? I'll get back to you in an hour."

There was another pause, then, "Think hard, Devon."

Devon did. A day ago he had left New York where he had been leading a somewhat miserable life that had rolled along in a monotonous, somewhat miserable way for many somewhat miserable years. There was comfort in being steadily but only somewhat miserable. You didn't have to think. Now everything was in crisis mode, and he had to think. And it was worse than being somewhat miserable.

CHAPTER 10

Devon got up and began pacing. A half hour later, thoughts were still whirling in his mind. When he felt capable of addressing the problem, he got into bed and attempted to strip reason from emotion. Something he had never asked himself before reared its unheralded head. At what point was he selling out his values? He had worked seventeen years for a low-paying journal because it had allowed him to do quality journalism. Most of those years, Andrews had been his editor. Andrews had always been about quality and integrity. He had contested innumerable issues with Devon, but never that.

This was different. When it looked as if he were going to be without a job, he, "Devon the Ethical," had almost shit his pants. Now, after a terrible journalistic performance, *Walden* was giving him a second chance. Why? Because they needed him! Had *Walden* not needed him, he most likely would have been fired.

Things were becoming clear. The issue for him now was keeping his job; the issue for *Walden* was survival. Everything else – ethics, integrity, whatever – was in the bullshit pile. Did money really trump everything he claimed to have valued his whole career? He tried to think of a single story he had covered that was of such magnitude it warranted that kind of sacrifice. None came to mind. The Gittleman article was the acid test of what he had held precious for so long.

Then again, maybe it was only his perception that this was about integrity. Any other journalist at *Walden* would do the story. But then, he didn't respect any other journalist at *Walden*. The truth was, he knew the story *Walden* wanted and Alessandra Gittleman probably wasn't going to give it to him. She was going to finesse him with half-truths or outright lies that would be difficult to check under the circumstances in which he was working. It was her agenda or nothing. And if he didn't get the story, he was probably going to end up on the streets, a place he had already visited in his mind.

Other than my career as a journalist, what do I have in my life? My marriage is a wreck. I hardly know my kids. Jesus, there has to be some kind of an alternative justification, or yes, you've sold out.

Devon sat up in bed. His palms were wet and he wiped them on the bottom sheet. They remained wet, so he grasped the top sheet, wiped them dry, and asked himself a question.

What's the worst that can happen if I return to CASE and try to interview Gittleman?

The answer he decided upon after plowing through the issue: He could find himself humiliated. Humiliation wasn't the worst thing that could happen to a journalist, as long as the result was truth. In reality, literary compromise was done every day. No one called it lack of integrity. Gittleman had a right to keep some things off limits. If he hadn't been given strict instructions on how to proceed, he'd have pushed those limits, but in the end, he would have respected most of her territorial demands. But his editor was demanding that he acquire information about her personal life. And now he had a gun-to-the-head economic interest in getting it. That bothered him. Then, an idea! He could ask her for just enough background information to interest readers. If she went along with the idea, a fact-checker could dig further, and he could publish the new information they dug up. That was his right. Hell, that was his obligation! If the fact-checker found something less than admirable in her past, but not serious, *Walden* didn't have to print it. If it was egregious enough, Devon would write it, and they could send it to press and rip her heart out. That could be a hell of a story. That was the answer!

"I'm not selling out if I do this right," he said aloud, getting to his feet. "I quit when I considered my integrity challenged. Giving in to Gittleman doesn't mean I lose my integrity – if I do it right."

And thus he stood for nearly a minute, at the end of which his brain puked.

God, that's so bad!

The conversation with Andrews began to gnaw at him. It was as much cloak-and-dagger as revelation. Details were absent, and it was details that would allow Devon to make a truly meaningful decision. It was time Clark Andrews told him the whole story. Time to place his call.

As soon as Andrews answered, Devon started in. "Clark, it's Devon. Look man, I've been wrestling with this, and I'm willing to do the Gittleman article as long as I'm not turned into a complete flack. But you're withholding information; I can smell it. Now give me the goddamn facts."

The squeaking of Andrews' chair ceased.

"Devon, I can only go so far with this conversation."

"Uh-huh. This investor *Walden* wants doesn't exist yet, right? I'm not going back to CASE and conform to what that old bitch wants if it's just to feed H-T's crazy dream. Now, what's with this so-called 'angel'? Honest answers, or I don't do the fucking story."

Devon heard the squeaking begin again.

"Okay. H-T really does have someone interested. Remember Lillian Scheidler?"

Devon's silence brought a memory-jogger from Andrews. "The dowager with the estate in the Hamptons?"

Nothing.

Andrews became irritated. "You were at that party Scheidler held at the request of the mayor. Her dead husband was one of the first billionaires in electronics."

Devon remembered. The party was supposed to be a celebration of the arts, when truthfully, it was Lillian Schwartzfelt Scheidler's clandestine fundraiser for a museum with some urgent needs it didn't want made public. He had written a hideous article that, when he looked back on it, could have been a puff piece for rich preening assholes who wrote big checks for a chance to be seen with the mayor and the super-rich. He'd hated the story, but justified it because it supported what he considered a worthwhile cause.

"Yeah. What's Lillian Scheidler want with *Walden*?"

"Ms. Lillian Schwartzfelt Scheidler loves *Walden*. She's considering a twenty-five million dollar buy into the magazine. Unfortunately, she feels *Walden's* slipping, and she's reluctant to associate her name with a downhill enterprise."

Devon began pacing the floor.

"She's right. We've been dog shit for years. We lost Harry Cusp, George Carroll, Edwina Linz – three of our best writers – because of salary. H-T replaced them with hacks. And the writers who quit are making twice what I'm getting now."

"Yeah, and most of the stuff from the replacements is crap. The loss of an editor didn't help either."

"So?"

"H-T thinks a great piece on Gittleman just might induce sweet Lillian to commit."

"That's preposterous! You expect one article– "

" –and there's a time issue. We have to play our hand before she decides to fund *Eleanor*. Ms. Lillian is an old libber and *Eleanor's* CEO's been sniffing around. *Eleanor* is in as bad a shape financially as we are, and they got an edge on us because they're oriented toward today's women. But! *Eleanor* has only been around fifteen years and *Walden* goes back eighty. We're an American institution. That's our strong suit with the old, rich and snooty. That means there's going to be a struggle for Ms. Lillian's money at a time when the quality of our writers and our commitment to today's women are in question. In Alessandra Gittleman, we cover a strong woman who fights for justice for women, and with you, we demonstrate quality writing. H-T wants this piece on Gittleman in the next issue."

Devon stopped pacing.

"Next issue! A ten-page article! Researched, written, and edited! In three weeks!"

"Uhh ... actually, two weeks and six days."

Devon leaned against the wall and ran the process through his mind.

"Clark, Shakespeare couldn't accomplish what you're asking in twenty days!"

"I ran the time line. You got ten days to get the information, two days to write it up – perfect, of course – some bullshit in-house, then off to the printer – if you start work today."

"Just kiss Gittleman's ass, and write hell out of whatever crap she gives me! That it?"

Devon heard a rattle, then a clicking sound. He recognized the noise. Andrews had opened a desk drawer and was squirting nitroglycerin under his tongue.

He's having an angina attack!

"Clark...Clark...are you okay?"

No answer. Andrews' deep breaths were followed by his wheezy voice. "Yeah, I'm OK. I'd never ask you to sell out, man. If Gittleman's not straight with you, walk away. It'll hurt, but I'll back you. Where you can, though, cut me some slack."

Devon was about to say he'd give it a try when he had an epiphany.

"Tell you what, Clark. I'll do it under conditions."

A sigh, then a defeated voice. "What conditions?"

"Tell H-T I want a ten percent bonus this year instead of a lousy two percent. Second, if this piece brings Ms. Lillian on board, I get a $20,000-a-year raise and a permanent annual five percent increase. And that's to be part of the deal H-T makes with Ms. Lillian. In the legal document that's signed by Ms. Lillian and the old fart. If she buys into *Walden*."

"Or what?"

"Or I don't do the story."

"Goddamit, you'd be making more than I make in a couple of years!"

The smile on Devon's face radiated as though he had just seen God. He'd never before negotiated anything important from a position of power. It felt great! He almost sang his answer. "I know that, Clark. But there's a major difference between you and me."

"What?" Andrews shouted into the phone, knowing it was he who would have to argue the case for Emmanuel's raise with the tight-fisted H-T.

"Alessandra Gittleman wants me, and she doesn't give a flying fuck about you. Do we have a deal?"

Moments passed, then Andrews started chuckling. "I like you, Emmanuel. I came clean only to have you turn into an extortionist. Yeah, we got a deal. Know something, man? I really do like you. But you're a fucking snake."

CHAPTER 11

Devon saw the woman at the desk reach for her telephone. Chairs scooted, some people stood, and an eerie silence broken only by knowing whispers slowly descended upon the room. The human energy surrounding him heightened his anxiety as he swept past the front desk and climbed the steps to the second floor. When he reached the top of the staircase, he set down his valise, dried his palms on the sleeves of his coat, picked up the valise again and raised his free hand to knock. The door opened before his knuckles hit wood.

Alessandra looked stunning. She was dressed like a 1950's Park Avenue divorcée meeting a rich potential suitor for dinner. Her hair, slightly unkempt at their first meeting, was now silky, lustrous, and meticulously coifed in the same style as when he had first seen her. Her light gold linen dress was form-fitting and buttoned high at the neck, with transparent sleeves in matching color, ending in an elegant linen cuff with gold buttons. Her shoes had two-inch heels. Her make-up was subtle but enhancing. Somehow, age, while not banished, had mostly fled before a face that nature seemed to have blessed from birth. Alessandra Gittleman at seventy-four was beautiful.

"Good morning, Devon," she cooed. "It's good to see you. Come in. Please."

Devon crept carefully through the door as if entering a minefield. The apartment was immaculate. An embroidered tablecloth had transformed the coffee table. In the center was a silver tea set flanked by a wicker basket covered with a rose-patterned napkin. Next to the basket was a crystal pitcher filled with orange juice. Two small plates hand-painted with tiny roses were set out.

Alessandra lightly took Devon's hand, led him to the coffee table, then gestured toward the chair he had occupied the previous day. The arms and headrest were now covered with white lace doilies.

"Sit. Please. I trust you had a good night?"

Devon looked warily from the coffee table to his hostess.

This isn't happening.

Alessandra's subtle smile deepened. She sat on the side of her recliner and tilted her head toward the table.

"I hope you like cheese danish. I'm partial to it myself." She picked up ornately engraved silver tongs, selected a cube of sugar, then paused. "Do you take sugar in your tea?"

Devon just sat. He was about to say something when she spoke.

"One lump or two?"

"Uh – n-no sugar. Please."

Alessandra delicately lifted two cubes from the elegant ceramic sugar bowl and placed them in her own cup, then began pouring the tea. When Devon's cup was half-full, she stopped.

"I'm sorry. Do you take milk?"

"No – just tea. Uhh – did you – uh – have a good night?"

Alessandra ignored the question, extended the basket of pastries toward him, and drew back the napkin. "Danish?"

Devon slowly reached into the basket, made his selection, and placed it on his plate, unaware he was extending his little finger. Suddenly, he recovered cognition.

"Mrs. Gittleman, I don't understand. When I left yesterday, I had the impression you would have enjoyed watching as I was eviscerated with a dull knife."

Alessandra tilted her head slightly to one side and laughed. Not an ordinary laugh, but a joyous, mischievous laugh. She picked up the pitcher and motioned toward his glass. "Orange juice?"

"I – I'm not sure. Later maybe."

Alessandra poured her own juice, then, with Victorian grace, raised her cup and saucer, sat erect on the edge of the recliner, crossed her legs and took a sip of tea.

As she centered the cup in the saucer, she looked directly into Devon's eyes and spoke in a soft voice. "Yesterday, I treated you quite rudely. I work in this building with volunteers and clients. They respect me; some perhaps even love me. But in the evenings, they leave, and there is no one in the building but me and a security guard who remains on the first floor. On the days that I do leave CASE, I'm usually on my way to do battle with officials whose views are in conflict with my own. Most of them dislike me intensely. It seems I've forgotten how to interact with another person on other than a business or an adversarial basis."

Alessandra's soft, throaty voice mesmerized Devon. He began to re-evaluate his own behavior of the day before. He had been exhausted and frustrated when they first met. Perhaps he had misjudged her. Then again, her comments to Clark Andrews didn't call to mind a saint. Caution returned to his mind. He felt like a cat creeping through a strange yard in which there might be hidden a large mean dog.

Alessandra's eyes shifted to her teacup as she raised it to her lips, took another sip, lowered the cup into the saucer and dreamily spoke in the same soft voice. "Somehow, Devon, I failed to separate you from all the people I've mentioned. You're from a world I left many years ago. A society where people are expected to treat one another with time-honored social graces, even in matters of conflicting opinions."

Alessandra set her cup and saucer on the table, leaned forward, and added tea to both their cups.

"Please forgive me for yesterday," she said, her eyes searching his face. "You impress me, you know. Few people impress me."

A cautionary neuron fired in Devon's brain.

Why do I impress her?

"Why do I impress you?"

Quiet settled upon the room, accompanied by Alessandra's fleeting smile. When she broke the silence, her voice was almost a whisper. "You risked your job for principle."

Alessandra took a bite of danish, then sipped more tea.

She gazed absently at the sugar bowl, raised her eyebrows and spoke as though musing. "The value of a person's principles, I believe, can be measured by the risks they're willing to take to hold them inviolable. You're wearing a wedding ring. I assume you're married, possibly have children."

Devon wasn't sure if she had asked a question, but he answered anyway. "Yes, a boy and a girl."

Alessandra nodded slightly, her eyes fixed on his. "Yet you risked your job in spite of your responsibilities. You did so because you thought your work was being compromised."

"That's true," Devon said in a strong but non-threatening tone, unaware his jaw had squared in defiance. "The integrity of my work means a great deal to me."

Alessandra placed the cup and saucer on the table, sitting erect with her chin tilted upward, her hands folded in her lap.

She spoke again in a soft voice. "What you did takes character. I would like to continue the interview, which I believe will benefit both of us. There are some things, however, that I would prefer to hold – to hold to myself. I'm sure we can work together, if you would be willing to accommodate me in some of those areas. Nothing major, just small accommodations."

Devon's entire emotional being screamed, *"Say yes!"* He was about to assent when he stopped. What "small accommodations" could she be talking about? She had gone from fishmonger's wife to seventy-four-turned-forty-year-old seductress and was toying with him. Knowing all the while he had to suspect what she was doing. Yet she seemed confident she could do it. And she was getting away with it! How?

The woman was a female Machiavelli. She was not one of Ulysses' sirens. Not at seventy-four, regardless of how attractive she made herself. She was using him as a tool for God-knows-what purpose. But why him and why *Walden*? She could have gotten herself interviewed by a person and an organization with bigger names than Devon Emmanuel and *Walden*. One of the TV magazines. Perhaps even *60 Minutes*. Something about his personal involvement had to be important in getting what she wanted. Small accommodations? How could he say no?

"All right, Mrs. Gittleman. That sounds fair enough."

Alessandra's chin rose coquettishly and a smile graced her lovely face. When she spoke, her voice resembled the low, soft, husky tone of Lauren Bacall.

"Call me – Alessandra."

Still suspicious of his subject's motives, but relieved the interview would take place, Devon began eating. Then he remembered; he didn't like cheese danish. He wondered what to do next. Moments passed without a word. Alessandra sat across from him, looking completely comfortable with the silence – still erect, chin up, managing to appear elegant while munching pastry, sipping tea and drinking orange juice.

"Your outfit – your dress – it's very beautiful, Mrs. – I mean, Alessandra."

Alessandra beamed as her hands moved over the fabric, smoothing it from her chest to her hips. "Why, thank you. Do you know it's many years old? My husband had it made for me in Paris at a small, outrageously expensive, establishment. He made me a full wardrobe and refused to let me see what he paid. I spent many hours with the designer while these clothes were created. I wear many of them to court. They never go out of style. They're classics. I have minor alterations done as necessary to keep them relatively contemporary. Jurors love them. Come, I'll show you."

Devon rose and followed her past the dining room table and chairs to a closet with double doors, which she threw open. An array of women's clothing blossomed before his eyes. Alessandra pushed aside clumps of hangers and moved items apart. Devon knew nothing about women's clothes, but even he recognized these were expensive. There were suits in fine knits and solid colors, slender dresses in what looked like linen and other fine fabrics, jackets conservatively designed in beautiful solid colors or understated patterns.

A faraway look and glistening tears came to Alessandra's eyes. "A few months later, my husband died."

Devon felt like crawling under the marshmallow chair.

I have to get out of here and think; she's tying my brain in knots!

"Could you excuse me for a few minutes, Alessandra? There's something I have to do. It shouldn't take more than twenty minutes."

"Of course," she said, brightening. "You have to take care of business. And I have a bit of housework to do." She nodded toward the coffee table.

Once outside the building, Devon began walking briskly down the gritty street. He had no destination. As he wandered, his mind began to clear, and he assessed his interactions with his adversary. Ruminating on the morning, he heard himself agree to altered interview parameters – but not greatly altered. He would still be responsible for decision-making. That responsibility was power, but his promise to grant Alessandra minor accommodations would lie hidden subconsciously in his mind as he sat at his computer and pounded out the story.

He had already violated two of his "inviolable" rules: 1) Never allow an interview subject to emotionally blackmail him; 2) Never bargain with an interview subject. In other words, no preconditions. And there had been none he could think of in his career until this aged combination Marlene Dietrich-Betty Davis-and-Lauren Bacall stroked his sensitivity cock. On the other hand, what difference did his promise make as far as the facts of the story were concerned? There was going to be a fact-checker. If his subject lied or evaded, he would find out.

Devon turned on his heel and began walking toward the Hobbit door. Alessandra Gittleman was clever, but his skills had been developed through seventeen years of print journalism. His path was clear. Do a hard-nosed interview, write the rough each night, and get someone to check the facts. He couldn't be both writer and fact-checker under such a tight deadline. He had to come up with a way to check facts rapidly. But how? The problem gnawed at him.

Devon was still anxious as he approached the Hobbit door, yet relieved that he at least had set a course. His instincts told him there was something special about Alessandra's story. It was time to get to work and find out exactly what that was.

CHAPTER 12

W hen Devon re-entered the building, he became aware of a murmur that eventually evolved into words, mostly English, with an occasional burst of Spanish. He rounded a corner and saw Alessandra moving between tables with two young women in tow, one white, one black, both dressed in jeans and white tees that read:

CASE
Because We Care

Three Hispanic women were maneuvering toward Alessandra, who was surrounded by the time Devon reached her. She spoke to him over the women's heads.

"After you left, I decided to see what problems we were facing today. These women are all volunteers at CASE. They have a variety of backgrounds. None are lawyers, although Jennifer and Cleo–" she gestured toward the young women in t-shirts "– are law students. Mariana, Carmen, and Dahlia have been with Gabriela and me for years, and they handle the initial stages of many problems. Without them, CASE couldn't function."

Alessandra addressed the women directly. "My friends," she said, reaching her arms out to them, "this is Devon Emmanuel. He's doing a magazine piece on our organization."

There were smiles and nods among the group.

Alessandra turned toward him. "We're in the midst of discussing new cases, Devon."

Devon sensed this was set up by Alessandra to demonstrate how the organization worked. He played along.

"Shall I listen in?"

"Yes," Alessandra answered. "Get the flavor of how we operate. What you're going to hear is typical of our day. Mariana, why don't you discuss the matter you're working on, please. Just don't use our clients' names."

Mariana fingered her gold necklace and seemed uneasy in Devon's presence. "Mrs. – my client – is new on public assistance," she said in heavily accented English. "She had a surprise visit from the County. There was a cousin visiting her – a man – and the county worker asked if he was living in the apartment. She said no, but the worker didn't believe her, even after she saw the cousin's out-of-state driver's license and one of his pay stubs. The worker went through everything in the house – the closets, dresser drawers, medicine cabinet – even the refrigerator. When the worker finished, she accused the client of fraud. She said it looked to her like the man was probably living in the home, and the client had not reported this. The worker threatened her with jail and said she would lose her welfare benefits and maybe her kids."

Alessandra spoke briefly in Spanish to Mariana, then asked her in English, "How do you plan to handle it?"

"I will request an immediate hearing if they attempt to end her assistance. In the meantime, I will gather proof that the cousin is actually living and working in another state. I think I should do this now, because the cousin is still here. Then if the County cancels her aid, we will have the evidence we need to go to a hearing."

"I agree," said Alessandra. "When you get the evidence of where the cousin lives, you'll show it to the County immediately, right? With a little luck, we won't have to take it to hearing. Do any of you have anything that could wind up with criminal charges?"

"I'm pretty sure mine is going to," said Carmen.

"Then we'll talk about it later in private." Alessandra glanced at the remainder of her co-workers. "Anyone else have something that's going to be touchy?"

"Nothing touchy," said Dahlia. "But the kids want to know when we're going to have our picnic?"

"Tell them Sunday three weeks from now. How is Enrique doing in his engineering courses, Dahlia?"

"Wonderful! He is handling a full load and he told me that he will get mostly A's. I am so proud of him. Things are going well."

Dahlia paused, then raised her eyebrows and added with a smirk, "You look so beautiful today, *Señora*. Is he your new boyfriend," and she looked toward Devon with a smile.

Devon could hear women laughing around the room.

Alessandra blushed a little and laughed with them.

"Afraid not, Dahlia. As I said, he's from *Walden Magazine*. Well – Mr. Emmanuel and I have to get back to the interview," she said awkwardly, then moved toward the stairs.

The women smiled at each other as the two walked away. "Nice to meet you, Mr. Emmanuel," one of them called in a suggestive tone, as the others giggled softly.

Alessandra laughed and shook her head.

CHAPTER 13

The first thing Devon noticed when he entered the upstairs apartment was the marshmallow chair. It had been moved to Alessandra's side of the coffee table, close enough that their legs might touch if she sat on one side of her recliner. The table was clean and held a small basket of red roses. From somewhere in the room came the faint dulcet tones of *Claire de Lune*.

Devon seated himself. The changes in the environment gave a sense of intimacy that was at once pleasant and disturbing.

Not this time. Not this time, Alessandra.

He shrugged off the intoxicating atmosphere and put his microphone in place while Alessandra arranged her own.

"Ready to start?" he asked, adjusting himself carefully in the more intimate spacing.

Alessandra smiled and raised her eyebrows. "Whenever you are, Devon."

"Mrs. Gittleman, I'd like to– "

Alessandra reached over and touched his knee. "–Alessandra. Please."

Her insistence on familiarity shook Devon. "Okay, Alessandra. Let's start again with your background."

Alessandra sat on the edge of her recliner, crossed her legs with an air of elegance, then folded her hands in her lap. Her physical demeanor slowly changed from relaxed and calm to one that suggested anxiety. She sat stiffly. She unfolded her hands, opened them in a finger-tip-to-finger-tip position, then folded them again. She swallowed nervously, and without moving her head, turned her eyes away from her interviewer.

"I haven't spoken about this in over thirty years. I had...problems the last time I talked about it. It's extremely private. I don't know if I can stand..."

What the hell! Right off the bat!

Devon stiffened in his chair. "I'll do the best I can, Alessandra. I'm not here to humiliate you."

Alessandra smiled weakly and removed a cigarette from her pack. Her fingers were trembling. Devon leaned over and lightly cupped his hands over hers while she lit it. She inhaled deeply and breathed out the smoke. With the exhalation, her body seemed to relax.

"I was born Alessandra Angelina Asencio Matreoni in the Bensonhurst section of Brooklyn, August 12th, 1936. It's hard to believe that was seventy-four years a–"

Devon heard nothing after the word Bensonhurst and interrupted loudly. "– I grew up in Bensonhurst! Eighty-second and Fifteenth!"

"You're kidding!" Alessandra whooped, throwing her arms upward. My father's business was on Eighty-second, near Thirteenth."

"I was raised a couple of blocks from your dad's business!"

There was happy, burbling laughter between them as Alessandra clapped her hands.

"It truly is a small world," she said, as the commotion waned. "Raised two blocks from each other. At different times, of course," she noted hurriedly.

Devon shook his head in amazement as Alessandra returned to her story.

"My parents immigrated to America in the early 1930's from the town of Indigio. That's in Calabria, south of Naples and high in the mountains. Indigio was poor even by Southern Italian standards. Young people left as soon as they could catch a boat to America. My parents were about twenty when they emigrated."

"Just…came over? Any particular skills?"

"My father had worked in my grandfather's bakery since he was a small boy. When he decided to leave Indigio, he was given a little money by his grandmother, plus a few dollars more from his father, along with two tickets on a freighter. He opened a small bakery and deli in Bensonhurst only a year after he arrived. He was known as the best baker in Bensonhurst."

Devon remembered the delicious aromas emanating from the small Italian bakeries in his old neighborhood. A trip through Bensonhurst while fasting on Yom Kippur was atonement enough for any sin.

"What was Bensonhurst like in the 1940s?" he asked.

Alessandra looked away for a moment as though trying to envision the Bensonhurst of her childhood. A nostalgic smile slowly spread on her lips, then she looked again at Devon.

"To understand – to appreciate the essence of the community – it's important to know that the neighborhood at that time was mixed Italian and Jewish. I never knew anyone there who wasn't one or the other."

Devon nodded. "It was still pretty much that way when I was a kid."

Alessandra cocked her head slightly to one side. "There was probably a difference, though. I'm talking about the '40's, and you were growing up in what? The '60's, I'm guessing?"

"Pretty much. What do you see as the difference?"

"The people. Regardless of whether they were Jews or Italians, in the '40's, most of the adults were immigrants, many fresh off the boat. In some parts of Bensonhurst, you had to speak two languages in addition to English or you couldn't communicate. If somebody you didn't know shook their head, you'd switch languages. Italian and Yiddish – that's what you heard in the streets. Except for the kids. The kids spoke only English outside the home, because that's what their parents demanded."

"What did you speak at home?"

"Italian, of course. Everybody in the neighborhood knew everyone else. Your customers were your neighbors."

"Your dad make anything besides bread and sandwiches?"

Alessandra's voice filled with pride. "He made almost everything Italian that could be baked. But his deli specialty was the hero sandwich. You could buy a half or the entire loaf. A family of five could share one, and everyone would be full."

Devon laughed and held his hands wide apart. "We used to have one of those a week when I was a kid. You know what happened later after all that cheese."

Both of them laughed. When the laughter subsided, Alessandra leaned back, readjusted her recliner, folded her hands, and continued her story.

"We lived above the bakery. Two bedrooms! I had my own room. We had a shower and hot water. Even the furnace worked! My parents were so proud of the plumbing and heating that they mentioned it in every letter to Italy."

Devon remembered similar stories from his grandparents. The only difference was, their letters went to Poland.

"Do you have brothers or sisters?" he asked.

Alessandra sighed. "I had a younger sister, but she died when I was two. I never knew her. My family memories are as an only child. Something must have happened to Mama when my sister was born. I'm guessing, of course; it was never discussed. I remember Mama looking sad when a customer would leave the shop yelling at her brood. She'd tear up, but never comment." Alessandra waved her hand as though sweeping away her mother's despair. "In any event, I was an only child."

The music changed from Debussy to Gershwin. Devon paused momentarily to enjoy the beautiful sounds of *Rhapsody in Blue*, unaware that his head had begun moving slightly, flowing with the elegant composition.

Suddenly, he realized he was losing touch with his subject and returned almost brusquely to work. "Tell me more about growing up in Bensonhurst."

Alessandra shrugged. "What's to tell? I was the daughter of an immigrant family that came from a country that went to war with their new country only a few years after they arrived. It wasn't an easy time for Italian-Americans, especially recent immigrants. It helped that we were living in an Italian neighborhood."

The distant look returned to Alessandra's eyes, and her words came in the manner of someone musing rather than telling a story.

"You could always tell the greenhorns. If they could speak English at all, they spoke it with a thick Italian or Yiddish accent. To the day she died, Mama's English never progressed beyond a couple hundred words. We rarely left the neighborhood. My father's English was just good enough to get us around if we needed to take the subway. Happened maybe – two-three times a year."

"You heard only Italian at home. Where did you learn English?"

"In the streets and in school. By the time I reached second grade, I was speaking with a Bensonhurst accent."

For Devon, the interview had taken on the feel of a conversation with a friend. The talk of family awakened a sense of loss in him. He hadn't thought about Bensonhurst in years.

Mom and Dad and I were so close when I was a kid. Sonja and I saw her parents ten or twelve weekends a year. Mine, Thanksgiving and Passover. How did I let that happen?

"Bensonhurst is changed now," said Devon. "It's more Russian than Moscow. How come you don't have a Bensonhurst accent?"

Alessandra's eyebrows rose. "California judges. You have a New York accent in front of an L.A. judge and jury, and you're screwed. I cultivated the California non-accent, and after forty years, I sound like any other home-grown Angeleno. They have no accent."

Devon was startled as Alessandra's hands suddenly flew up in the air, and her eyes widened. "Can you imagine? If you want to hear an accent in California, you can only find it in recent immigrants. What kind of place has no special accent?"

Devon laughed. "It's true. Tell me, how does a born-and-reared Bensonhurst girl adjust to Los Angeles? Every time I come here, I wonder where they hid the community. Does a New Yorker ever get used to L.A.?"

Alessandra slipped off her high-heel shoes and wiggled her toes. "I still haven't. I think you have to be born in Los Angeles, or you're condemned to spend the rest of your life here in a kind of limbo."

Devon scanned the face of the woman who only yesterday had been his tormentor. This was no monster. She was bright, funny, fun to be with.

She had spent years hidden under a harsh exterior. He wondered if anyone really knew her.

"What's going through that head of yours?" she asked.

Devon was jolted back to the interview. "Just thinking. Where did you go to school?"

"St. Cecelia. Parochial school, of course. Like all Southern Italians, we were devout Catholics. My parents went to Mass every morning. When things weren't going well, my father went to novena at night. When Papa spent so much time at church, I knew something was wrong."

Devon smiled. "My father did something similar with shul. Tell me about St. Cecelia."

Alessandra sighed. When she spoke, her voice was nostalgic. "St. Cecelia Elementary School was only a half block from where we went to church and a couple of blocks from our bakery. Those three places were my whole life."

She stopped for a moment, sat up, and poured more tea. She took a sip and made a face. "Cold. I'll be back in a moment."

Devon used the time to get out of his chair, stretch, and wander the room. When he approached the outer door, he could hear someone reading to the kids. *Charlotte's Web*. The passage was one his father had read to him many times. He could almost quote E. B. White's lines from memory. Somehow he couldn't recall having read it to his own children.

There was the sound of an inner door opening, and Devon returned to his chair. Alessandra looked different to him now than when she had left the room, but he couldn't decide what had changed.

"Where were we?" she asked, after moving her tea cup to the end table.

While Devon sipped his tea, she sat on the recliner and adjusted its position until she was comfortable.

"Parochial school," he said.

"Oh, yes. I got a wonderful education during those years. Talk about strict! All my teachers were nuns, and God help me if I brought home a note saying I did something bad or wasn't doing well in my classes. I never even got to speak in my own defense. I got my bottom spanked. The nuns never even let us out of the classroom to go to the bathroom unless it was recess or lunch. After a few weeks of first grade, I figured out if I didn't drink much before school, I could make it till recess without peeing my pants."

Devon laughed. "I've heard that before from friends who went to Catholic grade schools. So! It was pretty much a normal Bensonhurst life, huh?"

"Not the way you're thinking. Mom and Dad were immigrants, remember? I worked. I became a delivery girl for the bakery when I was seven. Neighborhood, of course. There was no danger; my parents knew I was safe."

Alessandra stopped. "You know, I'm making it sound like I grew up in a straitjacket. My mother and father loved me and were very kind to me. Italians and Jews still had large families in those days, so there were lots of kids my age to play with when I wasn't in school or helping out. No playgrounds of course, just the streets."

Alessandra moved to the edge of her recliner, sat very straight and flexed both arms to show her biceps, eyeing one of them with pride. "You're looking at the champion seven-year-old stickball player in the Eighty-second and Thirteenth Street neighborhood. You should've seen me hit. DiMaggio could have eaten his heart out."

The shared laughter made Devon feel warm and happy.

"Sounds like you had a good life – except for maybe an occasional bathroom accident and a spanking or two."

Suddenly, the conversation ended. The Gershwin music changed to the slow, mellow tones of Barbara Streisand. *"Happy days are here agaain, the skiiies above..."*

Devon saw tears glisten in Alessandra's eyes and she began speaking in a halting voice.

"Everything changed...everything...one day...I was eight. My mother and father had gone to Flatbush to see a friend. The visit was a big deal, since they rarely left Bensonhurst. At the subway exit, they entered the street just as a driver lost control of his truck. It killed them both. From that moment, my life..."

"...are clear agaain...so sing a song of cheer agaain...happy days are here agaaain."

Streisand's slow, mournful interpretation of the song seemed to make it difficult for Alessandra to continue. She struggled to hide her emotions, but the pain was obvious. The song, the image of the orphaned child, and the pain-wracked woman before him undermined Devon's journalistic exterior and, for an instant, made him want to take Alessandra, the child grown old, into his arms.

He had no idea where to go next. He was about to ask if she wanted to stop, when she sat up straight at the edge of her recliner, folded her hands in her lap, and again raised her chin in a regal manner.

"Devon, if you don't mind, I'd like to break for lunch. Go down to our kitchen. I'll meet you there in about twenty minutes."

CHAPTER 14

There were perhaps thirty kids standing in front of Devon as he took his place in a lunch line that snaked from the children's bathroom to a food service line outside the kitchen. The food was arrayed in stainless steel steam tables and served by two Hispanic women in hairnets and white aprons. Occasionally a child would not move forward, and more food would be dished onto the waiting plastic tray. No one actually asked for more; they simply didn't move.

"Mr. Emmanuel."

Devon recognized the voice of Gabriela, the assistant who had engaged yesterday's insistent intruder at Alessandra's apartment door.

"I am sorry you have been waiting in line," said Gabriela, taking Devon's arm and pulling him gently. "Come with me. I have a special place for you. We will bring you your lunch."

Devon felt embarrassed to be given special treatment in front of hungry children.

"It's okay," he said. "I can wait my turn."

Gabriela shook her head. "Please. *Señora* Gittleman has a table where she has lunch with guests."

The table was in the farthest corner of the adult side of the room. From this vantage point, Devon could view the entire floor. Almost immediately, his lunch arrived, two cheese enchiladas covered in a brick-red sauce with rice and refried beans. He was nearly finished eating when he saw Alessandra descend the stairs. She walked toward him with a slow ambling gait, her shoulders slightly hunched. He wondered if she was in pain. He stood as she approached.

"How did you like your enchiladas?" Alessandra asked, wearily sitting down opposite him.

Devon was so surprised by her haggard appearance, he was slow to answer. When he did, he stammered. "G-great. I...I watched the kids. They ate like they were famished."

Alessandra twisted in her seat and scanned the children's side of the room.

"Twenty-third," she whispered.

"Twenty-third?"

She motioned with her head toward the children. "Today's the twenty-third. Last week of the month is coming up; their families are running out of food. Not much to eat in their homes, so they load up at CASE."

"Don't they get food stamps?"

The question went unanswered. Alessandra twisted again to gaze at the children. When her food arrived, she nibbled at the enchilada.

"Some do, some don't," she finally answered. "You can still be very poor and not be eligible for food stamps. And many counties make food stamps hard to get. There are dozens of ways to do it, and bureaucracies are experts at making eligibility harder, even when the law tries to make it simpler. Workers 'lose' documents," she said, and made imaginary quote marks in the air. "They leave applications for weeks – sometimes months – in pending files, then claim the client has failed to cooperate.

"Counties constantly understaff the offices where people apply, and many workers are simply unable to keep up. When they falter, it becomes the client's fault. Even if someone is successful in applying for food stamps, it requires multiple office visits, often with three-to-five-hour waiting times. Sometimes months go by, and the applicant doesn't get a response to an application. When they check, they often find their application was denied, but no one has told them. Since they didn't know it was denied, they've lost time if they want to restart the process. And they have to start from the beginning. Counties are masters at denying aid to the poor. And the rest of California doesn't give a damn, especially our beloved political leaders."

A cynical expression appeared on Alessandra's face as Devon stared at her questioningly.

"Stick around, Bubby. You've got a lot to learn. Right now, I want to make you an offer."

Devon smirked. "Hopefully, not an offer I can't refuse."

Alessandra smiled as though the act created pain. "You'll never know how many times I've wished I were friends with the Godfather."

Behind Alessandra, Devon watched the children mopping their plates with flour tortillas. He wondered how many were children of undocumented parents. Then he remembered Alessandra's comment about food stamps. He knew from previous reading that undocumented persons were ineligible for them. Still, it must cost CASE a lot to feed everyone who came for help.

"You let them go through the line a second time?" he asked.

"No, my food budget's almost depleted by this time each month."

Alessandra ate a little more of her enchilada. "You interested in hearing my offer?"

The question was asked so softly Devon could hardly hear it.

Jesus, her eyes are glazed, and she's squinting..

"Always up for a deal," he answered casually.

Alessandra leaned forward, slid a hand over his and spoke quickly. "You've proven to me you're a *mensch*. I can work with you. *Walden* wants something from me and I want something from *Walden*. Let's talk about what I want. Since the economy crashed, my work has almost doubled, but my budget hasn't. I need something that will bring in money. I'm hoping to get it from your rich readers."

Confusion descended on Devon. He stalled for time.

"There's a lot of different parts to what you just said, Alessandra. What specifically do you have in mind?"

She pushed her tray aside. "When *Walden* publishes the CASE story, I want it to be the only one in that issue."

Devon's mouth fell open. "Alessandra, we do ten-page stories, three per issue– "

"– Page one to the last period. And I compose the title."

Devon jerked his hand from under Alessandra's as he came to the edge of his chair and his voice rose. "You want to write the title of my article!"

Alessandra leaned back in her chair and smiled at him. "Did the *mamzers* at *Walden* tell you I demanded that you write the story?"

"Yeah," Devon shot back angrily. "You asked after I quit!"

"Bullshit! I asked for you when I first contacted them. Picking you was no accident; I checked a year of *Walden* issues. Most of your writers have the literary talent of a warthog. You, on the other hand, have talent, Bubby. That's why I chose you," she said, looking proud of herself even as she squinted at him.

Her brazenness confounded Devon, then outraged him. "You–drove– me–out–of–CASE!"

Alessandra waved her hand, moved her chair close to the table, and leaned forward. "Forget that; it's no longer relevant. I had to get a feel for what made you tick. Listen to the deal. I know *Walden* didn't send you to Los Angeles to learn about suffering Hispanic women. *Walden* sent you to Los Angeles to get the life story of a hell-raising bitch who terrorizes politicians and is an object of curiosity. Especially among highly educated, wealthy, liberal Americans like those who read *Walden*."

Alessandra let her comments sink in for a few seconds, then said, "You were told to get my life story or basically not come back alive. Am I right?"

Devon stared in disbelief.

She set me up! When I walked out of CASE yesterday, it was a test to see how far she could push me! This woman is Machiavelli with a vagina.

As Devon stared speechlessly, Alessandra grasped his upper arm in a lightning move. "Am I right?"

Devon searched for an evasive response, found none, then heard himself say weakly, "Yes."

Alessandra giggled. "*Mamzers.*" She released his arm.

Immediately, Devon became unsure of what he had agreed to.

"I need to go over what you're proposing. You're asking that an entire issue of *Walden* be dedicated to CASE, plus the right to dictate the title. Is that it?"

"No. I also want you to feature some women who are poster children for what I've been fighting for thirty-eight years. Other egregious problems I'll summarize."

At first, Devon was so enraged by her proposal he couldn't respond. Then words began rolling out of him in a low, but angry voice.

"*Walden Magazine* has been in existence for over eighty years. We've been the benchmark for excellence in intellectual journalism since we began. We are not literary whores! Who do you think you are, issuing orders? You can keep your damned interview; *Walden* doesn't need it."

Devon rose to leave, but Alessandra grabbed his coat sleeve and held on tight. He slowly eased back into his chair and glared at her.

"Calm down and listen," she said urgently. "This isn't a deal for personal money on my part. It's an agreement with the magazine to allow a certain amount of latitude in telling the story. And it's a story *Walden* wants to tell. A story *Walden* readers need to see. Furthermore, it's a signal to your readership and advertisers that *Walden* is stepping into a new age with a bold new format. And it's starting the change with a compelling, important story. *Capiche?*"

Devon continued to glare at her.

"Is that it?" he asked in an acid tone.

"No. I want the article out in the next issue. Now you have the whole package."

With that, Alessandra massaged her eyes with her fingers, then turned and watched the children.

Devon slumped back in his chair. Minutes passed while he considered how to respond to something so radical. Finally, he decided on a few answers. It was time to set limits. He reached out and tugged her sleeve. She turned toward him expectantly.

"To begin with, Alessandra, you will not, repeat, *not* dictate the title of this article."

Alessandra started to speak, but Devon cut her off.

"I won't argue the point! That's the way it's going to be, or I quit now. Is that understood – yes or no?"

"Yes."

"Okay, now we can talk. Do you know how hard it would be to turn out a thirty-page *Walden*-style article in a couple of weeks? Even if I could gather the material and write it against that deadline, there's only one person at *Walden* who could authorize doing it. And he'll refuse. Your proposal is right out of *Alice in Wonderland*. By the way, what exactly does *Walden* get in return?"

Alessandra took a deep breath, tilted her head to the side, then exhaled and spoke in a hoarse tone, her eyes cast downward.

"You get the old broad's personal story beginning to end and a guarantee your readers will orgasm."

At first, Devon was amused, then sobered as possibilities began to stir. The concept intrigued him. Alessandra was controversial. A mystery woman. The stuff of spy novels. An article like the one she was proposing could have mass-market appeal if it were picked up by other media. If Andrews was right about the need for something that could deliver *Walden* its angel, this was it. But H-T would first have to bounce it off Ms. Lillian and take the risk she wouldn't like the content or the enormous change in format. If she objected, that would be the end of what was surely *Walden's* best chance for an investor.

Devon's next thought was more personal. If it turned out to be a great story, it wouldn't necessarily matter if Ms. Lillian didn't like it; it could still be useful to him in getting another job, because it would carry his byline. But then, there was the problem of the deadline. It would only work if he could make the deadline! A lot of "ifs." Too many.

"Alessandra, I'm a working journalist. Anything this big would have to be blessed by *Walden's* publisher, Halden-Tennsley. His approach to publishing is set in mid-1950's cement."

Alessandra patted Devon's hand. "I know that. But you're not powerless. You can promote the idea when the brass asks your opinion, which they will, because it's such an outrageous idea. Meantime, I've arranged for you to see one of the people you'll be covering in the article. She'll give you an idea of what to expect from the CASE part of the story. That will help in your arguments."

Devon, who had been sipping his drink, barely managed to keep from spraying a mouthful. "You've already set up an interview?"

Alessandra squeezed his hand. "You liked the story of my early years. You were into it; I could tell. Little Italian girl...orphaned at eight...becomes a lawyer...regularly beats the crap out of the power structure of mighty California. How I got to where I am is ten times better than that story you covered on the bum who left eight million bucks to the University of Chicago. *Walden* got enough mileage out of that little feel-gooder to keep its readers happy for most of a year. Am I right?"

Devon stared into the glazed eyes of his combination hope and nemesis. What she said was true. He hadn't even liked the Chicago story. It was a living cliché, more in keeping with *The National Enquirer* than *Walden*. Then, sudden clarity.

This wasn't dreamed up on the spur of the moment. She must have been planning this for months. It's a great idea, and a superb set-up. She can load it with high drama. There's no way to write and research her background and meet the writing deadline and still fact-check every statement she makes about her past, no matter how fast everyone works. I'll be flying blind in some substantive areas where I don't even suspect a problem. The close deadline gives her an enormous advantage to embellish or withhold information. On the other hand, every story inevitably poses the same risk. The risk here is just greater. It comes down to trust. How can I trust her, given my experience with her so far? I can't, but there is one thing that suggests hope. She gave her life to CASE, something that offered her only ignominy instead of fame, penury instead of fortune. That's enormous. But there's something deep she's hiding. I can sense it. It's risky as hell, but I want the story. I need it. Seventeen years as a cleaner-than-a-hound's-tooth journalist, and I'm on the cusp of becoming a flack to save my ass. What does she really want? What difference does it make at the moment? I'll try one more thing.

"Alessandra, you haven't been straight with me. You could have had stories like this written any time in the last twenty years. Why now? Why such a rush?"

Alessandra's arms flew apart. "This I have to explain to a boy from Bensonhurst?"

She looked around as if to see if anyone was listening, then spoke in a hoarse whisper. "I'm broke, Devon! A few more months, and I won't be able to pay the taxes on this place. I spent thirty-eight years building CASE, and it's about to collapse. What's going to replace CASE when the doors close?"

Devon stared unblinkingly at Alessandra. She stared back. It was as if their locked gaze were a wrestling match with both sides exerting maximum effort and neither gaining an edge. Finally, Devon looked down at his tray.

"You're being melodramatic."

"Melodramatic! For thirty-eight years, CASE has been a relentless defender of poor women, Hispanic and non-Hispanic, in Los Angeles County. If we go under, it would be a terrible loss. Our leaders are not standing in line to speak for the poor, Devon. Politicians are looking for a career; they don't give a damn about their constituents. The only time they notice poor people is when they need their vote. They're all liars, every damn one of them."

Devon jumped on the generalization. "How do you know they're all lying?"

Alessandra rubbed her forehead, and delivered her answer in a harsh whisper. "Their fucking tongues cluck. You ready to deal or not?"

H-T will never go for it.

"I'll see what I can do."

"Mazeltov! Now go back to your hotel and start selling the idea to your editor – that Andrews guy. His knees buckled when I demanded that you be sent back to do the story or I was quitting on *Walden*. I looked him up; he's smart. Work with him before you take it to the executive suite. I'll see you tomorrow. Your interview with one of my clients is at ten. Check in with me first, and we'll have coffee."

Alessandra pushed away her tray and started to rise.

All right, lady, you're not in total control of this relationship. I can guess some things about you, too. Let's see how you respond to this.

"Hey, wait a minute," Devon said. "How did things go with that District Attorney? Did you get Judge Wexler off the case?"

Alessandra's head jerked as she lifted herself into a standing position with one arm on the seat of her chair, the other on the table top.

Ignoring Devon's question, she began weaving her way through her constituents toward her apartment. "Tootle-ooh, Bubby," she called over her shoulder.

Devon smiled inwardly with satisfaction.

CHAPTER 15

Devon returned to his hotel room and took a long hot shower, emerging rejuvenated. Toweling off, he commented to himself that, although traumatic, it actually had been a good day. But a lot more lay ahead of him. He dressed, sat down at the desk and considered whom to call first, Clark Andrews or Sonja. It was 4:50 in the afternoon in New York; the editor would be free of meetings. A good time to reach him. When Andrews failed to answer, Devon left a text message indicating he'd call again in twenty minutes, giving an excuse to end any lengthy harangue by Sonja.

Devon sighed as he touched Sonja's land line on his cell phone. In his mind, he could see the tall, slim, dark-haired woman who looked younger than her forty-four years. Her oval face, once exquisitely beautiful, was still attractive enough to turn male heads, yet for years, it had failed to arouse sensual feelings in him. He knew her high-pitched "hello" would be annoying. The mental image of his wife irritated him, and as if by reflex, he rose from his chair and began pacing the room.

If Sonja were home, Devon knew she'd be curled up on the couch reading, cell phone beside her, cordless landline within reach. As soon as she knew who was calling, she'd pick up the phone, leave the couch, and start walking through the clutter.

Her "hello" was exactly as Devon had imagined it.

"It's me, Sonja. Sorry I didn't call yesterday, but I've been underwater. What's going on?"

"The usual stuff. Are you in the hotel *Walden* set up for you?"

"Yes."

"What's it like?"

The Twilight Zone entered Devon's mind. Thinking levity might ease his way into a less traumatic call, he delivered his answer in the sinister voice of the show's narrator. "Imagine if you will a single-story Bates motel with a postage-stamp-sized grungy-bottomed swimming pool. Inside the building, a man is standing in a room with two queen-size beds, one for him, and one, he assumes, for the cockroaches."

"Not funny. You told me you were going to interview Alessandra Gittleman. She interests me. I know you won't tell me, but I'd like to know more about her. She's very intriguing to the intellectual community but she never interacts with us. I'd like to meet her. You constantly meet interesting people in your work and never discuss them with me anymore. I never know who you've interviewed until our issue of *Walden* arrives and I learn that you've just published on a Nobelist."

Sonja's harangue grated on Devon. "Maybe it's because you haven't finished an article I've written in years. We used to discuss them, but today I could interview Vladimir Putin and you wouldn't care enough to read the whole thing. I got tired of it. Besides, I told you who I was interviewing before I left, and you acted like you never heard of her and didn't care."

Sonja's voice rose. "I was so angry you were leaving, I didn't think about it. When was the last time you asked about my work?"

Devon knew she was right. He had seen the art she loved so much. He hated it and couldn't pretend he liked it. That always irritated her. She interpreted his reaction as disdain for the importance of her work. It had been years since they had shown an interest in each other's professional lives, and that was partly the reason for the absence of their once lively discussions. He was undoubtedly the guiltier of the two in this regard. He often went out of his way to avoid letting her know what story he was working on.

"You're right about my ignoring your interest in my work, Sonja," he said, trying to placate her so he could end the conversation on a good note. "That's one thing I can improve on. I'll try. I've started my interview with Gittleman, and at the same time, I'm trying to figure out how I'm going to write the story. It's been all work and a lot of anxiety."

"Devon, L.A. is now one of the country's great cultural centers, and you're seeing it through the image of a seedy hotel. Sample the local cuisine. I've heard there are many fine restaurants out there. Go out and relax in the intellectual community."

Devon rolled his eyes. When he imagined the contents of Sonja's mind, he pictured hand-painted Volkswagen buses, Simon and Garfunkel, and Woodstock. He couldn't stand any of them.

"Thank you for that suggestion, Sonja. I'll go out for Ethiopian food tonight. It makes you thin. How are the kids?"

"Is it true? Is that really true?"

"What?"

"That Ethiopian food makes you thin?"

Devon stopped pacing. "Have you ever seen a fat Ethiopian? How are the kids?"

"I was just talking to a woman at work who comes from Southern India. A staple of her diet is chickpeas. You should see her; she's beautiful.

Her skin is perfect. The people from Ethiopia have beautiful skin. Do you think it's because they eat chickpeas?"

Devon's shoulders slumped. "Without question. How are the kids?"

"It would be wonderful to explore some of those diets. Find out everything– "

"Goddamn it, Sonja, how are the kids?"

Sonja paused for a moment, then asked, "Why are you getting upset? I just want us to be healthy. Californians eat healthy, probably because– "

"Aw, for Christ's sake, Sonja, how are the kids!"

There was a peculiar sound, and Devon decided Sonja had kicked something out of her path. When she spoke, the irritation in her voice was equal to his. "The kids are fine, except they're making the house a wreck. Thank God for summer school; at least it keeps them busy. David had the gall to tell me to clean up my own mess because he was tired of cleaning up after me. I'm sure he's starting puberty. Now there'll be two men in the house reducing it to dreck. I'll be spending all my free time cleaning. When you get back, we're going to discuss the division of labor in this house."

Devon let his head fall backward, then brought it forward until his chin hit his chest.

You dumb shit, why do you provoke these battles? All you had to do was be a little nicer; now you've set her off. That means your kids are going to catch hell instead of getting through the next week or so without dealing with a pissed-off mother who doesn't like being a mother. Brilliant, Emmanuel.

"Sonja, I have to go– "

"You're not going until you tell me about Alessandra Gittleman. Is she really brilliant? I looked her up on Wiki. Did you know she's from Brooklyn? They say she lives a cloistered life. Do you think she might speak at my Mensa group if she comes to The City?"

Devon glanced at his watch. It was 5:15 in New York. He needed to call Andrews.

"Sonja, Alessandra Gittleman is delightful, probably has an I.Q. of 160, was born and raised in Bensonhurst, and doesn't leave CASE headquarters except to raise hell with the establishment. The odds of her speaking to a Mensa group I would put somewhere between my teaching quantum physics at MIT and space aliens landing on the White House lawn. Tell the kids I love them and I'll be back soon, which will be several days from now. I'll bring you a menu from an Ethiopian restaurant if I go to one. Bye."

Devon touched Andrews' name in his cell phone before Sonja could attempt a return call.

After the third ring, a familiar voice answered. "Devon, are you going to bother me?"

"Yeah. Are you alone?"

"No, Devon, I'm in bed with Marilyn Monroe, Rita Hayworth and Mae West. What the hell's so important?"

Devon grinned as he retreated to his bed. "Don't you know any live actresses?"

"Not necessary. Those ladies were so hot, their asses are still warm. Whatcha got?"

"I'm not sure. I've had a day unique in my seventeen years at *Walden*. Alessandra Gittleman fits Winston Churchill's description of the Soviet Union – an enigma wrapped in a riddle. I've never met anyone like her. She goes from seventy-four-year-old vamp to meek, submissive little girl, to wounded warrior, and somewhere in the mix, from being one of God's favorites to a she-devil straight out of hell. I vacillate between considering her one of the most honest humans I've ever known to suspecting she out-performs Richard Nixon as a liar."

Devon waited for Andrews to assimilate the information. It was Andrews' way, and there was nothing you could do to hurry him.

Ten seconds later, the editor barked, "You got all this stuff on the computer, right? I've been so busy I haven't had time to check my Alessandra file."

"Yeah, everything's there. Clark, if I can capture this woman on paper, it will attract more angels to *Walden* than the Virgin Mary. There is a caveat."

"The part about out-performing Richard Nixon as a liar?"

"Yeah. But there's more. She wants to make a deal. Her personal story, birth to present, in exchange for our publication of the travails of indigent women caught up in the justice system, plus a summation of other bureaucratic indiscretions. Whadaya think?"

The sound of Andrews' swivel chair turning from side to side came to an abrupt halt. "Not possible. You can't cover all that in ten pages, Devon."

"Not a problem. She insists on the entire issue."

Devon heard a rolling sound followed by a thump, which he assumed was Andrews' body flying forward in his chair and slamming into his desk.

"What!"

"Entire issue. The *next* issue!"

There was silence followed by a response that carried a touch of anger.

"You – you're certain this is a valid proposal? Why the hell's she giving this interview anyway?"

"Money. She's doing the interview to interest rich readers so they'll contribute to CASE. And yeah, the proposal is real."

There was another thump. Devon knew the editor's elbows had just hit the desktop, and one hand was holding his head. It was among Andrews' favorite intimidation poses he had used repeatedly on writers over the years until it had become habit. "If it's money she wants, she might lie her head off to make sure this piece pours bucks into her coffers."

He gets it. He cleared the road. Now, I've got to sell him on the tough part.

"And it'll be our asses if she does and somebody discovers she lied," Devon said.

"Yeah!" There was another pause, then, "The single-issue part is an incredible idea, though. But only H-T can make that decision. If he says yes, you think there's a chance in hell we could cull it to thirty pages and get it ready in time for press?"

Devon had been staring at a bad Old Master print on the hotel room wall while waiting for his editor to speak. The question jarred him.

"I don't know. I'd have to write up each day's material that same evening. You'd have to edit right behind me. I don't have the details worked out yet, but I think it's possible – if we can get what we need."

Andrews' response was immediate. "Fact-checker?"

The man is good. His life may be a disaster, but he's great to work with.

"Absolutely," said Devon. "Especially about anything that touched her personal life. We need somebody great with a computer who's willing to push the envelope to get information that's buried in computer files – stuff long past and protected. Someone who isn't worried about – well – let's say...whatever."

Andrews' laugh had a touch of bitterness in it.

"Devon, H-T is holding onto every buck. One of our great editors, Izzy Schwartz, who from this point forward will be referred to as Izzy the Schmuck, quit yesterday after hearing *Walden* had money problems. He ain't being replaced. As a result, I, Clark Fucking Andrews, represent fifty percent of *Walden's* working editors. I have inherited Izzy the Schmuck's current projects because, according to our glorious leader, I have 'broad shoulders.' Both fact-checkers have just been laid off and there is no way in hell that old fart will put out a dime for another one. That places the burden of verification totally on the writer. Uh – that's you."

Everything Andrews said made sense to Devon. With the magazine in desperate financial trouble, H-T wouldn't hire extra help to verify Alessandra's story. Yet, if they went to press with the story, and Alessandra had lied, *Walden's* competitors would kick the magazine around like a literary football. The results, given *Walden's* perilous state, would be bankruptcy. The simple truth of Devon's previous consideration of the matter returned to haunt him. No journalist could spend several days interviewing Alessandra, write a feature story on her life against a backbreaking deadline, and still have time to verify what she said. There was only one way to get the job done, and that was to hire a fact-checker who was cheap, fast and motivated.

"Clark, you still there?"

"Squirting nitroglycerine under my tongue."

"Remember that intern we had a few weeks ago?"

Devon heard Andrews' chair turning again. "My sister's kid?"

"Yeah. What was his name?"

"Lindsay Culbertson."

"Yeah. I'll bet he'd like to pick up a couple hundred bucks a week checking facts using online sources. Tell H-T my problem and see if he'll spring for Lindsay. Two weeks max. Whatcha think?"

The squeaking stopped. "I think you're out of your fucking mind! The kid's seventeen. He doesn't have the slightest idea how to do what you're asking. And he's a real prick. No way, Devon, we need a pro."

Devon took a deep breath and blew it out through pouched cheeks. He was about to pitch something that might destroy him professionally and take Andrews with him. "I don't agree. A pro can't get us answers fast enough. We need an arrogant little computer geek who's snooty enough to think he can get to any data cache. While your nephew was at *Walden*, one of our lousy writers who was a computer nerd told me the kid could hack any system. That he was amazing."

Andrews' response was immediate and loud. "Yeah, but Lindsay don't know shit about being an investigator! He gets thrown out of every school he enters! His only interests are computers, sex and hamburgers – in that order. The reason he was at *Walden* was because he fucked up, and a judge ordered him to get a job after the school year ended or his ass would be sitting in juvenile hall. My sister leaned on me, and I terrified him into it. Is that what you want for a fact-checker?"

"Does he like money?"

"To the extent it'll get him another piece of computer equipment, ass, or a hamburger."

"Then I want him."

Silence.

"Well, he meets the computer and budget requirements," said Andrews. "But I still don't understand how we'll use him."

"Checking out stuff using his geeksmanship. I'll guide him. I'll go over his findings daily. At least we'll know if Gittleman's lying...maybe."

Devon could hear deep breathing. He knew that giving the editor time for a well-considered response to a difficult question was dangerous. A negative from Andrews after he had seriously considered an issue could be reversed only by God.

"If we don't do this, we may be walking right into a disaster, Clark. Think what could happen if she's lying and we're in print. I'll call you back tomorrow morning after you've talked to H-T."

"Yeah. What you going to do for the rest of the evening?"

"Have dinner at an Ethiopian restaurant and start writing. Later."

CHAPTER 16

D evon had never eaten Ethiopian food and decided to give it a try.
He called the front desk.
"Is there a decent Ethiopian restaurant in L.A.?"
"Absolutely, sir. I recommend the Queen of Sheba. It's walking distance for you since you're from New York."
"How far is it?"
"Out the front door, turn right, and it's about a hundred yards ahead on this side of the street."
"What has New York got to do with it? Wouldn't someone from L.A. walk there?"
"Angelenos can't walk that far, sir. Our legs have atrophied since the invention of the automobile. It's an evolution thing. Try the *yebag siga alitcha*. It's great."
An evolution thing. Funny.
The desk man was right; the *yebag siga alitcha*, a spicy lamb stew served on spongy bread, was delicious. Devon finished the main course, then relaxed on pillows in his private alcove, ordered coffee and a sweet milky dessert, and mulled over the proposed story. The enormity of the task, if H-T went for the idea, was daunting. Get a thirty-page effort into the next issue of *Walden*? At first, he thought the idea was impossible; then the challenge began to intrigue him. The more he thought, the more fascinated he became.
He spooned the dessert slowly. Then he stumbled on a possible solution. Compartmentalize. Each day's interview would be written as an independent "chapter." As more chapters were completed, he and Andrews would cut and paste from one part of the story to another, eliminating the chapter divisions as the article progressed, constantly smoothing the manuscript. When they finished, they could have an excellent rough, hopefully good enough to turn into a print-ready final in about a day. He rolled the idea around in his mind. It was an overwhelming plan, but the best he could devise, given the limitations.

The interviewing, writing, and constant re-writing would be exhausting. He needed additional time – some breaks in the interview process. Alessandra had intimated she might have to interrupt their time together. What had first appeared as an impediment began to look like an advantage, provided he could still acquire all the relevant information. His writer's instincts helped him envision what he wanted as a finished copy – Alessandra's story, tenderly told, interspersed with short bursts of the cold reality of her clients' lives.

His biggest worry was Alessandra. She had sounded desperate enough to say anything to get her hands on money. A computer guru was absolutely essential as a rapid means of fact checking. If H-T wouldn't pay Culbertson, regardless of Andrews' reticence, Devon decided he would pay the kid himself. First thing in the morning, he would call Clark and get Culbertson's number.

Devon took a sip of coffee and stretched out his long legs. His mind wandered away from the article, eventually settling on money. The draconian prospect of losing his job was hard to shake. That led to reflections on his personal life, a world he had previously avoided.

How the hell did we go from where we were when we got married to where we are now? We had such fun at the start. Rolled around in bed four or five times a week. Laughed like fools when we played out some of those crazy fantasies she dredged up. We were happy. The easy access to money had something to do with it. That apartment her folks picked out for us as a wedding present was beautiful.

The apartment appeared in Devon's mind as if he had just stepped through its door for the first time. Two bedrooms, a dining room, two baths, walk-in closets and furniture he knew cost a fortune. Sonja's mom had leased it in her name and refused to allow the landlords to reveal the cost, but Devon knew it had to be several thousand a month even back then. He had gone from lower middle class Bensonhurst to way upper middle class Manhattan.

The Schechters were giving it, and I liked it, and I took it, and I didn't argue. Sonja and I went out at least four times a month. Broadway theater, opera, dining at the best restaurants. Some of those nights cost five hundred bucks.

Devon rearranged himself on the cushions, then massaged the cramp in his calf until the pain left. He continued his musing.

Work was easier in those early years. Writing for large magazines kept me New York bound. I learned a lot on rewrite. It was fun showing my work to Sonja. I passed some of her suggestions along to the editors, and a lot of them were used. Those recommendations probably helped get me the job at Walden. I was on top of the world. I was a Walden writer. Loved the snob appeal of writing for Walden. They had some great young writers. I'll never forget Clark Andrews putting me through the wringer. He made me a real journalist. He could have picked one of the other young guys to mentor. I owe him. Seventeen years ago...seems like a century. Sonja and I were so close...how could we wind up like this?

Devon shifted on the pillows and caught the waiter's eye.

"Can I have a warm-up on my coffee?"

The tall, bronze-skinned man answered in unintelligible English, then left and returned with another cup of coffee and a small spicy candy. As Devon sipped his coffee, his mind eventually returned to his domestic problems. He wandered through his marriage until he identified what appeared to be the beginning of the inexorable downhill course.

That stock disaster. How could the Schechters be so naïve as to put their money in the hands of a speculator? They went from an experienced advisor who protected their inherited assets to that nutcase who promised them the sky. In one year, they lost everything. Sonja and I left a swanky Manhattan apartment for a one-bedroom in a seedy part of Brooklyn. Then she discovered she was pregnant. Fortunately, she got the museum job about that time. Kept us eating and got us out of that piece-of-shit, one-bedroom, and into our lousy three-bedroom. Butt-ugly part of Brooklyn, but at least it's not violent.

Deeper reflection brought Devon to the first of the great disasters in his marital life, an event he had thought at the time was wonderful without measure – a promotion to senior writer. Andrews kept feeding him plum interviews, but those interviews required a lot of travel. He found the work exciting. He began getting job offers. One in particular came to mind.

That one offer was almost double what I was making. I was an idiot not to take it, but Walden was my dream. And we were doing okay. Sonja became the museum's Girl Friday, and they added a third day to her week. Fucking museum got a hell of a deal. They were getting chewed up by the competition, and she turned things around for them. I remember how excited she was with her first "Important New Artists" opening. I shouldn't have been out of town that day. She never forgave me. Sarah's birth saved the day.

He remembered how much they both loved Sarah. That should have brought them closer together, but somehow it didn't. Sonja's world became Sarah and the museum. She had Sarah and the museum, and he had *Walden.* They began living separate lives. To him Sonja seemed to have lost her anchor. She became more and more involved with the museum, eventually drifting away even from Sarah.

Sarah had more of a home at the day care center than she had with Sonja and me. We didn't even recognize what was happening to us until Sonja got pregnant with David. That was the single most destructive event in our marriage. She didn't want the baby, and I did. I have no idea why I wanted another child. I just...wanted the baby. She finally agreed. That was the last time we had sex. So many years ago. I'm not even horny anymore. Used to have a few one-night stands on assignment. It's been months since I got laid. God my life is such a mess.

Devon waved to the waiter, who came to the table.

"Check, please."

Devon paid the bill, then stood up and stretched. He had to stop dwelling on his personal life. Everything had to wait until the angel was on board and *Walden* was stabilized. On his way out, he picked up a menu handwritten in Amharic script with a broken English translation. He folded it, stuffed it in the hip pocket of his jeans, and went to his hotel to begin work.

CHAPTER 17

Devon awoke at six the next morning. First on his to-do list was the call to Andrews. He was met by a growling "Whadayawant?"

"Sorry about interrupting your morning routine, Clark, but I wanted to get you before you met with the suits. I've gone over this thing *ad nauseum* and the only conclusion I'm left with is that we don't have a choice; we've got to hire your nephew. If his computer talent is as good as that writer told me, he's our best option."

A sniff and a squeaking chair were Andrews' response.

"You're no-bullshit serious about this, aren't you?"

"I am. That brings me to the reason for this call. If H-T refuses to put the kid on the payroll, I want the right to pay him myself for purposes of this article. And I want to start today."

Devon heard Andrews' chair roll, then a thump.

He put his elbows on his desk.

"I worked this thing over last night and grudgingly came to the same miserable conclusion. There may not be any other choice, Devon, but I promise you big problems. You can't control the little shit. You're going to have to terrify him into believing if he gets out of line, retribution will be certain castration. I'm not joking. Don't be nice to this kid; he'll take it as a sign of weakness. I'll work on H-T today. Now if there's nothing else, I need to get back to editing one of Izzy the Schmuck's lousy writers."

"One thing more. I need Lindsay's cell phone number."

"Text it to you later."

"Okay."

"Can I go now?"

"With God."

Devon's entrance at CASE later that morning was warmly greeted by the inhabitants. Anita Salazar smiled widely.

"Buenos días, Señor Emmanuel."

"Buenos días, Señora Salazar."

The exchange exhausted Devon's knowledge of Spanish. As he strode toward the stairway leading to Alessandra's apartment, other women smiled at him.

Definitely making progress.

He ascended the stairs at a trot and rapped on the door. It was a vivacious Alessandra who appeared in a sleek brown suit with tiny flecks of pastel blue and yellow threaded through the fine fabric. A scarf with soft blues and yellows was perfectly arranged like a cloud that rose from her collar to just beneath her chin. She wore gold earrings shaped like tiny waves and embedded with pale blue stones. Once again, her makeup was understated.

"Come in, Devon," she said, gesturing toward what he had come to consider his chair. "I have coffee and pastries."

Gone was the tea set. Roses now joined a coffee pot on the lace-covered table amid an array of cups, saucers, napkins and a pastry basket. Alessandra's demeanor was almost distant. Her eyes were dreamy, and she smiled absently as she uncovered and extended the basket.

"You didn't seem to like cheese danish, Devon," she said. "I took the liberty of buying cherry and blueberry pastries for today. Perhaps you'll like those better."

Devon was starving. He hadn't had time for breakfast. He devoured one of each kind of pastry along with two cups of coffee.

"This is great," he said through his last bite. "Thanks for the breakfast."

Alessandra had been munching daintily, watching Devon as he ate, her face a mask of serenity. Finally she asked, "Did you pass my proposal on to the high muckety-mucks at *Walden*?"

Devon refilled his cup and took another swallow of coffee.

"Sent it through the editor to whom you spoke so sweetly after I quit."

Alessandra laughed and sipped her coffee. "I suppose I was a little hard on him. Ready to interview one of my clients?"

"Yes. Do you think she'll object to being hooked up to a mike?"

Alessandra picked up her office phone. "Gabriela, has Maria arrived? ... Good ...Where did you set them up?...It'll do...Mr. Emmanuel will be right down. I'll come a little later."

"We're meeting downstairs?" Devon asked, setting his cup on the table and wiping his hands on a napkin. "Won't your client be bothered by the lack of privacy?"

Alessandra rose from her chair. "It's rare that anyone other than Gabriela enters this apartment, and that only happens if there is pressing business. This is my sanctuary, my place to think about my cases, or let my mind rest and lick my wounds. You'll be in a corner downstairs, close to where we were yesterday. It's private enough. Don't start the interview until I get there. It's not that I don't trust you; I just don't want to open up any areas that should remain privileged. And you can't use Maria's real name in the article, okay?"

"Got it."

Three chairs surrounded the small folding table, and Devon chose the one affording the best view of the room. Gabriela informed him the interview subject was making a quick phone call and would be present shortly. He passed the time watching the children. Regardless of the problems of their families, they were enjoying themselves. He could also hear the constant murmur of voices on the other side of the room as CASE clients worked with the aid of volunteers. Minutes passed, and Devon grew restless.

Where the hell is that woman?

A few minutes later, a short, wide-eyed, Hispanic woman whom Devon guessed to be in her mid-thirties exited the bathroom and started toward him. She was slightly overweight, and her thin-striped, spaghetti-strap jersey top revealed deep cleavage. As she approached, Devon's eyes fixed momentarily on the cleavage before descending to her tight black capri pants that flared slightly at the calf. His eyes ascended to the woman's face, again hesitating at her cleavage. She was pretty. A soft blush highlighted her brown cheeks, and she wore a rich, dark, berry-colored lipstick. What fascinated Devon were her eyes, which were heavily outlined, her upper lids looking almost bruised. Brows had been penciled on in rounded surprise. Raspberry-painted toenails protruded from her wedge sandals, and earrings, reminiscent of those he had once seen in a Moroccan bazaar, swung as she walked. Initially, Devon wondered what such casual, revealing attire was intended to convey to a stranger such as he, to whom she would be telling her story. Then he realized her clothing made a clear and simple statement. *I'm a woman,* it said, *a Latina. I'm sexy and I make no apologies.* She did not make eye contact, however, even as Devon rose to greet her.

Just then, Alessandra descended the stairs and walked quickly toward the two of them. She and Maria embraced, briefly conversing in Spanish. Finally, Alessandra placed her hand lightly on Maria's shoulder and introduced her to Devon.

"*Buenos días,*" said Devon, extending his hand and adding two more words he had recently learned. "*Mucho gusto.*"

Maria smiled in acknowledgment of the greeting, but her body movements suggested she was becoming nervous. Devon gestured toward a chair and spoke softly as he fitted her with a microphone.

"You can call me by my first name – Devon," he said. "May I call you Maria?"

Maria nodded and folded her hands in her lap.

"Before we start, is there anything you would like to ask about what we are doing?"

Maria spoke English with a thick Hispanic accent. "What will do you do with this recording, *Señor*?"

Devon glanced first at Alessandra, then quickly back toward Maria. "Hasn't Mrs. Gittleman told you what this interview is about?"

"Yes, the *Señora* did explain," said Maria, her voice rising as she defended Alessandra, "but sometimes I mix things up. Could you tell to me again, please?"

Devon glanced again at Alessandra, who sat in her chair, palms together, fingertips positioned beneath her chin. He wondered if perhaps she had left Maria uninformed about the purpose of the interview to demonstrate how much her clients trusted her.

"Maria, I'm a journalist. I write for a magazine named *Walden* and I live in New York City. We are doing a story on CASE and some of the people *Señora* Gittleman helps. That's why I'd like to talk to you. When I leave Los Angeles, I will return to New York City and write an article that will be published in *Walden Magazine*. It will be read by many people. The things you tell me will be discussed in the article. I will not use your name or tell anyone your address. Do you understand what I have said, and do you still want to do this interview?"

Maria stared at the center of the table. "*Si, Señor.*"

"I will not use this information in a way that will cause you harm."

Maria's head rose, and she stared coldly into Devon's eyes. "*Señora* Gittleman ask me to do this. The *Señora* would never do me harm. If the *Señora* say is okay, and this maybe help other women, then it is what I do."

A fleeting smile crossed Alessandra's lips.

"Well, then," said Devon, settling back in his chair, "let's begin."

Maria took a breath, moved her hands from her lap to clutch the arms of her chair, and began speaking in a voice so soft Devon had to strain to hear her.

"Uh, excuse me, Maria," he interrupted, "could you speak a little louder?"

Maria cleared her throat and began again.

"I am from Mexico. Ten years ago, I meet my husband in Guadalajara when he visit his family. He is United States citizen, he is born here, and he have a good job and make good money. We get marry, and I go with him to United States. We have two children and are doing good, then he start to drink. He lose his job and we must get for the children welfare."

Maria fell silent, her eyes filling with tears.

"It is very hard with no money. I want to work, but I do not have papers. Jorge never make me papers even when I ask him many times. He is citizen and we are marry, so it is no hard for him to make me papers so I can work. But Jorge say he no want me be like American woman, only he want I take care of the house, the kids, and take care of him, so I do not need no papers or job."

Devon turned to Alessandra. "How easy is it for a citizen to get papers for their spouse?"

Alessandra motioned with her head toward Maria. "Just listen."

When Maria spoke again, her voice broke.

"Finally Jorge get one job, but the hours are no good and the pay is not much, so we have to keep on welfare for the girls. He go out at night and do not tell me where he go. One night Jorge come home drunk and beat me with his fists until my face is black. I think maybe he try to kill me. I am so scare."

"Did you call the police?"

"Jorge is my husband. I do not want him to go to jail, and I am afraid if he go to jail, he will hurt me bad when he get out and maybe the kids."

"I see. So what happened?"

Maria shifted uneasily in her chair. Her voice quivered.

"I do nothing. But one night... one night Jorge he come home again very drunk. He smash everything and take a...a... "*Señora...Como se dice pierna de una silla?*"

"Chair leg."

Tears and sobs poured forth. "Jorge he take a chair leg and beat me. I try to fight back, but he is too strong and hit me in the head. I play like I am dead, then he leave. This time I call to the police. My neighbors take me to the hospital, and after I get out, the social worker from the hospital take me and my girls to a shelter."

Devon handed Maria his handkerchief and turned away as she used it. The story was heartbreaking, but not uncommon. Alessandra had to know that. Devon wondered why she wanted him to do an interview that would have so little traction with readers.

"Is that the first time you met *Señora* Gittleman – when you were at the shelter?"

Maria blew her nose. "No. It is many months later I meet the *Señora*. The people tell to me in the shelter, Maria, you must separate or divorce Jorge because he is drunk and violent. I do not want, because I am without papers. I cannot work and make money alone."

Maria pursed her lips as she fought for control of her emotions. When she continued, there was anger in her voice.

"They say to me, if you do not divorce or leave Jorge, it is possible the social work take your kids."

Maria paused. When she spoke again, her anger had abated and was replaced by sadness. She glanced down at her lap and squeezed her fingers into the arms of the chair.

"But they say also to me I can make my own papers to become a legal resident, because of what Jorge do to me. The law allow this because I am a – a– "

Alessandra finished the sentence. "Victim of domestic violence." Turning to Devon, she explained. "There's a federal law that allows a victim of domestic violence to petition on her own to adjust her immigration status, if she can meet certain requirements. One of those requirements involves proving that a spouse who was a citizen or legal permanent resident kept a woman from getting her own legal residency as a means of controlling her – which is exactly what Maria's husband did."

Maria began again. "I do like they say me. I live in the shelter with my children and when I get the first papers from the immigration, they let me work. I get one job cleaning hotel rooms, but my girls still get food stamps and health care. Everything go okay. I save money to pay for apartment. Then it is time for my divorce."

Devon interrupted. "Where was your husband all this time?"

"In Mexico. That make me happy, because he is no longer part of my hair."

Devon smiled at the mangled English expression. He wondered when Alessandra would spring the trap he now felt certain awaited him. "So...what happened next?"

Maria started to sob. "I go to the court to get my divorce papers, and they tell to me wait, then two policemens come and put on me handcuffs and take me to jail. They keep me four days. I understand nothing why I am in jail! My children are alone at the shelter! Then I go in front the judge and he say you take money from welfare but you husband and you do not report income, and this happen one year ago. I say no, I report everything. They say the County tell me this in one letter long time before. I tell them I do not get this letter. They say that is too bad because if I answer I can make...make..."

"What?" Alessandra asked.

"*Como se dice una audiencia, Señora?*"

"A hearing."

"*Si*, I can make a hearing and show I tell the truth. But the letter come to my home, and I am in the shelter and never receive, because it is the law this letter cannot be send forward and it is now too late. Now I must go in the court for the criminal."

To Devon, the woman's story sounded confusing and illogical. "Didn't you have a lawyer with you at court?"

"*Si*. The court give me one lawyer who tell to the judge that I am not guilty, that I do not do this, then they say to me there will be another court to say what will happen and until then I can go back to my children."

Maria's crying became uncontrollable, forcing her to stop speaking. Alessandra calmly watched her, making no move to comfort her, occasionally glancing around the room as if keeping tabs on the women still working with volunteers.

Devon was appalled.

My God, isn't she going to put an arm around the woman?

After a few moments, Maria wiped her tears and sighed. "The lawyer, he explain to me the paper. It say 'You have commit welfare fraud, and food stamp fraud, because Jorge is working two job and you do not tell us. Then you sign paper with this lie, so now this make three crime.' I tell the lawyer I never lie because I do not know Jorge is working two job. Only that moment I find out Jorge have two job, not one! And he never say me this! He keep all the money for himself. He go at night and never say where he go. I cannot ask or he will beat me! The lawyer say the County no care; somebody has to pay. Jorge is no here, so I must pay."

Devon held his hand up. Maria ceased talking. He turned to Alessandra.

"She can be held accountable for unknown acts of her husband?"

"When a wife and husband apply for public assistance, they are both responsible. If the wife is abandoned after the husband commits welfare fraud, she can be prosecuted for the crime even if she knew nothing about it. It's hard to prove she knew nothing, if she signed the monthly reporting form." Alessandra motioned again toward her client. "Listen to the rest of her story."

Devon turned back toward Maria.

"I am very frightened. I have no money. Then they change my lawyer, and now I have a new lawyer, and he say there is one thing only I can do. I must say to the judge I am guilty and then I no go to jail. The lawyer say I need pay only the money back and I have one small bad thing in the papers of the court. But I have no money, and I am not guilty, and I have no bad papers in the court until this. One lady at the shelter say if I go see *Señora* Gittleman, maybe she help me. I go. I tell the *Señora* my story, and she call somebody and she find I am saying the truth. The *Señora* go with me when I go to court and she talk to my lawyer."

Devon looked at Alessandra. "I assume this lawyer was a public defender, right?"

Alessandra's face became a mask of disgust. "He was. But he was a veteran who had slowly percolated through the public defender's office until he landed in welfare fraud in his later years. It was apparent he hadn't investigated her story, because he had no intention of fighting the charges; he was there to expedite a plea bargain. I met with her lawyer in the courthouse hallway. He was busy reciting the standard pitch for a plea bargain in a case like Maria's. If she accepted a felony conviction, the prosecutor would drop the perjury charge. She would still have to repay the entire amount of money – in this case about four thousand dollars, plus fines and fees. Once she paid it down to fifteen hundred, the felony fraud charge would become a misdemeanor. But the crime of deceit – whether felony or misdemeanor – is a death sentence for future employment. And it can kill an application to adjust immigration status or even lead to deportation."

"How the hell could she ever repay that much money?" Devon asked. "Even with a job, she'd have to work forever to pay off four thousand dollars at minimum wage and still take care of her kids."

"That was one of my arguments to the defense attorney, along with the evidence I gathered showing Maria could not have had knowledge of her husband's second job, that in fact, he kept it secret so he could have complete control of her. I explained that under these circumstances, intent – a key element of the crimes charged – was absent. Her lawyer looked worried. He knew my reputation and thought I might complain to his boss that he hadn't even considered a reasonable defense."

Alessandra stared past Devon as though watching a scene in a movie.

"When I finished, he suggested I accompany him to meet with the Deputy District Attorney and explain the case, then join them in the judge's chambers. I took him up on it. I actually thought we had a chance, because I knew things about this particular Deputy District Attorney that the public defender didn't. Now this is off the record, okay?"

"Agreed."

"Before she became a lawyer, she herself had been a victim of domestic violence. Her husband was Bernard Grantham."

"The financial..."

"The same. Big Bad Bernie got drunk and put her in the hospital for a week."

Devon shook his head in amazement. Bernard Grantham ran a multi-billion-dollar corporation, was a patron of the arts, and was known nationwide in financial circles.

Alessandra sighed. "Thought it was only indigent husbands who beat indigent wives, huh, Devon? Grantham tried to cheat his soon-to-be ex in the divorce settlement, but she had money of her own and hired a Hollywood weasel. The weasel's approach was to assure Grantham's attorney he would include an accusation of alcohol-related wife-beating, demand a criminal investigation, make exhibits of her purple face and closed eye, and make sure they, and the police report, found their way into the press. It would have destroyed Bernard Grantham. His wife got her half of everything the couple owned according to California law, along with a generous settlement from his half for her guarantee of silence."

"Tough weasel."

"That's the benefit of hiring a private defense lawyer who has time and money to make your case. Maria got a lawyer whose nickname was 'The Fly' for reasons I'll leave to your imagination."

Devon raised his eyebrows. "Are we back on the record?"

Alessandra nodded. "Anyway, the Deputy D.A. agreed with me on the domestic violence issue and said if the judge accepted the defense, she would agree to a dismissal, provided Maria paid back half the amount owed within a year."

"Why should she pay it back if the Deputy D.A. agreed she wasn't guilty?"

"The prosecutor knew what her bosses expected of her. She told the judge, 'We can't find the husband. And the People simply cannot agree to any settlement that results in a complete loss.' It was the best she could hope to get for Maria and she knew it. So the judge gave Maria several months to pay back the money and set the next date to review the case."

"How did Maria pay it back? I'm assuming she did, since she's here."

Alessandra said, "Tell him what happened next, Maria."

Maria swallowed. "When this happen, I am working already. But now I take a second job. I work at night cleaning buildings, and I have to pay my neighbor at the shelter to watch my kids. But I save my money. I go to the court and I pay the money and get a paper to say I pay. When time come for me to see the judge again, I take my paper, and I meet again my lawyer before we go inside. He ask me again to say I am guilty. I am so frightened."

The words were followed by another torrent of tears.

Devon frowned. "I thought you said there was an agreement."

Alessandra's stare was icy cold. "I had calendared the court date, so I went down there and found Maria in tears. Apparently, the public defender hadn't looked at the file since the last hearing. He didn't recall the deal. When I reminded him, he seemed disgusted. But he went to get the Deputy D.A., and wouldn't you know, it was a different one – not Grantham's ex-wife. The new Deputy D.A. hadn't looked at the case until that very moment, and the notes were not detailed concerning the deal we had struck. She got a little irritated when I stepped in to explain, because The Fly was busy trying to resurrect his notes. She refused the deal.

"I think The Fly was afraid of what would happen if he fouled this up, so he called for a meeting in the judge's chamber. And of course, it was a different judge, Judge Hartwell. The notes from the last judge who had agreed to the deal were not detailed. Judge Hartwell is a white ex-cop who went to a lousy law school. His legal knowledge is marginal, and his years on the police force made him a cynic. He doesn't believe anyone on public assistance is innocent, especially if they're Black or Hispanic."

"But you had a case. Why not take it to a jury?"

"First of all, it wasn't my call. I was a consulting attorney, not the attorney of record. But more important, there's a lot to be lost at trial. Judge Hartwell isn't the only one prejudiced against the poor. Many jurors come into a courtroom with false assumptions about welfare recipients, especially women of color. It's a risk to go before a jury. If you lose, your client could be looking at jail time and, in this case, immigration consequences. But also, we had a deal, and the deal was the best of all possible worlds, given the circumstances: Show proof that half the amount was repaid, and the Deputy D.A. would dismiss charges. The problem was, I was the only person in chambers who seemed to remember there was a deal at all."

"So what happened?"

"I made sure the judge knew exactly what the deal was, and that it had been documented by me from start to finish. I made it known that if the agreement was not honored, I would file whatever legal challenges were necessary against the public defender, the new Deputy D.A. and the judge."

"So they stuck to the deal?"

"Yes. They know I don't bluff. But most poor women like Maria don't have a strong advocate even when they're innocent, and they wind up with a horror story. Welcome to poor women's justice, Devon, California style."

Alessandra stood up, and Devon and Maria followed suit. Maria stood wiping her eyes with the wet, cosmetic-smeared handkerchief. Alessandra hugged her.

"Thank you for telling your story, Maria. I'll be in touch with you soon. How are the children?"

"They are fine, *Señora*."

"How are you coming with your papers?"

"Oh, I have now my papers with immigration, *Señora*! I am so happy! The lawyer you find for me, she help me a lot."

"That's wonderful!" Alessandra said, smiling.

"Goodbye, *Señora*. I must go to work now. *Mucho gusto, Señor Emmanuel*."

Maria hurried toward the door.

After Maria left, Devon turned to Alessandra. "You found her a lawyer to help with her immigration papers? Where did she get money to pay a lawyer?"

"She didn't. The immigration lawyer handled her case as a favor to me. But all favors require a return favor, Devon. You want justice in California, you pay for it, one way or another. Your education has only just begun, Bubby. I need to take a break now; there's something I'm involved in that won't wait. Let's meet again about two-thirty."

CHAPTER 18

I t was refreshingly cool in the hotel bar. Devon checked his watch. An
hour and a half until his meeting with Alessandra. Time to have a beer,
a sandwich, and make phone calls. While he ate, he stared at
photographs lining the walls. Sports figures and movie stars.

Where's all that L.A. culture Sonja gushed about?

He finished eating, then went to his room and called Andrews.

"Clark. What news from our world-class anachronism?"

"H-T jumped on the single-issue idea! I couldn't believe it! I've never
seen him like this. Rumors say something hot is coming down."

The answer elated Devon, who had felt certain H-T would say no.
Now the situation offered big possibilities, the kind that occasionally made
average careers bloom into greatness. Suddenly, Andrews' comment about
rumors leaped out at Devon.

"What rumors?"

"Wild speculation. Ms. Lillian is buying us outright... Ms. Lillian is
not interested...Ms. Lillian this, Ms. Lillian that...preposterous shit.
Something's coming down, though. It usually takes H-T twenty minutes to
wipe his ass, but he was on your proposal at the speed of light. Quote: 'Tell
him to write us the best story he's ever written.' Remember his eyes – lids
so droopy you can hardly see any white? The instant I told him about
Alessandra's proposal, his eyes got so wide he looked like he'd been
goosed with an icicle."

Devon's skin tingled. "Is he going to bring Culbertson aboard?"

"Not...exactly. Exactly, he's going to allow you to pay the kid."

Devon's electric feeling faded. "Did you tell him why we needed
Culbertson?"

"He didn't want to hear it. He was covering his ass in case the kid gets
in trouble. Old bastard's smart...creating deniability."

Devon silently fumed. The squeaking of Andrews' chair became more
rapid as the seconds passed.

"Hey, come on, big things are happening," the editor said. "Especially
for you, you sly son of a bitch. H-T says if everything works out – he

didn't define what he meant by 'works out' – you're going to get half of what you asked for in the way of salary, yearly raise and bonus."

Devon drove his fist into the air and yelled "Yes!" Then he remembered his original demand and mentally halved it. It was a long way from what he had asked, but still a pretty good package.

"Did you send me Culbertson's email address and phone number? I've been so busy I haven't checked."

"Done."

"You think I should tell the kid the background of this story?"

"No! Just tell him what you want done. And when you talk to him, tell him I said, 'Facts, no bullshit!'" A moment passed, then, "You're really going to fork over four hundred bucks to the little putz for two weeks' work."

"Unless you have a better idea."

Swiveling's stopped. Well...come on, say something.

"I'll half it with you, seeing as how my ass is hanging so far out. Know this, though; that money represents my two Yankee games for the year, Emmanuel."

"You're a fucking gentleman, Clark. And don't worry; I'll keep the kid in line."

A sarcastic laugh filled Devon's phone, then the tone changed. "You really think you can write the rough while you're still doing the interview?"

"How well can you edit a jigsaw puzzle?"

"What's that mean?"

"You'll have my copy the instant I finish a night's work. Edit it, get it back to me the next day, and I'll go over everything again. We're going to create a running rough. Can you finesse Izzy the Schmuck's lousy writers and concentrate on my stuff?"

The phone was silent for several seconds, then Andrews sighed and said, "Not yet, but I'm trying. I've never done anything like this before. New world, huh? Anything else?"

"Yeah, I'm having trouble getting face time with Alessandra. Her work keeps getting in the way. Actually, the free time is important to me because it allows me to write, but it's a double-edged sword. I have to get the interview done. I'd spend time talking to her at night but I have to write."

"Push like hell, Devon. This is our best – our only – future."

Andrews hung up.

Devon reclaimed Lindsay Culbertson's contact information and entered it into his cell phone registry. Then he hesitated. He had a sinking feeling. He was taking a terrible chance. If the plan went south, the ramifications could be terrifying. Culbertson was a minor. If the kid went too far and authorities caught him invading some agency's or organization's computer, he could get prosecuted. It wouldn't take a genius to make the case that he didn't actually know he was doing something unauthorized, since he was working for two professional journalists who should have known what they were requiring of him. Devon and Andrews were adults. Not only could they lose their jobs and reputations; they might be prosecuted. Culbertson's own uncle wondered if the boy was a sociopath.

On the other hand, if Alessandra lied to promote her cause, and the truth came out after the article was published – either way, Devon would be unemployed. He would at least have a shot at success if he used Lindsay. Devon had never gambled on anything in his life, and now he was betting his career, his family, and possibly his freedom, on a teenage sociopath. Then, without being consciously willed, his index finger pushed the Culbertson icon. The phone rang twice.

"Yeah."

Jesus, his voice just cracked.

"Is this Lindsay Culbertson?"

"Who the fuck's this?"

"My name is Devon Emmanuel. I'm with *Walden Magazine*. We met when you worked at *Walden*. I'm a close friend of your uncle, Clark Andrews. I need someone with your skills who can check facts. The job would take a couple weeks. It's all computer work. Interested?"

"How much does it pay?"

Culbertson's voice broke again on the word 'pay' and Devon suppressed a laugh. "Two hundred a week."

"Cash in advance?"

You little shit.

Devon called to mind the skinny, pimply-faced, hyperkinetic teenager whom he had found annoying when they had met at *Walden*. It was time to set the rules of their relationship.

Devon replied in a cold, rough voice, "I'll arrange for your uncle to send you a fifty-dollar retainer that'll reach you by tomorrow. Best I can do. You want the job or not?"

A few seconds of silence greeted Devon's icy bargain.

"When do I get the rest of the money?"

"When you finish the job. Is your computer state-of-the-art or a piece of junk?"

The answer was an angry shout. "I got the best computer in the Bronx! Nobody got one like mine! I fucking put it together myself. It's got power and speed like a small super-computer. I took eleven old systems, set them up in– "

"Good. Message from your Uncle Clark: 'Facts, no bullshit.'"

"What's that mean?"

"Facts only! Don't make stuff up if you can't get information. Show all your sources. I'll text your uncle to send the money today."

"What am I supposed to do?"

"You'll get your first set of instructions tonight. I need to know everything you dig up by the end of each day."

"You want me to start work before I get my mon– "

"Stop whining and just do the work, goddamit!"

CHAPTER 19

Alessandra was seated at a table with Gabriela and two young women when Devon entered the CASE office at 3:15 that afternoon.

"Go up and fix yourself some tea," she called to him as he stopped politely at the reception desk. "I'll be with you in ten minutes."

Devon headed upstairs, left the door of Alessandra's apartment open behind him, and set about locating the fixings for tea. The tiny kitchen was outdated and cramped, the appliances old, white, and enamel-chipped. The entire front of the refrigerator was covered by a day calendar, all twelve months showing. Most entries for past months were marked through by a black Sharpie. Occasionally, something would be highlighted in color. One such item was Devon's name. A message below it read, "CK OUT."

Devon found the tea and began heating water in a small pot while he searched for cups. In one cupboard, he found the mugs beside the elegant china he recognized from his and Alessandra's earlier breakfasts. He chose two mugs, hoping she would join him. Hunting through drawers, he found a tea strainer, filled it with tea, set it in a chipped porcelain tea pot and poured in the boiling water. The tea was ready when Alessandra appeared.

Pointing at the mugs, she said, "Rather not drink from dinky cups, huh?"

"Hate 'em."

"Fill the cups and I'll grab some cookies. We need to get started."

When Alessandra returned from the kitchen, she lowered her recliner within reach of the coffee table, adjusted her microphone, seated herself, then began munching a cookie and happily chasing it with sips of tea.

"Where shall we begin?" she asked.

Devon smiled mischievously.

Alessandra cocked her head to the side and set her cup on the table. "What's going on?"

"I think we should start somewhere...that will allow us to fill an entire issue of *Walden*."

Alessandra threw her arms in the air. "Your publisher went for it!"

Devon held up his hands in a not-so-fast gesture. "It's not completely confirmed yet. But having said that, I've been instructed to write the best story I've ever written."

Alessandra's response was a near-scream. "Wonderful! Lead on!"

At that exhilarating moment, the land line rang. The sound was like fingernails on a blackboard to Devon. No sooner were things going well than something always interfered. He sullenly muted the recorder and left for the back of the room.

From this vantage point, he watched as Alessandra cradled the phone to her ear, saying, "Wait a moment, Gaby."

She picked up a legal pad and ballpoint pen from the coffee table, scribbling on the pad to make sure the pen was functioning. "Okay, put him through... "Good afternoon, Charles," she said cheerfully. "I take it you come bearing gifts. What have you learned?"

Several minutes passed during which Alessandra's part in the conversation was reduced to listening except for: "I see...how long...yes...You can verify that? There are a lot of potential holes here, Charles; redundancy is critical. Find out everything you can as far back as it's safe to operate. If you think something might be risky, don't do it...You really think it's possible to explore that?... Okay, but that's far enough...No, that's too late; get what you can by tomorrow night and send it. I'll go over it, then we'll decide where to go next. Thank you, Charles. I owe you. Best to Helen."

Alessandra hung up and began writing on her pad as Devon returned to his chair. He sensed intrigue. It would be great material for the article, but it had all the earmarks of information Alessandra wanted to protect. He was on the verge of asking what had taken place, then decided against it. Things were going too well to take a risk. Maybe the story would come out later in the course of his interview.

"I noticed you asked Maria about her children," Devon said, as Alessandra laid aside the legal pad and paper. "All that turmoil must have been tough for them. Did that bring back any personal memories?"

Alessandra laughed. "Nice move, Emmanuel. Got where you wanted to go, didn't you."

Devon shook his head. "I just..."

"...wanted back into my life after my parents were killed."

Alessandra's eyebrows raised, but her smile remained.

"Devon, your mother wouldn't like it if you compounded that denial with another lie."

Devon laughed guiltily. "Okay, I want to hear what happened to you after your parents were killed."

"We're going there, but before that, you're going to learn a little more about the people I serve. I'd like it in the article."

Devon sighed and resigned himself to listening. "All right. But remember, we only have thirty pages. It sounds like a lot, but the space fills faster than you think. And I'm not trying to minimize what women like Maria have suffered, but frankly, her personal nightmare was not that easy to follow, and I'm someone who wants to understand."

"I was aware of that when I picked her to tell her story. That's part of the problem I want people to understand. The rest of this will be short. And it won't bore your readers. I have more riding on the success of this enterprise than you do, remember?"

Devon showed no reaction.

If you only knew.

Alessandra sat for a moment as though gathering her thoughts, then began speaking in an earnest, subdued tone. "You need to understand what's happening to these women, Devon. It's more than just poverty, it's a host of things. Poverty, of course, but also frustration at not being able to rise above it because of society's preconceived opinions of them based on things like race, gender, religion and misinformation that poisons our entire public dialogue about the poor. Then there's the constant uncertainty of what will happen in their lives from day to day, simply because they have no money or power. Will they break some law, knowingly or unknowingly, and wind up losing their kids? Maybe even go to prison! They want – they deserve – justice. As a writer of this story you need to understand – to feel, the basis of their fear. Fear for themselves, their kids, and the limits of their own anger.

"Americans give money, but ignore the lack of justice in this all too human dilemma. They don't understand that our country is sowing dragon's teeth by disregarding poor people's needs. Not only their need for financial help and education of their kids, but for honest justice. Remember that line in Deuteronomy? 'Justice, justice shalt thou pursue.' Americans sweep that Old Testament commandment under the court house mats when it comes to the people I serve."

Devon straightened in his chair and carefully chose his response.

"Alessandra, I'm no *Grapes of Wrath* Steinbeck or muckraking Sinclair Lewis. But I respect what you do, and I also want to help disadvantaged people. Everybody comes at this thing from a little different point of view, my readers included. That's why your personal story is so important to this article. I – we – need to understand why you've been fighting against a tide that never seems to ebb. And doing it for thirty-eight years."

Alessandra thought for a moment. "Actually, I like the fact that you're the one doing this article. Not just because you're a good writer. But after exploring as much as I could of your background – yes, I've checked you out – you're decent, well-intentioned, and stereotypically American. Your articles suggest you're possibly somewhat to the right politically. All of those things make it easier for you to address a larger spectrum of the public."

Devon's response was straightforward. "Alessandra, I'm here to interview you, to understand why you've spent your life doing things for disadvantaged people instead of just living blissfully in a Beverly Hills mansion. Spell out your ideas and I'll do my best to present them."

Alessandra took a cigarette from the pack on her coffee table, and Devon reached over and lit it. She took a deep puff, then lay back in her recliner.

"I guess it comes down to this. Americans think they are helping the poor. They pay taxes to help them, and can't understand why people like me keep complaining that the poor need more. What they don't realize is that the help they're giving is all tied up. Burdened, tangled, and rendered ineffective.

"I know public budgets have limits. But all the more reason why the help society gives should be easy for eligible people to get instead of being punitive, buried in systems that treat all poor people like criminals, and risk the food and shelter of fragile families. That's what makes me so angry! When you look at the system up close, it's designed to fail families like Maria's."

Devon had heard and read the comments of liberal advocates for years. Liberals, he had decided, were good at criticizing but never came up with a system that worked.

"How is society supposed to rescue people who are coming from so far behind? We can never make everything right for the poor. Immigrants – like my family about a century ago – they were on their own."

Alessandra's eyes flashed. "It's not the welfare money we give people that cripples them; it's that we've built human services systems that, by design, are not intended to help. In fact, they're dangerous and demeaning, and can leave people in worse shape than before they sought help.

"If hard work were all it took to make it in America today, Devon, there would be very few poor people. Poverty isn't about a failure of the work ethic. It's about millions of people battling forces over which they have no control. These are people who don't have enough money to live while they try to achieve self-sufficiency. But the systems that are supposed to give them a hand up are designed to treat them as if they are always at fault, and therein lies the story I need to tell."

Devon felt like turning away from the diatribe. He had heard all the reasons why America's economic system was failing. Globalization, deregulation, technology, demise of unions and all the other factors that were making it hard to live a middle class life, and he didn't want to hear it again. What Alessandra was laying bare chilled him. If it were true, it meant that perhaps hard work wouldn't save anyone. Indeed, only a few hours ago he had felt himself peering into a yawning economic abyss.

The ringing phone saved him. Alessandra took the call, listened, and said simply, "Okay, " then hung up and called to Devon who had, as usual, retreated toward the back of the room.

"My meeting's been moved up, and there are some things I need to get done, so we'll move on to topics you and our fellow Americans will find less turbulent. We left off with my parents' death."

Devon stifled a sigh of relief.

CHAPTER 20

Alessandra's brow wrinkled with concern as she shifted her recliner. "There are some things I'll share, and some I'd like to keep out of the article," she told Devon in a voice that seemed weaker than what he had heard in their earlier conversation.

"Is this what you meant when you asked me to grant you a few indulgences?"

She continued to fiddle with the recliner control, as if she were having a hard time finding a comfortable position. She looked tired and less in charge than she had before. To his question, she answered only "Yes," then closed her eyes.

Devon waited for her to begin. Time passed, and he found himself listening to the tick of the clock, which seemed to be getting louder with every moment of silence. Finally, in whispering, painful tones, Alessandra spoke.

"I was in class when one of the Sisters opened the door to our room and motioned to Sister Agnes, our teacher, to come into the hall. When Sister returned, she told me to go to the principal's office. Earlier in the day, I had chewed gum. That was a major offense at St. Cecelia. I was terrified."

Alessandra's right hand rose to her mouth, then descended to her chest, followed by a breath so deep it moved her hand upward. She began to speak softly.

***

I'm so scared. It don't seem right. It wasn't much I did. I know what's going to happen. Every kid at St. Cecelia's knows what happens when you get sent to Sister Francesca's office. I'm not going in. I'm going to walk right on past. If I keep walking, I can get out the back door. But they'll come get me, and I'll get a licking at home. I think I better just go in and say I'm sorry as much as I can. Ohhh, it's going to be so bad.

I wouldn't of chewed the gum if Donatella Santorini hadn't dared me. Ohhh, the steps...I have to walk up the three steps. I hate brown wooden doors with three steps and glass you can't see through and have to knock on. Blessed Virgin, help me. I've been a little bad, but I've done some good things. I helped old Mrs. Zantelli across the street the other day.

"Come in."

Ohhh...that's Sister Francesca in her black habit with the big white rim hat. I have to go to the bathroom. I have to do number one...maybe she won't let me. Ohhh...please, Blessed Virgin, help me. Sister Francesca's so tall and I got to go to the bathroom so bad and she just said "Come in" again. Oh, she's so big.

"Come here, dear. Did Sister Agnes tell you why I wanted to see you?"

"No Sister, but I already know and I'm sorry. I did a sin and I'm sorry. I did a terrible sin, Sister. I'll say fifty Our Father's and as many Hail Mary's as you want. I am so sorry."

Why's she looking at me that way? Why's she putting her hand under my chin...Sister's got tears! I didn't know it was such an awful thing or I never would of chewed it.

"I'm sorry, Sister. I didn't know it was so terrible. I'll never do it again. I promise I won't."

"You didn't do this, child. This was God's will."

"God made me chew the gum?"

What's wrong with Sister? She looks like she's going to fall down. "Sister, you look sick. I'll get your chair."

"Alessandra..."

"I got it, Sister Francesca...here it is, Sister...I didn't know gum was so bad. Honest I didn't. I promise I'll never do it again. You just sit. I'll get Sister Agnes."

"No...no...come here, Alessandra. Let me have your hands."

Why's she pulling me so hard? Her knees are squeezing my belly and I have to do number one. If she keeps pulling on me, I'm going to go pee.

"Alessandra, God has taken your Mother and Father. I'm sorry...I'm so sorry."

"God took Mama and Papa? He'll bring them back, won't he?"

Why's she crying? There's so many tears, they're running down her cheeks.

"Of course, dear, one day you'll all be together again in heaven."

"Not before?"

"No dear."

"Why's He taking them for so long? Without Mama and Papa, I won't know what to do. Tell Him to bring them back! I need Mama and Papa."

"He won't, dear. He won't bring them back. They've gone to a lovely place."

"He'll bring them back if He knows I need them. I'll pray for Him to do it. I'll pray all the time, and He'll give them back. Help me pray, Sister Francesca."

"God won't bring them back, Alessandra. They were killed in an accident a few hours ago."

"Mama and Papa are dead? Oh no...oh, they can't be dead...ohhh, Sister...ohhh, ohhh, ohhh."

"Put your arms around me, Alessandra. I'll hold you and we can cry and pray together...that's right, cry hard...cry hard, child. Cry to God for His mercy."

Ohhhh...pee's running down my legs. It's going on the floor by Sister's foot. I can't move with her hugging me so tight. Ohhh, Blessed Virgin...ohhh...

CHAPTER 21

Devon had watched in stunned silence as Alessandra's soft tones rose from her lips like a morning fog. Her face had become expressionless, her voice almost childlike. He listened as memories tumbled out of her, sometimes narrated, sometimes as though she were actually present in that long-ago nightmare. Through her, he heard not only her words, but the words of others who were part of those memories. He was shaking inside, feeling like an interloper who had gained entry into a private space. While listening, he had considered calling her name, but was afraid to interrupt and sat silent until she finished. Now she lay on her recliner, motionless as a stone. A vast reservoir of ... nothingness ... descended on him, smothering him like a pillow over his face.

Devon whispered, "Alessandra?" She didn't move. He spoke louder. "Alessandra, are you okay?"

Her eyelids fluttered, then opened slowly. She looked at him with the sadness of someone who had lost all hope. She swallowed again and again. Devon bolted out of his chair and got a glass of water from the kitchen. By the time he returned, Alessandra seemed more her normal self. She drank thirstily, finally stopping to catch her breath.

"I promised you my story from beginning to end," she said. "I keep my promises."

"But– "

"No buts," she answered, her voice tired but strong. "You wanted my past; you're getting my past. Now let's see you write it."

Devon felt numb. Alessandra had recounted the story in such detail, it was as if she had revisited not a place, but a time, a time in which she had been enveloped by profound sadness, reliving every moment, then narrating it as a dispassionate translation in the voice and words of a child, though spoken by an old woman. Sixty-six years ago, and he was there!

"Let's see you write it." How the hell do I write it?

Devon needed to get his bearings. "I think we should take a break," he said, and began to rise from his chair.

"No!" Alessandra barked, and he sank back into the pillows. "My story is going to take time, and your time with me is short. Every second we have together counts."

Alessandra closed her eyes again, her body sagging into the recliner. Again she pushed open the door to the dark room in her mind and went inside.

***

This ain't near home. I don't know anybody. There's Puerto Ricans and coloreds and whites but no Italians. The kids are mostly older than me. Why do they call it *The Mercy of Jesus*? The Sisters here aren't anything like Sister Agnes or Sister Francesca. Sister Agnes and Sister Francesca were Italian. All the nuns here are Irish. They're mean too, especially that Sister Doreen. The Sisters blame me for everything that happens to me, even when the kids call me dago and wop and other names. Luisa's the only girl here who's nice to me. She's Puerto Rican. I never met a Puerto Rican before. She's fun to play with, even though she's a year older than me. Her Mama and Papa are dead too.

I miss Mama and Papa so much. They never spanked me when I wet the bed. Sister Doreen paddles me. The big kids keep taking my food – the good stuff. What I got left to eat is awful. I can't eat it. Luisa gives me some good stuff, but I can tell she's hungry, too. It makes me feel bad to take it, but I'm just so hungry. I wish they hadn't sent me to that nurse's office. She said I had worms, but that worm medicine made me throw up. She got me in trouble, because after the medicine, I kept getting more skinny and they had to call a doctor. I told the doctor the other kids were taking my food. The doctor said I had maldurition and to stop the worm medicine and feed me. After we left the doctor, Sister Doreen yelled I was fed good, and everything was my fault, and that doctor didn't know anything, and *The Mercy of Jesus* was never going to him again. I got a licking from Sister Doreen and put in a room by myself. The room was almost empty. There were two beds, one on top of the other, a little table, a light bulb hanging from the ceiling, and a toilet. It was a nice toilet, except for a big chip out of one side.

At first I was really scared. One of the nuns would stand there while I said my prayers. I stayed in the room I don't know how long. It was terrible lonesome. I decided when the Sisters let me out, I was gonna run away. But there was a big high fence around the yard, tilted in at the top. I knew I couldn't climb over and didn't know what I could do to get past it.

When they let me out of the room, it was the same old thing, girls calling me dago and taking my food. One day at playtime, I was running near the fence and saw a little hole under it kind of covered with weeds. It was small but I thought if I digged some, I might be able to wriggle under.

It was the only way out I could think of, so if I was going to run away, this was how, and I had to do it at night to keep from getting seen. That was going to be really hard because all of us girls slept on the second floor in one great big room. I had to get out without waking anybody up, then go down the stairs and out the front door. It looked like there was just no way because they locked the front door at night.

A long time went by and no chance come, but I kept praying to the Virgin and finally she helped. One night, one of the Sisters come to check us in bed. When she went downstairs, I heard her lock the front door. I knew from the sound, it didn't lock. I waited what seemed like forever. Then, when I thought everybody was asleep, I put on my clothes. It was so dark. I couldn't see nothing, but I knew where everything was. There was this one spot where the floor squeaked when you stepped on it and I had to keep it from squeaking. I wriggled past it on my belly and got out the door of the sleeping room.

***

Alessandra's body began to move, writhing as though her muscles were contracting in place. Devon sat transfixed. He felt he needed to do something but had no idea what. He decided to just listen. Alessandra's eyelids fluttered.

***

The stairs come next. I kept on my belly and slid over them one at a time. The front door was a pretty good way in front of the bottom step. A light lit it to where I could just make out the knob. People were snoring and coughing, and somebody was walking. I was halfway down when footsteps come in front of me. It was Sister Doreen! She walked right past. I almost died!

Finally I was down the stairs and got to the door. I heard footsteps again, but they were going away. I stood up real slow, turned the knob and slipped out. I run to the hole near the fence and started digging. The ground was soft and it was easy making the hole bigger, but I jumped in before it got big enough and had to wriggle hard to get out. I could feel dirt on my dress and I was worried people would see it and know I run away from somewhere.

There wasn't much light from the street lamps, and the sidewalk had big broken lumps. I started running and fell a couple times. When I come to a bridge, I was out of breath and stopped. I wondered where I was. My hands and one knee were skinned from falling, and I was tired, but I knew they would come for me and I had to keep going. After I got my breath, I started running again.

The streets around *The Mercy of Jesus* were ugly, but this place was uglier. Every now and then, I'd see a man. They were old and walked like the drunk men I'd seen near home. Finally I come to a little park. I was really tired and lay down under a bush. I tried to hide under it but part of me stuck out. I went to sleep, and when I woke up, it was light, and a little white dog with shaggy hair was licking my face. It was a nice little dog and I reached up and got its floppy ear. Then I saw pant legs, and there was this skinny old man with a smile on his face holding a cane and big old bag. He scared me even though he didn't look mean. The little dog kept licking my face.

The man said, "Stop it, Liza Bell."

He put down his bag and picked up the little dog. The old man kept smiling at me. His face was long and wrinkled, and his hair was white, but his blue shirt and brown pants was clean. I didn't know what he was going to do.

Then he said, "What you doing here, honey?"

Mama always told me not to talk to strangers, so I didn't answer.

Then he said, "You hungry?"

I was, and even though Mama said not to, I figured I better say something this time, so I said "Yes, sir."

"Ain't got a lot, but you can have some of it. You rather have an apple or half a sandwich?"

I wasn't sure because I didn't know if the apple was beat up or not, or if the sandwich was made out of something I didn't like. The only way I was gonna find out was ask. "What kind of sandwich?"

"Baloney."

"Can I see it?"

He opened the big old bag full of clothes and stuff and got out a sandwich from inside a brown paper sack. It didn't look too bad, just a little squarshed. I could see the apple, and it looked old.

"I'll take the half a sandwich."

We were sitting on the grass eating, and all of a sudden, a police car turned the corner and come straight for us. Two policemen were in it, and one jumped out as it was coming to a stop and grabbed the old man and turned him on his face and yanked his arms behind him and began putting chains around his wrists. I didn't know why, but I ran over and pushed the policeman and told him to stop, but he stayed there.

The policeman asked me, "Did he hurt you, kid?"

And I said, "No, he gave me his half a sandwich. I was hungry, and he gave me his half a sandwich. He's my friend. You leave him alone."

But the policeman said, "Did he do anything to ya?"

And I told him again, "All he did was give me his half a sandwich," and I pushed the policeman. He still didn't move.

But then he asked me, "You wit him?"

I didn't know what to say. If I said I wasn't, they were gonna take me back to *The Mercy of Jesus*. I didn't know what was going to happen if I said I was, but if I went back to *The Mercy of Jesus* I knew I was going to get a awful licking from Sister Doreen and put back in that room.

The old man tried to say something, and the other policeman hit him with a big stick.

The old man yelled, "Don't hurt me. I ain't done nothing! I ain't done nothing!"

The policeman told him to shut up and opened the old man's bag and got his wallet and looked inside, then threw it back in the bag and stirred the stuff in the bag around and threw things on the ground.

I don't know why, but I yelled, "Leave my grandpa alone! You leave my grandpa alone!"

The two policemens looked at each other, and one said, "He's your grandpa?"

And I said, "Yeah, and you leave him alone!"

The policemen kept looking at me, and the one who had been talking said, "First you say he's your friend. Now you say he's your grandpa. Which is it?"

"He's my grandpa!" I yelled and started crying. "And he's my friend too."

The policeman said "bullshit" kind of soft, then the one who went through the bag shook his head. "I don't think this is the kid they're looking for," he said.

The other policeman kind of looked mad and said, "Well, I do. Her age is right. Look how grubby she is. I think we got our guy. Let's take him in."

Just then, the little dog grabbed the policeman's pant leg. The policeman kicked, and the little dog flew up in the air and landed on her back making a yip.

I yelled, "You leave Liza Bell alone! She ain't done nothing. You're just beating up on us. Here, Liza Bell! Come here, Liza Bell," and she did, and I picked her up.

Both policemen kept looking at me. Then one policeman started to say something, and the other one shook his head again, took the chains off the old man and started walking toward the police car.

The policeman standing beside me said, "Ain't we gonna take 'em in?" and the other policeman kept on walking. While he was walking, he talked to the policeman next to me.

"For Christ's sake, Joe! The kid knew the dog's name, the dog came to her when she called, the old buzzard's got more than fifty bucks in his wallet so he ain't a vagrant. What difference does it make whether she's his grandkid or not? She knows him and likes him. This ain't the kid, and this ain't the guy. Let's go get some coffee and a donut. I'm hungry."

CHAPTER 22

Alessandra lay still, her monologue having ended for no apparent reason. After a few moments, she opened her eyes and sat up.

A badly shaken Devon asked quietly, "Are you all right?"

Alessandra scanned his face. She seemed confused as she looked about. Finally she spoke, and her voice had returned to normal.

"Did you ever consider what happens to kids who go to an orphanage?"

Devon shook his head.

"It's a relevant question, since some of our political leaders have recommended that all children on welfare be placed in orphanages rather than be raised in poverty by their parents.

"You learn quickly why you're there. It's usually because no one wants you. Each day is survival, each night loneliness. In my case, I had experienced home, love, and the touch of family and friends who cared about me. You look for these things everywhere in an orphanage, desperate for one more minute of affection from someone who loves you, and you find none."

Alessandra put her hands to her temples. She swallowed, grimaced and mumbled, "We stop here...more tomorrow. Let yourself out."

"Alessandra – "

"Tomorrow."

"I– "

"Go!"

CHAPTER 23

Escaping the apartment was a relief to Devon, who stumbled down the road toward his car, grateful for his freedom, but exhausted emotionally and physically. Questions arose so quickly in his mind, he was unable to keep track of them. How was he supposed to write the story in view of what he had just seen and heard?

Regardless of the strange state Alessandra seemed to have entered while recounting her past, she had appeared in control of her faculties when she emerged from the trance-like episode. Yet Devon was unsure of what he had witnessed. Maria's narrative would be easy to write, but Alessandra had given him something Dickens would have struggled to bring to life. Except for time and gender, it was Oliver Twist lying on that recliner. *Walden* wanted Alessandra's life story, and she was giving it. Should he call Andrews and tell him *Walden's* last hope was beyond his skills? Maybe Alessandra's memories were flawed by age or emotional illness? He had no way of knowing; he'd just met the woman. Nobody knew anything about her except that she was brilliant, combative and a superb legal counsel. All he could really vouch for was that her clients and co-workers seemed to love her.

Devon's walk to the car became a mental march. Sorting through Alessandra's story, he found it somehow tethered to reality. People under hypnosis often could recall past events in minute detail. Even people operating from a completely unaltered mental state could sometimes recall occurrences of long ago. He could remember entire conversations from his childhood, and he hadn't been traumatized. Alessandra had warned him there might be problems with the personal part of the interview. He had never imagined the problems he had just observed.

Fortunately, finding a parking space had been difficult when he arrived that morning, and by the time he reached his car, he was calm enough to make a decision. He would stop playing Sigmund Freud and just do his job.

He slid into the driver's seat and relaxed, then began to develop an orderly plan. The call to his fact-checker on speaker phone began before Devon pulled away from the curb.

"Yeah?"

"It's me, Lindsay. Devon."

"Yeah?"

"Your money's on the way."

Silence. Devon waited for a response, but none came.

"Something wrong?"

The pause continued, then, "I got it. It was only fifty bucks."

The adolescent attitude grated on Devon. His answer was icy. "Fifty bucks was what we agreed on. Fifty now, and three-fifty at the end of two weeks."

"Whatchawant?"

"I got some facts I want checked."

"Yeah, well, I want fifty more bucks before I – "

The pressure pot blew. Devon screamed into the phone.

"Listen, you pimple-faced little shit! You got fifty goddamn dollars earnest money, and you're either going to do this work or I'm having your Uncle Clark come to your house and squeeze your nuts until they're the size of BBs!"

The voice that answered was shaky. "I – I'm telling my mom and dad what you just said."

"I don't fucking care if you tell the Pope! Number one! Using that so-called amazing computer of yours– "

"My computer is great! You don't know– "

" –and I don't give a rat's ass. Shut up and listen! Check the New York City records and see if they show the birth of an Alessandra Angelina Asencio Matreoni. I'm looking for the doctor who delivered her, the date and year of her birth, the names of her parents, and address of her family at the time of birth.

"Two: Check out her mother and father. Where they were born, when they came to this country, when and if they became American citizens, and what the father listed as his occupation on the birth certificate."

"Slow down, I c-can't keep up."

"I'll send you a follow-up email telling you what I want and where to look for the information; if you miss something now, don't worry about it. I just want you to know what's coming.

"Number three: Find out when, where, and how the mother and father died."

"Why I gotta check on dead people? They're fuckin' dead?"

Christ, what if the old records haven't been scanned into computer files? Can't worry about that now. No way to go but forward.

"You do it because I tell you to do it."

"But– "

"Shut up and do as I tell you."

"O – Okay!"

"Four: Check what Catholic diocese Bensonhurst is part of and see if a Sister Agnes and Sister Francesca worked at a Catholic girl's school named St. Cecelia – and if Alessandra was a student at the school. She'd have probably been in the first through the third grade. Get– "

The car weaved, and Devon yanked it back into its lane.

"Get St. Cecelia's address and find out if it's still in operation. And find out if those two nuns are still alive."

Devon considered what more he wanted.

"That it?"

"No. Check the Catholic diocese records in and around New York and find out if there was ever an orphanage by the name of *The Mercy of Jesus*, and if there was, whether Alessandra Angelina Asencio Matreoni ever lived there. That would have been in the 1940s. See if you can find out what happened to her. That's it."

"This is a lot of work."

"Yeah."

"But it's a lot of work and..."

"I don't care and I don't want to know your problems. That's why you're getting four hundred bucks. You'll get my email within the hour. Get started!"

"I'm telling Uncle Clark you treat me like shit."

"Go ahead. He's putting up half the money. Clark Andrews will skin your pimply ass alive if you fuck up, and I'll tell him the instant you do. I want this information by tomorrow night!"

"Asshole!"

The phone went dead.

CHAPTER 24

Expurgation of his piano-wire-tight emotions was a relief to Devon, and he roared down the freeway like a native Angeleno. Minutes later, at the hotel bar, he ordered a beer and called Andrews.

"Clark. Devon. I had a wild, amazing session with Gittleman. Wait until–"

"I listened. It's terrific. Man, she sounded exhausted. Reliving that nightmare must have been a killer. What was it like being in the room with her?"

Devon took a swallow of his newly arrived beer. "You can't even imagine. At first I thought she was faking. Next, I decided she was somehow mentally reliving that part of her past as if she were watching a movie. Then I thought maybe she was just nuts. In retrospect, I'm not sure she isn't nuts."

"Screw it. She's famous, and no one knows anything about her. This is Pulitzer stuff. Keep pushing the old girl. Stories about her clients will jerk a few tears, but Alessandra's life is pure gold. What a story!"

"Clark, this is an old woman – maybe a sick old woman–"

"Who wants her story told! Get it!"

Devon stared across the bar room at a painting. The image entered his eyes but stopped there. What his brain saw was the body of Alessandra Gittleman lying on her recliner. He became unaware of the passage of time.

"Devon…you there?"

"Yeah – sorry, spaced out a little. She'll probably want to return to poor women's issues. I don't want to go there, but things regarding her life are moving so well I'm afraid to argue with her. I think I should just ride along until I'm forced to do otherwise. What do you think?"

Andrews did his contemplation routine and Devon relaxed, grateful for the respite. The beer tasted good.

"Stay flexible."

Devon sipped more beer as Andrews talked at length about the challenges of working together at a distance and editing each other's copy with the clock running.

He really loves this story. Wonder how he'd respond if I told him I didn't have any idea how to write up what I just saw and heard.

At Andrews' next pause, Devon interrupted. "Clark...something strange is going on with Alessandra you need to know about."

The editor's chair stopped squeaking.

"What?"

"Headaches. The other day she acted as if she had an incredible headache. She had the same thing today. She sent me away while she was literally squeezing her temples."

Dead quiet except for Andrews' heavy breathing.

"What do you think is going on?"

"I don't know. I've considered migraines."

"Did she say she had migraines?"

"No, but I've known people who've had migraines. They describe spots before their eyes, nausea, vomiting...Alessandra's headaches come on incredibly fast without her mentioning symptoms of any kind."

Several seconds passed before Andrews responded.

"Don't worry about it. Things are going smoothly. I want to keep it that way. Has she said anything more to you about why she wants *Walden* to do this piece?"

Devon washed down the handful of mixed nuts he had been eating, then gasped out an answer. "Only that she wanted to air the plight of poor women in the justice system and use the entire *Walden* issue as a fund-raising mechanism."

"That smart old broad may say that, but I'll lay odds she has a hole card. It doesn't mean shit to us, though. We should stop thinking, and you start writing."

"Started last night. Writing this is going to be a ball-buster. You should have sent a novelist. I'll email you what I have as soon as I finish this evening's work."

"Anything else?"

"Yeah. Your nephew is bitching he was underpaid with the fifty-buck deposit for the research. I worry he might dog it on us."

"Leave Lindsay to me. If I know Lindsay, he hasn't told my sister about the money. I'll call the little putz and give him the message that if he gives us any crap, I'll tell his mother about the money. She'll take it away from him and put it in his education fund. When I finish with Lindsay, he'll kiss your hemorrhoids."

"Thanks, Clark. I'll be looking– "

The sound of a broken connection stopped Devon in mid-sentence.

Jesus, no one in the fucking Andrews family says goodbye.
Number three on Devon's call list filled him with dread.

"Emmanuel residence."

"It's Dad, David. How are things going?"

"Awful!"

Devon immediately conjured up traffic accidents, meningitis and kidnapping.

"What happened?"

"Mom."

"What about Mom?"

Hesitation.

"She won't do anything. The place is a dump. The only thing we've eaten since you left is cold pizza and Chinese takeout. I – "

There was the sound of a struggle, then Devon heard his wife's voice.

"...give it to me...give me the phone...David, I want the telephone, now give...it...to...me..."

The sound of a crash told Devon the phone had hit the floor. The remainder of the conversation between mother and son continued so loudly he could hear it.

"...That's right, throw it! That's all you know how to do, throw things and talk back! Why don't you try doing something constructive? Clean up your room! You were supposed to do that three days ago!"

David's answer was shouted. "I did it yesterday! It's the bathrooms, kitchen and everything else that's a dump. The dishes haven't been done since Dad left!"

"Then do them! You're not paralyzed! I have other work!"

"Like what? Hanging out with those creeps that never take a bath?"

"Those people are geniuses. They do great art. What can you do?"

"I can take a freakin' bath."

"Get out! Get out, or so help me...!"

Running feet, a slamming door, then the phone scraping against something.

"Devon, are you still there?"

Devon felt sorry for David but knew better than to try to defend him from three thousand miles away.

"I take it things aren't going well with David."

"He's starting that adolescent crap."

Devon heard a distant female voice.

"He's not old enough yet, Mom. Boys don't start puberty until they're almost thirteen."

"Sarah, this is a private conversation between your father and me!"

"I was just trying to help. You don't have to make a roark out of it!"

Devon rubbed his eyes with the tips of his fingers. The swishing sound of cloth on cloth told him his wife was back on the couch.

"They're driving me crazy! I come home tired, and all they do is gripe. The house is a wreck...what can you expect, four people living in a three-bedroom flat with a large closet for a third bedroom. I didn't go to Sarah Lawrence to be a housekeeper. We need to hire someone who can clean and make dinner."

"Sonja, we can't afford a housekeeper. When I get back we'll make some kind of arrangement that will make things easier on everyone when I'm out of town. I know we've tried it before, but there have to be ways we haven't tried that will ease the pressure on us all. Meantime, this is a good chance to spend some quality time with the kids. You know, do a little bonding, maybe take them to a movie or something."

"Oh, I haven't bonded with the children? I carried them inside my body for nine months, at the end of which I went through the hell of childbirth. I have permanent stretch marks. You leave for work and don't come home until seven or eight. Everything falls on me. You're gone for what now, nine days? I'm sick of it, Devon."

"Aw, for Christ sake, Sonja, just try to get through until I'm back. When I get home, I promise to take some of the work off..."

The connection broke.

Goddam it! Everybody hangs up on me!

Devon looked absently across the bar and thought of home. Where and what was home? He stared at the liquor arrangement, almost willing his mind to lose itself in the strangely beautiful bottles that reproduced themselves in the mirror behind them, shimmering in the light like a French impressionist painting. Sonja, the woman to whom he had been married for so many years, wouldn't leave his thoughts. The vision of the gorgeous young Sonja played in his mind. The day he first saw her.

He had been so insecure around girls when he was young. Every girl intimidated him then. Asking Sonja for a date had taken all the courage he could muster, and he had felt certain she would refuse. She had accepted. With enthusiasm! Later he discovered the reason. He had been given tickets to an exhibit at the Museum of Modern Art by a friend whose mother was trying to broaden her son's intellectual tastes. His friend hated modern art. So did Devon, but he had accepted the tickets, hoping they might interest Sonja. The tickets turned out to be the keys to her heart. To Sonja, "The true value in human existence lies in freedom from society's bondage." It was an aphorism she had repeated to him many times over the years. Modern art somehow fulfilled Sonja's quest for freedom.

Devon laughed as he recalled their first sexual encounter. He had been inexperienced and clumsy. That was not the case with Sonja Schechter. Had sex been boxing, she could have served as his promoter, manager, trainer, sparring partner and opponent, with enough energy left to invest his winnings.

To nurture their relationship, Devon had feigned a love of modern art and gone from one exhibit to another until he thought he would vomit. Sonja's parents loved him, funded his and their daughter's interest in the arts, and decided he was the perfect mate for Sonja. He was intellectual, literate to the bone, and liberal (they thought, and he had not given evidence otherwise). He was Jewish, attended an Ivy League school, and most important, he was poor, at least in their eyes. For whatever reason, Sonja's parents felt poverty and worthiness were synonymous. In a couple of years, the Schechters had a son-in-law. Devon sighed. Those days were gone forever.

CHAPTER 25

Devon was late getting to CASE the next morning. As he entered, he heard a familiar hum he was beginning to associate with the organization. People were milling about, occasionally laughing, children acting up a little, adults speaking softly to a neighbor or legal helper.

Devon approached the reception desk.

"Good morning, Ms. Salazar."

The receptionist's colorful dress and heavy make-up flicked his libido.

"Sorry I'm late. Nothing moved on the freeway for half an hour."

Anita laughed. "Welcome to Los Angeles, Mr. Emmanuel. The *Señora* is waiting for you," and she tossed a glance toward a small table in the corner where Devon had interviewed the previous subject. A white woman who looked to be in her '40's sat next to Alessandra.

"Come have some coffee and Mexican pastry," Alessandra said, beckoning Devon.

Devon moved quickly to the table. "Sorry I'm late again. I hit traffic." He eyed the pastries, coffee and orange juice.

Alessandra held a protective hand over the pastries. "Before we eat, I want to introduce you to a friend of mine. This is Ms. Loretta Wilson. She's agreed to tell you her story. Loretta, Devon Emmanuel, a man who has discovered the joys of L.A. gridlock."

Loretta laughed politely, then shook Devon's hand. "Hello, Mr. Emmanuel."

Loretta was tall with an attractive figure. She had blue eyes, a freckled face and a long, blond ponytail. Her simple, short-sleeved, V-neck white dress showed evidence of wear in places, leading Devon to wonder if it might be her only special-occasion outfit. Small beaded earrings, a matching beaded bracelet and what looked like a birthstone ring completed her ensemble. She seemed nervous, folding and unfolding her hands, eventually locking her fingers and placing her hands in her lap.

Alessandra motioned Devon toward a chair and began filling his coffee cup. As she poured, he chose three kinds of baked goods and ran a quick survey of his hostess. Her hair was neatly coiffed, soft shiny waves behind her ear on one side, tumbling to her shoulder on the other. Her face had regained its youthful appearance. She was dressed in tailored black pants and a long-sleeved, high-neck black blouse tucked into a belted waist. Black patent pumps accented by a thin line of shiny gold piping outlined the curve of her medium heels. Rich black from chin to toes, the effect enhanced by pierced disk earrings, their gold surfaces battered to look like ancient coins. A large gold obelisk dangled from a chain around her neck and came to rest at the top of her breast.

The femme fatale has returned.

Alessandra crossed her legs. "I have a brutal day ahead; let's make short work of this little repast and get going."

Devon ate quickly. He had never eaten Mexican baked goods before and found them delicious. As he was taking his last couple of bites, Alessandra spoke. "Loretta and I go back a few years, Devon. Her story makes some points I'm interested in your hearing."

When things were in place, Loretta straightened in her chair and took a nervous breath. Her eyes met Devon's, then drifted away. When she finally spoke, her high-pitched voice carried a slight tremor, and Devon detected a Southern accent.

"Mr. Emmanuel, the first thing you need to know about me is that I'm a good person. Like all good people, I've made mistakes. I moved here from Arkansas as soon as I graduated from high school. I had just turned nineteen and wanted to have some fun. I looked for a job as soon as I got here, but I had no work experience. I couldn't find anything. Finally I got a call for a sales position. I really wanted it. I had one good dress that really wasn't right for an interview, and no jewelry or cosmetics. I was certain they wouldn't hire me if I showed up looking like a dishrag. I was broke, so I went to Dumfy's department store and stole a white blouse, some make-up, and a black skirt – the kind of things they tell you to wear to an interview. It totaled about thirty-five dollars. When the police came, I confessed."

Loretta sighed deeply, then composed herself.

"This was my first offense, and I begged my public defender to talk to the D.A. or the judge and tell them my story. The public defender tried, but the D.A. didn't care, and the judge said he wouldn't do anything different for me than he'd do for any other thief. I already felt bad about what I had done, but now I lost the job interview and had a record for petty theft. My sentence was community service and a few hundred dollars in fines. It took months to pay that off, since I wound up getting a job in a fast food joint that paid less than what I would have made as a sales girl. I couldn't get a better job unless I could get rid of my conviction."

Loretta stopped and caught her breath.

"The public defender's office had told me that if I kept a clean record and paid all my fines and finished my community service, I could get the conviction expunged. So that's what I did. The paralegal said the court would take the conviction off my record and I wouldn't have to tell anybody I did anything wrong."

"Loretta, why didn't you call your folks back in Arkansas? Wouldn't they would have helped?" Devon asked.

Loretta bit her lip and looked away.

"My mom and dad were a mess. Living with them was hell. Dad was a drunk, and he and Mom fought all the time. I couldn't stand it. I had to get away. I wanted to see California, especially Los Angeles and Hollywood. I didn't call my parents when I got in trouble, because I knew they wouldn't help and they'd make me feel worse."

Loretta continued, "After the expungement, things started going pretty good. I got a sales job in a clothing store and the boss really liked me. In three years, I got to be head of a little department and was making a pretty decent living. When I was twenty-seven, I met a man and fell in love. We moved in together. I got pregnant. We had talked about marriage; we just hadn't set a date. When our little girl was born, he seemed to love her so much...I thought he did anyway. We were a family. He said he didn't want to get married until we saved enough money for a down payment on a house, so we just kept on living together. A lot of young people did that then, you know."

Devon nodded.

If this story gets any more like a soap opera, I'll have to pay Clark to keep on reading.

"We were so happy with our little girl that a couple of years later, I got pregnant with my son. My job was going great. I got a nice promotion with benefits. Dale, my husb...whatever...had a good job as a mechanic, so we were putting aside some money. We had each other and the kids, and I had an honest-to-God happy family for the first time in my life...I thought. Then one day, Dale came in and said he met somebody and was going to marry her. Out of nowhere! I didn't suspect anything! When he left, we divided up our savings, but it wasn't until later I realized he had already taken most of the money."

Devon looked intensely at Loretta, trying to hide any signs of the disinterest he felt sure his readers would experience to this point in her story. It wasn't that he failed to understand the tragedy of betrayal; it was the fact that it was all too common.

Tears welled up in Loretta's eyes. She continued in a raspy voice.

"I didn't have any idea he had been seeing someone else. It almost killed me! But I kept on going after he left. I still had my job and my kids. That is, until my boss made a bad business decision and went under. Even after I was laid off, I wasn't scared. I had my car, and I had saved money for emergencies so I could pay food and rent for a few months if I had to. Meantime, I had unemployment. I was sure I could get another job before it ran out."

Devon was beginning to see that Alessandra was trying to paint a picture of a woman who, aside from one small mistake, had been playing by the rules – working hard, saving money, taking any available job – robbing those who would judge her of the blame for errors they told themselves they would never make in similar circumstances.

Loretta seemed lost in thought. Devon was about to speak when she looked up. Her eyes were misty.

"Then came that recession. I couldn't get a job anywhere, and my car payments were killing me. My unemployment was running out, and then my son got sick. That broke me...drained my last savings. I swapped my three-year-old car for a Cadillac with 200,000 miles on it. The guy gave me fourteen hundred dollars to boot. Without car payments, me and the kids were still okay, because I moved to a smaller place. I got another fast-food job, but the hours weren't steady and the pay was terrible. I had to apply for food stamps. Things kept going downhill, and pretty soon we were living in the car."

Loretta shook her head slowly and repeated, "Living in the car. God, I was terrified the police would find out and take my kids. They do, you know. Child Protective Services! Protect...ha!"

The saga unfolded in Devon's psyche like a heavy blanket. *That's the problem with poor people. It's never just one thing. It's one thing, and then another, and then another.*

Suddenly he realized why Loretta had been selected by Alessandra as someone to be interviewed. A person with a budget close to the bone had no buffer against things that go wrong in life, whether caused by individual mistakes or forces beyond one's control. Devon knew Alessandra was counting on him to make people like Maria and Loretta matter to his readers. He forced himself to dig deeper.

"Tell me what it was like – living in the car?"

Loretta's tears came instantly, and Alessandra handed her a small pack of tissues. She politely blew her nose and answered.

"Devastating. Especially for my daughter. She was almost thirteen. Her friends wouldn't have anything more to do with her. My son was almost ten and hardly ever spoke."

Loretta gave a deep sigh. "I was ready to start dumpster diving when a miracle happened. I got a part-time job at Canfield's department store, stocking merchandise in the children's department. It was only two days a week, but that and the fast food joint gave us a little more money. Sometimes, I could pay for a night in a cheap motel, so the kids could shower and watch TV. Then L.A. had a terrible cold snap. We were okay in the daytime, but it got really cold at night. I couldn't run the Cadillac engine to keep the heater going, because I couldn't afford the gas and was scared we'd die of fumes. We were damn near freezing. Next day, I tried to slip out of Canfield's with two coats for the kids and got caught."

Loretta turned away from Devon, torment in her eyes. "I can't do this," she said, starting to rise from her chair.

Alessandra touched her arm lightly, speaking softly but firmly. "Remember what we talked about, Loretta. It's not just about you; it's about all the women like you who will never be allowed to tell their stories."

Loretta stared into Alessandra's eyes for a moment, then sighed and settled back into her chair. She breathed deeply.

"I was fired, and they pressed charges. Since I didn't have any money, I got another public defender. She said the prosecutor was charging me with petty theft with a prior. I told her there was no prior, because it was expunged. She told me the file and expungement papers were there, but it didn't make any difference; I still had a prior, no matter. And petty theft with a prior – that was a felony. The prosecutor was asking for prison time."

The other shoe just dropped.

Devon looked at Alessandra. "I thought expungement wiped a crime off your record."

"Just listen."

Loretta stood up. "I need a minute," she said, and walked a short distance away.

The instant Loretta left the table, Gabriela pulled her chair next to Alessandra. They conversed in low voices, Alessandra's hands moving constantly.

"I don't give a damn what he wants; the Sheffield case is crucial. We take this one to court."

Gabriela gestured in exasperation, her voice rising to a loud whisper. "How? How can we take it to court? Who's going to help you work up the Sheffield case if they decide to fight? You're overbooked, the paralegal on that case is moving to Modesto in two days, and there isn't enough time for you– "

Alessandra slammed her palm on the table top. "We don't back off this! We do, and they'll pull this shit on every case like it. If they want to fight, we fight!"

From the corner of his eye, Devon saw Gabriela shake her head, then get up and walk quickly away. His thoughts returned to Loretta, who was wandering the interior of the room.

"Alessandra, how could Loretta be charged with petty theft with a prior conviction if the other charge had been expunged?"

The anger in Alessandra's voice was still colored by her interaction with Gabriela. "Because the law allows it! And poor women do not make the law!"

Alessandra beckoned Loretta to rejoin them, then answered Devon's question.

"Decades ago, a statute was passed to deal with petty thieves who were chronic offenders, but the amounts stolen in each incident couldn't qualify as grand theft. Now that statute is used to make felonies out of small thefts that are years apart. It's great for the D.A.'s felony conviction stats. But it's really hard on poor people who occasionally steal out of desperate necessity."

"You making a case that every poor person should be allowed a few petty thefts?" Devon asked wryly.

Alessandra bristled. "No. I think stealing is wrong. So do most of the poor. But real life is filled with stories of people so afraid of losing something – their job, their home, their kids – for lack of some small but essential thing they have no money to buy, that they steal. The question in such a case is not whether it's wrong to steal. The question is whether the punishment should be a felony that can imprison you. And even if you aren't given a prison term, you're still sentenced to a life of poverty, because you'll never get a decent job again."

"But – I still don't get it. Isn't expungement supposed to clear your record?"

Loretta, who had sat down again, rolled her eyes.

"Today's background checks will turn up all crimes, even those expunged," said Alessandra. "And if you're ever charged with another crime – in this case, another petty theft – it doesn't matter how many years in the past it occurred, expungement will not protect you. The old crime rises anew."

"Then what's the point of expungement?" asked Devon.

"That's what I'd like to know!" said Loretta, bitterly.

"That's not the most important point of Loretta's story," said Alessandra. "Let her finish."

Loretta began with new energy. "I went to the courthouse and my public defender sat me down in the hallway and started reading me all the things I was being accused of, and I'm getting more and more scared. Finally, she gets to the possible prison sentence the D.A. is going to ask for."

Loretta's eyes teared up. "And I'm thinking, what about my kids? What about them? They've got no place to go. We're close, my kids and me. We've been through so much together. We love each other. Two coats on sale were about twenty-five dollars total, and my kids don't have a mother? And I have no future?"

Loretta sighed deeply. "I was so afraid. My public defender said I would get maybe six months. But when I got in front of the judge, he said, 'You people are always thinking you can get away with this kind of crime. I want you to understand that you can't.' That's what he said. He gave me a year in prison."

This is straight out of Les Miserables. I don't know how much I can do to make this come alive. Miscarriages of justice are common stories in the media. I'll talk it over with Andrews.

Devon rose, glad the interview was over. "Loretta, I want to thank..."

Alessandra stood up quickly. She lit a cigarette and began pacing, each puff sucked to the bottom of her lungs, followed by smoke that exploded through her mouth and nose as if she were a black-clad dragon.

"Is that where you're going to end this interview? You can't think of a follow-up question? Goddamn it, you're a big-time journalist, Emmanuel. Isn't there anything more you want to know?"

Devon turned his palms up. "What?"

Alessandra stopped pacing and yelled.

"Loretta was away from her kids for a year, for God's sake! Her children! Goddamn it, ask about her children!"

There was sudden silence in the room as all eyes turned toward Alessandra, who returned to her chair.

The dressing down angered Devon, but he swallowed it and turned toward Loretta.

"What happened to your children, Loretta?" he asked tonelessly.

"When I got out of jail, I tried to find them. Their father promised before I went to prison that the kids could live with him and his wife. But not long after they moved in, he and his wife broke up. One day, he asked his neighbors to watch the kids for a week and he never came back. No one has seen him since. The kids were farmed out to foster care and both of them ran away. No one knew what happened to my kids."

Loretta began crying, then slowly regained her composure.

"No one knew where my children were. Nobody! After I got out of prison, I went everywhere in Los Angeles looking. It took months to find my daughter. She was living with a small time drug-dealer. She was so high she barely knew me. I couldn't get her to go with me, and even if I could of, I didn't have a place for her to stay. A few months later, she died from bad heroin."

Tears began running down Loretta's cheeks, making small beads on her jaw.

Devon felt numb. It was different hearing or reading about a tragedy of this kind and sitting two feet from someone who had actually lived the horror. He started to say, "I'm sorry," but it sounded pathetic. Then he remembered.

"Your...son?"

"Two gangs were shooting, and somehow he was in the way. Lost my life and both children over sixty dollars worth of clothes, cosmetics and two cheap, marked-down children's coats."

Tears flowed in torrents, ending with the exhausted woman limp in her chair.

"Well, that's my story, Mr. Emmanuel. Mrs. Gittleman says it's up to you to print it or not. I hope you do. I didn't get justice. I got cheated out of my life. If you print this story, maybe somebody will change the law and another woman won't end up like me."

Devon turned and faced Alessandra. "Who do you hold accountable in a case like this?"

Alessandra ground out her cigarette.

"The prosecutor's office will say the loss of Loretta's children was tragic, then cleanse their souls with a reverently delivered denouement: 'The fact remains, the defendant shouldn't have been stealing.' No government body gives a good goddamn about the outcome in a case like this. Or anyone else's case, unless the defendant has the money to fight. If you're poor, prosecutors want to count your conviction among their victories – use it to advance their careers – and be done with you. A defendant has a better shot at a good outcome if they're white, but race usually doesn't make a whole lot of difference if they're destitute. I've heard the same story from Hispanic, black and white."

Alessandra stared blankly at the room full of busy women.

"Routine for poor women," she muttered. "Justice is just another name for fucked if you're destitute and female. Most Americans sit in their armchairs and say, 'You stole something. You broke the law; now you pay the price.' They never ask, 'Have we created the circumstances that force people to do wrong in order to do right for their families? And do the consequences meted out by our justice system make our society better?'"

Alessandra lit another cigarette and sat, radiating anger.

"When life happens, and a parent or any person falls to the bottom of the economic heap because there is no one to help, no way to stop the slide, they're forced into a position where they have to survive. Survival often involves breaking the law, because the law doesn't account for situations in which your children are freezing in your car at night. The law doesn't care that you're afraid to tell anyone because you've been told by social workers, shelters, and nonprofits that failure to provide the necessities can cause you to lose your children. So you break the law, because you place a higher value on keeping your children. Hoping times will get better.

"The problem with the safety net, Devon, is that it doesn't catch you until you are so far down the economic ladder that you may never be able to rise again. And even when you seek help from safety net programs, nearly half the people who are qualified never get that help."

Devon started to ask a question, but Alessandra continued, her eyes fierce.

"The real penalty for the crime is that children are condemned to a life of poverty. The parent can never recover from the criminal record, the loss of family life, and the stigma of criminal conduct. The kids are caught in the web – the stigma of poverty and poverty itself."

With that, Alessandra rose from her chair, signaling the interview was over.

"Thank you, Loretta. By the way, I may have a lead on a better job. I'll call you later."

After Loretta left, Alessandra sat down again and looked coldly at Devon.

"Well, what did you think?"

"I think the term 'justice system' might be a misnomer. In her case, anyway."

Alessandra smiled grimly and tapped ashes from her cigarette into her saucer. "You've still got a lot to learn, bubby. Will you use her story?"

"Yes."

I've been pounded enough today.

"Do you happen to have any antacids around, Alessandra? Those Mexican pastries gave me heartburn."

"I've got some in my apartment."

"Good. I'd like half a bottle. Then I want to know what happened to the little girl and the old man after the cops left them in search of coffee and a donut."

CHAPTER 26

Alessandra reminded Devon of a black swan as she slipped off her shoes, made a nest in her recliner, took a swallow of coffee, and relaxed. A languid smile slowly settled on her face. "You know, I still miss him."

"Who?"

"The derelict."

Alessandra searched Devon's face for recognition. It came just as she said, "In the park. I spent about a month with the old guy. He said his name was Joe. When I asked him his last name, he said it was Schmo. I'd just turned nine; I thought he meant it."

Devon and Alessandra shared a laugh. Then she turned serious.

"He wasn't a drunk, and he wasn't crazy. Not some schizophrenic babbling incoherently through the streets, although he did have his problems. I'm not sure what you'd call him. 'Derelict' is the best I can conjure up. He gave a new definition to the term 'street smart.' He knew where to get good cheap food, the least dangerous places to sleep, where to get safe drinking water and a bath – all the necessities. He carried a cane I'm pretty sure was iron-filled on the end."

"What makes you think it was iron-filled?"

"Because he used it on a guy who grabbed for me one night. It was almost dark and I didn't see the hit, but I heard the thud, followed by a scream, then another thud. More screams of 'My leg! My leg!' and I could see the guy against the night sky as he hurried away, dragging his leg until he disappeared into the dark."

Devon watched as Alessandra changed position in her recliner, her tight-fitting black clothes seemingly alive as her body moved. When she found her preferred position, she tilted her head back and stared at the ceiling.

"Initially, Joe was clean but disheveled. After a few days with me, he began taking better care of himself. He took great care of me. Showers, clean clothes, decent food. We went shopping. He bought me underwear, socks, a pair of shoes, two dresses and a carrying bag. Oh, and my first purse."

"Where did he get the money?"

"From a bank. I was with him when he made a withdrawal."

The comment surprised Devon. "And he was on the street?"

Alessandra gave an I-don't-understand-it-either shrug. "My guess is he got checks from some kind of pension. He had a post office box, too. I know he got at least one piece of mail, because I saw him take it out of the box."

Alessandra's face lit up, and she smiled as though she had experienced the pinnacle of happiness. "I was so proud of that purse."

Then she chuckled. "My hair was a mess when I first met him, and after a few days I asked him to cut it. He got a scissor out of his bag and trimmed it to about an inch above my shoulders. And he gave me bangs."

"Bangs! I can't imagine you in bangs."

"Bangs," she giggled. "He said it was the only cut he knew how to do for a girl. I wore my hair that way for years – bangs to mid-forehead, with wavy hair to my shoulders. I didn't change my hairstyle again until I was fifteen. I remember seeing myself in a store window one day when we were walking around, and I thought I looked rich and beautiful."

Alessandra's smile faded and was replaced by something that suggested a painful memory, as her facial muscles and eyebrows moved almost imperceptibly into sadness. Devon watched the changing persona and imagined her as a child. Bright, young, adventurous, wandering the streets of New York City with an old man and a shaggy little mutt. Surrogate grandfather, surrogate granddaughter, surrogate dog. A family. He was so lost in contemplation, he was startled when Alessandra spoke again.

"I lived a wonder-filled odyssey. Our only destinations were happy days and nightfall. Joe liked to talk, but it was hard for him, because he was extremely short of breath. Every word he delivered, though, was a gem. He never asked me much about myself. The little I told him seemed to make him kind of angry. He taught me all kinds of things – why the moon had phases, how trees grew, why grass was green. I loved listening to him and asking questions."

"The two of you just...wandered and talked?"

"That's about it. We went into museums on days when they were free, libraries, parks with swings and slides, and on the subway. I saw the Statue of Liberty! I loved it – and I loved Joe. He was the first adult who had treated me well since they took me away after my mother and father died. We never got very far in one day. He couldn't make it more than a block without stopping to rest. I was a typical kid, full of energy, and I wanted to run. He had to struggle to keep up and would yell, 'Slow down! We ain't on a speedway.' I think he must have been gassed in the First World War, because when I asked him why he breathed so hard, he said, 'Too much Belleau Wood.' That didn't make sense to me then, of course."

The clock chimes rang and Devon felt a chill. Alessandra's eyes fixed on him, but something was missing from them, something he couldn't describe. She stared at him, but appeared unseeing. Time passed. Then he heard the same change in her voice he had heard previously.

***

I woke up one night, and Joe was coughing and breathing real hard. I crawled over to him. "What's wrong, Joe? Are you sick?"

"Not feelin' too good, honey. Be okay. Don't worry yourself."

Light was coming from the street lamp, and I could see he was sweating. Then he started to shiver. "Joe, I think you're sick. You better go to the doctor."

"Don't need no damn...doctor. Be...okay in th' mornin'...go back t' sleep."

I curled up against his back and put my arms around his waist to keep him warm but he just kept shaking and sweating until my dress was wet. Then all of a sudden, he started talking strange.

"Let's go... let's go...over th' top, you sons o' bitches! Give 'em hell, boys...Roy, Jim...get some grenades into that goddamn machine gun nest."

I kept trying to talk to him, but he didn't answer. He just kept talking and shaking.

It was starting to get light, and I heard a siren. I didn't know what else to do, so I run out in the street waving my arms. It was a police car. It swerved to miss me, then screeched and stopped. A big policeman jumped out yelling while the other one talked into his police telephone.

"Whathehellswrongwityousekid?" yelled the big policeman. "You'll get killed in the middle of the street? What you doin' out at five-thirty in the mornin' anyways?"

I yelled back, "My Grandpa Joe's sick! I think he's real sick!"

The policeman looked at me funny.

"Grandpa Joe? Where?"

I grabbed the policeman's sleeve and pulled him toward the little park where Joe was sleeping and Liza Bell was licking his face. The big policeman felt around on Joe, then waved to the other policeman who got out of the car and come toward us.

"Whatchagot?"

"Stiff, I think. He ain't breathin' and I can't feel a pulse. Body's warm...looks like he just crapped out."

I felt awful. I started crying, and they kept saying nice things to me and asking who I was and what I was doing out at this time of the morning and stuff. I just shook my head and kept crying.

Then the big policeman said, "Look kid, we gotta know about your Grandpa Joe so we know who to tell he's dead. We need your help. Where's he live?"

I kept on crying and Liza Bell come over and I picked her up. She made me feel better. I knew I had to say something or they were gonna take me somewhere and maybe lock me up.

"Grandpa lives here," I said, and the big policeman smiled.

"The Bronx is a big place, honey. Where exactly is 'here'?"

I said, "I don't know."

The policeman kneeling beside Joe turned toward me and the other policeman and said, "He's got money but I can't find an I.D, Jake. Must have one hidden someplace in this bag, but I can't find it. What was your grandpa's last name, sweetie?"

And I said, "Schmo."

"Schmo?" They both said it at the same time.

"Yes, sir."

Then the big policemen knelt down beside me.

"Whatcha last name, honey?"

I didn't know what to say. I didn't want to tell him Matreoni because he might find out I run away from the orphanage. Then I had an idea. Donatella Santorini was always talking about a movie with somebody in it named Wilkes. That sounded good.

"Wilkes."

The big policeman rubbed his chin and stared at me. "Your mama was Grandpa Joe's little girl?"

I nodded, and he wrote Wilkes down in a little book.

The other policeman was giving me a funny look and it scared me. I hugged Liza Bell up under my chin and she made me feel better again just like before.

The big policeman smiled at me. "What was your daddy's first name, honey?"

"Ashley," I said, and the big policeman mussed my hair.

"That's a nice name. Where's Mama and Daddy now?"

All of a sudden everything come back to me. Mama and Papa and the funeral and how much I missed them and I started crying harder than I ever cried in my life. The big policeman picked me up and I hung onto Liza Bell. Next thing I knew I was in the police car and the siren was going until we pulled into this place I knew was a police station. At first I thought I was in trouble, but they treated me real nice. All the policemen did. They gave me bacon and eggs for breakfast. And they fed Liza Bell.

I had just finished eating when I looked up and there stood Sister Doreen. I tried to run but she was too quick. She yelled and grabbed me.

"Ye little witch. Ye wait 'til I get ye back t' *Th' Marcy a Jesus*! Slip out th' door, will ye? Well, we'll be seein' how ye'll be slippin' out th' door I'm puttin' ye behind."

I knew what was coming no matter what I did, so I hauled off and kicked her hard as I could in the leg. She let out a yell, and when she grabbed her leg, I twisted away and ran for the door. I was almost out when a policeman grabbed me. I yelled and kicked, but he was too strong.

When we got to *The Mercy of Jesus*, a policeman carried me inside and Sister Doreen showed him the room to put me in and it was the room where they kept me before. I knew after the policeman left that Sister Doreen was gonna come with her big paddle and give it to me, so I prayed to the Virgin and for a while it helped because Sister Doreen didn't come back.

That night I didn't get anything to eat. There was nothing the whole next day either. Then here come Sister Doreen with her big paddle, slapping it down hard with a popping sound into her hand. Her face was all squenched and her eyes was real big. In her black habit she looked like a devil. I was really scared.

"Ye little witch. Ye made a fool o' me but ye'll not be doin' it again. T'day ye start larnin' th' County Cork catechism. Now, hike that dress, pull down those panties and bend over."

When Sister Doreen stopped paddling, I hurt so bad I couldn't touch my behind. All I got to eat after that was biscuits and water. Lucky for me there was a bathroom because I stayed in that room three days – maybe more. I kept praying and asking the Holy Mother to help me and I guess she did, because I got out.

***

Alessandra shifted her position on the recliner. She was facing Devon now, and he watched as her eyes rolled about. He felt certain she didn't see him. Then she began speaking.

***

Running away from *The Mercy of Jesus* made me lots of friends. All the kids wanted to know what I done, and when I told them about Joe Schmo, they really liked it, especially how Joe died, and about Liza Bell, and they asked where they were now. I told them I didn't know, but that wasn't all true. In the police station, after the policeman grabbed me, I kept yelling for them to give me Liza Bell, but Sister Doreen said to get that scruffy thing away from me and that was the last time I saw Liza Bell. Nobody ever told me what they did with Joe either, but I guess it didn't make much difference, him being dead and all. I missed them both and said prayers for them.

Things were better than they were before I run away, until a big new Irish girl named Ginger Finnegan, who was really mean, come to *The Mercy of Jesus* and started calling me a wop and dago and some names I never heard before. One day she hauled off and knocked me down and jumped on top of me and started pounding. I tried to fight back but I didn't have much chance against her.

Then all of a sudden, here come this Puerto Rican girl, just a little bigger than me and she and Ginger really went at it. The Puerto Rican girl was Luisa Blanca Maria Benitez, my friend from before I ran away.

***

The unearthly atmosphere in the room disoriented Devon. To him it was a time of Dalian watches draped limply over wooden fences and long-necked giraffes singing the *Ode to Joy*, the notes soaring soundlessly into the void. Nothing he had just witnessed was part of the world he knew. It was a world sequestered in another universe.

Alessandra was silent and still. Devon wondered if he should call Gabriela. Then Alessandra raised her chin and put her hands on the seat of the recliner. She appeared dazed, but slowly became more in the moment. Eventually she made eye contact.

"Are you okay?" Devon asked. "I was a little worried about you."

Alessandra slowly gathered herself, ignoring his question. "Devon, I'm going to have to work on a case for the remainder of the day. Perhaps tomorrow we could begin a little earlier."

"I'll try to avoid gridlock," Devon said, trying to lighten the atmosphere.

"This is Los Angeles, Devon. Start earlier."

CHAPTER 27

Devon's feet had hardly cleared CASE's Hobbit-threshold when he called Andrews. He was startled by the editor's shout.

"Great fucking day's work! Great stuff!"

"How much of today's interview you read?"

"All of it! Listened and read in real time. Is this old woman amazing or what!"

Devon had his car in view and picked up his pace. "Clark, today's interview was one of the weirdest experiences in all my years in journalism. You had to be present to understand."

"Understand what? I heard everything as it was being recorded."

"But you weren't sitting an arm's length away from her. There are times in which she becomes – I don't know – stuporous, I guess you'd call it. It's like her mind leaves her body and goes back in time."

"Huh? I could tell she spoke a little odd. You telling me she's out of contact with reality?"

"No. At least I don't think so. She told me earlier she had problems talking about this. I'm not sure what's going on, but it's troubling. I don't even know how much of this shit's true."

Andrews' voice carried a hint of irritation. "It doesn't make any difference. We have a fact-checker. Have you talked to Lindsay yet?"

"Yeah. We should be able to prove or disprove some of the stuff she's giving us, if he lives up to his reputation. But an in-depth check of her personal life is impossible under these time constraints, regardless of Lindsay's talent."

Andrews' voice remained irritated. "So what? Who's going to say it didn't happen? Most people from her youth are dead. And she's the next thing to a hermit."

Devon reached his car, got in quickly, and started driving, continuing his conversation as he motored down the frontage road toward a newly discovered entrance to the freeway.

"I have worries about Lindsay too, Clark. It doesn't bother me that he's a little shit, but as you said, he's inexperienced. And what we're asking him to do could very well involve something illeg– "

"Forget that! You were right to begin with. I was being too cautious. Don't rethink your original idea. This stuff's too good not to publish."

Devon entered the freeway ramp and gunned the engine. "Where do you think we ought to go next?"

There was Andrews' usual pause. "I want to know her mannerisms, the way she eats, fidgets, writes, whatever. And get all the information you can about her sex life."

Devon nearly lost control of the car. "Sex life! You're out of your goddam mind! This woman wouldn't tell God about her sex life! She's seventy-four! Her husband died fifteen years ago, and nobody's been in her apartment overnight since. Sex life…sweet Jesus! Don't goddamn say that to me again, goddammit!"

Silence.

"Clark?"

No answer.

"Clark? Awe, fuck. He hung up!"

CHAPTER 28

It was past one o'clock in the morning when Devon pushed his laptop away, rose from the small desk in his hotel room, stretched and lay down spread-eagle on the bed. His brain felt like oatmeal, but he had completed the changes on Andrews' previous day's editing and a rough of the last interview. He added suggestions about how the first and second day's efforts might be meshed to create a more literary draft. Finished. Send. Time to clean up, relax, and get some sleep.

After showering, he placed a wake-up call for 5:30 a.m. on the house phone, set the alarm on his cell phone as a back-up, poured himself a shot of bourbon, turned on the TV, propped himself up in bed and began vegetating. When the wake-up call came and the phone alarm sounded, he found the television on and the bourbon untouched. He made coffee, drank the pot, made another, and poured himself another cup. Then he called Lindsay while shaving.

"Yeah."

Devon laughed at the sulking teenage voice, then answered in his approximation of an Irish accent. "Top o'th' marnin', Lindsay m' lad. Are we havin' fun?"

The response was teenage rage. "You said you was gonna call last night. I worked my ass off yesterday. How come you didn't call?"

Devon laughed louder. "You're my fact-checker, Lindsay. Stop sounding like my wife. How much of what I asked for were you able to get?"

"All of it. That was a lot of work!"

Devon lifted the razor, then hesitated. "Give it to me."

"Okay. Mrs. Gittleman's whole name is Alessandra Angelina Asencio Matreoni Gittleman. She was born on August 12th, 1936. Her dad was Enrico Arturo Fedele Matreoni and her mom, Beatrice Serafina Magdalena Denezzi Matreoni. They came to America from some place in Italy called Indigio. Mrs. Gittleman was born at home in Bensonhurst, and the doctor's name was Dr. Markus Feldstein. Her dad was a baker, and his business was on Eighty-third Street. That was their home address too. Her dad became a citizen in 1939. I don't know about her mom; I couldn't find where she had. Both of them was killed by a truck May 16, 1944, in Flatbush. They got run over coming out of a subway."

A warm sensation swept through Devon. So far, Alessandra was telling the truth. "Get anything else?"

"I got it! I already told you I got it! The Catholic school was named St. Cecilia, and it was tore down in 1967. It was on Seventy-ninth in Bensonhurst. Those two Sisters – Agnes and uh…"

"Francesca."

"Yeah. They died in a Catholic nuns' place. One in 1985, the other in 1987. *The Mercy of Jesus* orphanage was in the Bronx but got tore down in 1987. Alessandra Matreoni was there from 1944 'til 1950. There wasn't much record on what happened to her there except she ran away twice, the last time in1950. They brought her back the first time, but the second, they couldn't find her. She hit some nun in the leg with a bat the second time. It broke."

Devon sprayed a mouthful of coffee on the mirror. "The bat or the leg?"

"Leg," Lindsey answered innocently. "There was a letter in Alessandra Matreoni's police file from the nun who got hit that said Alessandra Matreoni was…wait a minute…'an incorrigible monster' and that the only thing to do was put her in a 'juvenile correctional facility.' Reform school, right?"

"Right. Who signed that letter?"

"The nun that got her leg broke. I don't remember her name offhand, but I can get it."

"Does 'Doreen' sound familiar?"

"That's it!" said Lindsay. "Sister Doreen. Boy, was she mad. She said Alessandra Matreoni tried to kill her, then run off."

A thought jolted Devon. "Lindsay, you're supposed to be getting everything available online. You're not…uhh…doing anything else…are you?"

"I didn't break into no place if that's what you mean. They scanned in their old records. Everybody scans in their old records. The Catholics, the cops – everybody."

The first part of the comment reassured Devon, but the last part brought uneasy questions.

"Juvenile police records are supposed to be in secure files, Lindsay. How did you get into the police department's secure files?"

"Same way I got into their main hard drive. The cops' computers is dinosaurs. A idiot could hack 'em."

Devon's concern subsided, then began undulating in his psyche like a small boat in a rough sea.

"Can they – they can't – trace you – can they?"

There was a pause during which Devon's gut torqued.

"It's possible if they had the right software, but they ain't. I could've busted their firewalls when I was eight. Nobody can find me. A super computer couldn't find me unless they had information on me that triggered on my kind of computer language and they can't because I wrote my own protection in a language I made up and then coded that. Nobody knows my language but me and nobody with a regular computer can crack it."

Devon knew nothing about computers beyond typing on them. The explanation sounded like super-nerd shit so he decided to accept it.

"What else you got?"

Lindsay sounded disappointed. "Nothin'! That's all you asked for. S'matter? You ain't satisfied?"

"Absolutely satisfied and you're right, you got it all. It was a great job! Nobody could have done it better."

"Ha! Nobody else coulda done it! You want something else?"

Legal cases in Los Angeles came to Devon's mind, but he decided to hold off on them. What he needed was more information on Alessandra's personal life. The legal stuff was easy to get and less time-consuming.

"Send me what you've got, then learn everything you can about Alessandra Matreoni. Check and see if you can find a record of the marriage between her and anybody with the last name of Gittleman. Run all of her names just in case there's more than one Alessandra Matreoni. Get everything you can. Don't leave anything out even if you think it isn't important. You're doing a great job, Lindsay."

Silence.

"Lindsay...Lindsay...? Fuck!"

CHAPTER 29

Devon navigated the freeway to CASE like an Angeleno, cell phone in ear, weaving through traffic and disregarding the rant of his infuriated spouse until she hung up in apoplectic rage. The surreal chaos, coupled with lack of sleep, had numbed his psyche. Alessandra met him at her apartment door, appearing equally drained and rubbing her temples.

"Headache?"

Alessandra nodded, eyes half-closed. "Have a seat. I need to go take something," she said in a whisper.

As she walked toward her bathroom, Devon sat in his usual chair. He hadn't eaten for hours, and when he saw toasted bagels, lox, onions, cream cheese and a pot of coffee, hunger overtook him. The wait for his breakfast companion became painful. He turned when he heard a noise.

Alessandra was walking toward him in a wobbly gait, her left arm moving strangely at her side. When she reached the table, she poured coffee using her right hand, surveyed the serving platter, picked up half a bagel, sat down and moved her recliner into a semi-upright position.

"Better start eating," she whispered, and looked at him through nearly closed eyes. "I love this stuff…my headache subsides, I'll go into a feeding frenzy."

Devon was building his culinary creation before Alessandra finished her sentence.

"Where did you get bagels this good in Los Angeles?" he asked, savoring his first bite.

Alessandra nibbled her bagel.

"Some Bronx transplants own a Jewish deli in Brentwood. I helped one of their employees stay out of jail about five years ago. Once a week since then, they send me bagels, lox, cream cheese and all the trimmings."

Alessandra's elegance momentarily took Devon's mind off his food. She wore a long-sleeved white blouse with button cuffs that went halfway up her forearm, then opened into loose sleeves and soft shoulders rising into a tight-fitting collar. The blouse was tucked into high-waist, sharply creased, cuffless black pants that resembled a style Devon had seen in a decades-old photo art display. Her shoes also reflected that era, black suede pumps with two-inch heels, rounded toes and small silver buckles. Her face was framed by hair in soft waves slightly tousled over one ear. The look was classic, professional, and very feminine.

"I know that headache's killing you. Maybe being told you look fantastic will help."

Alessandra raised her eyebrows weakly and smiled. "Thank you. Nice compliment for an old broad. And don't worry; my headaches usually subside fast."

"I wasn't trying to flatter you," Devon said after finishing a mouthful of food. "You really do look lovely."

She smiled graciously, so he pushed forward into her personal life.

"How come you have so many friends, considering your reputation as The Dragon Lady?"

Alessandra's answer was nonchalant. "I've been doing this work almost forty years. You make friends; you make enemies. I do what I do. People who hate me can go piss up a rope."

Devon laughed, thinking as he did that he saw a sly smile mixed with the Betty Davis persona.

"What about you? Don't you make enemies?" Alessandra asked.

"Only. That's why I envy your ability to make friends when you've lived your life on a battlefield."

"You know, Devon, many people are offended by injustice, but they don't do anything about it. They don't want to get into the ring, because when you do, you get hit. I get into the ring, and some people support me because I win. A few of them end up being my friends. That's my secret to making friends."

Alessandra patted her lips daintily with a napkin, then leaned back in her recliner. "I have to go to a meeting at three and need to prepare for it, so let's get started. We left off with Luisa, didn't we?"

"She'd just fought Ginger Finnegan to protect you."

Alessandra lay back on the cushion, massaged her forehead with her fingers, and pressed the heels of her hands into her temples.

"Ah, Ginger. Ginger was a piece of work. Ginger couldn't believe she hadn't licked Luisa. She'd lost face with her subordinates. The only thing that would make her top banana again was another fight, which took place a couple of days later. This time, it was a brawl that would have done justice to a Hollywood western."

"Who won?"

"The kids thought it was a draw. I didn't. Luisa came out of it bloodied and grimy and was immediately snatched away to see Sister

Doreen. I didn't know what happened in that office, but I felt sure when Luisa didn't come back that they'd put her in the room."

Alessandra sat up and cast her eyes idly about. Her gaze stopped at the top of the coffee table and remained fixed there for several seconds. Then she lay back.

"What did the nuns do to Ginger?"

"Nothing."

"Nothing? What were you doing while Luisa was away?"

Alessandra sighed and seemed to melt into the recliner.

"I felt so terrified without Luisa. I was all alone again. I didn't have a clue about what was going to happen to me. And I was worried about Luisa. I'd lie in bed at night and try to make a plan, but everything I thought about seemed impossible. During the day, I tried to hide from Ginger and her brigade."

"How could you hide? The place was crawling with kids."

Alessandra tilted her head back and closed her eyes. "I know. Then one night I made a decision. I had an idea, and I was going to start the next day."

Devon waited for Alessandra to continue, but she lay motionless and mute as she had in previous interviews. Time rolled by. He was becoming accustomed to these hiatuses. He watched her breathing slow. Finally she began to speak.

***

I talked to every girl who wasn't Irish and tried to get them to side with Luisa and me against Ginger. I knew that when Luisa got out, she was going to get beat up again by Ginger, and me along with her. I could only talk to somebody when they were alone, because everybody knew if they were caught talking to me, Ginger was gonna beat the stuffing out of them. A couple days later, Ginger did catch me talking with a girl, and me and the girl both got pounded. Then here come Sister Bridget, Sister Doreen's friend.

Sister Bridget looked around at the kids and said, "Who started this fight?"

Ginger pointed at me and yelled, "She did! She's always doin' stuff to everbody. I had to fight her...ain't that right?"

And she looked at the kids and they all started saying things like, "Alessandra's always startin' fights," and "She says bad things about the Sisters!" And one yelled, "She calls the Sisters the B-word."

"That's not so! I never said any of that! Ginger's been calling me dago and wop."

"She's lyin'!" Ginger yelled, and turned around quick toward Sister Bridget. "Ask 'em! Ask any of 'em!"

And Sister Bridget did and all the Irish kids started yelling I was lying and none of the other kids said anything. Sister Bridget gave me a scary look.

"You fight, you lie, and Good Lord knows what else. C'mon, we're going t' see Sister Doreen."

I was really scared. I thought if Sister Doreen paddled me again, I would die. When I got to her office, I just stood there while she yelled.

"Did ye niver hear o' juvenile haall, young lady?"

I could see she was getting madder and madder while she talked and her face was big and red.

"Ye know what they do t' ye at juvenile haall?"

I didn't, but I figured it couldn't be any worse than getting paddled again. Sister Doreen shoved me into a chair then stood in front of me real close. She was tall and kind of fat and her boobs stuck way out.

"They'll beat ye 'n they'll starve ye. Think ye'd like that? Ye won't git good food 'n a waarm bed 'n education like here. I've a mind t' have 'em come 'n git rid a ye once 'n fer aal. Waant me t' do that?"

I didn't know what to say. Juvenile hall sounded about like *The Mercy of Jesus*. While I was thinking, I was looking straight up at Sister Doreen's face. Her eyes kept getting wider and wider when I didn't answer, and I kept getting more and more scared and couldn't talk.

"Well, ye little vixen, what'll it be – juvenile haal or *Th' Marcy a Jesus?*"

It was then I made up my mind. Maybe they would beat me and starve me, but if I stayed at *The Mercy of Jesus*, Sister Doreen and the Irish kids were gonna beat me up too and take away what I had to eat. It couldn't be any worse.

"I want to go to juvenile hall," I said.

Sister Doreen kind of rose up in the air and when she come down, she grabbed my hair and pulled me to her desk and bent me over it and started using her paddle. All I could do was scream. I thought she was never gonna stop. I don't remember what happened after that, because next thing I knew I was in the room with Luisa, laying on the floor with her face about a foot from mine.

"How y' doin'?" she asked.

I didn't say anything right off. I just lay there curled up with my knees under my chin. My butt hurt so bad I started crying.

"Sister Doreen beat your butt?"

I snuffled and nodded. Luisa being there made me feel better and I said, "I've been wondering how you were. Are you okay?"

Luisa smiled. "Yeah. It ain't so bad here. That bitch Ginger ain't around and them mick friends of hers. When we get out, you know Ginger's gonna come for us. Whether we win or lose won't make no difference. Ginger will say it was us started it, and Sister Doreen'll beat the shit outta us and throw us back in here."

I was getting to where I could think straight. "I know for sure Sister Doreen'll beat the shit out of me." It felt funny saying that bad word out loud.

Luisa touched my back and legs, and I jerked.

"Can you move your legs?"

I put one leg out straight and got a pain in my behind. I reached back and touched it. It hurt. "I don't know if I can get up." I straightened out the other leg. That really hurt and I yelled.

Luisa shushed me and I quit yelling. She took the side of her fist and wiped the tears from my cheeks.

"You got a lot of lickin's here, and it ain't right cause you ain't done that much."

And I said, "Yeah. Everybody hates me."

"I don't. I like you. The other Puerto Rican kids and colored kids – they all like you too. It's just the Irish kids hate you, and I don't think they would if it wasn't for Ginger. They're scared of her. Turn on your belly and let me see your butt."

I hated anybody looking at my butt. Luisa put her hand on my shoulder. "I'm just gonna take a quick see. You got a skinny butt. Sister Doreen might of hurt your tail bone and that's why it hurts to move your legs."

I rolled over and pulled my panties down. It hurt bad doing it. Luisa looked, then said to pull them back up.

"Am I okay?"

Luisa shook her head. "Your bottom's all black and blue and blood's coming out of little spots where it was stuck to your panties. Can you walk?"

I tried to get up but there was this terrible pain and I yelled. Luisa got my arm and I got up again but just went back down.

"You're hurt bad, I think. Maybe all the way through."

I thought about Ginger and Sister Doreen and getting beat again and it about scared me to death. Somehow I had to get away from *The Mercy of Jesus* but I couldn't figure out how.

"What you think I ought to do?"

Luisa said, "I don't know. But if you get out where Ginger can get hold of you, she'll get you sent to Sister Doreen again for sure. Next time, you might be hurt so bad you can't ever walk. I think we better try and stay in here. Sister Mary Alice has been bringing my food, and she seems nice. Maybe we can ask her."

I said, "I don't know Sister Mary Alice. I only saw her once, and she never said anything."

Luisa said, "I didn't know her neither 'til I got in here. She's new. She puts more meat on my plate than the other nuns. If she comes tonight, I'm gonna try and get her to let us stay put for a while. You lay curled up when you hear the latch and don't say nothin'."

It was near lights out when there was a peck at the door. I was on the floor and kind of raised my head. Luisa put a finger to her lips. I could hear the key turn in the lock, then the door squeaked. Out of the corner of my eye, I saw this little bitty nun come in and put down a tray. I was so hungry, I wanted to dive for it, even though I knew moving quick would hurt. Sister closed the door behind her and whispered. She was hard to understand because she talked Irish so fast.

"Eaat queek. Lights oot 'n five minutes."

Luisa and me started eating fast, but there wasn't too much. I gulped mine down, but Luisa didn't eat all of hers.

"Ain't you gonna eat it?" I asked, and kind of looked at her.

"Naw, I saved it for you."

"But it's yours."

"It's a gift. You gotta take it 'cause you can't turn down a gift."

I looked at Sister Mary Alice. "Is that right, Sister?"

Sister Mary Alice looked away and I decided that meant yes. I tore into the stuff left on Luisa's tray. While I was eating, Luisa whispered in Sister's ear, and Sister whispered back. Then she picked up the trays. Suddenly, the lights went out. There weren't any windows, and it was really dark. The door squeaked, a little light come in from the hall as Sister went out, and then it was dark again. Keys rattled and the lock clicked.

I reached out, trying to find Luisa. She was kneeling beside me, and my hand hit her on the nose.

"Owee!"

"I'm sorry, and thanks for letting me eat your stuff. I was really hungry."

Luisa sniffed. "I thought it would make your butt feel better."

"I think it does. What were you saying to Sister Mary Alice?"

"I told her your butt was all black 'n blue with blood stickin' to your panties and maybe you was hurt all the way through. I told her as soon as we got out, Ginger was gonna get us, and then Sister Doreen was gonna get us, and if she used the paddle on you again, you might not be able to walk. Then I asked if she could keep us here 'til you got better."

That got me excited. "Wha'd she say?"

"She said she'd ask Sister Doreen if she could keep us here and teach us catechism. She said she'd pray for us, too. I told you she was nice."

***

Alessandra lay still and silent for a while. Then her eyes opened slowly, and she stared at Devon. "Spaced out again?"

"Yeah. Do you remember where you were?" Devon asked cautiously.

"Yes, I do. I was in the room. I was with Luisa."

I believe her. This is a person reliving the past in real time. If I write that, though, I'll be laughed out of the profession, unless I can anchor it in something concrete. But what?

Alessandra checked her watch. "We have to stop. I need to work on a case."

Devon was more than ready for a break. He felt drained, his thoughts going to the horrific beating Alessandra had received at the hands of the nun. The sounds of her screams echoed in his imagination. He cleared his throat and spoke, his voice barely audible. "Was Sister Mary Alice successful in keeping you out of harm's way until you recovered?"

"She was, but there's a lot more to the story. I have to be in court tomorrow and won't get back until early afternoon. Then I have to see clients. You like Italian food?"

"Love it."

"Meet me at Angelucci's restaurant at six. You can Google the address; there's only one Angelucci's in L.A. We'll work after dinner, if we're still sober."

"Tomorrow evening at Angelucci's."

CHAPTER 30

Andrews' call came as Devon was walking toward his car, the editor's voice exploding in his ear. "Can you believe this story? Jesus Christ! I love it!"

Devon laughed. "You've been listening in real time again, haven't you?"

"I couldn't help it. This is Little Orphan Annie meets Attila!"

"How does H-T feel about it?"

"He hasn't seen it."

Devon jerked upright, his head hitting the door frame as he was getting into the car.

"For Christ's sake! Clark, the piece is already long. If H-T refuses to accept the way I'm developing the story, I'll never finish on time!"

Andrews feigned the voice of a preacher. "My son, I'm making it safe so you can lie down in green pastures. There is evil lurking in the fucking valley!"

"What's that mean?"

The editor's voice carried an edge. "I mean every turd-faced, mediocre *Walden* writer's going to be running into H-T's office the instant the news of the single-story issue breaks. They'll be screaming for their article to be published this month as planned. Right now, nobody at *Walden* except you, me, H-T and some scared-shitless suits know what's really coming down. I want pure gold before I show H-T the story, because he might leak it to one of his favorite ass-kissing writers. We've got to make the old fart believe that Lillian Schwartzfelt Scheidler's acquisition of *Walden* leads only through the vision of Andrews and Emmanuel. Excellence and absolute secrecy are our friends, Devon. Transparency is our mortal enemy. I intend to keep everything hidden until the time is right."

Devon roared out of his parking place, raging at Andrews.

"I understood everything was a done deal, and now I find out we still don't know if H-T is going to approve of my work. You bullshit me, Clark! You're my friend, and you bullshit me!"

Andrews replied calmly, "I never made promises. I gave personal opinions."

"Personal opin – fuck that!"

"It's unimportant. Stay with me, Devon. Remember, my ass is on the line as well as yours. Besides, if H-T doesn't go for it, we're probably screwed anyway, because this magazine will go under. Rumor says we're in more trouble than I first heard at the briefing."

Devon had a sick feeling in his stomach. "What the hell is happening back there, Clark?"

"Nobody's talking, but from the faces on the suits, I have a hunch the rumors are true."

Devon tried to break in again, but Andrews cut him off.

"Listen to me. Whatever is coming, there's a few things we know for certain. H-T is pragmatic. Unless the whole organization gangs up on him, we can pull this off. I can keep *Walden* in the hunt and the two of us with it, if we do this right. You've got to trust me, Devon."

Devon was deliberating as the editor made his argument. The point about the other writers putting pressure on the old man had precedent. Devon remembered the time H-T had folded when his writers complained bitterly about one of his decisions.

"Clark, have you talked to Lindsay today? Clark...Clark...aw, for Christ's sake!"

CHAPTER 31

It was nearly 5:30 the next evening when Devon hit the "send" button on his computer, delivering an updated version of the article to Andrews. The break in his meetings with Alessandra had given him time to catch up on the writing. He felt tired, relieved and hungry.

He showered, shaved, and put on the "New York dinner clothes" he packed for all important trips – tan Armani suit, Egyptian cotton shirt, expensive tie, and loafers so costly he had rarely worn them in ten years. They still carried a faint smell of new. He got Angelucci's Restaurant address off the net and made one last check of his appearance.

He felt good as he left his hotel room. The article was coming together. If there were no big setbacks, making the deadline was nearly a certainty, although the last few days would be a killer.

Christ, what I wouldn't give for another week on this story.

His cell phone rang as he entered the freeway. Lindsay.

Devon ignored the niceties of salutations. "What'd you learn?"

The absence of a greeting whizzed unnoticed past the kid.

"Stuff. When she ran away from the orphanage the second time – the time she broke Sister Doreen's leg – she was fourteen. I can't find nothin' more 'til she's twenty-four. That's when she married old man Gittleman. He was fifty-two, and she was twenty-four."

Lindsay's comment brought to mind the photo on Alessandra's small bookcase. She had looked to be in her early twenties, and the tall man beside her was easily fifty. The background was the Grand Canyon.

Honeymoon!

The voice on the phone broke into Devon's thoughts. "You still there, man?"

"Yeah."

How could she have vanished for so many years? She broke an Irish nun's leg. Most New York cops back then were Irish; they'd be all over the case.

"Did you run her entire name through those files?" Devon asked. "All of her names?"

"Yeah. And I did combinations. Ran that Puerto Rican girl's too...Luisa Blanca Maria Benitez. Nothin'. I found Alessandra after she ran away from the orphanage. Then I found her a second time when she was gettin' married to Gittleman."

Devon took the freeway off ramp, checked his directions for surface streets to the restaurant, then asked, "What else you got?"

"There ain't a lot. She went to Columbia Law School. She was a magma cum lawd."

"That's *magna cum laude*. She graduated with high honors."

"She's smart, huh?"

"Yeah. Smart as hell. Anything else?"

"That's it. I couldn't find any more."

Devon saw the sign for Angelucci's Restaurant, slowed and pulled into the parking lot. Time to put a little balm on the wounds he had inflicted. "You did good, Lindsay."

"You want I should keep lookin' for what she did after law school?"

What good would it do to go into her law practice? I can get that any time I want.

"Keep looking for her between the ages of fourteen and twenty-four. People don't just disappear for ten years. Run variations on the spelling of her name. Do the same with the Puerto Rican girl. I'll call you tomorrow."

CHAPTER 32

Angelucci's was a modest-sized restaurant with decor nearly identical to expensive dining establishments Devon had enjoyed in Rome. The ceilings were high, and a few beautiful paintings of the rugged Amalfi Coast were nicely arranged on the off-white walls. Fresh-cut flowers in small glass vases spread their colors at the center of each table.

Devon stopped at the maître d's desk and searched for Alessandra amid the sea of white linen tablecloths, eventually finding her in a secluded booth, chatting and laughing happily with an overweight man in a chef's uniform that included a pleated chef's hat.

A tuxedoed host walked up briskly. "You have reservations, sir?"

"I'm with Mrs. Gittleman. No need to walk me back; I can see her."

The maître d' looked at him as if he were a peasant. "As you wish, sir."

Devon moved between tables occupied by casually dressed Angelenos, his fashionable clothes making him feel black-tie-at-a-picnic. As he approached Alessandra's table, he heard a stream of Italian as the chef spoke to her, gesturing energetically.

Alessandra looked beautiful, her age nearly hidden behind flawless make-up, her wavy hair parted, one side brushed behind her ear, the other gathered under a clip fashioned like a small tangle of tiny gold-leafed vines. A black turtleneck knit contrasted with a long-sleeve, collarless olive jacket set off by a design of overlapping, thin black circles. As he drew closer, Devon could see black boots and a swath of black skirt beneath the table.

My God...she's gorgeous.

Alessandra smiled and waved him toward her. The chef turned in mid-sentence and followed her gaze. His demeanor became taciturn when he saw Devon. Alessandra coquettishly introduced Devon to the chef, seeming to enjoy the possibility that two men – one at the threshold of middle age, the other at the sunset of it – might still vie for her attention.

"Leonardo, this is the young man interviewing me for the magazine. Devon Emmanuel…Mr. Leonardo Angelucci, owner and head chef of Angelucci's, the finest Italian restaurant in which I've ever had the pleasure of dining."

The two men exchanged cold pleasantries and handshakes. Angelucci excused himself and returned to his kitchen, casting Devon a disapproving glare over his shoulder.

With the chef gone, Alessandra concentrated on Devon.

"So, what have you been doing with your free time, my elegantly dressed Mr. Emmanuel?"

Devon unbuttoned his coat and took a seat across from her in the booth. A waiter appeared from nowhere to snap open a napkin and place it on his lap.

Alessandra addressed the waiter. *"Arturo, una bottiglia di un vino special, per favore."*

"Si, Signora."

The waiter left, and Alessandra again turned her attention to Devon, who smiled and answered her question.

"What have I been doing? I've been writing an elegant story about you. And speaking of elegance, you define the word tonight. You look fantastic."

Alessandra beamed. "Thank you."

Devon nodded as his eyes again journeyed over her.

How does she look like this at her age? It's incredible.

"So…how did things go at CASE?"

Alessandra sighed. "I pounded away on that case – the one where the D.A. was backing down on our deal. I also had to help my co-workers with the daily load. It's enormous. One client after another. Nowadays, some are former middle-class women who've lost their jobs and are facing everything from repossession to eviction."

"Sounds exhausting. Sure you're up to the evening?"

Alessandra straightened, took a deep breath and spoke enthusiastically. "I hereby banish all evils of the day," she said, and swept her hands apart. "Tonight we eat, drink and celebrate life. What suits your palate? Main course if you were God?"

Devon shrugged. "How can I answer without a menu?"

Alessandra raised her eyebrows. "God does not need a menu."

Devon laughed. "I only look like Him."

The waiter returned with a small basket of bread and a bottle of wine. He presented the wine label to Devon, who nodded unknowingly. When the cork was offered, Devon deferred and gestured casually toward their glasses, which were quickly filled.

"Could we get a menu– "

"The menus were already offered," Alessandra interrupted. "I declined." She raised her glass. "Salute."

Devon clinked her glass.

"This wine is from Leonardo's special wine cellar. It's a perfect selection for what we're going to eat."

Devon took a sip. It was superb. He leaned back in the comfortable booth and smiled at his companion.

She orders my wine. Refuses to let me see a menu. Probably didn't even occur to her to do otherwise. That was some look I got from Leonardo. Hope the kitchen help hides the knives until we're gone.

"Why did you refuse the menu?"

Alessandra tilted her chin up. "We're in Angelucci's. Do you like Italian seafood?"

"Well..."

"Prepare to be amazed," she said, sweeping her arms above her head. "Leonardo presents his creations in repertoire. Never the same delights on successive evenings. He personally selects all the seafood and meats he uses. What you're about to experience is not dining. It's wonder – it's simplicity – it's – breathtaking. Two of his finest pastas appear tonight. One is pasta with fresh swordfish and cherry tomatoes, something you may not have had in New York. The other is delicious too – rigatoni with homemade Italian sausage and ricotta. Which would you like for the *prima piatti*?"

She's a symphony by Mendelssohn. It would be a sin to interrupt her.

"No idea. You order for both of us."

Alessandra's smile was almost grateful. "Excellent! We'll start with some *antipasti*. A little *bottarga* butter on – "

" – *bottarga* butter?" Devon interrupted warily.

"Stewed carp intestine," she answered nonchalantly.

Devon's mouth dropped. Alessandra laughed riotously.

Amazing. Stressful day, and she ends it with mischief and vivacity.

"*Bottarga* butter, as they call it in Calabria, is a paste made from the eggs of a tuna. It takes months to prepare. It's kind of pink in color. It's served on little toasts called *crostini*. Living in New York as you do, you're surely familiar with unusual Italian culinary gems."

"Some, but not sophisticated dishes prepared by top chefs."

"Tonight we educate your taste buds." Alessandra hesitated, then asked, "You...follow the kosher laws?"

"I'll eat any part of a pig."

"Wonderful. You'll be able to try some grilled figs with goat cheese, prosciutto and balsamic vinegar. And perhaps some *funghi sott' olio*?" Seeing Devon's blank stare, Alessandra explained. "They're the most wonderful wild mushrooms. Preserved in oil with garlic, peppers and fennel. We'll need a small bowl of cracked green olives, too. Now those I remember from my childhood."

Devon rolled his head. "Alessandra, I came here hungry, but what you're describing will fill me up before we get to the main course."

"Not to worry. We're not going to wolf down this meal. We're going to eat the old Italian way, slowly, as if we're at Sunday dinner and we don't have to think about anything until tomorrow. There's no TV, no phone, nothing but good company and good conversation."

Devon reached into his jacket and pulled out his phone. "Just turning it off," he said, returning it to his pocket.

The waiter, Arturo, took the order in Italian, nodding in acknowledgment but writing nothing down. He refilled the wine glasses, removed the basket of bread and left the table. Shortly, the array of *antipasti* appeared.

Devon gazed in contemplation as the feast began.

"Is something wrong?" Alessandra asked, a note of worry in her voice.

"Everything's fine," he reassured her.

"It's just that…seeing a meal like this laid out in such careful order reminds me of Shabbos when I was a kid. I remember Mom standing and beckoning the Sabbath 'bride.' The quiet rituals that went with the meal. I've missed all that. I've missed the peace that descended on the room – on the family. It was wonderful. I didn't appreciate it back then. I guess no kid does."

"You don't follow any of the Jewish rituals in your own family?"

"No," he said, his eyes avoiding hers. "It seems I've gotten away from a good number of family rituals."

Alessandra said nothing. Instead, she waited in silence, as if expecting he would explain. He found himself wanting to speak of his childhood, but decided against it.

"The subject of this interview is you," Devon said, shaking off his reverie.

"The subject of this interview is trust," Alessandra corrected him. "I didn't share my story with just anyone. I chose you, because I thought I could trust you to understand it. It's a little different when the tables are turned and somebody's asking about your life, isn't it?"

Devon sipped his wine.

"I've had a few challenges."

"Hmm," she responded, never taking her interested gaze from him.

As the moments passed, the wonderful food, wine and his delightful companion wore away Devon's resistance. He found himself sharing some of his own life journey, including youthful dreams of his young adulthood. Alessandra was an intent listener, drawing him out in spite of his uneasiness. It was almost as if they both had a repressed desire to know each other better. They took nearly an hour working their way through the delicious appetizers.

They were so engrossed in conversation that Devon was startled when the pasta was served. He tasted it.

"Fantastic."

Alessandra smiled broadly. "Take your time, my friend. It's going to be a long evening with delectable cuisine prepared by a great chef."

Back they went to laughing and talking, with Alessandra savoring the stories of people Devon had interviewed in the past. No sooner had he mopped up the last of his pasta sauce than two waiters appeared, one removing the plates after patiently awaiting Devon's final forkful, the other setting down a platter with an elegant rack of lamb garnished with deep green leaves and small bright flowers.

The waiter attempted to serve Alessandra, but she raised her hands. *"Just uno, per favore, e patate molto pochi. Sembra delizioso, ma sono certo che posso mangiare molto di più."*

"Naturalmente. Se si desidera che più tardi, volentieri io ti servirò."

The waiter placed before her what looked like a tasting plate, with portions the size of spoonfuls.

The food was served sizzling hot. The waiter artfully prepared Devon an ample plate of lamb, potatoes, artichokes and peas.

Again, time retreated. Devon sat enthralled as Alessandra, the undernourished, abused child of his imagination was transformed into a fascinating, erudite, funny, older, yet still beautiful woman.

By now, the restaurant was packed, but to Devon, it seemed as if he and Alessandra were alone. The restaurant patrons had faded into silence, as Devon listened to a woman in total command, fearless as a titan, who gave and took as she pleased in the world of men without regard to their desires or needs, and only as she wished. Feelings that he hadn't experienced in years arose in him.

Suddenly, Alessandra's face turned white, her head drifted downward, and her left arm began to move aimlessly.

Devon lurched across the table. "Alessandra!"

Alessandra raised her head slightly, smiled and whispered, "Nice evening, eh, Bubby?"

"Great evening. What's wrong?"

Alessandra's smile became more faint. She absently studied her arm, which continued to move, watching it as if it were no longer part of her body.

"Don't know," she answered in a mumble. "Haven't thought about…fifty years…the dawn…hold back dawn."

The rambling speech and bobbling limb sent Devon reaching to help. Alessandra knocked his hand away, then lifted her arm from the table as though she were a robot and lowered it into her lap.

"I have a headache."

Devon frantically waved to the waiter, who had already noticed something wrong and was staring in horror. Devon beckoned him with animated but silent gestures, trying hard not to upset the other guests. The waiter quickly came to their table.

"I will call an ambulance," he whispered hoarsely.

Alessandra had maneuvered to the edge of the booth. With difficulty, she wobbled upright, stiffened and pointed a wavy finger at the frightened waiter, who had begun working his cell phone. Her voice was weak, but commanding.

"No!"

The waiter turned his palms up and looked pleadingly at Devon.

"No," she said again, firmly but softly. "No ambulance."

Arguing will only make things worse. Get her home and deal with it from there.

"I'm driving you back to CASE, Alessandra," Devon said quietly.

Alessandra lifted her chin. Her words seemed to tumble out of her mouth, but were clearly discernible. "You can...chauffeur."

"Bring the check," Devon said urgently to the waiter.

The waiter was so frightened his body lurched at the request, and he reverted to broken English. "Everything is...ah...ah, not charge. Onna house from boss. Issa like always – like always."

Alessandra struggled puppet-like to assume an imperial demeanor. When she spoke, her words were clearer and louder.

"Ask Mr. Angelucci...if we could see him, please."

Guests began watching. Some appeared alarmed but were calmed by waiters who quickly engaged them in earnest discussions of menu items. Moments later, an apprehensive Chef Angelucci appeared, sweat and concern on his face, his white apron stained with the evening's work. The conversation between the two friends took place in Italian, Alessandra speaking in a halting staccato. They kissed lightly on both cheeks, and Alessandra, standing with knees trembling, handed him her car keys.

Angelucci turned to Devon. "Alessandra...she say you drive-a her home in-a you car. She leave-a here the car. Tomorrow my people bring." The restaurateur hesitated for a moment, staring coldly at Devon. "Alessandra... Alessandra she is saint. You know Saint? You are Catolica?"

Devon shook his head. "No, but I understand saint."

"Then you write 'bout-a Alessandra like-a she's-a saint."

"I understand," Devon answered, feeling Angelucci's command contained more than a hint of hostility.

Getting Alessandra to the car and into CASE was an effort. By the time they reached the stairs, Devon and the security guard were mostly carrying her.

"My chair," she mumbled, as they struggled through the door. "Dim…lights. Press down…dimmer switch."

Fear showed on the security guard's face. "*Señora* Gittleman, let me call for you a doctor."

Alessandra shook her head. "Migraine." Through glazed eyes, she looked at Devon. "My headache medicine…kitchen…top cabinet as you enter."

Devon left with Alessandra's staccato voice fading behind him: "*Voy a estar…bien, Jorge. Gracias…por la ayuda. Buenas noches.*"

"*Buenas noches, Señora Gittleman. Estoy abajo, Señora. Llamame si usted me necesita y estere' aqui rapidamente.*"

While Devon searched for the medication, the security guard adjusted Alessandra's recliner. When Devon returned to her side, he was forced to kneel beside her in order to see her in the dim light. Her eyes were closed, her head tilted to one side. Coming face to face with her so closely, he was appalled by what he saw. It was as if she had aged forty years. When he recovered emotionally from the shock of her appearance, he noticed her arm was no longer shaking.

"Alessandra…how many of these pills do you need?"

Alessandra opened her eyes slightly. "Four."

She took the pills from Devon's palm with her right hand, put them in her mouth, reached for the water with a wavering left hand, then stopped, switched hands and washed down the pills.

"What's wrong with your left arm, Alessandra?"

"Weak," she said so softly Devon could barely hear her. "Gets that way sometimes when I have a bad migraine. Be okay tomorrow."

I never heard of a migraine doing this, or coming on so suddenly.

"You're bullshitting me," he accused her in a firm voice. "How about the goddamn truth!"

Alessandra laughed weakly and handed him the glass.

"Fine language from only man alone with me…this apartment at night…fifteen years," she whispered.

"I'm not leaving until you're asleep. I'm going to carry you to your cot now and don't try stopping me."

Alessandra closed her eyes and shook her head. The whisper in her voice continued. "Never sleep on the famous cot. It doesn't exist. This is where I sleep."

"Then, I'm going to sit in my chair. When you're sleeping and things look okay, I'll leave."

Alessandra's eyes opened and wandered about his face. She rested her right hand on his forearm.

"You're getting...too close to your subject, Bubby. Those professors in your fancy college...wouldn't like it. Bad journalism."

As Devon rose to his feet, Alessandra's hand caught the sleeve of his coat. "We're not making enough progress. Running out of time. Long as you're staying, we talk."

"You can't mean that. You're in agony!"

Alessandra shook her head. "Feeling a little better. I've had worse migraines. Mine sometimes hit hard...clear fast. Like this since I was in my twenties."

"I don't believe you. We can work tomorrow. We don't have to work now."

"Can't work tomorrow. Personal business. Three of my clients will– "

"Personal business?"

" –be here tomorrow. Listen to all three. Write up the one you want. After that, everything will be my story. Fit me with my microphone. Let's get started."

CHAPTER 33

Devon stumbled about, setting up the microphones he had left in her apartment from the last day's work.

This is crazy, but I'm pushing against the deadline and have a long way to go. She knows it. If she can talk, I'll let her, but I'm only going so far. What an end to a beautiful evening.

While Devon scrambled, Alessandra removed a cigarette from a pack and attempted to put it between her lips. Devon saw it fall from her trembling fingers into her lap. She stared at it as though it were a curiosity. He retrieved the cigarette, lit it, then gently placed it between her lips. She took a puff and inhaled deeply. He removed the cigarette and placed it in an ashtray within his easy reach. Alessandra hadn't exhaled, and Devon was becoming concerned, then a stream of smoke flew from her mouth and her head slumped against the recliner.

"Do you remember where I left off?" she whispered.

"You and Luisa were locked in that room in the orphanage. Sister Mary Alice was going to try to convince Doreen to let you stay in the room to learn catechism."

"Ah, yes." Alessandra's voice was weak. "We spent three weeks in the room. We had fun even though we had to learn catechism. Sister Mary Alice also brought our school books. When she wasn't at prayers, she taught us our other courses. I'd never thought of Luisa as smart, but she learned fast. Except for catechism."

"Why would you have thought she was – uh – slow?"

"I don't know. Ignorance maybe. Little prejudice picked up from the streets in Bensonhurst. Luisa loved math. As soon as the light came on in the mor…morning, Luisa would start teaching me math."

"You like math?"

Alessandra gave a short laugh, then frowned in pain, and her wavering left hand went to her forehead. "Got to…remember not to laugh. No. I was, and remain ... mathematical retard."

"Know the feeling. Did anyone say how long you were going to be locked in the room?"

Alessandra beckoned for the cigarette, took another puff, and motioned for Devon to knock the ashes off.

"No. The first we heard about regaining our freedom, which for...most part we didn't want, was from Sister Mary Alice who woke us early one morning...Never forget her frightened little face in...light from the hall. And that...thick Irish accent. Remember...every word.

"'I'm needin' all ye school books 'n paaper queeck. Study ye...catechism like madd, garls; it's ye gettin' ouut day. Stuudy...like ye've niver stuudied befar. If we're lucky, I c'n keep Sister D'reen involved 'til...afternoon, then she's goin' t' waant t' heer what ye know. Cramitin, garls, if ye doon't, aall three of us...in troouble. Terrrible, terrrible, troouble! Saints be with ye.' Then she shut the door and was gone."

Alessandra stopped, raised her head and looked about. Devon saw hollow cheeks and wide, nearly lidless eyes with expanses of white, punctuated by large black marbles.

She's terrified. All these years and she's still scared.

Alessandra's head sank slowly back onto the cushion. She motioned for another drag off the cigarette, which Devon provided.

"...Starting to feel better. Anyway, that afternoon the lock on the door turned, and...Sister Doreen entered. She stood in the doorway like an immense black and white tiger...holding her...big paddle....Didn't even glance at Luisa – just me – and her voice – I can still hear her voice."

"A' right, little Miss Alessandra Italiana, let me har ye catechism. We'll staart th' questions from...b...begginin' 'n keep goin' 'til I tell ye t' stoop. And I'll hear Hail Mary's 'n Our Father's first."

Alessandra glanced about in panic.

Devon reached for her arm. "Alessandra..."

"I fell to my knees...started saying Our Father's and...Hail Mary's. Don't know how many I said, but I knew Sister Doreen wouldn't hit me while I was praying. We started on catechism. S...surprised me how much I remembered. Questions seemed to go on forever. Finally, she said, 'Enoough.' She turned to Luisa, who fell to her knees and started with Our Father's and Hail Mary's. Then Sister Doreen began the catechism."

Alessandra's eyes widened wildly again, and she began breathing fast and deep. Devon placed his hand gently on her arm until her eyes slowly closed. Time passed. He ground the cigarette into the ashtray and waited. He was about to leave quietly when Alessandra continued.

"Luisa didn't get far into the catechism before she looked up at Sister Doreen and said, 'I can't remember any more.' Her face was serene, like she was walking through a meadow on a summer's day. The calmness of her voice is as incredible to me now as it was then. At that moment, I considered her...beyond courageous. Terrified for her."

"What do you feel when you think back about Luisa's composure – from the vantage point of sixty years?"

Alessandra's eyes opened instantly and she stared at Devon as though he were mindless. "Same way I did then."

Silence.

Then from a face devoid of expression came a whisper. "Luisa was a unique human being."

"What do you mean?"

"I mean...there are some humans who rise above what nature ordinarily allows. Far above the rest of us."

"Who would you put in that category?"

The clock chimed, causing Devon to jump. He glanced at his watch. Once again, the chime had sounded at no particular point of the hour. He felt his heart skip a beat, and his breath came fast. Everything in the room had a sinister feeling. The dim light appeared to make things move as though the air were filled with ghosts.

Calm down. Nothing's going on here but exhaustion, headache, and a screwed up clock!

In the subdued light, Devon watched as Alessandra developed a countenance that approached the angelic; her words came as an ethereal whisper.

"Nelson Mandela, Vaclav Havel, Gandhi, Martin Luther King, Joan of Arc."

"Incredible list. What puts Luisa in that lofty category?"

"I've read about them. Their life stories. Their courage. Luisa...had that kind of courage. She understood...things, sensed them, even though she had little formal education."

In the quiet that followed, Devon began to relax, actually enjoying the absence of the outside world as he sat alone with Alessandra. But the quiet was also intense. There were moments when he felt they were isolated in another universe.

"What about you? You've taken on some of the toughest guys in California and won. You're smart, and you have courage – don't you think?"

Alessandra's face remained serene. "Enough, I suppose. But it's not natural. In the years we've been talking about, I was constantly terrified. I developed courage later."

The quiet descended again.

She looks so weak...frail.

Suddenly Alessandra opened her eyes and looked unblinkingly at Devon. Her voice rose. "Some people are born with great courage. Born unafraid and willing to act, regardless of the consequences."

The clock inexplicably chimed again.

Devon moved uncomfortably in his chair.

"Then there are the rest of us," Alessandra added.

The eerie silence descended again. Alessandra's eyes had closed; her chest rose and fell slowly with deep breaths.

She's doing better. I'll keep going a while longer.

"You really believe some people are born without fear?"

Alessandra's eyes opened. "I do. In my lifetime, I've witnessed the spectrum of humanity. Occasionally, courage occurs through determination. Myself, for example. But there are few natural heroes. The only one I've ever met personally was Luisa."

"What did Sister Doreen do when Luisa said she didn't know any more catechism?"

"Nothing. She seemed stunned by Luisa's lack of fear. She glared at her, but Luisa remained impassive. Sister Doreen looked so angry, but she did nothing."

"Why didn't Doreen go after her?"

"Probably because there were other people around, and also Sister Doreen was a bully who was not prepared to deal with Luisa's courage. In retrospect, Luisa's failure to show fear probably made her Sister Doreen's ultimate target."

"Why do you think that?"

Alessandra thought for a moment. "Wasn't so much what Sister Doreen said; it was the sound of her voice and the way she turned away from Luisa. She wanted to denigrate Luisa's gift of courage, needed to, but something stopped her. I can still hear that black-clad bitch from hell. 'Whut I expected. Ye're n'turally slower. 'Tis th' cuarse a yer paople.' Then she boomed out, 'Sister Mary Alice!' 'Here, Sister D'reen.' Doreen spat out, 'Ye did goood, 'specially with th' Italian. Other laarned somethin'...good as c'n be expected, I suppose. I waant ye t' keep warkin' with 'em. Make sure they toe th' line 'n if they give ye troouble, let me know.' I hated Doreen for saying those things about Luisa. They had to hurt her. I still hate bullies."

"So she let you and Luisa go back with the other kids. What happened when you did?"

"Things went well for about a year. Sister Mary Alice watched out for us constantly. Luisa and I began making a lot of friends, all the new Puerto Rican and colored kids and even a couple of Irish girls. Most of the Irish stayed away from us though. Then one day, I knew something was going to happen, because the two Irish kids that had been friendly began to avoid us. I could feel Ginger's malevolence in the air."

"That must have been frightening."

"It was, but nothing bad happened...until one afternoon I was coming onto the playground. Luisa was sick and Sister Mary Alice was on an errand for Sister Doreen. We were playing kickball when someone hit me in the back and sent me sprawling. I tried to get up, but Ginger was on me in a flash, punching away with both fists. I don't know how long she punched, but it seemed forever. Then Sister Bridget yanked Ginger off me, got hold of the back of my blouse, and half-dragged me to the office."

Alessandra became silent and pursed her lips. Devon waited for tears, but her face relaxed and she moved her head from side to side. The movement was so slight he wasn't certain it had occurred.

"When I got to the office, I was bleeding all over my skirt and blouse and couldn't see out of one eye. I could see Sister Doreen though. She was holding the big paddle and my fear made her seem to grow bigger. She shoved me so hard into a chair, it would've fallen over if it hadn't slammed against the wall. I began crying. Her voice was like a clarion from hell. 'Queet cryin', ye miserable little wretch. Coodn't stand proosperity cud ye? Well, this time thar'll be no Sister Mary Alice t' coddle ye. This time, ye're goin' t' larn things my way! Get up 'n bend over th' desk!' I froze and she grabbed me, flung me over the desk and started beating. Each whack felt as though it penetrated my body."

There was another slight movement of Alessandra's head, and the whisper returned. "I must have fainted, because the next thing I remember was waking up in the dark. The pain was terrible. I couldn't get up. I started crawling around until I came to the toilet and found the nick in the porcelain. It was the room all right, but it was in total darkness. I thought it was after lights-out and crawled onto the bottom bunk and fell asleep."

Alessandra quit speaking. The scene she had described seemed such a nightmare, Devon couldn't think of anything to ask. He sat watching her. The quiet began closing in again, disturbed only by the tick of the clock. He took a deep breath and heard it enter his chest. Then Alessandra spoke.

"When I woke up, I was starving. The lights hadn't come on. I crawled to the door and listened. Nothing. I hurt all over, cheekbones, nose, ribs, but mostly my bottom, where pain was shooting up my back and down my legs. I was so terribly, terribly lonesome and scared. I started crying, then told myself crying wasn't doing me any good. I needed to get control of myself, so I decided to think about fun things."

"You've just been beaten until you can't walk, and you decide to think about fun things?"

Alessandra's eyes opened, and she seemed to consider the question. "When you're locked up and all alone, crazy things happen to you. They happen because you need them to happen."

"What fun things does a twelve-year – "

"I'd just turned thirteen."

"Okay, thirteen. What things?"

"When Mama and Papa were alive. All the people who used to come into our bakery. The kids I played with at St. Cecelia. Donatella Santorini and her crazy stories. I missed Donatella. I thought about Sister Agnes and Sister Francesca and how nice they had been to me."

Alessandra's breathing deepened. At first, Devon was alarmed that she might have lost consciousness. Her face began to change expressions, almost as if she were responding to images in a dream. He sat transfixed as she began speaking in the strange child-like voice that now sounded so familiar. In the low light of the room, he felt drawn into her past. Lost in time. Her time.

***

I could hear somebody at the door...light...Sister Mary Alice.

"Oh, Sister, I'm so glad to see you."

My legs buckled under me and I fell and grabbed her habit and held on. Sister shoved the door shut with her foot and wrapped her arms around me, pulling me tight against her. I felt her fists in the middle of my back.

Then she sort of shook me. "Listen. It's daytime. Thare's no boolb in ye light's why it's daark. They'll be 'round with soomthin' t' eaat, but not mooch. Hide these apples 'n when ye eaat them, eaat caar 'n all. I'll try t' get other stoof, but noow all I c'n get is apples. I know what happened on th' playground, child. I'll do what I kin. I'll pray for ye. Ye pray also. Pray too for Sister Doreen and Sister Bridget when ye pray for th' others. Remember, ever bit o' th' apples! Lord bless ye."

Sister Mary Alice squeezed two apples into my hands. That's what I had felt pushing into my back when she hugged me. Then she lowered me down on the bed and slipped out of the room. I ate both apples, then prayed for me, Luisa, Sister Mary Alice, Mama, Papa, Joe Schmo, Liza Bell, and other people. But I couldn't pray for Sister Bridget and Sister Doreen. It bothered me I couldn't.

Then the door opened and Sister Bridget was there with a tray. She said, "I have ye dinner. We've decided t' give ye some light – not that ye desarve it."

Sister Bridget set the tray on my little table then screwed in the light bulb. I looked at my plate. Four slices of bread and a pitcher of water. It wasn't much, but Sister Bridget could see I was hungry.

She said, "Thar'll be no eaatin' 'til ye've said ye prayers and asked Jesus fer forgiveness. On top o' that, I waant ten Hail Mary's and ten Our Father's."

I crawled out of bed and got on my knees and started praying. I mentioned every sin I could think of, which I hadn't done, but with Sister Bridget standing over me, I knew I had to have a lot of sins so I could ask for forgiveness. As I started my Hail Mary's, she left, but I kept on praying because I figured she was standing outside.

Before I finished the Our Father's, my throat was so dry I could hardly stand it. I drank some of the water. It tasted good. I started to eat the bread and stopped. Four pieces of bread ain't a lot. I knew I had to do something to make myself feel full, or I was still going to be hungry when I finished. I decided to make myself believe I was full. I closed my eyes and imagined my fingers was a fork and that when I tore off a piece of bread with my fork-fingers, I was really diving into the biggest plate of spaghetti ever, covered with Mama's special sauce. I ate and ate, and by the time I finished the four slices, I was so full I couldn't eat any more.

It was getting lonesomer and lonesomer. Then I thought of something. If I could imagine my fingers being a fork, and a little bit of bread a big gob of spaghetti, I could imagine other things too. I'd been missing Liza Bell a long time. I tried to imagine her up, but no luck. Then it come to me I wasn't using anything to be Liza Bell. My bread plate was right-sized for Liza Bell so I started imagining it was her, then I remembered they would take the plate away! That would be awful if it was Liza Bell! Then I remembered my table. They wouldn't take it away. It was little, but still too big for Liza Bell, so I shut my eyes while I imagined, so I couldn't see it. That worked, and pretty soon, there was Liza Bell and after that, I didn't have to shut my eyes to make the table small. I petted and talked to Liza Bell and she cuddled up to me. I tried to talk to Joe Schmo too, but he wouldn't come out, so I pretended he was there anyway. It got to where I could see Liza Bell any time I wanted, even with my eyes open.

My light bulb made shadows and I started pretending the shadows were all sorts of things like trees, fire plugs, lamp posts and a lot more. Suddenly I could see Joe Schmo and we started talking right away, him telling me all the things he did when he was a kid and me telling him about Mama and Papa and Donatella Santorini. Then he started doing a little dance and got Liza Bell doing it too. Then Liza Bell learned to talk, and the three of us wandered all over New York. It turned out Joe had been a prince and a wicked witch put a spell on him and took away all his money and his dad's kingdom. Liza Bell was his big horse and the wicked witch turned her into a little dog. I felt sad for them, but they said they were happy and they told me I could be happy too. All I had to do was set my mind. I told them I'd already started and was happy. I was having fun when there was this noise and the door flung open and someone come flying through, stumbled to the back of the room, and fell and hit their head on the toilet."

"Ye c'n rot here far as I'm concarned, ye little Puerto Rican witch! I'm caallin' th' police and seein' ye t' juvenile jail," said Sister Doreen as she stood at the door.

She left and I crawled over to whoever was laying by the toilet. It was Luisa, and she was skinned-up, her hair mussed, and her blouse torn. Blood was coming from where her head hit the toilet.

"Luisa...Luisa, it's me; it's Alessandra." Luisa didn't move, so I got some water from the pitcher and rubbed it on her face. "Wake up, Luisa. Please wake up."

Luisa opened her eyes, raised herself on one elbow, and stared at me. "Alessandra?"

I said, "Yeah. How ya doin'?"

And she said, "My butt hurts. But I got her for you, Alessandra. I got her good!"

"Sister Doreen?"

"Naw. Ginger. I got her good!"

Luisa wasn't making much sense. "What are you talking about?"

"Me and the Puerto Rican and colored kids. You remember that big colored girl named Ellie Jenkins that come in a while back?"

"Yeah."

Luisa grinned and said, "Boy she can fight. You know how Ginger always has those three or four Irish girlfriends with her?"

I slid down until I was flat on the floor and looking into Luisa's face. We were so close, I could feel her breath. She smiled at me and I could see blood in her teeth.

"Yeah."

Luisa said, "They're really good fighters."

"The Irish girls?"

She shook her head. "Naw, Ellie Jenkins and the colored kids, and the Puerto Ricans. I figured somethin' out about Ginger. That's how I got her. You know how it's always Ginger goes after you and not you goes after her?"

"Yeah."

"Well, it come to me it ought to be us comin' after her. She always does the same thing – gets you alone with her friends and beats the snot out of you."

I couldn't figure out why Luisa kept talking about it, because I already knew all that.

"How's that figuring out something?"

She grinned again and some blood come on her lips.

"Because it's the way to beat Ginger. I went to the Puerto Rican kids and asked them if they would help me in a fight with Ginger – hold off her friends while the fight was goin' on. All of them said yes 'cause Ginger don't like us Puerto Ricans. But they wanted the colored kids to help because there were too many Irish. I went to Ellie Jenkins and asked if she would talk to the other colored kids and get them to help hold off the Irish girls. She said yes 'cause Ginger was always calling the colored kids nigger."

That sounded like a good plan, but it had a problem.

"Luisa, you fight good, but Ginger always beats you up."

"I know, but it ain't because she's so strong. It's because she's got lots of help. I figured if Ginger knew she didn't have any help, she might not fight good. Today I got where Sister Mary Alice couldn't see me, 'cause I knew it was then that Ginger would jump on me. Sure enough, here she come, the Irish girls with her, and she started."

I looked at Luisa's face. "And she beat you up like this?"

Luisa said, "She might've, but then here come the Puerto Rican and colored kids. I thought they were just gonna hold off Ginger's friends, but that's not what happened. They started beatin' the snot out of them. Ginger saw what was happening and tried to get away. I was really mad, and sure enough, Ginger didn't fight good. I pounded her. Sister Mary Alice and Sister Bridget and Sister Monica come running, but they couldn't stop the fight 'cause everybody was so mad at the Irish kids, they just kept fightin'. It was then my clothes got all ripped and dirty."

"How'd it end?"

"The Irish kids were beat up bad and screaming it was always us startin' fights, but this time all of us screamed back they was liars. Ginger was scraped up bad and screamin' loudest of all. I knew Sister Bridget was gonna listen to her and not us, no matter what I said, so I hauled off and made the best punch I ever made right on the end of Ginger's nose. Blood just busted out and went flyin' everywhere, some of it on me. I tried to run, but the big new nun – Sister Monica – grabbed me, and Sister Bridget told her to take me to Sister Doreen's office."

Luisa didn't have to tell me anymore, because I knew what had to have happened. After Italians, Sister Doreen hated Puerto Ricans second-worst.

"I don't know how long Sister Doreen paddled me. It was a long time. She slapped me in the face a lot too. But I got Ginger for you, Alessandra. I got her good!"

I didn't know what to say. I kept thinking Luisa could have stayed around her Puerto Rican friends and the colored kids, and she would've been a little safe anyway. She did all this for me. I looked at her face again and I could see the welts where Sister Doreen had slapped her.

"Luisa, I sure thank you for taking up for me. You're really brave. How bad is your bottom?"

Luisa reached down and touched it. "Hurts a lot. Sister got me good."

"Can you walk?"

Luisa made a face when she tried to get up. I wanted to help, but she pushed me away and got up on her own, took a few steps, wobbled, then fell sideways onto my bed. I kept laying on the floor. We didn't talk for a while, then I thought about what Sister Bridget said before she left the room.

"Luisa, what's a juvenile jail?"

"Jail for kids. Some of the girls from my neighborhood got sent there. They said you really had to fight good or you'd get beat up every day. I don't care. I know how to fight."

I felt sad because Luisa just kept lying there staring. I didn't know what was going through her head. It was strange laying there on the floor looking up at her. I could see the littlest thing. It was like I had never seen her before. She had long hair that was so black it shined, and she had a pretty face too. The nicest thing was her eyes which were big with a lot of white and coal black in the center. Suddenly she turned her face into the mattress until all I could see was her hair. Time went by, then she turned toward me again and tears were trickling down her face. I'd never seen Luisa cry before.

"Luisa, are you hurting terrible?"

Luisa shook her head. "My boobs are growing. And I don't know how to take care of myself the way girls are supposed to at their time of the month and I got nobody to ask."

I had thought about that because I was going to have the same problem. There was only one person I could think of to ask.

"Luisa, when Sister Mary Alice comes, we'll ask her."

Luisa made a face. "Sister Mary Alice is a nun. Nuns don't know nothin' about girl stuff."

"Sister Mary Alice was a girl before she was a nun. When I was a kid, I remember girls older than you who went to be nuns and already had boobs. I'm going to ask Sister."

That evening, Sister Monica came by with bread and water for both of us. After I ate three pieces, I told Luisa I was full and she could eat my last slice. She argued, then gave in and ate it. It got to be lights-out, but no Sister Mary Alice. Then the lock clicked. I rolled off the bed just in time to catch her as she stumbled into the room and fell into me. A couple of things hit the floor, and from the sound, I was pretty sure they were apples. In the light from the doorway, I could see she had a whole armload. I took them from her and put them on the bed. She turned to leave and I held onto her habit.

"Sister, I need to talk to you."

"Can't taak now; have t' go afore they ketch me. When ye get oout, we'll taak," and she pulled away, kind of jumping out the door.

Boy, did we eat apples. There were ten, and we ate five apiece, core and all.

Luisa was still bothered. "I guess what you're sayin' is true about Sister helpin' me," Luisa said, "but what if they take me to jail before she gets a chance?"

I put my arm around Luisa, who was really sad. "I'll get Sister to go to the jail and tell you. I won't let you down, Luisa. I'm not ever going to let you down."

***

As the quiet settled in again, the room became unreal to Devon, warping out of shape, things moving, yet somehow remaining in their original space. He could hear the tick of the clock as it grew louder and slowed ... tick .... tick ..... tick ...... tick .... tick. Then the clock chimed and seemed to follow the cadence of the ticking.

Something's happening to me. I've lost track of time. I feel so heavy I can hardly lift my arms. I'm exhausted. I feel like these people are coming back to life. But this isn't a séance; this is real. Jorge is downstairs. I should call him...

Alessandra's eyes opened and moved about like doll's eyes.

"Alessandra."

"Huh? Happened again."

"Yeah. We're going to finish this tomorrow. You need sleep and so do I."

"We're getting short on time..."

"And you've been back at *The Mercy of Jesus* long enough. You have to stop."

"We need to keep going. There's so much to cover."

Devon removed her microphone. "That's it for tonight."

Alessandra caught his sleeve. "I won't be here tomorrow, remember? Three of my clients will talk to you. Do as I told you. Pick the one you want to write up, and we'll spend the remainder of your time in L.A. on my story. Thank you for a delightful evening, dear."

A weak smile crossed her face as her hand slid off Devon's forearm. Her eyes closed, and she waved goodbye with a movement of her fingers.

CHAPTER 34

Devon began writing immediately upon reaching his hotel room. Every line was mediocre. He knew what was bothering him. After deleting new text, he stopped, Googled "migraine" and read some articles. To his surprise, he discovered Alessandra's symptoms could actually fit with migraines.

He returned to work, this time weaving the story directly into the previous day's effort. He finished at five in the morning and turned on his cell phone, which rang immediately. It was Andrews.

"Devon. Sorry to be calling so early but I have news. I tried to get you last night but you turned off your fucking phone. I couldn't get anything but a recording when I called the damn room phone!"

"I was writing, Clark. This story is a monster and I didn't want any distractions. What's the news?"

"Bad! H-T met with Ms. Lillian at her home in the Hamptons. She said she was sorry, that *Walden* had been a great magazine, but it wasn't creating the energy needed to reinvigorate the women's movement. She told him that in her opinion *Eleanor* was better suited to that purpose and she was buying into it."

Devon felt weak. The horror he had experienced after envisioning being unemployed slammed its way through his brain.

"It's over, then? *Walden's* closing its doors? Is that what you're telling me?"

"The answer is 'probably,' but the old man got a vague commitment from her to hold off making the final decision until she reads your story. H-T's worried she won't wait long enough to see it in print. He wants to give her a proof. We need your copy in three days."

The pressure pot blew again. "Jesus sweet Christ! I've got two more days of interviews. I've been working at an insane pace! I just finished writing up yesterday's stuff when you called. I'm exhausted! I'm going to start turning out crap!"

Devon heard Andrews' desk drawer open, followed by a clicking sound. "You're pumping nitro under your tongue again, aren't you?"

The voice that answered defined the word "panic."

"Yeah. I need this fucking job, Devon. You're the only horse I have – we have – in this goddamn race. Please do this. Do it like you're approaching the open door of the execution chamber, and Alessandra Gittleman is your phone line to the governor. Keep sending copy back and I'll rewrite immediately. Your stuff's all I'm doing now. Fuck everything else. When you fly back, I'll meet you at JFK with a finished rough, and you can critique while we drive. H-T will take it to the Hamptons that evening. Are you with me, man?"

Devon's reply was a mixture of sarcasm, anger and fatigue.

"Do I have a choice? Go see your doctor before you fucking die and I lose my last chance at a job."

On his way to the bathroom to shower and shave, Devon caught a glimpse of himself in the mirror. His eyes were red, and his stubble beard accentuated the lines in his face.

I look like the last guy sitting in the dugout after his team lost the World Series. Got to raise myself to a higher level. Andrews is right. I'm the only horse we have in this race. And it's head of the stretch in a crowded field.

He thought of Alessandra. A horrifying youth, then as an adult, battling wealthy, politically and socially connected dragons that plotted her defeat. Every day, she faced the never-ending pain of her clientele while living on the top floor of an ugly white building in a violence-torn part of a large, congested, smog-filled city. Yet somehow, her life was fulfilled. If the photograph of her and her husband at the Grand Canyon was any indication, at least part of her life had been happy. She didn't have to ask if she had lived her life well; she was certain of it. And if she ever forgot, that security guard, the women she worked with, and those people she had helped would remind her.

The ringing phone brought him back to the moment.

"Hello, Lindsay," he yawned, and continued shaving.

"You don't wanta talk to me, man?"

"Lindsay, I was writing until five this morning. That's eight o'clock your time. I'm tired. I'm in a shitty mood. Just tell me what you found."

"Nothin' on Mrs. Gittleman, but I found that other chick."

A surge of hope shot through Devon. "Luisa?"

"Yeah."

"Where? Is she still in New York?"

"Yeah. In the cemetery. She's dead."

Devon's exhilaration plummeted. He began trying to salvage something from the discovery. "What did she die from?"

"The death paper said Hodgkin disease – whatever that is."

"Cancer. When did she die?"

"Uhh...I don't remember exactly, but it was a long time ago. It's in the email. I think it was maybe in the 1950's."

"Where? Did she leave a will?"

"She died in a New York Hospital. I tried to get in, but it's a really tight system. Everything I know came from that file telling about her death. I checked and the doc's dead too. I don't know about a will."

Devon quit shaving, walked to the bed, and sat down.

There has to be more than this.

"Lindsay, write this down."

"I record straight from the phone now, man."

Jesus, he's got all this recorded.

"How long have you been recording?"

"Since after you tore me up that time because I couldn't keep up with you. Remember?"

"Yeah."

Screw it. You're in so deep now, criminal charges wouldn't make any difference.

"Check the probate court records to see if a will was filed. I'll send you some information so you'll know where to start looking. After that, search for anything criminal against her. If you find something, hunt for evidence to see if it's tied to another person, institution, orphanage, church... anything. Especially Alessandra."

"Okay. That it?"

Devon thought for a moment. "Check to see if Alessandra passed the New York bar exam. Look for cases she was involved in before coming to California – City of New York, State of New York, anywhere."

Devon flopped backward onto the bed, gobs of shaving cream still on his face. His brain felt stuffed.

"That the whole thing?" Lindsay asked.

"Yes. No! Go back into the files of that orphanage and find out where a Ginger Finnegan came from, then search the name Finnegan in that part of town. She probably got married, so contact any Finnegan in that area and ask if they know of her. Track her down. I'll send you the details."

Lindsay's reaction was immediate.

"Aw, come on man. I ain't gettin' paid to track down some old broad. I'm going to have to make a lot of calls, and nobody's gonna talk to me about somebody if they don't know me. And I don't know any Finnegans. I'm not doin' it!"

"Hundred extra bucks."

"One-fifty."

"One-twenty-five, you little shit, and I don't tell your mother!"

The enraged teenage voice cracked. "Uncle Clark already ripped me about that. He said you weren't going to say anything like that no more if I cooperated!"

"Do we have a deal or what?"

"Yeah, 'n you're the worsest asshole ever!"

"Worst! It's worst asshole ever! Learn some fucking grammar!"

CHAPTER 35

T he day was grueling. The women Alessandra had arranged for Devon to interview told stories so far beyond the routine failures of American justice and society that they drained his energy. He found himself dozing as he drove, until he was jerked into alertness by bumping lane dots and an angry driver in the next lane who lay on his horn and gestured wildly. The near-collision brought a supportive adrenaline rush. Devon made it back to his hotel room, set a wake-up call for two hours later, and asked that no calls be put through to his room. He turned off his cell phone and lay down across the bed.

When the wake-up call came, Devon wasn't aware of having slept, yet his watch said eight o'clock. He showered, then called the front desk. A voice familiar from previous conversations answered.

"May I help you?"

"I have a special order. I'm tired and have to work all night. In New York, they sell a coffee drink called a hammerhead. Does this hotel make them?"

The answer was proffered with offended pride. "Sir! The hammerhead was invented in California. Perhaps you'd care to try our 'Lightning Bolt'?"

"What's in it?"

"Six espresso shots with a cup full of drip coffee as its base. I believe you'll find it refreshing. Survivors have given it rave reviews."

Devon chuckled. "Will it get me through the night?"

"At the speed of light."

"How soon can I get one?"

"Room service will deliver one to your door in ten minutes."

The Lightning Bolt arrived as promised. When the door closed, Devon held the hot cup in his hand. For no reason, he felt like laughing, or crying, he couldn't figure which. He knew his emotional state represented not only lack of sleep but also the soul-sucking suffering of the women he had spent the day interviewing, along with the impending destruction of his own life.

He needed sleep. If he drank the Lightning Bolt, he would be awake for hours.

Devon removed the lid from the cup and peered into the black liquid, imagining himself as Hamlet contemplating suicide. He hesitated, then took a big swallow, lowered the cup a moment, then drained the remainder in large gulps.

What I'm doing is stupid. Lillian Schwartzfelt Scheidler has already made up her mind. Still, there's the chance that if the article creates enough stir, I might get a shot at another job. Got to stop thinking and just work!

Minutes later, a giant bolus of caffeine nearly lifted Devon into the air. In the next nine hours, he turned the saga of the three women into a short, gut-wrenching epic Dostoevsky would have admired, struggling at the finish as his caffeine levels fell toward normal. Then he remembered his cell phone and turned it on. As usual, it rang within seconds.

CHAPTER 36

"**D**ad?"
    The voice shocked him.
    "David?"

"Yeah, it's me, Dad."

"Is everything all right?"

"No! Mom's been on a rampage. The reason I'm calling is she didn't come home last night. We don't know where she is. Sarah and I are scared something might have happened to her. She turned off her phone. We couldn't get either of you. We don't know what to do."

Devon slid down in his chair. Seconds passed as he tried to think of a solution.

"Dad…are you there?"

"Yeah! Can you stay home from school today?"

"I guess. I have a test coming up in math though."

"I'll speak with your teachers when I get back. Let me talk to Sarah."

"Okay."

Devon waited anxiously. Eventually, both children's voices broke through the background of the television.

"I've got to get the shampoo out of my hair. Keep talking until I'm done…Did you tell him Mom didn't come home?"

"Yeah. He wants me to stay home from school. He wants to talk to you."

"Tell him I'll stay home with you. Now get out of the bathroom. Wait – ask him what we should do if Mom doesn't come home tonight?"

"Hello, Dad? What should we do if Mom – wait, she's here. She just came in…Mom, it's Dad. Here she is, Dad."

Devon knew what was about to happen. Sonja always attacked when cornered. Her tactics remained unchanged.

"Where the hell are you and when are you coming home?" she asked belligerently, her voice going from faint to caustically loud as she apparently wrested the phone from her son and put it to her ear.

The abrasive words ground into Devon as he thought about his children alone at night in a New York apartment while he imagined his wife sleeping in a wretched studio with some thirty-year-old-schizoid-paint-wallowing-bullshit-artist pretender. He fought to keep his voice calm and to phrase his words as inoffensively as possible.

"I'm still in Los Angeles, Sonja. I know you're under a great deal of stress, but I'll be back in two days and we'll talk. Please don't leave the kids alone again until I get back, okay? You love them as much as I do, and if anything happened to them, neither of us would forgive ourselves."

There was a brief silence.

"Two days. Then I'm moving out. I can't take it any longer. I'm moving out in two days! Two days, Devon!"

"I understand. I'll see you in two days, Sonja. Would you mind if I talked with David again, just to say goodbye?" he asked softly, careful not to incite her further.

There was no answer until his son's voice came on the line.

"Dad?"

"Yeah, David, I'm so sorry this happened to you and Sarah. I wish I could come home right now, but I'm in a fix. Mom says she'll stay with you till I come back. I'll be back in two days. You can call me whenever you want in the meantime. I'll answer, or I'll call you back as soon as I can."

After finishing the call, Devon slumped in despair. He thought of the years he and Sonja had lived together, wondering how everything had gone so wrong after what had seemed a promising start. He had been certain that Sonja had been cheating on him since David was a baby, but he had said nothing. He hadn't even considered bringing it up. Instead, he had engaged in a few meaningless affairs of his own. What the hell was wrong with him? He had been trying to evade the issue rather than confront the truth. He was more comfortable living a lie than doing something about it. He loathed his failings. He loathed his life!

Devon reflected on the three women he had just interviewed. He wasn't all that far from them. His marriage was over. Probably his job too. What would happen to him? What in the world was going to happen to his family? Amorphous thoughts slowly came into focus in his rapidly dulling mind. Going through a divorce would be horrible. The kids' lives would be turned upside down. He'd be broke, freelancing like his destitute friends, living on credit cards.

On and on his mind went, bringing forth nothing but pain and chaos. As he looked at his watch, he found solace. It was time to get cleaned up and return to CASE. Back to the great lady's story. So far, it had been filled with pain, but somehow he looked forward to being with her.

He showered, put on clean clothes, bought a Lightning Bolt for breakfast, then drove to CASE, drinking the bitter coffee as he wove in and out of traffic.

CHAPTER 37

Alessandra met him at the door in an Asian-style deep blue dress with a high neck and shimmering gold brocade. The tightness of the dress revealed her slender figure. Somehow, the sick old woman he had left sleeping that night had vanished, and once again, the beautiful woman with whom he had dined was restored.

How can she look like this now? It isn't possible.

Alessandra tilted her head to the side and smiled. "Don't just stand there, Bubby. Come in. I have more bagels, lox and cream cheese to honor your final days at CASE. To top it off, I made my special espresso. Just for you. Come."

Alessandra touched his hand and gestured him toward the elegantly arrayed coffee table. "Let's relax a little before we start. We have a lot to cover."

The Lightning Bolt was already making itself known to Devon. His palms were sweating, his heart was doing flip-flops, and every hair on his head felt as if it were preparing to leap from his scalp in a suicidal plunge.

I can't drink more espresso! But she made it especially for me. Wonder if there's such a thing as death by espresso?

He decided he had no choice but to drink Alessandra's espresso. He was also ravenous and began eating a bagel-lox-cream-cheese-and-onion creation, holding it in one hand while he clumsily put on his microphone and started the recording system.

Alessandra watched his assault on the food while adjusting her own microphone.

"How long since you've eaten?"

Devon stopped eating for a moment and actually examined the question.

"Day...maybe less, maybe more," he said, trying to make himself understood through a mouthful. "Since Angelucci's."

He continued eating.

Alessandra raised her eyebrows and said whimsically, "Jake used to eat that way during hiking days in the Sierras. He loved pastrami on rye.

Herschel's Delicatessen made them three inches high. They're out of business now. 1'd get one for each of us along with two giant dills and four cans of beer. I'd stuff it all in my backpack. We'd stop mid-day for lunch after several hours' hiking. You should've seen him eat. Amazing. I could never finish a whole sandwich, because they were so large. The moment I'd pause in eating, he'd reach over, grab the sandwich, then 'borrow' my beer."

Alessandra smiled and gazed at Devon, whose mouth was so full he had cheek pouches.

"Have you ever opened a beer can after it's bounced at ten thousand feet for five hours on a hot day?" she asked.

Devon shook his head.

Alessandra flung her arms up. "Foam...high in the air. We would share the hot beer and laugh like kids."

The over-caffeinated, gorging Devon had just picked up a kosher dill. He was so startled by Alessandra's flinging arms he threw the pickle high in the air.

After they stopped laughing, Devon resumed eating. Then – epiphany! He had just been given entre into the heretofore unattainable – the most concealed and stealth-bound images in Alessandra Gittleman's personal life. The desire to explore the opening was intense, but the possibility of offending her stopped him. He needed her to come to him with this cornucopia. One approach seemed to offer possibilities. Truth.

"Alessandra, I'm going to make anything you say about your relationship with your husband off the record unless you tell me it's okay. So – on the record or off? I'm obviously hoping for 'on.'"

Alessandra sobered, rose from her recliner and paced, while Devon sat in fear until she returned and sat down.

"I keep forgetting you're a journalist. You and I had a rocky start that I precipitated, but we've come to trust each other – to some extent. I feel as if I got to know you a little that night in the restaurant. I do not want my husband's name or my marriage sullied by public speculation of my critics. I've read your work, and I trust you'll handle my relationship with my husband carefully. I'm willing to put some of our relationship on the record. The operative word is 'some.' You understand?"

Devon nodded. He could not believe his luck. Then he remembered her comment. "You actually read my articles?" he said, resisting the urge to elicit further opinion on his writing.

Alessandra looked surprised. "Of course I read your articles. I told you that. Frankly, Devon, *Walden* may be an elite magazine, but with the exception of you, its writers are pedestrian."

Devon reacted immediately. "You chose *Walden* for this article solely because I wrote for them?"

"No – well, partly. There were other intellectual rags with decent writers that reached the audience I was looking for, but *Walden* was the oldest and had the greatest snob appeal. I decided it probably had the wealthiest, gag-inducing, sheep-following, elitist readers as a result, and if I could get a couple of the more important ones interested, the other sheep would follow. That was the main point in *Walden's* favor, but you sealed the deal, Bubby. You're a good writer – very good. You can reach these people, but I can't."

Devon smiled broadly, and Alessandra's eyebrows rose.

"Don't let it go to your head. And the decision to let you explore my life with Jake is mostly because a lot of people are going to make assumptions that are wrong when the article comes out. I want to preempt that."

"If you were looking for great writers in venerated magazines, why didn't you call the *New Yorker*? They have great writers and a huge readership. Many more people read *The New Yorker* than *Walden*."

Alessandra shrugged. "Great writers who are boring as dog shit. 'Mr. Sullivan briefly addressed his victims' family moments before Warden Rogers engaged the switch to the electric chair.' There's no goddamn juice in their writing! No, you fit my jaded requirements. You're honest, critical, and acid-tongued. You're never boring. I hate boring."

Alessandra eased her body backward in the recliner, then motioned with her head toward his empty plate. "You were starving."

Devon didn't answer. Instead, he loaded up his plate again. Both of them laughed when he finished his breakfast with an accidental but audible burp.

"Excuse me," he said. "Thank you for breakfast."

"You're welcome. How did your meeting go with Sarah, Elvina, and Margaret?"

Devon took a deep breath and blew it out. "Everything I've heard since I came to CASE has been rough, but yesterday was appalling. How can you stand dealing with this stuff every day?"

Alessandra thought for a moment. "This is the work, Bubby. My job is to help those I can, comfort those I can't, then go on to the next person. I don't let emotions get in the way."

She'll swing the sword for you, but if she loses, she's capable of cutting her losses.

It was almost as if Alessandra had read his thoughts.

"It's not that I don't care about people beyond helping with their case," she explained. "The important thing to me is that I *can* help, that I *can* do something. People who come to CASE have no one else to help them. If I were to feel defeat or discouragement at the fact that I can't help my clients escape poverty or pain, I'd never be able to go on. So I don't let myself feel that. And I keep on going."

"Why?" Devon asked. It was a question from his heart, not his job.

"Because that's what a life's work demands, Bubby. A job is just a job, but a life's work is something you sculpt patiently, like Michelangelo's 'David.' It involves sacrifice and endurance. If you want your life's work to become something wonderful that changes the world, you have to make the sacrifice, and you have to find ways to endure."

"Alessandra, why, after so many years of refusing to talk to a journalist, did you decide to tell your story?"

Alessandra's answer was immediate. "Money. I told you that."

"But what do you envision happening after the article is published? Where's all this money supposed to come from?"

Alessandra seemed perplexed that Devon needed an explanation. She made an "X" in the air and Devon hit the mute button.

"This is off the record. And the comments I made about why I chose *Walden* are, too. Understand?"

"I do."

Alessandra looked at him as though second-guessing herself about how far she could trust him. "The money's going to come from your readers. Many Americans know of me and what I do, but I've never given interviews. Among your readers are the very rich, who feel fulfilled by putting on charitable events for beneficiaries they have no desire to know. The rich love to sit next to someone like me, soak up exclusive reflected glory, then preen their feathers. They'll pay to do it. And I plan to make myself available. For a price."

She detests rich people.

"If you didn't need money, would you still have agreed to this interview?"

"Of course not!"

The Mona Lisa smile appeared. "But I admit it's been nice having you here, Bubby. You're a pain in the ass, but you're sassy. I like sassy."

Devon smiled and glanced at his watch. "We should move on."

He hit the "record" button.

"Where were we?"

"You and Luisa were in the orphanage pokey. Luisa was worried about being sent to juvenile hall; she was just reaching puberty and she didn't know how to take care of herself."

Alessandra gave a long nod. "Yes. I was going to ask Sister Mary Alice to help Luisa if she got sent up."

"What happened?"

"She got sent up. She was there almost a year. I'm sure Sisters Doreen and Bridget had a hand in the sentence."

"What happened when the two of you were let out of the room?"

"There weren't two of us, only me. They sent Luisa to juvey as soon as her face healed up."

"You lost your best friend. You must have been terrified."

Alessandra got comfortable on her recliner and lit a cigarette, which she smoked almost entirely before she spoke again. Devon sat quietly, afraid to rush her.

"Ginger tried to rally her troops to bully me. But Ellie Jenkins told the Irish kids that if any of them bothered me, they'd get beaten to a pulp. Then Ellie turned on Ginger and slapped her around in front of her soldiers. For a *coup de grâce*, Ellie pulled down her panties and made Ginger kiss her bare ass, then told everybody that if they told on her, she'd tear them to pieces when she got the chance. After that, everybody made fun of Ginger. She must have said something to one of the Sisters, because she began spending a lot of time in the nuns' quarters away from the rest of us kids. Ginger left me alone after that, but I always had it in my head that she was bent on revenge."

Alessandra looked away.

"Over the next year – the one Luisa spent in juvey – I actually had some peace and did well in my classes. I became close with Ellie. I tutored her in school subjects. She was bright and fun to be with."

"Did you get Sister Mary Alice to see Luisa in juvenile hall?"

"I did. As a matter of fact, she went on a weekly basis to teach Luisa catechism. I'd send along a letter for Luisa, and Sister would return with a reply. It was after Luisa got back to *The Mercy of Jesus* that things got bad again."

"What happened?"

It was some moments before Alessandra spoke.

"I think a headache's coming on. Could you get me my medicine? Bring a little water too; the pills don't go down well with espresso."

When Devon returned, she swallowed three of the tablets, then laughed. "Bubby, I don't know whether you're the headache or you just give me one."

Devon didn't laugh. Alessandra's left arm was rocking.

"Alessandra – are you really having migraines?"

The question seemed to irritate Alessandra, and she moved uneasily in her recliner.

"Yes, but it's mild now, just an aura. If I catch it early like this, they usually abort. Let's go on."

"You said things went bad after Luisa returned. How bad?"

"Very bad. Especially for Luisa. Sister Mary Alice got transferred back to Ireland. In one swish of the broom, we lost our only adult advocate. We were accused of all sorts of things, none of them true. We felt sure the accusations came from Ginger. Ellie was reluctant to deal with it, because the nuns were watching her. She'd taken her share of poundings from Sister Doreen and threats of being sent to juvenile hall. Juvenile hall wasn't pleasant for black kids in those times – still isn't."

"So you and Luisa faced a lot of punishment?"

"Luisa mostly. Sister Doreen would still paddle her and banish her to the room."

"What about you?"

Alessandra looked away in thought and sighed.

"I got a few beatings. Then the axe fell. We were always hungry. We stole some food from the kitchen and Sister Bridget caught us with a brick of cheese and a loaf of bread. She accused us of many other thefts. None of it was true, but she said *The Mercy of* Jesus had run out of patience with the two of us. They were going to ask the Monsignor for permission to contact the police. This was shortly after my fourteenth birthday."

"You were in real trouble."

CHAPTER 38

Alessandra barely nodded her assent.

"Yes, we knew we were in real trouble. We were sure they would call the police. It would be bad for me, but a disaster for Luisa. She had already been in juvenile hall, and they had warned her they would keep her until she was eighteen if she returned. I was desperate. Luisa was the only person in the world I cared about and the only person who cared about me, and she was going to be locked away."

"She was fifteen at this time, right?"

"Fifteen, yes. Luisa said she'd rather die than be sent back. I was afraid she'd kill herself."

Alessandra lay quietly. Devon thought to ask if she was all right, but before he could speak, she continued, her face rigid, save for barely moving lips.

"I was so frightened."

"That she'd kill herself?"

"That, or we'd be separated and I'd lose her forever."

"Did Doreen put the two of you in the room?"

"No," she whispered, "and that scared me even more. I thought it meant that bitch might be planning something else. So I did the only thing I could think of. I talked Luisa into running away. We set up a plan. It probably wouldn't have worked, but we had some incredible luck. A fire started in the kitchen at dinner time, and in the confusion, we made a break for the fence and climbed over."

She doesn't mention breaking the nun's leg. All the checking Lindsay's done to this point supports her story, but now she's being selective and evasive. Revisit it later.

"What did you do after you escaped?"

Alessandra looked at Devon as if he were an idiot. "We ran!"

"You had no plan for what to do after getting outside the fence?"

Alessandra brought her palms together and pressed her forefingers against her lips.

"We hadn't thought that far ahead. All of our thinking went to the escape. We didn't know how to get around in The City. The nuns rarely took us more than a few blocks from the orphanage. We just ran! Hid in the day and ran at night, sticking to the alleys as much as possible. We were too scared of getting caught to steal anything to eat, and the bums always beat us to the garbage cans. We were petrified each time someone saw us, because we felt sure they would call the cops."

Jesus...like running from a chain gang.

"The third morning...we were hiding near a car. The radio was on and tuned to the news. The announcer was talking about us. He gave our age, size, physical features, and a warning to contact the police if we were seen. I'll never forget his words: 'Do not try to apprehend these two young women; they may be armed and dangerous. If you see them, call the police at once.'"

Alessandra's eyes roamed the room. "It was like being a member of the resistance in occupied France in 1944...trapped in a blind alley...voices of the SS getting closer. I was constantly terrified, but every time I started to come unglued, Luisa brought me back. She would tell me all we had to do was keep our heads. When I'd start to cry, she put her arms around me. She comforted me."

Tears began pouring down Alessandra's face. Devon started to reach for the tissue box, but she got to it first and began blotting her tears.

She squeezed out her words in an anguished voice. "There was no one to be strong for Luisa."

Sixty years, and she still cries for her friend.

They sat silently for awhile, then Alessandra continued the story.

"We decided we had to get out of New York City, but we didn't know how. Then at dawn on the fourth day...some industrial section..."

Alessandra stopped, looking as if she were trying to recollect the story. As the delay continued, however, Devon noticed her eyes closing. She seemed to be asleep. He waited. When she spoke, he realized that once again, she was reliving events of more than sixty years past.

***

...of The City. Trucks everywhere. We dodged between them to keep from being seen.

"Alessandra, let's hide behind that big truck over there."

Once we were behind the truck, I started to calm down. Then I smelled it.

"Luisa..."

"What?"

"I smell pie."

Luisa sniffed. "Yeah, I smell it too."

"Maybe it's coming from that truck in the corner. The back doors are partly open."

Luisa peeked around the truck we were hiding behind. "Nobody's around. Let's go see."

We started running, and I beat Luisa to it. The smell inside was wonderful. Pie! All laid out on racks just like Papa use to put them. Dozens and dozens of pies. I climbed inside with Luisa right behind.

I started to grab a pie and she caught my hand. "If we just snatch pies and run, somebody might see us. But if we hide inside, we can eat pie, then get out when the driver stops for a delivery. It might get us to a place where they're not looking for us as hard as they are here. Go to the front of the truck. Hurry!"

I stood for a second, then she pushed me. "Go on before the guy comes out and sees us!"

I started moving between the racks with Luisa right behind until I come to the front. "I can't see anything back here."

Luisa said, "That means the driver can't see us neither. Scooch down and start eating."

I was about full when suddenly the doors closed, there was a clacking sound and everything turned black. No light at all. The next thing I heard was the truck door slam, then the engine started.

"Luisa, the driver's starting to go. What are we going to do?"

"Like I told you. Stay put."

"I'm scared."

"Nothin' bad's happened so far, Alessandra. If we're lucky, we'll get out of this part of The City. C'mon. Help me move these racks out of the way."

We eased the racks forward, made ourselves a space, lay down and waited for the driver to stop and make a delivery. But instead, we just stopped and started, stopped and started, and the doors never opened. Then the stopping and starting ended, and the truck just droned on. We'd hardly slept in days and fell asleep.

I woke up and the truck wasn't moving. I was terrible thirsty. It was dark as the bottom pit of hell Sister Bridget always talked about. I knew Luisa was near because I could hear her breathe. Pie smell was smothering me. I wondered if we were still in the truck and stuck out my hand. I touched one of the racks and I could still feel pies. I didn't know how long we'd slept, and I thought maybe the driver had found us and called the police. That thought really scared me. I began reaching around in the dark to find Luisa. I couldn't feel her, so I swung my leg, and my foot hit her.

She jumped and said, "Oh, God! Oh, God!"

"Shush, it's me – Alessandra."

"W-why are you kicking me?"

"Don't talk so loud. We've stopped."

I heard Luisa moving around. "Where are we?"

"I don't know. The racks are still in front of us, and they have pies, so the driver hasn't unloaded. The engine isn't running. It might be night. The driver might be sleeping. Or gone to get the police. What should we do?"

Luisa didn't answer.

Then I thought I heard a far-off voice. "Did you hear that?"

"I heard something. I ain't sure what."

We stayed quiet, but we didn't hear anything more. Finally I said, "I got to pee, and I'm thirsty. What do you think we ought to do?"

"I don't know. What do *you* think we oughta do?"

I couldn't think of anything. I kept waiting for Luisa to come up with something, but she didn't. Finally, I decided for myself. "I'm going to go see if the doors open."

"I'll go with you."

I moved forward. I hadn't gone far when I found out that only the three racks nearest us had pies. The driver had made deliveries, but he wasn't finished. We had slept right through everything. When Luisa and I reached the doors, I pushed on them, but they wouldn't open. All of a sudden there was a clack, the doors swung wide, and there in the dim light of dawn was a big man.

In a flash, Luisa jumped over his shoulder and he jerked back. I froze, then jumped too, but he grabbed my arm, flipped me to the ground, and stood over me. I could make out his face, and he looked like he was going to kill me.

He said, "You little whores – stowing away on my truck, eatin' pie. Well, by god, you're gonna pay. I'm takin' it out in trade!"

He grabbed me around the waist and threw me inside the truck, then jumped in after me. I tried for the open door, but he shut it and was on top of me before I could move. At first I was so scared I froze, then I screamed, and he clamped his hand over my mouth. I started fighting, but he was too strong. I felt his other hand run up my dress and grab the top of my panties. I knew what he was going do and fought as hard as I could.

"Rape! Rape! Rape!" It was Luisa.

The man let go of me and jumped to the door, shoved it open and started whispering loud. "Shut up, shut up, shut up! I'm not doin' nothin'! Go – get out of here! Go!"

But Luisa yelled louder, then I started screaming, "Rape! Rape! Rape!"

The more the guy tried to get us to quit, the more we screamed. Then he grabbed his wallet, scooped out money, and threw it on the ground.

"Take it! Take it and run!" he said. "Quick! People are gonna come! Run! Run!"

I was on the ground picking up money fast. Luisa had already picked up some by the time I jumped down from the truck, and in seconds, we had it all. Then we ran like crazy. I don't know how far we ran, but eventually we collapsed on the ground. We just couldn't go any farther. A few minutes later, I sat up. We were behind a wall. It had bushes all around it. It was getting light fast. I could hear birds and now and then a car.

"Wonder where we are," I said, still puffing.

Luisa puffed back, "Don't know. This don't look like any place I've seen."

"We got to find out."

"We can do that later. Right now, let's pee, then count our money."

When we finished counting, I had a hundred and thirty-three dollars and Luisa had two hundred and eighty.

"What do you think we ought to do?" I asked. "The truck driver is going to call the police. Nobody's going to believe what we say."

Luisa shook her head. "That driver's not going to tell the police. This is probably money he got for the pies. He's not going to say he lost it to two girls, especially if he thinks we're gonna say he tried to rape us and gave us the money not to tell. We're okay unless he finds us again."

We divided up the money equally and put it in our panties, then tried to figure out what to do next. The radio had talked about two girls, so we decided I'd stay behind the wall and Luisa would look around alone. She had gone through the change and had boobs and could pass for eighteen. People didn't think I was more than twelve.

It seemed like Luisa was gone forever. I was all alone and scared. I thought maybe the police got her. I knew she wouldn't tell them where I was, but I was still going be on my own. Where would I go? What was I going to do? I was hungry again, and it was boiling hot next to the wall. I had to get some water.

I started around the wall, and Luisa almost ran into me. She was carrying a big bag and some packages.

"Think I wasn't comin' back?"

"Boy I'm really glad to see you! I thought the police—"

Luisa broke in, "I brought some stuff – hamburgers, fries, soda and a whole bunch of fruit."

She started taking stuff out of the bag and putting it on the ground. We sat against the wall and ate until we were stuffed.

Then I asked her, "Where are we? What took you so long?"

"I've been looking around. We're in a town called Niskayuna. It's close to a bigger town called Schenectady."

I had never heard of either place. "Is Nisamuna close to New York?"

"I don't know. All I know is, it's a long way from *The Mercy of Jesus*, and people seem friendly."

That scared me. "You talked to people?"

Luisa finished a banana. "I had to. Not at the start. At the start, I just snuck around, but I had to talk to people to buy this stuff."

"Did you see the truck driver anywhere?"

Luisa grinned. "I think he left town. I walked all over and didn't see the truck. We must've scared him. What do you think of my new clothes?" and she got up and twisted and turned.

At first, I didn't know what she was talking about. Then I saw she had on a new dress and socks and shoes. I was so hungry and thirsty, I hadn't even noticed. Her clothes were really pretty.

"Where'd you get those? And you're clean. How'd you get so clean? Your dress was torn as bad as mine from going over the fence. Didn't anybody ask why your dress was torn?"

Luisa said, "Yeah, the store that sold me the clothes. I told them I'd fallen and tore it. I washed up in a gas station before I went to buy the dress. When I showed the sales girl my money, she forgot all about how I looked. I got you a dress, too, and some shoes and socks. Let's go to the gas station so you can get cleaned up and put on your new stuff. We ought to get some more clothes, too, because we're going to need them."

When we got to the gas station, I cleaned up and changed as fast as I could. The dress fit me perfect, and so did the shoes.

After we started walking again, Luisa moved close to me and whispered, "There are some things you have to remember. Your name is Maria Hernandez now, and you're my sister. My name is Consuelo Hernandez. If anybody asks, we're Puerto Rican."

"But I don't look Puerto Rican."

Luisa said, "My mother had me, then she married a white guy with a kid. He died, and my mom made you take the same name as me so everybody would know we were sisters."

"What do we say we're doing here?"

"We got an aunt and uncle in Schenectady who take care of us in the summers, and they're visiting friends. We didn't want to go and just sit around, so they dropped us off to go to the movies and gave us some money so we could shop. How's that?"

The whole thing didn't sound great, but I said "Okay."

***

The ringing telephone brought a glassy-eyed Alessandra back to the moment with a start, and she grabbed the receiver.

"What is it, Gaby? I'm behind on this interview...hang on. Devon, I have to take this call." She started to gesture toward the recorder.

"I know the drill," Devon said, and stopped the recording. He started toward the kitchen.

Alessandra shook her head. "This time, I'm going to have to ask you to step outside. Come back in five minutes."

"Okay. I'll check back in a little while."

Devon headed for the first-floor bathroom. He ruminated as he washed his hands. Alessandra's omission of breaking the nun's leg still bothered him, but the longer he considered it, the less deliberate it seemed. She was reliving traumatic events. She probably just forgot.

What difference does it make if she broke that super-bitch's leg? It isn't like she killed her. I'd have broken both her legs. And Sister Doreen is undoubtedly dead and hopefully residing in the bottom pit of Dante's hell. The story's the thing...just keep getting the story.

Gaby called to him as he exited the bathroom. "The *Señora* is ready for you."

Devon re-entered the apartment just as Alessandra was settling in her recliner.

"How far had we gotten?" she asked, as he seated himself and turned on the recorder.

"You were in Niskayuna."

"Niskayuna was a pretty little town," said Alessandra. "We wandered around, then we went shopping for a few more clothes and two suitcases. I loved buying clothes off the rack. I was so happy. We were clean and dressed nicely. People never questioned us, even when we asked directions to the bus station. Having the suitcases helped. Luisa was always thinking."

Devon leaned forward in surprise. "You left Niskayuna? Where did you go – Schenectady?"

Alessandra laughed. "That's a funny part of the story. Luisa bought some gum and a couple of candy bars at the gas station while I was in the bathroom cleaning up. When I came out, she was standing next to a rack of maps. We bought a map of New York, then went to a little park and studied it. We decided Niskayuna and New York City looked too close together for us to be safe. So we kept studying the map and decided the best place to go was Batavia."

There was a burst of laughter from Devon. "Batavia? Batavia's completely across the state. Why Batavia?"

"We thought the name sounded so odd no one would think we would ever go there. And as you say, it was on the other side of the state from New York City. Twenty-four hours later, we were in Batavia and starting a new life."

CHAPTER 39

Alessandra rose and began clearing the table. "I need a short break to clear my head; it's ten after eleven." Noticing Devon had barely touched his coffee, she gave him a disappointed look. "You didn't like my espresso?" Her tone sounded wounded.

Devon, who was saturated with caffeine, reacted as though he had sat on a cat. "No! Yes! I loved it! It's just – I've been drinking too much coffee."

"I thought you were antsy," Alessandra said, as they moved toward the kitchen. She stopped in the doorway, turned toward him and smiled weakly. "I'm going to miss you, Bubby. What's living in The City like now?"

For a fleeting instant, Devon considered divulging the chaos in his life, then squelched the idea.

"Why don't you come for a visit and find out – check out old haunts?"

Alessandra loaded the dishes into the sink.

"I left New York in my early thirties. I haven't been back since, except to change planes. There's nothing there for me now."

She sighed, then glanced about, as though in search of something, until her eyes fell on an array of canisters in a corner.

"I'm going to have some herbal tea. Care to join me?"

"Sure."

Alessandra scooped leaves from three of the canisters into a tea strainer, put a pot of water on a burner, then reached for a small teapot from the recesses of a cabinet. She moved through the kitchen with the grace of an Olympic skater, neatening things as she went. Devon leaned against the doorjamb and watched.

Look at her. Bluebird of Happiness on a summer's day.

Suddenly the tea scoop dropped from her hand. She picked it up and tossed it in the sink.

"Migraine?"

"No. Just a little tremor in my left hand. It gets worse after one of my bad headaches. It'll clear. I'm fine. Are you drinking so much coffee because you need to stay awake and work?"

"Yeah, I have to get a lot of writing done before I return to New York."

"I know what that's like. When I have a big case, there are weeks when I get maybe three hours' sleep a night. I get personality changes. Even Dracula avoids me."

Devon chuckled as he thought about his first day at CASE. "Turn into everyone's sweetheart, do you?"

The water boiled, and Alessandra turned off the gas, wrapped a dish towel around the pot handle, and filled the teapot. "Will my story make your next issue?"

"It better."

The conversation ended oddly, with Alessandra staring into the steeping tea. Finally, she turned toward him. "I asked if it would."

"Yes. It will. Why is it so important to you that it appear in the next issue?"

"Money. I'll give you more information if you'll keep it off the record."

"Agreed."

"Jake's trust fund has – perhaps – four months left. I protected the principal by putting it in T-bills to make certain the money was safe. I didn't get hit by the stock crisis, but the T-bills have been paying zilch. I've had to convert most of them. I have three small private grants left, but after that, I'll be reduced to borrowing against the building. When I do that, the people who want to destroy CASE will know immediately that I'm in trouble, and they'll squeeze me. They'll bleed me to death a drop at a time. CASE won't survive a year."

"Now you're being paranoid."

"Really? Why don't we take the tea to our chairs, and I'll tell you a couple of stories. Then you can decide for yourself if I'm being paranoid."

The tea was calming, the aroma relaxing.

"Ready for my paranoia stories?"

"Let's hear them – uh – on the record, okay?"

"Absolutely not!"

Devon sighed and clicked off the recording switch.

"CASE had been in existence about three years, and we were winning cases the county had previously breezed through. Now they had to fight if they tried to screw one of my clients. I was always nipping at their heels. Sure enough, BANG, I'm being investigated by the state Attorney General's office for misuse of funds. Fortunately for us, we never took public money of any kind, but they made us jump through hoops to show that money we received from donors was being used for the correct purposes. Then they threatened our tax-exempt status. We spent weeks defending ourselves. In the end, the Attorney General's Office found nothing wrong, but they drove us nuts. Then there was the investigation by the FBI. You remember Mr. Angelucci?"

"The chef who owns the restaurant?"

"Angelucci is an honest guy, but he had a brother who was in the mob. That brother had a kid who got involved in something. He was a good kid, and what he did was nothing big. Angelucci didn't want his nephew tarred by having family lawyers involved and asked if I could help. It wasn't a hard thing to work out, but the kid's father was very grateful to me and made a big contribution to CASE. One of my enemies got wind of it and reported it to the FBI. They went through my financial records. They found nothing, of course. Angelucci never forgot what I did, and ever since then, he treats me like some kind of goddess.

"Over the years, wealthy board members have slowly drifted away, because they were scared to be associated with me."

"Who were they?"

"I don't want to get into that, Devon."

No evidence to back up her claims, but what she says sounds like the truth. Can't publish it anyway. Someday I'm going to dig into this stuff.

CHAPTER 40

"We were discussing Batavia. I'd like to get back to it," Devon said.

A wan smile returned to Alessandra's face. "Choosing Batavia was incredible luck. This was still close enough to the war years that many young men were in college on the GI Bill, in Korea, or taking jobs in the major cities. Small towns were desperate for blue-collar workers. Luisa got work at an ice cream plant the day she applied. Changed clothes right at the plant and worked until quitting time. No Social Security number, no driver's license, no identification, nothing. The Happy Cows Dairy and Ice Cream Company."

"How could they hire her without identification?"

Alessandra shrugged. "Times were different. The country was flush with victory. There was a 'can-do' atmosphere. We had beaten the Great Depression and won the most incredible war in human history. Yankee Doodle was unstoppable. As for Luisa, she looked eighteen, spoke English without an accent, and looked healthy and strong. That was enough to qualify her. Back then, they didn't ask questions they didn't want answered."

"You were two kids alone in a strange town," Devon said. "You knew nothing about being on your own – paying rent, cooking, washing clothes, using transportation. How did you do all those things and manage to avoid the cops?"

Alessandra laughed. "Luisa. We used the rest of the truck driver's money to rent a little house. She picked a place just outside town near a school bus stop. She was determined I was going to graduate from high school. It was weeks before I realized she had to walk almost two miles to get to the dairy. Rain, snow, steamy upstate heat."

"What about the differences in your appearance? You don't look Puerto Rican. People actually bought that story about the mixed marriage?"

"Would you believe no one asked? I was Maria Hernandez, sister of Consuelo Hernandez. The lie we made up about a second marriage? We never had to tell it. People probably just came to their own conclusions."

Alessandra leaned forward. "Those were great times for the two of us," she said nostalgically. "We did as we wanted. No Sister Doreen, no Ginger Finnegan, no adult to order us about. Luisa was paid fairly well at the dairy, and everything was dirt-cheap in Batavia. I bought the groceries and cooked the meals. We had a wonderful life."

Devon looked surprised. "You cooked?"

Alessandra sat upright in righteous indignation.

"You're damn right I did! From the time I was three, my mother had me in the kitchen. I learned a lot before she died. And we were in farm country. Everything was fresh – produce, eggs, meat. The farm-fresh ingredients made up for my culinary inadequacies. I learned more as I went along. I'm a pretty good cook, Bubby."

Devon quickly nodded his head. "I have no doubt."

Alessandra turned wistful. "I became a great cook when I married Jake. You should have seen him eat my pasta dishes. Incredible."

"So you and Luisa lived safe and well in Batavia."

Alessandra's voice was full of youthful enthusiasm. "Like queens. To us, anyway. Luisa was a hard worker, and in a few months, they made her a supervisor. She made good money for those times. Everything was great – until Sven."

"Who?"

Alessandra sighed, and a look of sadness captured her face.

"Sven Jorgensen. He was a local boy who worked at the ice cream plant. Luisa went bonkers over him."

"This was her first boyfriend?"

Alessandra nodded. "You should've seen Sven. He was twenty-two, about six-three, blond. He had the most beautiful blue eyes. He was built like a Greek god. To this day, he remains the most gorgeous man I've ever seen. Movie star or whatever. All farmers with daughters kept a shotgun loaded for Sven."

Devon laughed. "What were you doing while Sven was wooing your roommate?"

"Staying home. Boys weren't interested in me until I was almost seventeen. By this time, Luisa had added three years to her original lie about being eighteen. And she really looked twenty-one. I was an ugly duckling. Then, in a matter of months, I changed. I would stand in front of a mirror and admire myself. I couldn't believe it. I was pretty! Unfortunately for me, Sven Jorgenson agreed. He played hooky from the dairy one day and showed up at our house. He knew Luisa was at work, and I couldn't figure out what he wanted. But he knew what he wanted and didn't waste any time. I put up a hellacious fight. He slipped and fell while we were struggling in the kitchen, and I grabbed a skillet and hit him in the face. He ran out screaming like I had delivered a mortal wound. I kept my virginity."

"What did Luisa think about all this?"

Alessandra clasped her hands together, making a loud clap.

"Oh, God! I told her as soon as she got home. She exploded! Everything you've ever heard about the Puerto Rican temper was true for Luisa. She accused me of leading him on, seducing him, lying to protect myself, and more things than I can remember. She screamed so loud, somebody actually called the cops."

"Wasn't law enforcement still looking for you?" Devon asked.

Alessandra's face came alive as she almost shouted her answer.

"Yes! There was even a picture of Luisa and me in the post office! Fortunately for us, it was taken when we first came to the orphanage. We no longer looked like that, but we were terrified when that patrol car drove up. It turned out one of the officers knew Sven. He thought this was a fight between sisters over the local dreamboat. I knew better than to say anything different. The cops left laughing and joking about the number of girls Sven had deflowered."

"Were you able to patch things up with Luisa?"

"It took a couple of months. What saved us was, regardless of what happened, we really liked each other. No, that's not strong enough – we loved each other. We really had become sisters."

Devon paused to allow Alessandra time to deal with her emotions. Then he asked, "What was Batavia like in those days for a couple of good-looking teenage girls?"

Alessandra rolled her eyes. "Boring! Boring in the extreme! There was nothing to do unless you liked high school sports, and we hated them. Luisa wanted to return to New York City. I thought it was too dangerous. Luisa was eighteen now – an adult – which meant she would go to adult prison if we were caught. At least, that's what we thought."

"So you stayed in Batavia for a few more years?"

"No. I could see it was impossible for us to stay together if I refused to go back to The City, and we were all the family each of us had. We started arguing about setting a date to leave. I finally agreed that in the spring, after I had graduated high school, we'd return. A year later, we were back in New York."

Devon sipped his tea. "Luisa was what now – nineteen?"

"Not quite twenty. She was amazingly beautiful. I saw men on the street actually stop and stare at her."

"Where did you live in The City?"

"Queens. We had saved quite a bit in Batavia, and we were able to rent a small apartment."

"Why Queens?"

Alessandra thought for a moment, her eyebrows arched.

"Actually, I remember our reasoning. In those days, Queens was cheap and a good distance from *The Mercy of Jesus*, making it less likely we'd be accidentally recognized. And our apartment was walking distance from a beautician school Luisa wanted to attend."

Devon knew the story of Luisa's illness was close and wondered if Alessandra would leave out the death of her friend. He thought it was possible she could have forgotten to mention the incident with the baseball bat. She had been very emotional when she told the story. The death of Luisa was different. Leaving out something that important would raise the odds she was avoiding other milestones in her life or ugly things she wanted to hide. He checked his watch.

Need to break soon and contact Lindsay.

"What about your names, Social Security cards, all the identification you needed. New York City isn't Batavia."

Alessandra nodded. "That was exactly what had bothered me about going back! Our luck held, though. In those times, there were no computers to instantly kick out information. We were very careful."

Devon set his cup on the table, leaned back in the chair and smiled. "Alessandra Matreoni returns to New York City."

Alessandra smiled whimsically. "I did. And so did Luisa Blanca Maria Benitez."

"What about money? You couldn't have put away all that much in Batavia."

"Money wasn't much of an issue. This time, it was me supporting us while Luisa went to beauty school. I felt good doing it. Luisa was my friend, my sister – my family. Without her, I probably would have been dead or in jail."

There was a catch in Alessandra's voice. "Luisa loved me and would go through hell for me. And I loved her and would have done the same for her. I took joy in watching her success. She graduated at the top of her beauty school class and got a job at a nice salon near where we lived."

Devon found himself fighting his own emotions. He had never had a friend like that, never anyone about whom he felt that deeply except for his kids and his parents. He thought of Clark Andrews as his friend, but their friendship had never really been put to a test – except for the challenge they both faced now.

"Do you remember the names of the businesses where you and Luisa worked?"

"Yes. Luisa worked at Helene's Salon, and my place was called Unique Creations of Loveliness. Mr. Simkas, my boss, was an elderly gentleman who had been in the dress business for years. His store was well-known in Queens as a fashion boutique. The upper middle class went there. Even some of the rich from Manhattan had dresses made there when they wanted something really nice at a fraction of what the elite Manhattan stores charged. He had a middle-aged Italian woman named Renata Marchesa designing for him. Some of her neighbors in Brooklyn did the sewing. The clothes were gorgeous. The dresses I sold would beat the shmatteh you pay a couple of thousand for now on Rodeo."

"So you learned the custom clothing business."

Alessandra nodded as she sipped her tea.

"More than that. Renata and I spent a lot of time together. She liked me because I spoke pretty good Italian, and our families were both from Calabria. She brought me books about design. I read everything she gave or lent me and picked her brain constantly. She was the one who pushed me into speaking correct English. I can hear her now. 'You want a good job in this business? You have to speak like a college girl.' She was always correcting me and telling me what books to check out of the library to broaden myself. Luisa and I had no TV in our apartment, so I became fairly well read."

Alessandra took another sip of tea.

"Mr. Simkas treated me wonderfully. He even gave me a little commission on everything I sold. A couple of months after Luisa started at Helene's, she began bringing in good money. Her clientele were the wives of doctors, lawyers, and well-to-do merchants. Back then, wealthy and upper middle class women had their nails and hair done every week. Luisa was good, and they began asking for her. Her base pay wasn't much, but the tips were great. When we put our two salaries together, we felt rich."

Alessandra's face had a faraway look. "We went to movies, nice restaurants, bought pretty clothes, even a little jewelry."

"No more boyfriend problems?"

Alessandra began laughing. "Oye vey, boys were the bane of our sisterhood! We both had boyfriends. Mine was a student at Queens College. And men were after Luisa like crazy. She settled on a Puerto Rican guy about thirty who had just become headwaiter at the best restaurant in Queens. He was gorgeous. They had a hot romance, and Luisa would occasionally stay out all night."

The issue of sex had come up twice. Devon didn't know where to go with it and found himself embarrassed and sitting silently.

Alessandra winked at him. "Trying to decide whether or not to ask the old broad if she was sleeping with her boyfriend, Bubby?"

Devon laughed. "I feel like a voyeur."

There was an explosion of laughter from Alessandra, and Devon could feel his face flush. This brought more laughter and a pointed finger as Alessandra sang a child's taunt.

"Bubby's hung up on se-e-ex. My Bubby's hung up on se-e-ex! Forty-something years old, and he still blushes. That's sweet, Bubby. A breath of fresh air in this stifling, hypocritical world. You think maybe it could increase interest in the article?"

Devon jumped at the opening. "Hell yes, it'll help. Everybody's a voyeur."

"Okay, I'll answer," said Alessandra, then her face sobered and her finger shot out at him. "I answer only what I choose!"

"Fair enough. Did you sleep with him?"

"Of course I slept with him. He was my first lover."

Devon could feel the scarlet in his cheeks deepen and wondered why he was so embarrassed.

Alessandra, meanwhile, smiled and enjoyed his discomfort.

"In retrospect, Morty wasn't much of a lover. But what did I know? I was probably his first lover too. All I knew was that what he was getting kept him coming back for more, and that was all that mattered to me."

"How did you pull off a love affair with hot-tempered Luisa around?"

Alessandra rocked her head back and laughed, then sipped more tea as she answered in a conspiratorial whisper.

"We had a system, Morty and me. As soon as Luisa would call and say not to expect her, I'd get on the phone. Morty lived almost three miles away, didn't have a car and couldn't afford a taxi, but so help me, he'd be at our apartment in twenty minutes."

Alessandra broke up, and Devon laughed with her.

"One night, we were going at it hot and heavy. Morty was like a madman. Suddenly I heard a shriek. I thought it was Morty having an incredible orgasm, and then I realized it wasn't Morty's scream. He thought it was me, because he stopped and looked at my face. Then I heard another shriek.

"Morty was off me in a flash, grabbed his pants and ran. He just made it out of the apartment, bare-assed naked with Luisa swinging at him with everything within reach. Talk about screaming! Morty in English, Luisa in Spanish, and me just freaking out. That was the last time I ever saw Morty."

By the end of the story, Alessandra and Devon were laughing hysterically.

"I'll never forget the fight that followed," said Alessandra. "Luisa was so angry, her words came out in Spanglish, her arms in constant motion. When she became rational, she glared at me from behind the couch."

"You kept the couch between you?"

Alessandra nodded. "She said...she said...'You're gonna get knocked up!'"

"I said, 'No! No! I can't get knocked up!'"

"She stared at me like I was crazy. Then she said, 'Why you so sure you can't get knocked up?' I told her...I told her..."

Peals of laughter rolled out of Alessandra along with gasps for air. "I told her I couldn't get knocked up...because I was using her diaphragm."

Devon laughed so hard he scraped his headset against the chair and it dangled from his ear. Across the coffee table, Alessandra gripped her sides with laughter, unable to speak. Both were exhausted when their laughter ended.

"You stole her diaphragm?"

Alessandra nodded rapidly. "She thought she lost it and had bought another one."

Devon sighed and shook his head. "You know, in some ways, Luisa sounds like a sister, but in others, she sounds like a surrogate mother to you."

Alessandra did not answer immediately. She seemed to be thinking.

"You're probably right. In some ways, she was like a mother to me. So protective. So anxious about my future. Other times, she was more like a big sister. We kept very few secrets from each other."

"But you kept some, right?" Devon probed.

Alessandra looked at Devon for a moment, almost as if she wanted to answer. Abruptly, she looked toward the clock.

"You'll have to excuse me; I have some calls to make. Let's start again at three-thirty."

She's evading again. Wonder if Lindsay's found anything.

Devon walked to the door, then turned before opening it. "Alessandra, I enjoyed this interview session so much."

The throaty voice that came back to him was pure Lauren Bacall. "See you at three-thirty, Bubbala."

CHAPTER 41

D evon returned to his hotel, asked the man at the front desk for a
wake-up call in one hour, then went to his room and passed out on
the bed. The ringing house phone startled him into an irritated and
confused wakening.

Got to sleep...can't go on like this.

Moments later, he ordered a Lightning Bolt, then started working. The
first call went to Andrews.

The usually acerbic editor gushed enthusiasm.

"Devon! Mighty savior of publishing companies, Thane of New
Fucking York! I love you, man! Nobody but you could've gotten that
tough old broad to talk about her sex life. You are the Once and Future
King of journalists!"

Andrew's congratulatory flood smothered Devon under a trench coat
of guilt.

"Clark, she's going to have the last word on how much of that stuff
appears in print." He paused, then for no apparent reason, and unaware it
was happening, he began raging. "That's the way it's going to be, and if
anybody ..."

A loud pounding on the door snapped Devon out of his maniacal fury.

"Hold on, Clark. My Lightning Bolt's here."

Devon gulped half the contents of the cup.

Andrews' voice was concerned. "Devon, are you all right?"

"No! I'm wiped out. The only way I can stay functional is drinking
Lightning Bolts. I'm taking in so much caffeine, I'm afraid of what it's
doing to my brain."

Andrews laughed. "I can tell that. For my edification, what exactly is a
Lightning Bolt?"

"Neurotoxin in a cup. How's the rewrite coming?"

Devon heard Andrews' chair squeak, followed by two thumps, and
knew the editor had rolled up to his desk and put both elbows on top.

"Devon, there's no other way to say this. The stuff is great! Tell Alessandra that, warts and all, it'll do more for poor women than anything since Christ defended Mary Magdalene."

Andrews' nail-tough compliments bounced off Devon without registering. As he swallowed more of his Lightning Bolt, a thought flashed into his mind.

"Did you ever talk to H-T about my financial demands – the ones we discussed?"

There was a pause, then Andrews answered in a concerned tone. "We've been over that already. You're going to get half of what you asked for in salary and bonus. I saw H-T today, and he told me to tell you – these are his exact words: 'Tell the greedy non-allegiant jerk that while I agreed, if the magazine folds, he can forget a letter of recommendation.'"

"Is non-allegiant a word?"

"Who the fuck knows? And why should you care? The editor of any intellectual rag who reads this copy will hire you if he has an opening – which they don't."

"Our plans – still the same when I arrive in New York?"

"They are. I'm picking you up at Kennedy in front of the baggage claim. Wear a scarlet letter on your forehead."

"Upper or lower case?"

There was no response. The call had ended. Devon downed the remainder of his coffee, noticing the time as he did. He was running late. He made the call to Lindsay while driving.

Once more the predictable greeting. "Yeah?"

"Lindsay! How's the greatest checker since Emile Zola?"

Breathing, then a sniff. "Zola – that the enforcer on the Red Wings?"

Devon laughed at the comment as he cut across two lanes of traffic, giving the finger to a honking motorist.

"Whatchagotforme?"

"Nothin' exciteful. You asked about a will for that Luisa. Couldn't find one, but I found out she had a police record. She was in reform school for a year and was wanted for aiding in a foleny. I couldn't find that they caught her. She run away from the orphanage the same time Mrs. Gittleman did. Oh, and Mrs. Gittleman passed both the New York and California bar. She was a public defender attorney in New York City until she went to California. She had a bunch of cases."

Devon cut off another driver and exited onto a side street. "What about Ginger Finnegan? And it's 'felony,' not 'foleny.'"

Lindsey shouted his answer. "I found her! I called an old Finnegan guy who lived in the neighborhood from the address in Ginger Finnegan's orphan file. He knew about her. She fell off the Coney Island Ferris-wheel. She's dead. When you gonna send me my money?"

"Couple days. Right now, you got more work to do."

The revelation brought an adolescent scream from Lindsay. "Bullshit! We're finished. We were supposed to be finished the other day, but you promised me more money for what I gave you today. This is bull– "

Devon screamed back, "You'll get the fucking money! You're making out like a goddamn bandit, and I hired you for two weeks anyway, so don't gimme any shit!"

A few seconds of silence later, a sniff, then, "Whatchawantdone?"

"Check on two sisters. Last names Hernandez, first names Consuelo and Maria. They lived in Batavia, New York, in the early nineteen-fifties. Consuelo worked at the Happy Cows Dairy and Ice Cream Company."

"What about the other sister?"

"Student at Clinton High. That's in Batavia. She graduated from there. They left Batavia about the mid-fifties. Check to see if the Batavia cops have anything on them."

"That it?"

"No. Find out if a Sven Jorgensen worked at the ice cream plant while Consuelo Hernandez was there, and see if he still lives in Batavia."

"That it?" Lindsay grumbled.

Devon was about to say "yes" when the name Ellie Jenkins popped into his mind.

"One more. There was a girl – Ellie Jenkins – a black girl at *The Mercy of Jesus* orphanage when Benitez and Gittleman were there. See if you can track her like you did Finnegan. If she's still alive, contact her, and ask if she remembers anything about Alessandra and Luisa's time at the orphanage. I'll email you everything I want."

Complete silence, then Devon grasped its meaning. "Same pay as last time. Are we good?"

A deep sniff. "No bullshit about telling my mom? Cross your heart and hope to die?"

"No bullshit about telling your mom, cross my heart and hope to die. If you get it done! And Lindsay…I'll check. Lie to me, Lindsay, and I'll fuck you over so bad your mother will spit on your head. How soon can you have it?"

The threat blew past Lindsay as if it had never issued.

"I dunno. Most of these old places are closed, and gettin' old records is hard sometimes, even if they ain't closed. Then I gotta track down Ms. Jenkins. It's a lot of work."

"Get it in two days, and I'll add another hundred bucks."

"Okay. And this time I want all my money!"

"Just do your job."

The conversation ended as Devon was walking toward the CASE building. He felt anxious. It was nearly four and he had a lot more to do.

His pounding heart and sweaty palms reassured him the Lightning Bolt would make it possible to finish.

A smiling Alessandra met him at the door. "You're late, Bubby. I'll bet you didn't eat."

Devon shook his head. "Had a Lightning Bolt."

Alessandra picked up her phone. "I'll see if there's anything left from lunch."

A brief conversation followed in Spanish. When she hung up, Alessandra leaned back in her recliner.

"Where did we leave off?"

"We were talking about your relationship with Luisa."

Alessandra became reflective. "It's interesting, you know. In all our years together, we only had two real fights, and both of them were about men. And sex."

Devon squelched a smile.

There was a rap on the door. Alessandra answered the door and returned with a tray bearing a paper plate heaped with chili rellenos, black beans, flour tortillas and a sweet Mexican drink. Devon was starving, and the food was wonderful. Alessandra watched as he ate.

"Bubby, you are the closest thing to an eating machine since Tyrannosaurus."

"I haven't had time to eat," Devon said, as he finished his last mouthful, set the tray on the floor and wiped his hands on a napkin. "Back to the story."

He quickly set up the equipment he had left lying on the valise near his chair, then settled back.

"After the incident with the diaphragm, how long did it take the two of you to become soul sisters again?"

Alessandra's face faded to sad. "Not long. We never stayed mad at each other long. Everything was going great until Luisa came out of the shower one day and said she had a lump under her arm. I felt it. It was half the size of an egg. Then we found a second lump in her neck. We started searching her body and found two more. We thought it had something to do with working with chemicals in the salon. The lumps got larger over the next few weeks. I begged Luisa to see a doctor, but physicians were expensive, and she didn't want to spend the money. When she finally went, a biopsy showed Hodgkin disease."

She told it the way it was. You, Emmanuel, are a doubting jerk.

Alessandra lay back in silence, shaking her head slowly. When she looked at Devon, tears were running down her cheeks. She wiped them and continued.

"Her doctors did more investigation. The disease had spread everywhere. Chemotherapy was in its infancy then, and radiation therapy, which they used with it, wasn't much better – very debilitating and phenomenally expensive. What both of us earned together paled in comparison to her medical bills. Luisa couldn't work anymore, and we exhausted our savings. She wanted to switch to a charity hospital, but I demanded she keep on seeing the doctors already treating her, because we were told they were the best in New York."

Alessandra's hands suddenly cupped her face, and she began sobbing. Devon wanted to put his arms around the broken-hearted woman and comfort her. Instead, he gripped the marshmallow chair so hard, the cloth almost tore.

Put your arms around her, and it'll destroy the last vestige of objectivity left in this interview. You have to wait it out.

Finally, Alessandra regained her composure.

"More than half a century, and Luisa Benitez remains so special to me. When Luisa died, I lost the last member of my family. We shared not one drop of blood, but the soul doesn't know shit about genetics."

Alessandra took a tissue, blew her nose, then sighed deeply.

God, I hate going on with this.

"What did you do after Luisa died?"

"It...was a long while before I was able to start my life again. I was emotionally incapacitated. I wanted to die. It was the last time in my life the Church did something for me."

"In what way did the Church help?"

"I thought if I killed myself, I was going to hell. Once a Catholic, always a Cath..."

A great gush of tears and sobs brought Devon vaulting out of his chair. His arms encircled her. She clung to him, her fingernails digging into his back, her body convulsing silently. He could feel the hot wet tears soaking his shirt. Pain welled in his throat. He couldn't speak.

Eventually, Alessandra's arms relaxed, and Devon gently slipped out of the embrace and returned to his chair. He couldn't concentrate. He was already exhausted, and now he found himself becoming too emotionally involved with his subject.

I can't write the rest of this story. I'm tangled up with this woman. I have to get Andrews to write up today's interview.

Unaware of Devon's inner turmoil, Alessandra continued her story in a subdued voice. "I visited Luisa's grave every day. Sometimes on weekends I would spend the whole day sitting there talking to her. I talked to her in my dreams. We had whole conversations. It was so much like when she was alive that sometimes when I woke up, I'd be calling her name."

The conversation paused. To Devon, the quiet in the room somehow acquired mass. It was as if he could actually feel the weight of

Alessandra's sorrow. Pounds of anguish pressed on his body, sometimes so strong it took his breath.

"How did you survive such a loss, given your past?"

Alessandra answered weakly, "I think it was by sitting at her grave and talking to her. Speaking the words aloud was self-administered psychotherapy. Hearing my own voice helped me." She sighed deeply. "After many months, I just...moved on. I had to change jobs, though. It was hard leaving Mr. Simkas, but I couldn't work there without thinking about Luisa."

"You were able to work while you were going through all this?"

"Kind of. Mr. Simkas knew what had happened and did everything he could to help me. I wasn't much of an employee during that time. He was a wonderful man. It was so hard to leave him, but he understood. Leaving the Unique Creations of Loveliness changed my life."

CHAPTER 42

T he chime of the clock and a child's squeal from the first floor brought Devon back to the moment. He checked his watch.

I'm wasting time, and I'm running out of it!

"Where did you go after you left Simkas? You had to make a living."

A smile began to play on Alessandra's lips.

"One day I was sitting at a bus stop when I saw a discarded copy of the local shopper. It had an ad for a small clothing manufacturer in Queens – 'Gittleman and Schechter.' They were looking for someone with design skills in young ladies ready-to-wear. It was a job for someone much more experienced than I, but I applied anyway. To my surprise, I got interviewed. The three guys who interviewed me were old-school, garment-district New Yorkers – foremen. They had begun their working lives on the Lower East Side when they were kids. The interview took place in their office, which was nothing more than a shack attached to the little factory. You could hear the sewing machines on the other side of the wall…people talking. The three of them asked me questions and listened to my answers without showing the slightest enthusiasm except for one, who kept looking at my boobs. After about twenty minutes, one of them waved his hand. I was in the middle of a sentence. He said, 'OK, we'll call if we want you,' then he turned away and began speaking Yiddish to the others. I understood a lot of Yiddish back then. They weren't even talking about me, except for the one who had been looking at my boobs."

Devon chuckled. "What did he say?"

"'The kid's got great tits.'"

Devon's chuckle became a laugh.

"Not exactly the response you were looking for. What did you do after realizing you didn't have a chance at the job?"

Alessandra's how-dumb-can-you-be look spoke for her, but she answered anyway in a tone that matched the look. "I started job hunting. What else?"

"Any luck?"

"Actually, there was a dry goods store that wanted me, but the pay was awful. I was going to have to move to some miserable little walk-up if I wanted to stay in Queens. I would've been forced to take the job, but I got a call from Gittleman and Schechter. To my amazement, they offered me the position. Good wages. Nearly as much as Luisa and I had made together. And it was only a mile from my apartment. I could walk to work. Jake Gittleman turned out to be the sole owner. Schechter was dead."

"Little did you know you had just gone to work for your future husband."

Alessandra smiled. "Nu?"

Devon thought about himself. Alessandra had faced outrageous fortune and become a force in the world. He had been given love, stability, education, everything one needed for success, and what the hell had he accomplished? He could write. Every once in a while, a story he wrote brought letters from readers suggesting he had engaged them in something important. But that was it.

"It takes guts to accept a job, knowing you're unqualified. Weren't you worried?"

Alessandra's eyes widened. "Out of my mind! It was very stressful in the beginning. They started me in the factory to get a feel for the business from the ground up. I was desperately trying not to let them see my ignorance. It took the old foremen about half an hour to figure out how little I knew. But they could also see I was working like my life was on the line. That made me their kind of employee. Actually, I needed the stress," she added. "It helped get me through the loss of Luisa."

"How long was it before you met Jake Gittleman?"

Alessandra smiled wistfully. "It was several weeks. Mr. Git – Jake. Sometimes, when I think back, I find myself calling him 'Mr. Gittleman,'" she said with a laugh. "I was terrified of meeting him. He could be really brusque. Eventually I discovered that Jake Gittleman was the most decent man I'd ever known. Employees told me all sorts of stories."

"Give me a sample of Jake Gittleman the man."

"Okay. He never held Christmas parties or gave out presents. If you were talking to someone, he'd just break into your conversation if he had something to say. And you were expected to work as hard as he did when you entered the doors of G&S. If he thought you were wasting time, he'd call you on it. Right there. Right then. But the other employees said not to let his manner bother me, to just watch, and eventually I'd see the real Jake Gittleman and learn to respect him as much as they did."

"Didn't his abrasive personality make some people angry?"

"Oh yes, but if they didn't get fired or quit, they came to understand and accept him. Gittleman & Schechter paid more than almost anyone in the garment industry, and that went from the janitor up. If something happened to a G&S worker – if they needed a little money to tide them over until the next paycheck – all they had to do was go see Jake. He didn't coddle anyone, but his employees were important to him.

"He had co-signed on notes for some workers' homes, paid some of their hospital bills, helped with college money for their kids, and God knows what else. He never talked about it. You were expected to pay the money back when you could, of course. If it took ten years to pay it back, then it took ten years. When you worked at G&S, you were valued – if you worked hard.

"He gave bonuses when the company made money. Not just to management, but to everybody. I never heard of another small company doing all those things for employees.

"He didn't speak against the garment workers union when they tried to organize the factory. His people refused to join – it was said, out of respect for him. The truth is more likely because G&S paid well above union wages, and there were no union dues."

Benevolent dictator.

"How did you finally meet him?"

Alessandra relaxed on her recliner for a short time, apparently lost in her memories. Devon was about to prompt her when she continued.

"It was about a month after I started. I had been spending all my time with the foremen in the factory. Jake called me into his office and told me he had a special assignment for me. I was to take two weeks away from the job and develop some clothing ideas G&S could produce competitively for middle class teenage girls."

"That must have been a challenge."

Alessandra rolled her head. "God, I was so scared. I didn't know the first thing about designing for teenage girls. I knew what they liked, though. The first thing I did was go through the New York department stores. What they had in that age range was dreck. It wasn't pretty and it wasn't cheap."

"Niche in the market place!"

"Yes. I decided, experience or no experience, I could design better clothes than that crap. I hardly slept the entire two weeks. I spent days reconnoitering and nights drawing up my ideas."

Alessandra's voice changed as she began to merge into the past, the same as Devon had seen her do so many times before. This time, however, her words became musical as if she were once again a happy young woman.

"I remember...

***

"...when I came back to report to Mr. Gittleman. He looked up at me from his desk.

"What the hell you mean 'They're all dreck?'"

"If we could sit down together, Mr. Gittleman, I could show you."

"Of course you can sit down. Get a chair."

I couldn't move. I felt paralyzed. He glared at me.

"Well, don't just stand there. Get the damn chair and sit down, or come back when you have something to say."

Oh, God, if he yells at me again...

I got the chair. "Mr. Gittleman...please, just listen for a couple minutes. Don't say anything. Then look at what I have to show you. Will you do that?"

"Why would I do anything else? I've been paying you for two weeks. I want to see what I'm getting for my money."

Oh, God, he's got that you're-an-idiot look on his face. They say he gets it just before he throws you out of his office. There go his feet up on the desk...just like they said...opening the desk drawer...eating those damn M&M's. A whole handful! Who eats whole handfuls of M&M's and chases them with a bottle of warm Coke?

"Miss Matreoni, you asked for two minutes. You got a minute and a half left."

Tell him and make it good!

"Mr. Gittleman, I've been working like mad since you told me what you wanted. I went through stores in every borough that handle the kind of merchandise we talked about. What I found were ugly, over-priced, poorly designed dresses made with cheap material. In not one store – not one – did I find anything that I would buy for my daughter – if I had a daughter. Every night when I came home, I worked on designs. I have a friend who helped me. She knows fashion, and what it takes to market. What I designed, her suggestions made better. It's all here in the folder – all the designs, each one front and back with some alternative suggestions for the patterns."

Well, at least he's looking at the designs instead of my boobs. Why doesn't he say something? He's been looking for fifteen minutes. I don't care what he says; they're beautiful. If the bastard doesn't like them, I'm gonna take them somewhere else.

"Miss Matreoni, who did you say helped you design these clothes?"

"A designer who worked in the dress shop where I used to be a sales girl. I learned a lot from her. They sold high-end dresses in that shop."

"You worked for old Isadore Simkas. Am I right?"

"Yes, sir."

"I know the designer. Renata Marchesa. I tried to hire her once. Offered her top dollar, but she only wanted to work high-end. These clothes are beautiful. She designed them, right?"

That made me angry. "I designed them! I told you that! You think I stole her ideas, just say so, and I'll get the hell out of here. I need this job, but I don't need it enough to let somebody call me a thief!"

***

Alessandra suddenly roused from her mystical state, looked about, then stared at Devon. "Have I…"

"Yeah. Do you remember what was happening?"

"I was talking to Mr. Gittl…Jake."

"You told him off when he implied that your mentor designed the dresses you presented him. Remember that?"

"I talked...about that…?"

"Blow by blow. Alessandra, you frequently space out when you talk with me about your past. Does it happen when you're talking about these things with other people?"

Alessandra rubbed her eyes. "I haven't talked to anyone about these things – ever – other than with Jake."

A little shot of fear streaked to Devon's heart. There would be no one to corroborate her story. That would force him to rely completely on his moody teenage fact-checker.

Alessandra looked at Devon as if waiting for him to comment.

"Are you having a headache?" he asked hastily, covering for his lapse of attention.

Alessandra spoke coldly. "This is business. Go on."

From wilted flower to barbed wire in an instant.

"You were reading Jake the riot act when we left off."

"I remember. I got up and left his office. I went to accounting to pick up my wages."

"You really were leaving then?"

"Yes. Nobody was going to mistreat me again. I'd put up with that shit most of my life. I learned from Luisa how to stick up for myself."

"Obviously you patched things up with Jake."

"He knew I'd pick up my wages before I left, if I were really quitting. When I got to accounting, they told me to wait, that Mr. Gittleman wanted to talk to me."

"What happened?"

"I lit into him again when he showed up. Right in front of everybody. He just shrugged it off. Then he convinced me to go to lunch with him and continue our conversation."

"Did he apologize?"

"No. In all my years with Jake Gittleman, I never heard him apologize. He listened to what I had to say, then we went back to his office and went over my designs. I had been in such a huff when I walked out, I'd forgotten my folder in his office."

"What did he tell you?"

"He said my designs were gorgeous, but he couldn't make them for the price the competition was charging for dreck and still make a profit. I asked him for a chance to talk to the guys in the factory and he gave me permission."

Devon smiled knowingly. "The old foremen?"

"Yes. They listened to some things Renata had told me – ways to simplify the manufacturing process. Mr. Simkas had wanted everything hand-made, since his trade was upper crust, so Renata never got a chance to put her mass-production ideas into action. Now I had the chance to try them, and I was sure she'd give me advice."

"You were the new kid on the block. Weren't these tough old guys insulted when you, a kid, pushed your ideas?"

Alessandra shook her head. "Gittleman & Schechter was facing tough competition, so they listened, especially after I told them the manufacturing ideas came from Renata. They all knew Renata. She was from their world, and they respected her."

"How did you go about things?"

"The three foremen and I spent several days pouring over the problems of how to mass produce the designs using Renata's cost-cutting suggestions. The foremen were excited about the project and brought all their years of factory experience into the equation. I talked over their ideas with Renata almost every night. It was exhausting, but we were finally able to put together a workable plan. Then we had to sell it to Jake."

"And that wasn't going to be easy."

"It wasn't. But remember, these guys were on a first-name basis with the boss. They knew him from when they were kids together, swiping candy from neighborhood stores and brawling alongside him in the streets. They argued with him full throttle. When I returned to talk to Mr. – to Jake – all three of them went with me."

Devon laughed. "Had your back."

Alessandra lit a cigarette. "Front, back, both sides. Absolutely!"

"Did you convince him?"

"At the start, he resisted, but we harassed hell out of him."

Alessandra laughed, her eyes roaming the room as if she were viewing the old dress-making factory right in front of her.

"You could hear the arguments between Jake and the factory guys from one end of the old building to another. Half Yiddish, half English. Talk about swearing in Yiddish; these guys were professionals. Later, I asked one of them what he had said, because as a kid learning Yiddish, I had never heard those words. He laughed and said, 'Oye veh, such talk I don't make in front of young ladies.'"

Devon laughed along with Alessandra.

"So, what was the outcome of all that arguing?"

"We never let up until Jake agreed to come into the factory and see what we were proposing. He gave it an honest assessment. Jake was always honest; he never bullshit. He said what we were proposing was going to cost up-front money he couldn't afford. If it failed, it would wipe out all G&S profits for a year, maybe more. But Jake Gittleman had guts. He gave us the go-ahead on the dresses, because he agreed it had huge upside potential. Then he gave me another job while things at the factory were getting started. I was supposed to figure out a marketing strategy and decide how to deploy it."

Devon sipped some cold tea and found himself contemplating Alessandra. She had changed again, perhaps from the memory of a happier time as a young woman. She looked so beautiful in the subdued lighting. Black hair, lustrous, framing an oval face. Shoulders, an elegant pedestal for her head. Slender arms extending to delicate fingers. Her body, straight and strong. At seventy-four, still a vision.

I'll miss her...

"Knowing you, I feel sure you made the marketing plan happen. But how?"

Alessandra cocked her head. "Such confidence he has in me! Renata gave me marketing advice, and I used it, together with stuff I thought up myself. I busted my ass. I went store to store, constantly improving my schtick. I convinced the buyers to keep the initial price the same as they charged for the dreck, and let the kids push their mothers into buying the new product. I had cut our price so much, G&S lost money on the first production run. A few months later, our merchandise swept through the young middle class female market in the Bronx, Brooklyn, and Queens. Then the upper middle class girls discovered our line, and everything just exploded. All over greater New York. We had to rent extra factory space, put on more workers, operate on round-the-clock shifts. You can't imagine how we worked! The Gittleman & Schechter name started showing up in New York Times ads. It was like the big stores were marketing for us. Our name was gold in New York."

"And a romance was born."

Alessandra nodded. "A few months after I went to work for the company, Jake and I were dating. He was fifty-two and been a widower for many years. They never had kids."

"He was so much older than you. Didn't you have reservations?"

Alessandra reflected. "When we got married, I was twenty-four. Time is a funny thing, Devon. Would I have liked Jake to be twenty-four? Of course. But I had nearly twenty-five wonderful years with him. The happiest years of my life. And I wasn't looking for a father, either. He was my husband in every sense of the word. And I couldn't have loved him more. I learned so much from him – literature, art, we traveled. He was self-taught, but he knew more than any college graduate I've ever met. You never knew that when you were working with him. He never showed off. But living with Jake was always exciting. He was the one who insisted that I pursue my education."

Devon felt uneasy but ignored it. "I want to explore your education and law school decision more before we stop, but right now, go ahead with your story."

"Things were happening so fast during those years, it's hard to keep them straight. You're going to have to work the time line yourself when we're finished, okay?"

"Sure."

"During the next couple of years, Jake and his foremen turned the business into a real teen clothing force in New York City. One day Jake got a call from Greenbrier. They were nationwide, and they wanted to merge with G&S, with Jake and his foremen staying on to manage the expansion. That would have required a huge commitment of time and effort, but the money eventually would have been enormous."

"So...you're telling me he didn't join forces?"

"Jake was mid-fifties by this time, and so were his foremen. They knew it was an opportunity to become extremely wealthy, but when they got together, the four of them agreed they didn't want to work that hard any more. They asked Greenbrier to make an offer for the company. To everyone's amazement, Greenbrier offered $20 million. Jake took twelve, the three foremen a million and a half each, a cut for Renata, and the rest went to the employees. Can you believe they gave that much to the workers? And those schmucks fought over how much each person should get!"

Alessandra waved her hand as though she were swatting flies. "I don't want to talk about that. I still get so damn mad, I can't stand it."

And H-T wouldn't even spring for a juvenile fact-checker to help save his fucking magazine.

"It was Jake's company," Devon said. "Why did he give so much away?"

"Jake's father was an Eastern European Jew who had spent his life in America as an organizer for the garment workers union. He was a socialist, of course. Jake never really left his roots. The way he divided up the money was in keeping with his political philosophy. And frankly, his philosophy of life. He said doing the right thing was more important to him than the money. He felt these people had earned what they were getting, that he wasn't 'giving' them anything."

Devon checked his watch. Four-thirty. He had to check in at LAX at nine-thirty, and before that, he had to drop off the rental car. Getting to the airport meant going through Los Angeles traffic with rush hour gridlock that would be made worse if anything unforeseen happened. He needed to leave CASE by six to be absolutely certain of getting on the flight. Regardless of what else happened, he had to make that flight.

"Something wrong? You seem preoccupied."

"I was running through my schedule, reviewing what I need to get done before I leave."

"While you think, I'm going to the kitchen."

Alessandra left, and Devon began making a mental hierarchy of what he needed to cover in the time remaining. He was deep in thought when he heard the crash. He raced to the kitchen and found Alessandra on the floor.

CHAPTER 43

For a moment, Devon froze in mute horror, then leaped forward and dropped to his knees.

"Alessandra!"

Alessandra waved her hand dismissively. "Migraine," she rasped. "In the cabinet...white pills...you know where. Get three."

Devon grabbed the pills, a glass of water, a wet washcloth, and a kitchen towel. Kneeling beside her, he pushed the pills into Alessandra's right hand, then sponged her face gently as she fought him to sit up and swallow the medicine.

"How did this happen?" he asked as he helped her hold the glass to her lips. "I never heard of a migraine coming on this fast."

Alessandra shoved his hand away. "It may have been coming on for a while, but sometimes they come on faster. Headache and light-headed this time...no real warning. Lost my balance and grabbed for the oven handle and missed."

Devon's knees were touching Alessandra's side as he dried her face with a kitchen towel. She glanced at where their bodies made contact. "Bubby, we keep meeting like this – people will talk."

Exhausted by falling caffeine levels, sleep deprivation and deadline stress, Devon found himself fighting back tears. "We're from Bensonhurst. What do we care? Let's get you back in your chair."

In the process of lifting Alessandra into her recliner, Devon's face came within inches of hers. He was shocked. He'd been so busy helping her, he hadn't seen the obvious. The migraine had turned her into a haggard woman who looked even older than her age. And yet, he was drawn to her, unable to pull away. As he eased her into the recliner, he lingered a moment longer, one arm under her shoulders, the other under her knees. He suddenly realized that if they had met when she was a younger woman, he would have loved her as much as Jake Gittleman did. The realization caused him to yank his arms from under her body, and in doing so, he fell backward, catching the edge of her recliner and saving his head from crashing to the floor.

Alessandra smiled weakly as she looked down at him. "Thank you, Bubby. That look on your face was sweet."

Devon was lying on his back looking up at her.

She knows!

Somehow, some way, he had fallen in love with a woman old enough to be his mother. All pretense of objectivity fled his mind.

I need to get the hell out of Los Angeles.

He chose humor to mask his feelings as he struggled to right himself.

"You've just witnessed the Emmanuel family's amazing dexterity and athleticism."

"Is that what it was?" Alessandra laughed softly, then appeared to sadden. "Let's get on with the interview. You have to leave soon."

Devon took his seat, checked the microphones to see if everything functioned, then resumed his work. He watched as Alessandra revived at the mere mention of her husband's name, as if the name alone were enough to ease the migraine's throb. She brought the recliner into a more upright position, let her head lay back and began speaking. Her voice was soft, yet strong.

"How do you convey the fullness of a relationship? To many, Jake was an abrasive, fiery man, capable of hurting you intentionally. He was far from perfect. We had some magnificent fights, but our life together became – an intertwining of souls."

Alessandra rubbed her temples, then continued. "Jake had a heart like no other. Some of those factory workers tried to cheat him after the company was sold. Imagine! After he gave them money to which they had no legal claim! When an opportunity arose to strike back at them, he wouldn't."

"What happened?"

"I won't answer that; I get too emotional. It enrages me."

"If it didn't bother him, why does it bother you?"

Alessandra rubbed her temples again. "I asked myself that at the time and couldn't answer. Eventually I came to understand that Jake had something in his soul I didn't possess, and I was jealous. Jealous of my husband! Can you believe that? But I gloried in the knowledge that such a man could love me. Me, the miserable little orphan waif from hell. I must have cried a hundred times thinking about that since he died. And about the fucking creeps who hurt him! I knew he was hurt too, but he never let me or anyone else see his pain. I wanted to blow their fucking heads off!"

"You would have retaliated if it had been you?"

Alessandra rose on her elbows, her eyes open wide. Then she sagged back into the recliner, closed her eyes, and her voice softened.

"I had been hurt...so much in my life. I suppose I became incapable of the grace Jake displayed. Over the years, I came to admire his philosophy and his determination to practice it against all odds. I practice it now...to an extent, but I've never been able to embrace humanity's failings with true forgiveness."

"What is 'true forgiveness'?"

Alessandra raised her chin and opened her eyes slightly. "True forgiveness...is the quality Jake Gittleman held in his soul. Forgiveness is when someone does something to you that really hurts, but you don't want anything bad to happen to them."

The words twisted inside Devon. Many years had passed since death had separated Alessandra from her husband, yet she continued not only to love, but to worship, Jake Gittleman.

Devon's voice became harsh without his realizing the change in tone.

"Let's get on with the story."

There was a note of surprise in Alessandra's eyes.

"As I told you, I was helping bring on the new line of clothing, working every day with Jake. Some days we'd spend fifteen hours two feet from each other with nothing more than bathroom breaks. No lunch, no coffee, just planning and deciding when and how to execute the next move. Ideas would leap from our heads. We'd thrash them out until what remained added to the creations. We got so far ahead of the factory, the foremen began to complain. Jake decided we should slow down and take lunch and coffee breaks."

Devon folded his arms across his chest.

Jake Gittleman found a woman who cherished him, working in his run-down factory. And I found a woman who detests me who had never dipped her fingers in dishwater.

"At first, the two of us began having dinner together to discuss future ideas for the new clothing line. I didn't even realize we were dating. After work, we'd just go to a cheap little restaurant down the street from the factory, then he'd walk me to my apartment."

A puzzled look crossed Alessandra's face.

"You're not going to believe this, but I'm not even sure how it turned romantic. I honestly didn't fathom that Jake was romantically interested in me. I know that's naïve, but it's true. One night he took me home as usual, and he kissed me. Out of the blue, no hint it was coming. I was shocked. I liked him, but I never thought of him as a boyfriend. Anyway, one thing led to another, until one night I found myself in bed with a man more than twice my age."

Devon sat like a stone, and Alessandra seemed annoyed.

"In those days I was attractive." She shook her head angrily. "That's nonsense; I was beautiful."

"What did you think about your May-December relationship?" Devon asked. There was a hint of acid in his tone.

"It's called a May-September relationship," Alessandra snapped. "What did you think?"

Alessandra closed her eyes again, and the enigmatic smile returned. Her voice became almost frivolous.

"At the start, I thought it was just a fling. A middle-aged boss sleeping with a pretty young employee who liked him. The sex was great. Unlike the young men who had been in my life, Jake was a wonderful lover. I have to admit, I also enjoyed the attention he lavished on me. And he did lavish! Dinner at the best restaurants in New York, opera, theater, symphony. New York came alive to me as I never knew it existed. Our relationship continued to grow. Then one day, a revelation! At twenty-three, I was in love...for the first time in my life."

Alessandra's expression became whimsical and far away. "I already knew Jake was a strong, decent man, but he revealed himself to me during that time as someone who thought Alessandra Angelina Asencio Matreoni was a smart, beautiful, and worthwhile human being. You can't imagine how that felt to someone coming from where I did. I began thinking of myself as a woman who deserved respect. And I did my best to return that respect."

Alessandra's smile broadened. "It was wonderful, my new world. Jake and I did everything together. There was only one thing wrong. I was in love, and he never brought up the subject. I was afraid to ask him how he felt or tell him how I felt. I was afraid of the response."

"Still figured he was just having a middle-aged fling with a beautiful young woman?"

Alessandra sighed, her face sad. "I was kind of coming to that conclusion. It hurt, but I never let him see it. Then one day he asked me, if I could do anything I wanted with my life, what would I do? This, while we were struggling with a marketing problem and arguing like hell."

Devon laughed and checked his watch. "What'd you tell him?"

"I didn't know what to say. That thought had never occurred to me. What I knew was survival. I told him I didn't know. He said to think it over, that he was interested. But that it had to be a 'no bullshit' answer."

"What did you do?"

Alessandra raised her eyebrows. "I thought! For several days."

"About what?"

"About the things that had happened to me in my life. And to the people I knew. The kids at the orphanage, Joe Schmo, and all the abuse powerless people suffer because no one takes their part. I decided if I could do anything, I would be a person who rose to their defense. I wanted to become a powerful advocate for the poor."

"What happened when you told Jake your decision?"

"He told me to quit my job and go to law school."

"And you agreed?"

Alessandra shook her head. "I told him I didn't have the educational requirements, and even if I did, I'd never have enough money for law school."

"What did he say?"

Alessandra's eyes became teary. "He said, 'Your education will be my wedding gift.'"

I knew that was coming! Fuck you, Jake Gittleman!

"Wow. Shocker."

"It was to me. At first, I thought he was joking. When I realized he was serious, I didn't know what to say."

"His proposal, it was in some joint near the office?" Devon asked sourly.

"No," she said softly. "It happened on a beautiful summer evening. We were walking through Central Park. We had just finished dinner at one of the fanciest restaurants in New York City. It was the sweetest proposal a girl ever got. He told me he knew he was an old man in the eyes of a young woman, but he loved me with all his heart and would be everything to me that he knew how.

"He said whatever I decided about going to law school had nothing to do with his marrying me, that it would be his privilege to fund my education regardless of whether I accepted his proposal. That his marriage proposal was offered out of love. More than sex and more than vanity, all he asked was that I not reject him out of hand. That I take a few days and think it over."

The room began to close in on Devon. He decided it was too hot, then opened his collar and loosened his tie. It was still too hot. His agitation grew as he waited for Alessandra to continue.

Why doesn't she speak?

Finally he spat out, "And?"

Her eyes darted toward him. "Are you having a problem with this?"

"No!"

Alessandra looked at him quizzically, then shrugged and continued.

"I did some real soul searching. I knew the age difference would eventually mean I'd be alone again one day. I'd probably outlive him by many years. But I really loved him. So I decided to stop thinking and just do it. A few months later we were married, and I became a pre-law student."

The story was destroying Devon. It was devoid of the cynicism that layered all his conscious thoughts. His resentment of Jake Gittleman increased to hatred. He tried to force back an ungracious remark but was unable to stop himself.

"You never regretted marrying an old man?"

Alessandra cast Devon an angry glance, but held back in her response.

"Age wasn't an issue after we married. We didn't have children for reasons I won't go into, but the years I had with Jake were more than I ever hoped for and more than most women ever experience. He's been gone a long time now, but every day, I look at that picture of Jake and me at the Grand Canyon – the one on the bookcase. We were on our honeymoon. I was so happy, I thought my heart would burst. When I look at that picture, the years come flooding back. He's still with me, and will be until the moment I die."

The phrase "and will be until the moment I die" burned in Devon's brain. He had heard the cliché so many times…movies…books. Except for his parents, who revealed almost nothing about their relationship, it was always bullshit. Now, for the first time in his adult life, it was real. He wondered how it felt to be loved, or to love someone, that much. He choked back the knot building in his throat.

"So, you went to law school. Where?"

"Columbia. I went through my undergraduate studies in two years. I wasn't as well prepared for law school as my Columbia classmates. They had attended Ivy League schools as undergraduates and before that, prep academies. I had to work my ass off, but I graduated with honors. Still, the only job open to me was public defender. In those days, if you were a woman, you got no respect in the legal profession. I was determined to change that."

"How?"

Alessandra's jaw squared, a look reinforced by the malevolence in her voice.

"I worked up my cases like a warrior preparing for battle. Eventually, my male opponents began to take notice as I kicked their butts in court. They made disparaging comments about me, questioned my sexual orientation, my motives. You can't imagine the shit they threw at me. I never answered. I just let it fester inside me."

Alessandra's eyes turned icy cold, and her voice became a whisper.

"I never forgave! I'd lie in wait until I could catch my adversary in a legal mistake and bring it out in open court. Then I'd grind it in for the remainder of the case, humiliate them every chance I got. By the end of a year, the message went out from the prosecutor's office: 'Don't fuck with Gittleman; she's the arch bitch of New York.'

"I enjoyed my practice, but I wasn't getting what I wanted from the law. I found myself changing from a poor people's advocate into a lawyer searching for a chance to kick hell out of my opponent for the sheer joy of inflicting pain. I was becoming like the very people who abused me. Also, many of my cases were defending people I detested – rapists, thieves, con men. I returned guys to the street I would have given odds were guilty."

"You ever ask them if they were guilty?"

"Never!"

Alessandra thought for a moment.

"But I also helped a lot of people who I thought were innocent."

"What did Jake think of the fact that you were becoming harder as a person?"

"All Jake ever asked was, 'Are you happy?'"

"And your answer?"

"Always 'yes.'"

CHAPTER 44

*A*lways yes.
Devon hated the answer. The marshmallow chair began to feel uncomfortable.

I hate this fucking humiliating chair.

He stared at Alessandra, who looked at him peacefully. Her features were still those of an old woman, captive of the headache Devon felt sure was yet tormenting her. He tried to understand his own feelings, to at least name them, but all he came up with was turmoil.

Goddamn it, let it go. Alessandra Matreoni loved Jake Gittleman. Stop this bullshit, finish the interview, and get the hell out of this godforsaken place.

He snapped out his questions.

"Why did you tell him 'yes' if it wasn't true? What more did you want from the law? Did you already have some kind of concept of CASE in mind? I don't understand…"

Alessandra gave him a strange look. She waited for the conclusion, and when none came, she moved her head further back on the recliner cushion until she was staring nearly straight up.

"I told him yes, because I was so happy in my personal life. Our marriage was wonderful. And I loved the law in spite of my problems. The fact was, I really didn't know what kind of practice would fulfill me; I just knew I wanted something other than what I was doing. I decided I needed to live somewhere outside the State of New York for a few years. I wanted us to move to Los Angeles."

"Why Los Angeles?"

"This is embarrassing. I'd never been to California. All I knew about it were the orange groves, the Pacific Ocean, the mountains, the great California parks, and the magnificent trees, all of which I had seen in magazines and movies. I asked Jake if he would consider the move. Jake was born in New York, and although he had traveled, he would forever be a New Yorker. I know it must've been hard for him to leave The City, but he never mentioned it. You have to remember, the Los Angeles of that time was much different than today. It was an intellectual desert. A hick town built for, and operated by, freebooters. For this, Jake, who was now retired, independently wealthy and able to afford the best food, entertainment and cultural venues in the world, gave up his beloved New York."

Devon slid his legs out and looked at his feet. "The two of you just…took off?"

"Yes. We bought a beautiful home in Pacific Palisades. In my wildest dreams, I never imagined living in a home like that. It was something Jake wanted to give to his love. He furnished it, too. That antique dreck behind me is a small part of it; I keep it because Jake chose it especially for me."

"You never liked it?"

"God, no. It's gaudy. Jake didn't know anything about furnishing a house. I'd come home, and another piece of dreck that cost a fortune would be sitting there."

"And your reaction?"

"How much I loved it. It was an expression of his love."

I goddamn hate you, Jake Fucking Gittleman!

"So! You're in sunny California. What did you do?"

"I passed the California Bar and began practicing with a woman I had known in New York. She had moved to L.A. a couple of years before me. I didn't find the practice at all satisfying. My partner was mostly concerned with making a lot of money, which Jake and I already had. One day, a Mexican-American woman came into the office with a story of spousal abuse. Before she finished telling me, I asked her why she didn't have her husband arrested. She answered that the reason she had come to me was that her husband had had her arrested. The story she told enraged me. I took the case *pro bono* over my partner's objections and lost."

"You lost?"

"I could not believe I lost! But my client lost a lot more, her children and her freedom. She killed herself. That was the transforming event in my career. It enraged Jake, too. Shortly after that, he bought this property. We renovated the building, and while the work was going on, I became proficient in Spanish and read everything I could about California criminal and poverty law.

"I also sifted through the dirty laundry of the power structure of Los Angeles, their connections at the city, state and even federal level. When everything was ready, I opened my legal doors to the women in this community. Free if they couldn't pay, with a request they give something back when they were able. Mostly that came in the form of helping others here at CASE."

"And that was the start of CASE."

Alessandra shook her head. "Not really. I thought justice should be on the side of my clients. Society had stacked the deck, so I decided I'd attack the forces arrayed against them by any legal means available. The politicians' only interests were staying in office and stealing. And to a large extent, they controlled what was reported in the press. Whenever my clients were being screwed, I trotted out the dirty linen of those who took advantage of them. The story was always picked up by the newspapers, and then TV had to cover it. The more I was hated by the power structure of Los Angeles, the more effective I became. CASE was already a nonprofit, but when the women I served came to believe in me as their true advocate, that's when CASE came to life."

Devon glanced at his watch. "I'm going to have to leave soon, Alessandra."

Alessandra seemed not hear him.

"Those were heady days. Jake gloried in what I did; it went to the heart of his philosophy."

The passion that had rolled out of Alessandra as she spoke of CASE and her life with Jake induced a mixture of anger, admiration and jealousy in Devon. He tried to recall a single moment comparable to what he imagined Alessandra had felt in her life. The birth of his children? No. His parents' pride when he graduated *magna cum laude* from college? No. His feelings of failure ballooned, and he changed the subject.

"You couldn't work all the time. What did you and Jake do for fun?"

Alessandra looked at Devon a moment without answering. Finally, she said, "You're really having problems with this, aren't you, Bubby?"

"No," he groused. "I'm tired, and my Lightning Bolt is waning. Now, tell me what you and Jake did for fun."

Alessandra's eyes ranged over Devon from his thick brown hair to the sneakers he wore for the first time since arriving in Los Angeles.

"I worked nearly seventy hours a week at CASE, but took off some weekends and holidays. I also took two ten-day vacations each year. That was the usual year. Every third year, Jake and I took an entire month and traveled the world. One year, we took three months and lived in Rome. I love Rome. We took a trip south and looked up my relatives in Calabria."

The change to light-hearted conversation lifted Devon's spirits.

"Did you remember enough Italian to make yourself understood?"

Alessandra gestured as she tried to paint her words on an ethereal canvas.

"It was the first time I had used only Italian to communicate since Mama and Papa died, except for when I worked with Renata. I was amazed at how much I remembered. And the people – I think I'm related to half of Italy."

Devon smiled. "You went to the little town your mother and father came from?"

Alessandra became ecstatic. The vivacious woman returned, and the years began to slowly recede from her face.

"We did! My relatives treated us like royalty. We ate bread from the very bakery that had belonged to my grandfather, the same place where my father learned to be a baker. We ate so much homemade pasta and sausage that we gained weight like pigs. It was wonderful!"

"Jake didn't mind pork? He was Jewish, wasn't he?"

"Of course he was Jewish. You think he got the name Gittleman in Dublin? Religion didn't play a part in Jake's life."

"What about religion in your life?"

The question sobered Alessandra. She folded her hands in her lap and spoke in a whisper.

"When Luisa was going through her treatments, I spent so much time on my knees, they bled. I wouldn't use the kneelers in church. I knelt on the floor, hoping God would notice my pain, forgive my sins, and let Luisa live."

"You really thought – "

"Her death did something to me. I'm not sure what, but that, coupled with the terrible years at *The Mercy of Jesus*, ended my association with the Roman Catholic Church. I wish I were still a believer. I wish the Church still meant something to me. You know, Bubby, it isn't easy being old without a God. I wish I could meet Him. There are so many things I would like to ask."

Devon smiled. "I see God is still male."

Alessandra broke up. When she composed herself, she raised her eyebrows.

"Once Italian Catholic, it's hard to conceive of God any other way than male."

Same when you're Jewish.

"What would you like to ask God when you meet Him?"

Alessandra pursed her lips. Her eyes became deeply sad, and her voice cracked.

"Why He gives so much to so few when so many have so little. Why He allows so many assholes to exist happily, while many so good people die miserable and young."

Alessandra sighed deeply. "So many times I've doubted things I've done – and things I haven't done."

"Like what?"

Alessandra looked startled. Devon felt the reaction was her realization that she had lost control long enough to almost say something she regretted. He started to follow up, but she brushed aside his question abruptly.

"We're getting away from our story. My bone of contention with the Church is irrelevant. You asked what Jake and I did for fun, and I've only told you a small part. Jake learned to love California. We walked the Pacific Crest Trail – not all at once, but over time about two thirds of it. He stayed in great shape, while I spent so much time on my ass doing law, it was hard to keep up with him."

Alessandra smiled. "I remember one time...we passed a guy on a high mountain trail. I was probably thirty feet behind Jake. The guy says, 'Better wait up for your daughter.' I thought Jake was going to kill him. Lucky for Jake, he was about sixty-five at the time, because the guy who said it looked like a professional football player. He tried to apologize after Jake yelled, 'That's my wife, goddamit!' But Jake just stood there swearing at him until he walked off. Jake was far from perfect, but for me, he was the perfect man."

Devon was tired, and his dissatisfaction with his own life continued to mount as Alessandra described wonderful, happy, productive years with Jake. It made Devon bitter to think that Jake Gittleman, a hardnosed, rough-hewn man, older at the time than Devon was now, had found a captivating twenty-four-year-old Venus because of a want ad in a throw-away newspaper, a woman who embraced life with gusto and energy, who could look past her husband's failings and see his inner worth, while he, Devon Emmanuel, a highly educated and accomplished writer, had wound up with Sonja, a woman who had become a stranger to him and reminded him every day of his inadequacies. Somehow, he knew the fault was his.

Devon was so lost in thought he was startled when he heard Alessandra's voice.

"You're wondering how Jake died, right?"

"I wasn't, but I was thinking about you and your husband. How did Jake die?"

Alessandra crossed her arms and appeared reflective.

"We were at twelve thousand feet on a hike to the summit of Mount Whitney when we stopped along the trail to eat and enjoy the view. In the middle of lunch, Jake was staring into the distance when he suddenly turned toward me and said, 'You've given me so much in my life. Thank you.' Then he slumped over, and that was it. Just like that, he was gone. Just like he came into my life, he was gone from it."

The clock chimed, once again off the hour, followed by a deep silence.

Every question Devon thought of to revive the conversation seemed trivial. He stared at Alessandra, and she stared back. She shed no tears. Her face remained impassive.

Devon glanced again at his watch and cast a questioning look at Alessandra.

"You're wondering what happened to me after Jake died – what happened to CASE, right?"

"Yes, but I'm also worried about the time. We could finish by phone after I return to New York."

Alessandra shook her head. "Hun-uh, I want to tell you now. It won't take long. With the death of Jake, I sold the house in Pacific Palisades and put the money in the trust Jake had set up. I renovated the upper floor of CASE, moved in, and I've lived here since six months after his death. My life has been one thing since Jake died – CASE. I rarely see anyone socially unless it's at Angelucci's."

"What's going to happen to CASE when – when you can no longer run it?"

Alessandra laughed. "My Bubby can't bring himself to say 'die.' You're funny, Bubby. That's why we're going through all this now. I have to be able to be replaced, and it takes money to do that. I work without salary; I doubt anyone else can."

Alessandra put her hands on the arms of her recliner and pushed herself up.

"Well, that'll do for now. You can always call me if you have any questions."

She took a few steps toward the door and turned back toward him.

"Write me a great story, Bubby," she said, barely above a whisper. "At the end of it, tell your readers that the fight for justice for poor women is in its infancy. Someone has to pick up my sword and wield it after I'm gone, or the people I serve will have little justice. I've learned that the law and the Constitution are wonderful, but they only work well for those with a clenched fist. Those who are not able to fight in America are doomed."

Alessandra clasped her hands and gave a quick sigh. "It's getting late. Better get your stuff together and be on your way. It's been a pleasure knowing you Bubby. You're a *mensch.*"

Devon rose with difficulty from the marshmallow chair. The thought occurred to offer a handshake, but somehow, it didn't feel right. Instead, he stepped toward Alessandra and embraced her. He felt her hug him back.

"I'm going to make this the best damned story I've ever written," he said, unable to think of less cliché-ridden words to express the feelings that were roiling in him. "I'll miss you, Alessandra. Of all the women I've known in my life, none has touched me the way you have."

Devon gathered his equipment, put it in his valise, and walked to the door. He was about to leave when he stopped, put down the valise, and turned to Alessandra. He put his arms around her and kissed her lightly on the lips.

She looked surprised. "That was sweet, Bubby." Then she squeezed him. "*Vaya con dios*. Don't forget me."

"*Shalom*, Alessandra. I could never forget you."

CHAPTER 45

Devon watched as the woman with the screaming baby shuffled her way onto the aircraft. He had never been able to sleep on a plane when children cried, and it was no different now with the six-month-old in the seat in front of him. Los Angeles to New York…through the night with no sleep for a mind already exhausted.

Despite the noise, Devon managed to read Clark Andrews' edited version of the story. It portrayed Alessandra with clarity and honesty, her times, her clientele, and the flavor of CASE. Above all, it captured Alessandra's essence. He judged it to be more than just good writing. It was literature.

The day had ended with Devon's request for Andrews to write the rough of the final interview, which was not yet available for review. When Devon finished his work, he closed his eyes, but couldn't sleep. Across the aisle, a passenger stuffed a copy of the L.A. Times into the seat pocket in front of him. Devon tilted his head to read the headlines.

"Care for the paper?" the passenger asked as he turned and caught Devon trying to read at an angle.

"If you don't mind. I've been busy for several days and have no idea what's going on in the world."

The man handed Devon the paper. "If you're looking for good news, don't read it. The whole world is turning to crap."

Devon chuckled. "Well, it's been turning for years. Slaughter's still going on, huh?"

"Yeah. Gets worse every day."

"Thanks for the paper."

Devon finished the sports section and was sorting through the paper to get the front page when he saw: "SUPERIOR COURT JUDGE ACCUSED OF MISCONDUCT. Relieved of Duties Until Matter Resolved."

The article explained that evidence had surfaced that two years earlier, Judge Henry J. Wexler had financially benefitted from a land transaction after handing down a reduced sentence to the son of a land developer. The evidence had come to the reporter via an anonymous tip, and the reporter's follow-up revealed the accusation to be bona fide.

Devon felt as if he had been clubbed in the head.

Alessandra! That has to be the case she was working on that took so much time away from us. Wexler was the guy who wouldn't go along with the plea bargain blessed by that judge who died. Alessandra's client was going to be destroyed. I remember when she was on the phone talking to somebody who was supposed to be digging up information. It had to be about Wexler. So that's how she planned to get him off the case. My God! Can't think about this now...too tired. I've got to sleep. There goes that kid again. So help me, if he keeps screaming, I'm going to strangle him.

A few hours later, Devon disembarked from the plane and looked for Andrews at the entrance to the gate. No Andrews. Devon began walking, his mind conjuring up worrisome scenarios. Maybe Andrews was stuck in traffic. Suppose he didn't show. What would Devon do? He didn't know where to go. Matters easily resolved now seemed monumental. He decided to sit a few moments on a bench along a passageway and consider the problem. His mind jumped from one strategy to another, sometimes forgetting what he was deciding in the middle of an exploration.

I'm not accomplishing anything. I'll pick up my baggage and if I still haven't made contact with Clark, I'll call him.

Proud of his plan, he approached the conveyors and heard someone calling his name. Turning, he saw a man waving his arms.

"Devon! Where the hell you been? Bags from your flight have been moved to storage!"

The words didn't make sense. At first, Devon couldn't remember the name of the fat man, then realized this was the person who was supposed to pick him up.

"I just got off the plane. Never JFK fifteen baggage minutes. You didn't you meet...?"

Andrews stared at his writer and tried to make sense of the garbled sentences.

"It's been an hour since you landed!" Andrews interrupted. "We were supposed to meet here at the baggage claim. I saw your luggage and checked with the airline. They said you were on the flight. I searched and couldn't find you. I was just now heading to security. Have you read the copy?"

Total confusion descended on Devon, who managed to answer "yes," which was followed by unintelligible babble.

Andrews stared for a few seconds more.

"We're going to my place as soon as we collect your bags. You're going to sleep, shower, then read the last of the copy."

The next thing Devon knew, he was being shaken out of a deep sleep. He glanced about the room. He had never seen such disorder.

"What is this dump?" he muttered.

"My apartment," said a voice from the doorway. It was Andrews. "You're in my bed. Can you hold a cup well enough to drink coffee?"

"How did I get here? How long have I been asleep?"

Andrews pushed forward a cup of lukewarm coffee. "Several hours. Drink this, then go shower. I'll have the edit finished by the time you return."

Devon drank the coffee, then entered the bathroom. The shower stall took up a third of the dirty, six-by-eight-foot space. The room's only redeeming quality, he decided, was a near-empty bottle of cheap vodka sitting next to a toothbrush. Since there was no evidence of toothpaste, the purpose of the vodka seemed apparent. He picked it up, and on closer inspection, noticed cloudiness in the bottle. Andrews' "toothpaste" was growing something.

Finger-brush my teeth with plain water. This is me in a few months.

He turned on the shower and let it get hot.

Unbeknownst to Devon, Andrews, who could hear the shower running, was waiting until he estimated his writer was lathered up. Then he turned off the hot water. Devon's scream, "Turn on the fucking hot water!" was the editor's evidence his plan was working. He did not turn the hot water back on.

Ten minutes later, clad only in boxer shorts, Devon, furious but fully awake, stood in front of his host in the smallest and grungiest kitchen he had ever seen.

"Your goddamn shower almost froze me to death! Why do you live in this shithole?"

"Because it's what I can afford. Your Cream of Wheat and raisin toast are ready."

Devon ate while Andrews read him the remainder of the copy. Eating was uncomfortable. Devon's belly was pressed against the soiled tablecloth of a round, wooden table. Improving the situation was impossible, because the back of his chair was up against a yellow wall, and the back of Andrews' chair on the other side of the table nudged a sink full of dirty dishes.

Nobody lives in a place like this. It's horrible.

"Whadayathink?" Andrews asked when Devon finished reading.

Devon followed a lumpy spoonful of Cream of Wheat with a bite of raisin toast to avoid gagging.

"The last part's a good draft, but it needs work. How long have I slept?"

Andrews glanced at his watch. "Let's see...got here at nine. It's one-thirty...four and a half hours...you been up half-hour...four hours. Have you read what I emailed you?"

"Yeah. It's great," said Devon.

"Agreed. Last part definitely needs your hand. Drink the rest of the coffee in the pot and start rewriting. We got a five-thirty deadline."

Devon glared at Andrews.

"Screw that! I'm exhausted."

"H-T wants the final in his hands when he goes to see sweet Lillian tonight."

The scheming bothered Devon, and he commented in a tired, grating tone, "Lillian Scheidler has already told H-T she's going with the other magazine. What difference does it make which day she reads the story? *Walden* is on life support, man. *Walden* is dying! The only importance of this article is our hope that it's going to get us jobs at another magazine. Fuck H-T and fuck Ms. Lillian! By the way, I insist the article go out under both our names. You wrote the last part."

Andrews stood up and looked about.

"See this place," and he turned slowly and scanned the kitchen. "This – 'shit-house' – is the only thing between me and the streets. I could live a little better, but that would require my kids to drop out of Princeton. They're the only humans on this planet who truly care about me, and me about them."

Andrews suddenly realized what he had just said. "Except for you, of course."

Devon gave Andrews a wry smile.

The editor continued. "I want my kids to finish Princeton before I croak, Devon. The health insurance at *Walden* is good, and I don't have it if I lose my job. I've been having bouts of angina, and they're getting more frequent." Andrews hesitated, then added, "Think I've plugged off a stent. Nobody's going to hire me at my age with my health record, regardless of how well this story is received. I know *Walden's* odds of getting picked up by Miss Lillian are almost zero, but until she pulls the plug, I'm going to fill *Walden's* goddamn oxygen bottle if I have to hook it up to every tree in Central Park."

Devon's silence brought an acid, "Given that you're a half-fucking-inch from being my roomy, Emmanuel, I suggest you start work."

Now is the time. Do it now or forget about it.

"Clark, something has happened that you need to know before we finish this story. Alessandra..."

"What?"

A few minutes later, the Wexler incident was out in the open.

"How do we handle this?" asked Devon. "She got a Superior Court judge removed from the bench by less than honorable means. This story makes her look like St. Joan."

Andrews tapped a spoon on the table as he considered the problem. "How do you know she was the one who blew the whistle?"

"Aw, come on, you've heard the story. Who else would have dug up that stuff? It had to be her."

"How do you know for certain it was Alessandra Gittleman who blew the whistle? Give me some goddam proof!"

"I don't have any proof, but..."

"But you're going to indict and convict Gittleman. Why don't you just conjure up Torquemada? For Christ sake, this is an example of your great journalistic integrity? Journalists get tips all the time from unnamed sources."

He's right. I don't know for certain. And I did learn about Wexler when we were off the record. But then again, she talked about how she got dirt on people who opposed her and punished them with it. I don't know. There's no time to think; there's no time to dredge up the answers. This whole thing is such a mess.

"You want to just ignore what happened then?" Devon asked.

"Hell, yes! Let's get to work."

Three hours later, the two men high-fived one another as Andrews pressed the "send" button that delivered the manuscript to H-T's email. They were finished. A wonderful feeling of calm enveloped Devon. He lay down on Andrews' bed and fell into a deep sleep almost immediately.

When he awoke, he checked his cell phone and discovered he had forgotten to turn it on when he arrived at JFK. It was three in the afternoon! There had been several calls, all from Sonja and Andrews. He had slept almost a full day.

With a sense of foreboding, he pressed the button beside Sonja's name.

CHAPTER 46

It was almost as if Sonja had been lying in wait.

"Devon! Where the hell have you been? You promised you would be here yesterday."

"Sonja, I'm sorry. When I got to Kennedy, Clark Andrews picked me up, and we finished the story. After that, I fell asleep and..."

"... and I'm moving out of our apartment as we speak. The kids get home at four-thirty. I suggest you be here, because I'm going to be gone. And don't call me. My lawyer will contact you!"

The connection broke, and Devon sat on the edge of the bed, rubbing the smooth glass face of the cell phone across his forehead.

So it begins. After child support, legal fees and what Sonja will demand, I'll be lucky to live as well as Clark. I'm in a nightmare, and I can't wake up.

He wondered what he would do when *Walden* closed its doors. The story, along with his past work, might save him. Merciful God, it had to save him. Devon showered, shaved, and readied himself to see his children. He checked his wallet. There wasn't enough money to take a cab, which meant he'd have to take the subway and get home as much as an hour late. Panic! Just as he grabbed the doorknob to leave the apartment, Andrews was putting his key into the lock. The door flew open, and the editor threw his fat arms wide and enveloped his writer.

"My Chaucer, my Rabelais, my Shakespeare! He whose computer doth touch and sooth the philanthropic hearts of rich old women! God in His infinite mercy has delivered you to me! Kiss me!"

Devon laughed and drew back. "To what do I owe these accolades?"

Andrews threw his arms into the air, and his fat knees propelled his body off the floor like a cheerleader. He landed with a thud and gestured wildly.

"Sweet Ms. Fucking Lillian liked the article so much she's buying forty percent of *Walden*! She wants to meet with you, me and H-T to go over the needs of the organization. And she wants to meet Alessandra. She said – and I quote, 'Ms. Gittleman is the benchmark that all American women must measure themselves against if they aspire to enhance the role of women in today's society.' Her exact fucking statement!"

Devon was stunned. The words had tumbled out of his editor so quickly they were hard to understand. Comprehension was made more difficult by Andrews' insane movements, his arms above his head, hands flapping at the wrists as his pear-shaped body pirouetted out of the apartment door into the hallway, then back again.

Devon checked his watch. The kids were probably home.

"Clark, give me a lift to my apartment."

Andrews' ballet ceased. "I don't have a car; you know that. I'm a New Yorker. I borrowed the one I picked you up in yesterday."

"I've got to get home fast. I'll have to take a cab. Lend me forty."

"You're leaving without getting drunk?"

"Sonja has moved out, and the kids are home alone. I really need the forty bucks, Clark. Hey, where did you sleep last night?"

Andrews reached in his wallet and handed Devon two twenties. "On the fucking floor. Tonight, my man, I am bringing to your dwelling alcohol. And we are going to drink like print journalists from the old school. I am also bringing food, not only for you and me, but for your brood. What kind of stuff do they like?"

Christ, I don't even know what shape the kids are going to be in. Their Mom and Dad splitting up...me not around for over a week. On the other hand, it can't hurt if they get some food they really like. I have to learn about parenting sometime.

"You know a good Thai restaurant?" Devon asked.

"Sure. There's a great one a few blocks from where you live."

"Yeah? Get some satay for all of us, a beef dish of some kind for David, something veggie for Sarah, one of their curries with beef for me, whatever you want, and four quarts of Thai beer."

Andrews gave Devon a disappointed look. "That's only a quart apiece."

Devon laughed. "Bring the kids soft drinks. See you about eight?"

"Eight it is!"

Devon was apprehensive about going home. He knew he was going to have to talk to his kids about the breakup. To his surprise, things went easier than he had anticipated. Sarah did everything but ask why it had taken them so long to get a divorce. In the middle of a heartbreaking part of the discussion (Devon considered it heartbreaking), David asked if it would be all right to ride home from soccer practice the next day with Barry Schneider. Neither child shed a tear. Their main concern seemed to be how they could still see their friends and participate in school activities if their time was split between both parents.

As Devon finished the conversation, he was on the verge of asking if either of them gave a shit that their parents were divorcing. When David's face clouded up, Devon was actually consoled by the show of emotion.

"What is it, son?" he asked in a comforting voice. "Ask me anything."

David looked away, then his eyes met Devon's. "Can we get some fresh take-out tonight? That stuff in the refrigerator is two days old."

The sound of his editor kicking the door and bellowing were all that kept Devon Emmanuel from crying.

Andrews entered, carrying a twelve-pack of beer and a smaller bag that he raised in the air.

"The Thai Tooth Fairy hath arrived," he yelled. "Make way for glad tidings and vicious heartburn." He stopped and looked around. "Where do you people dispose of toxic material?"

Devon laughed. "We'll put it on the table. Sarah, can you set the table? David, give her a hand."

Sarah moved to get the dishes while David took the packages of food.

"What'd you get?" he asked.

Andrews looked at him quizzically. "You're David. I haven't seen you in a while. You, I got Thai beef. It's not hot, but I brought some ground pepper if you want it."

"You got my favorite! Dad, he got my favorite!"

Devon motioned with his head towards Andrews. "A thank-you would be in order."

"Yeah, thanks," said David, as he turned to set the food on the table.

"Kids seem to be taking it well," Andrews observed.

Devon snorted. "Too well."

"They're at the age where they can take a punch. Mine were older when I got a divorce, but they still handled it better than me. Let's eat and get to the drinking."

In less than an hour, the food was eaten, the dishes cleared, the kids off to homework, and the two men left to savor their journalistic triumph. They opened their beers, clinked bottles, and laughed like teenagers.

"Did you ever think we'd make it?" Devon asked, as the laughter subsided.

Andrews put his leg up on a kitchen chair. "I did. I really did. Now, how do we rebuild *Walden*?"

They brainstormed and came up with two first-rate writers and one editor culled from a group of New York journalists. Next, they discussed what it would take to bring the writers and the editor aboard. By the time they had finished five beers apiece, they had settled on the necessity of eliminating *Walden's* mediocre writers as well as H-T's cronies, who had surrounded the old man for forty years. It was time for the old guard to retire. As a matter of fact, H-T himself should step down as publisher.

It was nearly eleven when Devon felt his cell phone vibrate.

Sonja.

Devon looked at his friend. "Got to take this, Clark," and he walked to the bathroom.

But the number on the cell phone was not Sonja's. Devon recognized it. There could be only one reason for this call.

"Lindsay, I'll be out tomorrow and give you your money. I just got home yesterday and I've been too busy to get there. Don't worry; you're going to get your money."

"How come you never say hello?" the whiny voice asked. "Anyway, that ain't why I called. Remember the old woman you asked me to find?"

"Ginger Finnegan. You said she was dead."

"Ginger Finnegan is dead. The other old broad – Ellie Jenkins."

"The black girl from the orphanage?"

"Yeah. First I tried her the way I did Finnegan, but that didn't work. Yesterday I tried another way and found her. We talked on the phone. She remembers Alessandra Matreoni and Luisa Benitez."

The revelation excited Devon, but the article would be in print before he could dig out her story. No matter what Ellie Jenkins told him, it would be impossible to change things now.

"Great job, Lindsay! We don't need to know anything from Ellie now, but that doesn't take away from your work. Awesome! I mean that."

"I'm glad you feel that way 'cause Ms. Jenkins said Alessandra Matreoni was a 'ho.' Said she remembered her well, and knew what had happened to her, and that she was a 'ho.'"

Devon thought he was having an out-of-body experience. His first reaction was to tell Lindsay to forget everything Ellie Jenkins had said. He actually tried, but couldn't bring himself to say the words.

"Lindsay...does Ellie Jenkins seem...normal? I mean...does she seem like she might be crazy? Did you see her?"

"I didn't go to her place! She lives in the worst part of the Bronx. You want somebody to meet Ms. Jenkins, you do it yourself, man. And don't bother offering me no more money 'cause I ain't goin'!"

Devon stood frozen in place.

"You still there, man?"

"Yeah. Could you send me Ellie Jenkins' address and phone number?"

"Already have. Can I get my money tomorrow? And if you're goin' to see Ms. Jenkins, I'd like it before you go. If you get killed, I'd be workin' for nothin'."

CHAPTER 47

Devon hadn't seen another white man in blocks, and he was certain he could not have been more conspicuous if he had been carrying a burning cross. He was relieved when a patrol car pulled up as he was checking the few legible street numbers on a building. The black cop in the shotgun seat leaned out the window.

"Whatcha lookin' for, man?"

Devon took his driver license and *Walden* I.D. out of his wallet on the way to the patrol car and presented them to the cop. When the officer looked up, Devon handed him a slip of paper with Ellie Jenkins' name, address and phone number.

"I'm looking for an apartment in this building...I think it's this building."

The cop glanced at the paper, then scanned Devon's face as though memorizing every detail. "You score shit there, you won't get it out of the building. Some kid will take it off your body before you get two floors. Do me a favor and get the hell out of here. Stories about cheap dope in this part of the Bronx are bullshit."

Devon stared into the cop's eyes. "I'm not here for drugs. I'm looking for a woman named Ellie Jenkins. She'd be mid-seventies and is supposed to be living at that address. I need to see her."

The cop behind the wheel leaned toward the open window. "You city, state, or fed?"

"Journalist. This lady – Ellie Jenkins – she's important to my story."

The cop in the shotgun seat looked at his partner. "Wanna call Tiebo?"

"Think Tiebo'd do it?"

"Ha! Twenty bucks and Tiebo'd sell his mother."

The cop in the shotgun seat put his arm on the window.

"There's a junk-ball named Tiebo who sleeps under the stairs in that building," he said. "I'm gonna tell him you're offering twenty bucks to take you to the apartment and back. Don't pay him until you see the old woman. You got two tens?"

"Yes."

"Good. Give him ten when you get to her apartment, then ten when he gets you back on the street."

Devon nodded. "Thanks. Can I have his number and my paper back?"

"No, I'll make the call to Tiebo. That way, you may get back to the street alive." The cop pointed to a bus stop. "If you make it outta the building, go straight to that bus stop, get on the first bus that comes along regardless of where it's going, and stay on it until you're outta this part of the Bronx. Don't fuck up my day by turning into a corpse. Paperwork takes forever, and I got tickets to the Mets game tonight. And don't buy shit from Tiebo; it's been cut maybe fifteen times."

The gray-haired black woman who stared at Devon through the metal security door was over six feet tall and weighed perhaps three-hundred-fifty pounds. She wore a sleeveless tent dress in an African print. Toenails painted a deep purple peeked out from pink, fuzzy bedroom slippers. Her wrists were twice the thickness of Devon's. In her right hand was a fifteen-inch pipe wrench.

"Ms. Jenkins?" Devon asked hesitantly.

The woman didn't answer; she just glared at him.

"I'm the man who called you for an appointment...Lindsay Culbertson's boss."

"Show me yo' identification."

Devon removed his *Walden* I.D. from his wallet and held it close to the metal screen.

The woman looked from his I.D. to his face, then opened the security door, glancing behind him at Tiebo, a tall, extremely thin black man of about thirty-five.

"Whatchu be doin' here, Tiebo?"

Tiebo took a step back. "Excortin' yo' white boy fren. Whachu think I be doin'?"

The woman turned to Devon. "He bring you?"

Devon nodded.

"You pay him yet?"

"No."

"How long you gone be here?"

"Not long. I just want some information for a story I'm writing about the person I told you about on the phone. Remember?"

The woman eyed Devon suspiciously. "Tiebo, I calls you when it time t' come back."

Tiebo reared up on his toes. "I gets paid now!" he shouted.

The big woman moved so quickly, her body knocked Devon several feet before he could get out of the way. She grabbed Tiebo by his t-shirt and wielded the wrench over her head.

"You paid when I say you gets paid. Now get gone till I calls, then you get yo' ass back up here quick. You paid when he get on the bus. That when you paid."

"Tha's bullshit!" Tiebo yelled, cowering from the menace.

Ellie Jenkins' glare widened into the psychotic. "You drugged out piece a shit! You says one mo' fuckin' word and I be throwin' yo' ass ovah that rail and watchin' it splatta when it hit bottom!"

Tiebo made a short scream as she lifted his body off the floor with one arm and flung him down the hallway. He grabbed the guardrail, righted himself, then bounded down the rickety stairs.

Having dealt with Tiebo, the woman turned to Devon, saying politely. "Folks calls me Ms. Ellie."

Devon nodded. "Ms. Ellie. Nice to meet you in person."

"Don' worry about what jus' happen. Ain't no other way to deal with Tiebo. Come in."

The interior of Ms. Ellie's apartment was clean, spare, and furnished with dark brown furniture. Against one wall of the living room was a couch that bowed in the middle. In front of the couch was a coffee table surrounded by three chairs. Ms. Ellie sat heavily in the middle of the couch and motioned Devon to sit in the center chair.

Neither spoke for several seconds. She stared at him, then raised her eyebrows and said, "You gone axe me somethin'?"

Devon responded quickly. "I need information about Alessandra Matreoni. She lived in the same orphanage as you. This would have been in the late 1940s or perhaps early 1950s. Do you remember her?"

"O'ph'nage *Mercy o' Jesus*?"

"Yes."

"S'posin' I do. What in it fo' me?"

"*Walden Magazine* doesn't pay its sources."

"Then *Walden Magazine* don' get shit! I wants a hundred."

Pay it, for God's sake! What difference does it make if you pay her? You're in so deep now, paying her for information is the least of your journalistic indiscretions.

"Fifty now, and fifty after I check out your information."

Ms. Ellie's huge body stiffened, and her eyes widened. "Hundred now, and twenty five if it check out. But you gone pay it all now."

Devon laughed nervously. "You're adding twenty-five bucks?"

Ellie sneered at him through her round face. "You doubtin' Ms. Ellie? Ms. Ellie don' like that! You thinks Ms. Ellie lies, you gets yo' white ass outta here. What it be?"

Alessandra's description of Ellie as an early teenager, her sense of pride and courage, centered in Devon's mind. The decision was easy.

"We'll do it your way."

Devon removed a shoe and extracted a hundred, a twenty, and a five-dollar bill, and slid them across the table. Ellie picked up the bills, held them to the light, then stuffed them between her giant breasts.

"Whatchu wanna know?"

Devon decided that for a hundred-twenty-five dollars, he would start from the beginning.

"When did you first meet Alessandra Matreoni?"

Ellie Jenkins rearranged her body on the couch and considered the question.

"It were late 1940s like you say. She hung out with a little Po'ta Rican spitfire name Luisa. They always be gettin' in trouble 'cause of the Irish kids, 'specially big Irish girl name Ginga. Nuns who run *Mercy o' Jesus* Irish and don' like nobody but Irish. They was from the ole country."

Ellie's eyes trailed away as if she were remembering.

"Ginga always gettin' Alessandra and Luisa in trouble. Mostly Alessandra at the start, then bofe. Them two big nuns really hate Italians. Like I say, Luisa, she Po'ta Rican. They always draggin' Alessandra in the office and wailin' on her ass, then throw her in this room didn't have no light and starve her. Luisa, she try to hep Alessandra. I knows tha's a mistake 'cause pretty soon Luisa in that room with her.

"They was this one little nun – a young one – who try to hep but they send her back to the ole country. I was with Alessandra and Luisa two-three years and don' know how they make it through."

Ellie paused to scratch a spot on her huge hip, then turned her attention back to Devon.

"That Luisa girl, she smart and she know I don' like what was happenin', but since it wudn't happenin' to me, I didn't do nothin'. Then Ginga start sayin' things about black girls, and Luisa and me got a bunch of us together an' beat the livin' shit outta her. Beat the shit outta Ginga's frens too. Them Irish kids scared to death when they sees either one of us, but even after that, Ginga still know how to make trouble."

"What did the nuns do after you beat up Ginger?"

Ellie looked at Devon as though he had asked the stupidest question in history.

"Whatchu think they done? All hail brake loose. It got real bad after that and them nuns sent Luisa to refoam school. When she get back, things's turn worse. This time, mostly Luisa gettin' it. I don' 'member how long it go on, but one day Luisa and Alessandra steal some cheese and get caught and I hear Ginga tell Luisa she goin' up fo' life."

Devon squinted in disbelief. "Life! For stealing cheese? And you believed her?"

Ellie shrugged. "That what Ginga say, and I don' know no different. I was a chile. One night Luisa come and say she and Alessandra gone bust out 'cause they doin' time if they stay. They goin' over the fence next night. She want me to start a fah in the kitchen at suppa time t' give them a chance t' run."

"I heard something about a fire," said Devon. "Why did you decide to help them by starting the fire? You could have gotten in big trouble. You could have gone to juvenile hall. You had to have known that."

"'Cause I be so mad! Them Sisters…they been wailin' on me too and I just be waitin' fo' a chance t' get even. I stole the softball bat we had fo' the playground and tol' Alessandra where I hide it near the door 'cuz she might need it when they go. That evenin' I set the grease on fah in the kitchen. Whoooee, cops and firemens everywhere. Big Mama nun screamin' that Alessandra take that bat and fuck her leg up when she catched 'em sneakin' out. I remember them cartin' her off in a ambulance screamin'. Man, that the beautifulest song I hear in my whole life."

Ellie Jenkins began laughing, and Devon joined politely.

"Did you ever see Luisa and Alessandra after that?"

Ellie sat up. "You wants some coffee?"

Devon took a fraction of a second to weigh the consequences of refusal, then said, "I'd love some."

Ellie eased into a sitting position, put both hands on the table, raised her large body from the sofa, locked her knees, then straightened into a standing position. Devon watched her wobble away and partially disappear into the tiny kitchen. She returned carrying two mugs of black liquid that resembled motor oil.

"I drinks my coffee black. Cream cost too damn much."

Devon took a careful sip. The coffee was wretched, but he smiled. "Good coffee."

Ellie glared at him. "It shit! Don' lie no mo' t' Ms. Ellie – 'bout nothin'. She don' like lyin'."

Devon held up his hands. "No more lies. The coffee's terrible."

With some difficulty, Ellie crossed her legs at the ankles and sipped her coffee.

"You was axing if I saw Luisa and Alessandra again. Not t' talk to. One day, long time back, I see a New Yawk paper and it have a pitcher of Alessandra, only she don' call herself Alessandra, she call herself Maria Hernandez. I know she Alessandra though. She real pretty in the pitcha. Got that sweet lil angel face an kinda secret smile."

"Why was her picture in the paper?"

"Alessandra, she got herself tied up with a rich man. I mean that boy Wall Street rich! Franklin James Stevens-Longworth. Ellie never fo'get that name. Paper say Franklin's wife find out he messin' 'round and d'vo'ce him. He be payin' Alessandra five hundred dollahs a fuck and he gettin' it steady. That girl makin' real good money fo' back then. Real good!"

Devon took a long sip of coffee. The awful taste helped to ease the pain he was feeling.

"Did you ever hear what happened to Alessandra after that?"

Ellie's eyes opened wide, and she shook her head. "That all I knows. Nevah saw nothin' mo' 'bout her. It like the world swallow her. I wanted to get in touch. Didn't want nothin', just kind of liked her. She nice to me in the o'ph'nage. So was Luisa. But it like the world swallow her. Whatchu know about them two?"

Devon gave a short laugh. "A lot less than I thought. Anything else you can tell me?"

"No, 's all I know. You ready t' go?"

"Yeah. I don't want to know any more."

"Okay. When Tiebo get here, I be the one do the talkin'. Whatchu payin' him?"

"Two tens."

Ellie picked up her cell phone and called. Seconds later, Tiebo knocked on the door, and Ellie waddled over and opened it, pipe wrench in hand. When she was sure it was Tiebo, she opened the door wider, poking her head outside to glance from one side of the hallway to the other. Then she turned to Devon.

"Give him half the money."

Devon complied, and Ellie again fixed Tiebo in a psychotic glare.

"Tiebo, you gone get half yo' money now an' the rest when he get on the bus. You puttin' the arm on him on the way to the bus stop…pull you a knife or a gun…when I get my hands on you…and I will…I gone fuck you up so bad yo' ears be sticking out yo' ass."

Tiebo's eyes became gigantic, and he started to object, but was stopped by Ellie's booming, "Shut the fuck up!"

Ms. Ellie then turned to Devon. "You get on that bus when it come, and you don' nevah come back down here. You does an' you on yo' own. I don' be heppin'. You got that?"

It was a crushed Devon Emmanuel who got off the bus and caught the subway to the Culbertsons' small, well kept, Brooklyn home. On the way, he decided to have Lindsay check the New York newspaper morgue files until he found what Devon was certain he would find. Maria Hernandez had been a hooker. A five-hundred-dollar-a-night prostitute at a time when five hundred dollars was big money. He had just written the best prose of his career about a woman who had offered her body for the comforts of life. He tried to turn his mind off, but it ignored his command, as if to say, "See what happens when a journalist gets too close to his subject?"

The stuff about Jake Gittleman was undoubtedly crap. Alessandra got her hands on a rich, lonesome, horny, middle-aged guy and charmed him into loving her so much he married her. He never checked her out.

Devon felt like someone had stuffed a baseball down his throat. He fought back tears and waited for the feeling to go away. It didn't. Maria Hernandez – Alessandra Angelina Asencio Matreoni Gittleman – the whore with a heart as big as her lies.

The next issue of *Walden* would be mailed to subscribers soon. There was no way to stop the publication now, because H-T wouldn't allow it until he was certain his deal with Lillian Scheidler was bound by all the chains of American contract law. If Alessandra's past came to light, H-T would blame Devon, a writer so desperate for a great story that he published without adequate research into his subject's past. H-T had nothing to lose. Without the story, *Walden* was going bankrupt anyway. The plight of *Walden* at the time of the publication would leak, and the desperate circumstances facing the author would enhance the probability of his deception. The story would not only carry Devon's name, but Clark Andrews' as well. Their reputations would be history. No magazine would hire either of them, regardless of their proven talents.

This fantasy had hardly cleared Devon's brain when a more appealing thought replaced it. It could be years before the prostitution story came out. Alessandra's true identity had not been discovered at the time of the divorce proceedings, or Ms. Ellie would have mentioned it. Apparently, Maria Hernandez was the only name used in the newspaper article. There had to be rabid newspaper scrutiny at the time if Stevens-Longworth was such a prominent society figure. The press would have been vying for a scoop. Nobody was going to waste time digging for facts related to the prostitute's life. The facts they cared about involved the scandal. The guy was important, he had been seeing a high-priced prostitute, and his wife was divorcing him. That was probably the extent of their inquiry.

That was the big story at the time. Even if the press finds her out now, Alessandra will still be an angel because of what she gave back to society. Joan of Arc would still be St. Joan today even if she'd laid her whole regiment. Andrews and I might just get away with it!

But what of the principles he'd lived by? Principles that had kept him seventeen years at lousy wages, neglecting his family. If those principals meant anything, he had to speak out. Tell the world that Alessandra Angelina Asencio Matreoni Gittleman made her living on her back as a young woman and took advantage of her looks and cunning to marry a rich man.

That's what you'd add to the article if you held to your fucking principles, Emmanuel.

CHAPTER 48

Devon's stop at the Culbertson home was brief and spent at the kitchen table lauding Lindsay. Mrs. Culbertson insisted on serving coffee. When Devon finished talking, she was convinced her son was a combination Steve Jobs and Sherlock Holmes.

Once outside the house, Devon paid Lindsay what he owed him and made a new request. He asked for all information available in New York newspaper morgue files concerning Alessandra Matreoni, Maria Hernandez, and Stevens-Longworth. Then Devon threw his arm around Lindsay's shoulder and spoke quietly.

"Lindsay...I don't have any more money to give you. I know I haven't always been nice, or even decent to you, and now I come asking favors. I need you to keep secret everything about Alessandra. She's a good person, and I don't want to destroy her."

Lindsay looked insulted and pulled away from Devon. "I know that. You don't have to tell me that. She's helped a lot of poor people. I like her. I ain't sayin' nothin'."

"How do you know about the people she's helped?"

"I read your story."

Devon was shocked. "What? How? It hasn't been published yet."

"I crashed your computer. Your protection's a pussy."

With that, Devon slapped the grinning teenager on the back and headed toward the subway that would take him back to *Walden*.

The *Walden* staff, all of whom now knew Devon had saved their jobs by rescuing the magazine from bankruptcy, greeted him with honors generally reserved for archangels. It was over an hour before he could escape the crush and get Clark Andrews free.

H-T, who saw them both leaving, shouted a cheery, "Out of here, you two! Take care of business and have a couple of cognacs on me."

Twenty minutes later, they entered Andrews' favorite watering hole. During the walk, Devon had spoken two words to his curious editor, who had pumped him for information.

"Later. Troubles."

While working on his second double scotch, Andrews addressed Devon, who sat slumped in the cracked red-leather booth, staring into the distance, his legs splayed beneath the table like puppet limbs.

"Give it to me."

Devon told his "Ellie Jenkins" story, eyes closed, without stopping, ending with, "We've unknowingly lionized and gilded a hooker, and our unsuspecting boss, even if he is an asshole, sold her to one of America's richest women as the righteous defender of feminine justice."

Clark Andrews reached in his coat pocket, produced a tiny bottle of nitroglycerin, squirted once under his tongue, and waited for his chest pain to subside. His next act was to gulp down the remainder of his second double scotch.

"What do we do now?" he gasped as he finished his drink.

Devon shook his head. "I have Lindsay looking up the story in newspaper morgues. You ever heard of Franklyn James Stevens-Longworth?"

Andrews raised his glass to the bartender and pointed into it with two fingers. The bartender held up a bottle of *Chivas Regal* and Andrews gave a thumbs-up.

"Sure. Surprised you haven't. He was involved in a scandal back in the late fifties. I remember reading about it while doing some background for a story I handled on rewrite. Franklyn's mother was a Stevens and his father a Longworth. Both families have been in this country since the late 17th Century. Both had relatives in the Revolutionary War, and both made a fortune in the Civil War selling arms to both sides."

Devon looked wide-eyed at Andrews. "They made their money as arms merchants to both sides in their own country's Civil War?"

"They did, indeed. After Appomattox, they went from arms to finance. Since that time, they've been connected politically from Congress through the White House regardless of the party in power. Both families are secretive, rich, and aren't bound by the norms of conscience. Sometime in the early Twentieth Century, a Stevens girl married a Longworth man; it had to be one of their progeny who was banging Alessandra."

It was Devon's turn to down his drink and signal for another. The phrase "banging Alessandra" caused him to consider the relative emotional relief to be gained by breaking his friend's jaw versus dissolving into tears. He had been in a funk before they reached the bar, but now he felt worse. Through his misery, a thought wormed its way into his alcohol-loading neurons.

"Clark. These people – the Stevens and Longworths – you say they were rich and connected? How rich?"

Andrews thought for a moment. "Together – probably in the top hundred families in the country. The Oval Office connection is a pretty good indication of their wealth. Whatcha drivin' at?"

Devon twisted in the booth to face his friend. "Why would a family with that much money, with so much to lose if there was a scandal, let this story out? Why wouldn't they pay a couple hundred thousand hush money and move on? Something doesn't make sense. That can't be the whole story."

"That answer, my boy, you will learn by reading the New York newspaper stories."

Devon glared at Andrews. "Fuck the New York newspapers! Tell me what happened."

Andrews ignored Devon and ogled an attractive woman who had just walked into the bar. His answer was delivered in a casual tone.

"The affair between our gal – of course at the time I didn't know she was our gal – and Franklyn Jimmy didn't stop with the divorce. FJ was a little kinky. He didn't like it when he didn't get his way. My guess is he wanted to get kinky one night and Alessandra said no. He slashed her throat. Somehow, Alessandra alerted the cops and managed to live. Franklyn James got five years, as I recall. Didn't this Jenkins woman tell you the rest of the story?"

Devon shook his head. He thought back to his meetings with Alessandra. Every article of clothing she wore on her upper body covered her neck. Now he knew why. He felt an urge to wreck the bar. He wanted to kill Stevens-Longworth. Then he wanted to kill that lying bitch. Right after he murdered that piece of shit H-T for no other reason than it appealed to him.

His thoughts then turned to the more immediate. Painful as things were, he had to protect himself. He considered what would happen if he went to Miss Lillian and told her the full story. It might help him survive, because he could make the argument that he was forced by H-T to make an impossible deadline. But what about Clark and CASE? Andrews was his only friend, and CASE was special. Regardless of its creator's past, CASE was special.

Andrews had been waiting patiently while Devon mused.

"How come Jenkins didn't tell you the end of the story?" Andrews finally asked.

"I don't know. She said she tried to get in touch..."

Andrews was giving Devon a stare that said, *You're not telling me what I have a right to know, and I want to know it now, because my life is going down the drain with yours.*

"My guess is, Ellie Jenkins didn't know Alessandra married Gittleman, and that was the reason she lost track of her. She thought she was looking for Alessandra Matreoni when she was still using the pseudonym Maria Hernandez. Or maybe Ellie was trying to protect her, and that was why she never mentioned the slashed throat. She made it sound like a high society divorce-prostitution scandal."

"That don't make sense. Why would Ellie cover it up after revealing Alessandra was a hooker?"

Devon smiled. "That, my friend, would be personal to Ms. Ellie. And I wouldn't go down there to find out if I were you. Ms. Ellie might choose to throw you over the balcony because you disrespected her friend, even though she hasn't seen her for decades. Ms. Ellie, she got principles. A bigger question is, how come Alessandra's real name didn't come out in the trial?"

"There was no trial. There was a plea bargain. My guess is a lot of important folks were paid off. Who knows? Anyway, a month after the initial media feeding frenzy, nothing more was heard about it."

"He only got five years for almost killing someone?"

Andrews chuckled. "My friend, are you really that naïve?"

Devon took a slow, deep breath. "Money. Just like Alessandra said."

Andrews was silent as Devon struggled with his feelings, then took a sip of scotch and used the glass to point to a woman at the bar. "My boy, I would like to call back thirty years and lay that."

Devon never heard the comment. He could only think of Alessandra. The image in his mind was of her scarred neck, which he had never seen, and the feeling in his chest was that of a broken heart. He no longer had any doubt that Alessandra Gittleman had been a prostitute.

"Clark, what happened to Stevens-Longworth?"

"He did a few years in a resort prison, and somehow got paroled. The Stevens-Longworth family was loaded, and money talks. And thus did Freaky Frankie become Free Freaky Frankie."

"What finally happened to Franklin James Stevens-Longworth?"

"Frankie James left the States, moved to Monaco, and eventually died of hedonism."

A contented alcohol-induced haze emanated from Andrews' face. "Devon, you cannot tell me that you would not like to pork yon specimen of female sensuality. I await the fullness of your imagination."

Devon ignored the comment. "Clark, I want to go back to L.A. Can you get H-T to spring for a round-trip ticket and one night's lodging?"

"Sure," said Andrews. "Looking for answers from Alessandra, right?"

"Yeah."

"To which questions?"

Devon hesitated.

"Time to lay everything on the table, buddy."

"This is personal."

"Bullshit!" Andrews shot back. "I'm in this too."

"I want to hear this stuff from her perspective. This woman has done some really great things in her life, a hell of a lot more than you and me."

Andrews' face became a mixture of concern and disbelief. "You're going to fly to L.A. to get her side of the story? Devon, she lied before. What makes you think she won't lie again?"

Devon put the heels of his hands on his forehead and rubbed. "Because I don't believe she will. And that is the pristine, immaculately cleansed, washed-in-the-blood-of-the-lamb-fucking-goddamn truth from the bottom of my wretched soul!"

Andrews' eyes returned to the woman at the bar. Suddenly, he raised his partly filled glass, waved to the bartender and again pointed into it with two fingers.

"How many doubles is that?" Devon asked.

"I don't know and I don't care," Andrews said, his speech slurring. "Death, be not proud!"

"You're going to be so shit-faced when you finish that next double, you won't be able to walk back to the office."

"I solve problems better after multiple doubles. Walking's not a problem to me. Not knowing what you're going to do after you leave L.A. is a problem to me. Have you called sweet Alessandra and asked her if she was a whore?"

Devon swallowed. "Don't call her a whore, Clark. Yes, I've called her cell phone. It's full, so you can't leave a message. I called CASE, and they wouldn't put me through to her. They said they had strict instructions that she was not to be bothered. That's not unusual for her."

Andrews started his next scotch by holding it at eye level. Finally he took a sip.

"Sorry about the whore crack. I don't know what she's actually done or not done. And you're right, the stories I heard from your feed certainly make her a better human than I've ever been. Go out to Los Angeles and find out what she says really happened. I would like you to do me a favor, though."

"Yeah? What?"

"Promise me you won't blow any whistles until we've discussed what you're going to expose. I'm talking about the Franklyn James Stevens-Longworth episode and all the other things she's probably lied about."

The request bothered Devon. "Are you thinking about Alessandra Gittleman's reputation or Clark Andrews' problems?"

Andrews let his head fall backward onto the booth cushion. "I'm thinking about Clark Andrews' kids. The instant sweet Lillian's attorneys know the article covered up this shit, they'll undo her *Walden* buy-in, and I'll lose my job immediately. I really don't give a fuck what happens to me. Those kids are the only worthwhile things I have to show for my miserable life."

The fat man turned his face toward Devon without raising his head from the cushion. "Y'know, Emmanuel, I like you. Unfortunately, you have integrity. You're the only person I know in this fucked-up world who I'm certain has integrity. And that scares the shit out of me, because you can never trust a man with integrity. What time will you leave for L.A.?"

"If you can get H-T to spring for a ticket and a hotel room, and if I can get the kids situated, I'll leave tonight on the red-eye."

Andrews took another large drink of his scotch. "What'll you do when you get there? I mean, how do you plan to unravel this mess?"

Devon waited for an answer to arrive in his mind. "I have no fucking idea."

CHAPTER 49

CASE was unchanged from Devon's last visit, but the response of its inhabitants to his presence could not have been cooler had he been a white-sheeted Klan member. No one looked at him again after a first glance. Silence drenched the room. Devon walked toward the desk.

"Hello, Anita," he said to the receptionist in a near-whisper.

"*Buenos dias, Señor* Emmanuel."

Formal. Not encouraging.

He decided to adopt a beseeching persona. "Anita, I've been trying to reach Alessandra. I have to clear up a critical point in the interview and she agreed that if I had any questions, I could call her. Could you please get me in to see her? I assure you, this won't take long."

Anita Salazar looked down to avoid Devon's eyes as she spoke. "I am sorry, *Señor*. The *Señora* is seeing no one."

Devon placed his hands on the desk, and with the face of a religious supplicant said, "Anita...*Señora* Salazar...this is really important. I've flown all night to get here and I'm exhausted. Could you at least tell her I'm here?"

Tears were in Anita's eyes when she looked up. "She is not in her apartment, *Señor* Emmanuel. And I have given my word I will not say where she is unless she calls first to me. You are a nice man. I do not like saying no, but my orders come from *Señora* Gittleman herself, and I would never break my word to the *Señora*."

Devon heard a sound behind him. He turned to see the guard who had helped him carry Alessandra into her apartment the night she became ill.

"Hello, Officer Aruba."

The security guard's salutation was pleasant and cheerful.

"Good morning, *Señor* Emmanuel. May I help you?"

Anita pressed the security alarm.

Devon felt a sense of foreboding as he shook the guard's hand and smiled. He glanced casually around the room. Everyone seemed to be studiously avoiding eye contact. It was obvious no one in CASE was going to tell him the whereabouts of Alessandra. The security guard made that a certainty.

"*Señor* Emmanuel...I must be getting back to my post. Would you accompany me, please?"

Outside, Devon checked his watch. Almost eleven. It was a bright, clear day, and he squinted as he looked in the direction of his car. The guard followed his gaze.

"Where did you park, *Señor*?"

"About three blocks up the street. Same place I used to park."

The security guard motioned with his head. "I will walk with you, *Señor*."

I'm being escorted off the fucking premises!

They walked in silence, the sound of their footsteps on the pavement grating on Devon's nerves. He considered saying something, then decided it would be useless. They were nearly at the car when the guard stopped.

"*Señor* Emmanuel."

Now a few feet ahead of the guard, Devon turned to face him. Aruba seemed nervous.

"Forgive me, *Señor*, but I must talk with you. A few years ago, my sister was accused of abusing her children. It wasn't true. Her ex-husband lied to the police. They arrested her and took her children away. She did not think she would ever get them back. The *Señora* fought for her, and the charges were dropped. Since that time, I have worked as a security guard at CASE when I can. Now I find myself troubled."

"What's going on, Officer Aruba?"

"*Señor* Emmanuel, I gave to *Señora* Gittleman my word that I would not tell where she is. I have thought much about my promise, because I think I have made a mistake. My heart is bothered. I will tell you where she is, if you will give to me your promise not to say how you found her, and you will tell me how she is doing."

Devon's answer was immediate. "You have my promise."

"*Señora* Gittleman is very sick. She was taken to the hospital. When I helped the ambulance people move her, she asked me to promise not to tell anyone where she is or what happened, and to say the same to everyone at CASE. I have tried to find out her condition, but the hospital will not tell me. I am very worried."

Aruba pushed a small crumpled piece of paper into Devon's hand. He checked the paper and saw the name and address of the hospital.

Devon's initial relief at finding Alessandra's whereabouts quickly turned to dread. He gripped Aruba's arm.

"I'll do my best. I'll respect your confidence, and whatever I learn, I'll tell you. Thank you, sir."

As he drove to the hospital, Devon thought about his feelings for Alessandra. The tears that flooded his cheeks were partly from love and partly from anger. He also considered the problems he would face getting in to see her. This became paramount as he neared the hospital.

He examined various possibilities. If he simply announced he wanted to see her, he'd get nowhere. The lower-level hospital staff probably wouldn't even confirm her presence in the medical center.

It'll be a miracle if I can bluff my way into her room, but I have to try.

By the time he reached the hospital parking lot, he had a plan.

CHAPTER 50

Devon's guess was right about what would happen at the admissions desk. When he asked to see Mrs. Gittleman, looks were exchanged among the three women present. Eventually, one of them said, "Janice, go ask Mrs. Glick to step in here."

"Janice" left the glass cubicle through the back of what Devon considered a beautified holding cell and returned with a slim, fashionably dressed, perhaps thirty-five-year-old woman who walked directly to the enclosed security window. She was not smiling.

"I'm Elizabeth Glick, head of admissions. How may I help you, sir?"

Devon kept his face expressionless, his voice flat, and spoke while taking his New York driver's license out of his wallet. He had decided that surrender of this icon would add a veneer of honesty to the lies he was about to tell. He dropped the license into the small tray that opened into the cubicle.

"Mrs. Glick, my name is Devon Emmanuel and I'm here to see Mrs. Gittleman on a matter of urgent business."

Mrs. Glick did not respond. Instead, she stared at the driver's license and appeared to be thinking.

"What issues will be involved in your visit, sir?"

Devon didn't hesitate. "That information is confidential, Mrs. Glick."

"Are you an attorney?"

He was prepared for the question, his answer predicated on the gamble that the security guard's remark about Alessandra being very ill was a reality. He pushed his luck.

"I'm not an attorney, but I assure you this matter involves issues that Mrs. Gittleman will want addressed as quickly as possible. I think we both know that, given her current condition, time could be an important factor."

Elizabeth Glick was forced into an uncomfortable position. A deeper verification of Devon's credentials would take time, and the hospital's classification of the patient was not good. The gatekeeper tried again for information, nodding toward Devon's satchel.

"I assume this has to do with signing documents?"

Devon's face remained expressionless. "Forgive me, Mrs. Glick; I can't speak to that."

Mrs. Glick hesitated, then removed a sheet from a note pad, wrote a floor and room number on it, then placed it in the small tray.

"Conclude your business as quickly as possible. Stop at this office on the way out, return this piece of paper, and we will return your license. You are not to confirm Mrs. Gittleman's presence in this hospital or divulge any of the information on that paper. Agreed?"

"Yes. Thank you for your cooperation."

The walk to Alessandra's room was nerve-wracking. Devon expected to see a guard lurking behind every pillar. He reached the correct floor and began checking room numbers. When he found the room, he felt a sense of both accomplishment and foreboding.

He was shocked when he entered Alessandra's room, even though he had prepared himself to be traumatized. The hospital bed was positioned at about a thirty-degree angle, and her legs were extended over the downward slope of the mattress. Her head was swathed in beige bandages, her upper body twisted to the right. Intravenous fluid flowed into her left arm. Other devices were attached to her in what seemed a helter-skelter manner. The top of her light blue hospital gown was level with the upper part of her breasts. She looked ancient.

Devon cautiously made his way to the bedside and watched her breathe. A long thin scar began below the angle of her left jaw and extended to her collarbone. Emotions he could not describe coursed through him, writhing and biting like a medieval torture device. He considered reaching out and touching her, actually began to do so, then withdrew his hand and let it rest on the bed rail.

Across from him, a computer screen monitored in insentient detail the functions necessary for life.

Suddenly the door opened, and a young nurse entered. When she saw Devon, her face became a combination of surprise and fury.

"Who are you, and what are you doing here? This is a neurosurgery floor! Mrs. Gittleman is not to have visitors!"

Devon handed the nurse the paper Elizabeth Glick had signed. The response was not what he had hoped. The nurse's eyes widened. She answered in a loud, acid whisper.

"I don't care what some idiot in admissions thinks! Get out! Now!"

He opened his mouth to argue and was slammed with one word. "Out!"

Arguing, he knew, might get him arrested. There had to be other avenues he could explore, and he couldn't do that locked up. He picked up his satchel, took the paper from the nurse's hand, and started for the door.

"Stay a while, Bubby."

Devon froze in mid-step. He turned back toward Alessandra.

The nurse stared at her patient. "Mrs. Gittleman, if I let him stay, I'll be in trouble..."

The hand bearing the IV moved gently back and forth and Alessandra motioned toward the door with her chin.

"Mrs. Gittleman, I have your meds. I need you to take them before I leave. If you'll do that, I'll leave the room – for a short while."

The nurse then looked from Alessandra to Devon and continued. "If he isn't out of here soon, I'm calling Dr. Chang."

Alessandra smiled at Devon after she swallowed her meds. "See what the women's movement did. Progress, nu?" Her eyes returned to the nurse. "He'll be out of here soon. And if you have any problems with Chang, I'll see that you go unscathed. I'd appreciate it if we weren't bothered."

The nurse left grudgingly, while Alessandra straightened in her bed. Forgetting her head was wrapped, she attempted to fix her hair with her fingers, then laughed when she felt the bandage. She motioned Devon to her bedside.

"To what do I owe the presence of my sweet Bubby?"

Devon didn't know what to say. Thoughts – fragmented, intertwined, some with meaning, others defying understanding – whirled and flashed through his mind. Harsh things, mean things, bitter things. Things he hated! He felt as if snakes were inside him, rolling into a knot and sliding up and down from his throat to his belly. His eyes closed tight as hot, deep, sobbing, nose-filling tears trickled down his face. He felt a hand slip over the top of his, and only then did he realize that he had been gripping the bedrail.

Alessandra spoke softly. "I know I'm responsible for those tears, and there's probably nothing I can do about them. It's best that I start the conversation. You know that migraine I've had off and on for years…what I've been having recently isn't a migraine. I have a brain tumor. I've just had surgery."

Devon's gasp broke Alessandra's explanation and she squeezed his hand harder. When she felt he was calmer, she continued.

"Shortly after you left for New York, I had a seizure. They brought me here and relieved the pressure in my head."

"What's going to happen to you?"

"The neurosurgeons have told me that if I go through a lot of bullshit, I can buy four or five extra months of what sounds like worthless life. Without the bullshit, I have maybe eight good weeks. I'm not interested in worthless life. I've had a great life – not always an easy life, but a great life. I'm going to take the shorter time, smoke my cigarettes, eat anything I goddamn well want, and piss off as many people as possible."

Alessandra shifted her position, grimacing slightly as she did. "Now that you know I'm dying, how much longer I have, and my plans, I expect you to be a mensch and ask me all the nasty questions that prompted your return to L.A. Keep it short, because that nurse doesn't like you. She'll call Chang, and he'll call security, regardless of my arguments. Around here, you have to die according to protocol."

Devon's mind refused to work. Everything his eyes fell on spoke of fear, pain, and death. He had an urge to smash the monitors. His entire life seemed like froth on a beer or a ten-minute snow flurry that never stuck to a tree or a house or the ground. Nothing. Nothing meant anything. Nothing the hospital, nothing the country, nothing the world or even the universe. Existence – especially his – nothing!

"Bubby, you need to say something."

The shout erupted from somewhere in Devon Emmanuel's viscera. "Shut up! Just shut up until I'm finished!"

Alessandra looked shocked. Devon fixed her in an angry stare. Then he looked aimlessly about the room.

Suddenly the door flew open and the battle-ready nurse, empty stainless steel bedpan cocked in her hand, burst through. Alessandra motioned her away. The nurse hesitated, then left.

Alessandra's gaze returned to Devon, whose momentary mental chaos began to clear. With clarity came words. He spoke as he watched repetitive bumps, curlicues, and messages move monotonously, mesmerizingly, across the monitor screen. His own voice sounded hollow to him, almost unearthly.

"How long have you known you were dying?"

Alessandra straightened the neckline of her hospital gown, then pulled up and smoothed the sheet covering her.

"Will honest answers lead to murder and loss of my eight-week debauchery?"

Devon's shoulders hunched in anger, and his reply was raspy. "Just answer the goddamn question."

"I've suspected."

"For months before I came to interview you?"

"Yes."

"Was your perceived soon-to-be-fatal illness the reason you offered *Walden* the interview?"

"Yes."

"You wanted to bring in money to help perpetuate CASE after you die?"

"Yes."

"Did you really ask for me because you thought I was *Walden's* best writer?"

"Yes."

"And your insistence on having me continue to do the interview after our fight– that fight was really a test to see if I would react in the manner you wanted?"

"Yes."

Devon ran a hand through his hair. "Were you a hooker in New York City in your early twenties?"

"I suppose."

"What the hell kind of answer is 'I suppose'?" he asked in a surly tone.

Alessandra slowly moved her head from side to side. "The answer one gives to imply the affirmative more than the negative – but leaves room for doubt."

Devon tried to assimilate the answer. Failing that, he ignored it. His next comment dripped sarcasm.

"Your law courses – they covered the philosophy and art of prostitution?"

Alessandra sighed deeply. She tried to look into Devon's eyes, but they were fixed on the monitor. Her voice was soft and carried pain.

"No, Bubby, I became proficient in the field of prostitution before I entered law school."

"Then how does 'I suppose' apply to prostitution?"

His question hurt Alessandra, and she bristled. "Set your ass down in that chair, shut up, and listen."

Devon turned from the monitor, made cold eye contact, and started to argue.

Alessandra preempted him. "Speak respectfully, goddamit! I earned that respect. Now sit down and shut up, or get the hell out!"

Devon pushed the blue vinyl armchair close to the bedrail, sat down, and crossed his arms.

"You undoubtedly know that I was the girl Franklyn James Stephens-Longworth was sleeping with, and that I was identified as the 'other woman' in his divorce proceedings. Twice, sometimes three times a week, we would meet in his cozy hideaway in Connecticut, and, yes, we would have sex. And, yes, I would be paid for that sex. Five hundred dollars a night. This went on for months."

Each word was a hot knife stabbing him. "Sounds like prostitution to me," he muttered. "I don't see much room for 'I suppose.'"

Alessandra lay there fuming. "Want to learn, Bubby, or adjudicate?"

Devon didn't answer, and Alessandra continued. "Doubt, sweet Bubby, comes in many forms. Our society would define my behavior as prostitution. Philosophically – ah, philosophically – think about Lady Godiva. In medieval times, she rode naked through Coventry to achieve a common good. That was frowned upon by the high-born British who had labels for such a loss of decorum. I had sex with a stupid, arrogant, perverted asshole to get money to pay for Luisa's therapy. She died anyway. She never knew I was the benefactor who paid her medical bills. She wouldn't have allowed me to do that. She thought I was sleeping over with my boyfriend. We had fights about it in which I argued that I was an adult, and if I wanted to sleep with my boyfriend, I would damn well do it regardless of her illness. I know it hurt her, but I didn't have any choice. Without treatment she would die, and without money, there would be no treatment."

Devon wasn't expecting the story. He felt humiliated.

"Didn't you tell her anything? 'I have a night job' – anything?"

"No. How much could I make in a regular three-night-a-week job that would justify leaving a dying friend? Luisa would have known that was a lie."

"You let her think you were out enjoying yourself while she was dying?"

Tears glistened in Alessandra's eyes, and she didn't answer.

Devon wished he were dead.

Alessandra leaned her head back, closed her eyes and took an enormous breath. When she didn't move or speak, Devon started to leap up, but his chair squeaked, and she raised her hand. He slowly lowered himself into the chair.

"After Luisa died, I was still thousands of dollars in debt and kept sleeping with Franklyn James until everything was paid off. After that, Franklyn James Stephens-Longworth was out of my body forever. So I leave it to you. Was I a whore?"

The snakes churned again. Devon couldn't think of a response. He started to speak and was cut off.

"While you're deciding my guilt or innocence, let me address other issues. If you know about my sexual indiscretions, you probably know that Sister Doreen accused me of breaking her leg. Sister Doreen's leg was broken, but I didn't wield that softball bat. Sister Doreen shouldn't have tormented a Puerto Rican girl. Puerto Ricans are good hitters. Remember Roberto Clemente?"

"Sister Doreen made the accusation against you. We have the police report."

Alessandra laughed derisively. "And you have the good Sister's signed statement. And there could be no doubt about the good Sister's word? The good Sister detested me so much she lied to the police, knowing I would be sent to juvenile hall. She didn't have to make up a charge about Luisa, because she already knew juvey was a done deal for her."

As if she were giving her closing argument to a jury, Alessandra said, "Let's summarize: I prostituted myself to a pervert in the hope of saving my friend's life. My best friend. A friend who was willing to be physically pulverized and go to prison for me. The only sister I ever had."

Tears filled Alessandra's angry eyes. "Sister Doreen, that blessed nun, attempted to frame a fourteen-year-old child with the intention of branding her a criminal and ruining her life. Sister Doreen felt free to do that, because she hated everything that wasn't like her."

Silence.

Then, a soft voice. "Tell me, Bubby, which of us was a whore? Which one, for valuable consideration – bigoted fanaticism in her case – fucked decency and morality?"

Devon didn't answer; he just sat. He once thought he had a philosophy of life. Now he was unsure of anything, especially his own life.

Alessandra stared at her confused visitor. The anger that had animated her face minutes before was gone, and in its place was a soft peace.

"Did you turn up any other information in your search into my past?"

Devon looked vacantly at Alessandra. "Like what?"

"Attempted murder."

"Stephens-Longworth's attack on you?"

Alessandra made a face. "What other attempted murder would I be referring to, Bubby?"

The conversation stopped. Devon kept trying to process the information, but his brain was already engaged.

Her real name. How did she keep it from being known?

"Yes, I'm referring to that incident," said Devon. "How did you keep your real name from becoming known after the scandalous divorce and the attack on you?"

"The Stevens-Longworth family arranged that. They discovered my real name and the fact that I was wanted for crimes as a juvenile. And, of course, there was the prostitution I could have been charged with. They made me a deal. I agreed to muddy my testimony against Franklyn James, and they agreed not to turn over what they knew to the authorities."

Devon slowly nodded. "And that was why he only got five years. The scandal and slashing...they all took place after Luisa's death?"

"Yes."

"What happened to Stevens-Longworth after he got out of prison?"

Alessandra raised her eyebrows. "Franklyn James lived the good life on the French Riviera until he died a few years ago. Right now, you're probably wondering how he came so close to murdering me when I decided to stop being his whore. Am I right?"

Devon felt his body tremble. He had come to Los Angeles thinking Alessandra had totally betrayed him. He discovered he had mistakenly lost faith in a woman who was far above him. He wasn't sure how much more he could take.

"Go on."

"When our arrangement began, I received an advance on my services. About five hundred dollars. When Luisa's bills were paid, I stopped seeing him. He wanted back the money he had advanced me. He had previously agreed that we were finished with our – arrangement – but he insisted on a meeting. When I got to his apartment, he decided to take the debt out in trade. I decided he wouldn't. Somewhere during the struggle, a switchblade appeared and he slashed my throat. He hadn't counted on anyone hearing me scream, since the house was pretty isolated, but somebody did and called the police. Frankie pleaded temporary insanity. It almost worked – but then, you know the whole story, don't you? Would you like to talk about the perversions little Frankie enjoyed?"

Devon got up from the chair and walked to the window. It was beautiful outside, palm trees, wide boulevards, glorious sunlight. And he was surrounded by instruments to delay or monitor death. And a dying woman who was successfully countering his every effort to – to what?

What do you want? Every answer she could ever give will cause you pain.

"No, I'm not interested in hearing about Frankie's perversions."

"Really? What are you interested in hearing about, Bubby?"

Devon continued to look out the window.

This brought a gut-level scream from Alessandra. "Turn the fuck around and look at me!"

Devon turned just as the nurse flung the door open again. In unison, he and Alessandra bellowed, "Get out!"

The nurse left. Devon returned to the bedrail and gripped it with both hands.

"Did Jacob Gittleman know about your past?"

"Every damn bit and in much greater detail than I've told you. My past didn't make any difference to him. It was our future that interested Jake."

"The two of you went to California because it was less likely your past would be discovered if you were living three thousand miles away from The City?"

"Partly."

"And you never gave interviews because of the possibility someone might do exactly what I've done – discover your past."

"Yes."

"And you destroyed Judge Wexler, didn't you?"

A look of disgust masked Alessandra's face. "No. Judge Wexler destroyed himself. I asked a well-connected person in Sacramento who was beholden to me to dig into Wexler's cases. He discovered Wexler, who was an unforgiving man to poor defendants, had only rapped the knuckles of a kid who was the son of a big developer. It was a drug thing and the kid could have gotten ten years, but he came out with a suspended sentence. Not long after, there was a land deal, and Wexler received a piece of the action in the father's company. The same Wexler who was willing to send my client to prison for years and take her children away for what was basically a minor offense. He had no problem with that. Guys like Wexler make their way happily through life. They're the scabs of our society. Fuck Wexler. I hope he gets ten years in some hellhole. He won't, though. He may not even go to jail, and if he does, he'll do a couple of years on a cushy penal farm. When he gets out, somebody will arrange for him to get a good-paying job. If my client had gone to jail, she'd be lucky to make minimum wage when she got out. And she'd probably lose her kids. You want justice in America today, Bubby, be rich, be connected, and buy a great defense. You'll get more justice than you deserve."

Devon watched the monitor as it ticked off one heart beat after another, a process that would, in a couple of months, end in a flat line. He felt a terrible sadness that he knew would remain with him for the rest of his life.

As Devon stood in silence, Alessandra scanned his face. "You know, Bubby, you get better looking the longer I know you. Love that hair."

Devon laughed. "You're impossible. With your dying breath, you'll still be conning me. Stop the bullshit."

"Bubby, Bubby, Bubby – what am I going to do with my Bubby?" and she reached up and stroked his hand. "It's not easy being a decent man, is it, Bubby?"

Devon began to feel tears accumulating again, but he noticed something else. The writhing snakes in his gut had disappeared.

"No. And that complicates my life. I've just completed an article and sent it to the printer. It leaves out the fact that the subject of my interview is a multiple felon, went to law school and was admitted to the bar in two states after having committed those felonies, and bullied one of the most famous literary magazines in American history into doing a story on her for the express purpose of furthering her cause after her death – all the while suspecting her demise was imminent."

Alessandra beamed. "Bubby! You should have gone into law. That was accurate, succinct and discerning."

Devon shook his head. "Alessandra, if our roles were reversed, would you sacrifice your professional integrity to protect such a person? Or would you retract your article and end not only your own, but maybe a hundred other people's livelihoods, as well as CASE, an organization that gives hope to those with little of it? Tell me how to deal with this."

The Mona Lisa smile appeared on Alessandra's lips. "Our roles aren't reversed, Bubby. You're staying; I'm dying. You're going to have to make up your own mind. There are some things you should remember in making your decision, though."

"What?"

"You're absolutely right about what you said. CASE really will cease to exist without the money this article could bring. That means people like the ones you met, who managed to start their lives over again because of CASE, will face a society that considers them worthless. And they will have one less strong advocate in a landscape in which there are too few already."

There was a knock at the door. The nurse entered and stood with her feet widespread, fists on her hips. She looked first at Devon, then at Alessandra. This time her facial expression spoke as forcefully as her words.

"The time is up!"

Devon leaned over the bedrail, and Alessandra's arms went about his neck. They kissed. What he felt at the moment their lips touched was a mixture of love, regret, and heartbreak. He tried to speak, but couldn't. Afterward, he gently released her, stood up, and picked up his satchel. He was almost out the door when Alessandra spoke.

"Good luck with life, Bubby. For your edification, if we were both young, you're the kind of guy I could've gone for."

Devon smiled. "You never stop. You're an impossible woman. We'd probably have killed each other. Goodbye, Alessandra. I love you. You're the only woman...I've ever really loved."

"I love you too, Bubby."

CHAPTER 51

The janitor stopped sweeping long enough to stare briefly as Devon walked through the narrow lobby. This was the guest who had become known among the hotel personnel as "Lightning Bolt Man," a human capable of downing two or more of the mind-twisting caffeine concoctions in a single day. Even the cokeheads were impressed. Yet he seemed different now. His clothes were disheveled, his gait halting, his eyes red. The janitor, an Angeleno, could think of only one reason for red eyes. Dude was stoned. Definitely.

When Devon reached his room, he poured himself a drink from the small refrigerator and sat down at the desk. The crying jag he had experienced in his car as he drove to the hotel had drained his work-weary body. He took a large swallow of the liquor from the plastic glass.

How could he have fallen in love with a woman twenty-plus years his senior? It stretched the imagination, yet it was undeniably true. Alessandra Angelina Asencio Matreoni Gittleman was the first and only real love of his life. And she would be dead in a couple of months.

The feelings Alessandra had aroused in him forced him to recognize that he had never really loved Sonja. She was beautiful and brilliant, and he had been insecure. She had made him feel like the kind of man who could attract beautiful women. She had boosted his self-image, and he had interpreted it as love. Love. What was it that singer called it? "A second-hand emotion."

The phrase hadn't made any sense to him before, but now he felt its meaning. Jake was able to push aside all of Alessandra's past and see the human being he loved so much. Maybe Devon had finally learned that lesson himself.

He poured himself another drink and slowly paced the room. There were other issues to consider, and what he chose to do about those was going to alter his entire life. He checked his watch. Back in New York, H-T, the man who had employed him for seventeen years, was publishing an article that his best writer and his senior editor both knew covered up lies.

If H-T had known the truth, would he have published anyway? Without question. But did that make hiding the facts acceptable? No. Journalistically, nothing but the truth would set things right. H-T didn't want to know the truth, because it would end his magazine by wrapping the angel's wings around another journal.

The real question was, what was Devon doing to himself? This wasn't like failing to report that a famous woman had a casual affair with a wealthy man when she was young and poor. These were illegal acts that, if had they been known, would have made Alessandra Gittleman ineligible to join the bar or maybe even resulted in criminal charges. Instead, she not only practiced law for over forty years, she had become a near-religious figure in the eyes of countless women who would have been thrown under society's bus without her aid.

If he said nothing? His career-long convictions of professional integrity would be compromised. If his omission were discovered, he would be condemned as a liar by his own credo in a profession whose main argument for existence was truth.

He checked his watch. Five o'clock in New York. Andrews would still be in his office. As miserable as Devon felt, it was time. He lay down on the bed and made the call. The first ring brought an answer.

"Devon?"

The panic in Andrews' voice was unmistakable.

"Yeah, it's me, Clark."

"Tell me what I need to know."

Devon sighed and tried to control his voice.

"Are you where you can get your hands on your nitroglycerin?"

"That bad, huh?"

"Everything Ellie Jenkins said about Alessandra was true. Alessandra was Stevens-Longworth's call girl. She got five hundred bucks a night. He slashed her throat when she refused to keep on servicing him. She used the money to pay for Luisa's therapy for Hodgkin disease. Alessandra claims she told Jake Gittleman everything before they got married."

With the exception of heavy breathing, there was silence on the other end of the line. Devon took another swallow of his drink as he waited. When Andrews spoke again, panic had returned to his voice.

"Was she servicing a whole troop of rich guys or just slasher boy?"

"I didn't ask."

Devon heard heavier breathing, then the pumping sound of the nitro bottle.

Silence.

"Ms. Lillian finished the deal with H-T. The lawyers just left after the signing. You got any idea what will happen if this gets out now?"

Devon's laugh was derisive. "Yeah, Clark, I'm pretty sure. Ms. Lillian will rescind the buy-in, or failing that, get rid of *Walden* in a fire sale. It won't make a hell of a lot of difference to you and me, though. We'll both be out of jobs after our next paycheck and out of journalism for life. Where are we now in the printing process?"

"Finished."

"What I thought," Devon sighed. "Well, the damage is done. The two big questions are, do we tell H-T? Or do we wait and hope everything just – goes away? I don't know the answers, Clark."

Devon again heard the pumping sound. "Clark…?"

"Pain's easing. I've been thinking, Devon. We should keep our mouths shut. I mean, for all her faults, Alessandra Gittleman is an incredible woman who has done more for human beings than either of us. For that matter, more than the vast majority of her fellow Americans. What the hell, the only reason she became a hooker was to help her dying friend. Nothing in her past invalidates what she did for people. I'm against exposing her. Gittleman's only interest in this article was to bring money into CASE. She's lived the life of an ascetic since her husband died. Christ, she's like Mother Theresa. And we don't have to worry about her talking. Furthermore, who in New York is going to remember her from those days? Six months from now, nobody will even remember the article, except for contributors to CASE. Meanwhile, a restructured *Walden* will turn out some really excellent journalism, and CASE will be saved from extinction. We'll have our jobs. You'll have your raise. I'll still have my health insurance, which also covers my kids, and maybe I'll get out of that shit-house apartment. If we expose Alessandra now, everybody loses."

"Hold on a minute," Devon said. He opened two more bottles of liquor from the refrigerator, poured them into the glass, swallowed the contents, then lay down on the bed.

"Clark, would you still say that if *Walden* weren't in trouble, and we weren't desperate to save our jobs?"

The answer came through quick, harsh and loud. "Don't give me bullshit! I don't know what the hell I'd say. What did Alessandra say about it?"

"She left that decision to me."

"She told you that?"

"I left Alessandra in the hospital where she just had surgery for a malignant brain tumor. She'll be dead in two months. She suspected she had the tumor. That's why she wanted us to do the story on CASE so quickly."

Andrews' silence seemed to last forever. Then he almost shouted in disbelief.

"Jesus Christ, she's fucking dying for CASE! And you're going to rat her out?"

That was the question Devon had been struggling with since leaving Ellie Jenkins' violent, drug-infested building. Until now, however, that question had been professional integrity versus expediency. Now it was about the woman he knew he loved and the organization she would go to any length to protect. He made his decision.

"Let's keep quiet, Clark. I don't know if that's right or wrong. I'll be in New York tomorrow. Don't pick me up."

Devon broke the connection without saying goodbye. He had one more phone call to make before leaving Los Angeles. He punched the number on his cell phone and waited.

"Hello."

"Officer Aruba, this is Devon Emmanuel. I saw the *Señora* a couple of hours ago."

"*Señor* Emmanuel…"

"I have bad news, sir. The *Señora* has a tumor in her brain."

"*Señor* Emmanuel…"

"It's incurable, sir. The prognosis…"

"*Señor* Emmanuel…*Señora* Gittleman *está muerta*."

CHAPTER 52

" Just stay on the path to where it divides, Mr. Emmanuel. Fifth row, fifth grave on the left. You'll see the roses. Someone sends them every week. They just put fresh ones on the grave this morning. You can't miss it."

Devon thanked the woman behind the counter of the cemetery office. He started to leave, then turned and pointed to an item on a small shelf.

"I'd like to buy a pack of those pebbles, please."

He tucked the packet into his shirt pocket and began wandering the path. It was hot, and Devon was glad he'd worn a short-sleeve shirt and light pants, and was grateful for the shadows cast by the old pepper trees. The path split, and he stayed obediently left.

Eventually a pink headstone came into view, its base adorned with white roses. He stopped, took a deep breath, exhaled, then began cutting across graves.

It had been almost three years since he had left Alessandra's bedside, but the emotions running through him were nearly as painful as they had been on that dreadful day of her death. As he stood in front of her grave, his eyes fell on an adjacent black headstone.

He read the inscription, gave a little smile of recognition, then whispered, "Hello, Jake. Guess we finally meet. Alessandra described you as a hell of a man. She loved you to the bottom of her soul. I guess that's why I was so jealous of you."

Devon gazed across the rolling landscape to let his emotions settle. In the distance, the sun angled over low mountains, and skyscrapers were visible through the haze. When he turned back toward the graves, his sadness returned. He opened the pack of pebbles and placed one on top of Jake's headstone.

"Forgive the monologue, Jake, but your wife said speaking aloud to graves was excellent therapy for troubled souls. At the moment, mine falls into that category. Want to hear something absurd? You're dead, I'm living, and I'm still jealous of you. I fell in love with your wife in less than ten days. That picture of you two at the Grand Canyon is still etched in my brain. I'd give a year's life to have been you when that photo was taken – walking the trails, laughing, arguing, then making love in some cabin."

Devon sat down at the foot of Alessandra's grave and wrapped his arms around his bent knees. He was silent for a moment, then chose a pebble from the pack and tossed it against her headstone.

"Pink Italian marble. Nice touch. Complements Jake's black marble."

He picked at the grass, then looked again at Alessandra's headstone.

"I apologize for not going to your funeral. Even the thought of going was too painful for me. I almost didn't come today, but I was in L.A. plugging your book. Didn't seem right to leave without seeing you. I'm still trying to get used to the fact that you're...not here."

He was about to speak again when he was struck by the absurdity of what he was doing.

It's stupid to sit here and talk to her grave. You've been talking to her for three years, for Christ's sake. Put a pebble on her headstone and leave.

Devon tried to stand but suddenly felt as if a hundred-pound weight were pushing him down. He eased back onto the ground, and the weight slowly dissipated. Exhausted, he lay back on his elbows to rest.

His mind roamed over the three years since Alessandra's death, the events crammed into a kaleidoscope of memory. His divorce, the fear that he had emotionally scarred his children, the shock and apprehension when both David and Sarah chose to live with him. The inadequacy he felt on becoming the person most responsible for parenting and his surprise at the pleasure it afforded him. Sonja's willingness to be a weekend mother, and the amazement of both parents that this reconfiguration of family life led to her building a stronger relationship with the children. He remembered his relief as he watched the kids become happier teenagers.

His thoughts turned to the exhausting months helping Andrews restructure *Walden,* while sifting through Alessandra's life and writing on the book. He revisited the anxiety he had felt after leaving his job at *Walden* to finish the manuscript and help publicize it – his fear the book wouldn't sell and he'd be penniless with two children to raise. He looked again at the pink headstone.

"I wrote the story of your life, Alessandra. The whole megillah. Things you told me and stuff I discovered after you...after you died. I dug into your past with a vengeance. When I'd start pounding away on the computer, I could feel your presence. The book is selling like mad. Since I knew you'd ask, yes, I'm giving a slice of my royalties to CASE."

Devon tried to continue speaking, but his vocal cords felt as if they were being ripped out. Sobs came, tears poured, and his chest felt like it wanted to expel his heart. When his tears were finally exhausted, he sat on the grave wondering what to say next. Somehow, he felt comfortable in this lingering, one-sided conversation, as if Alessandra were alive and they were sipping tea and catching up on old times.

"Remember Judge Wexler? Things went the way you said they would. He got three years in a cushy prison. It didn't even have fences. He was paroled in a year and now has a high-paying job with a developer.

"Oh! Sister Mary Alice...little nun who helped you when you were locked in that room...she was given a major award in Dublin for her work in the education of indigent children. I wrote and asked for a phone interview and she granted it. Mary Alice is very old now, but she remembered you and Luisa. She was sad about your deaths but happy when she learned you had held an important position in American society. I told her about Luisa breaking Sister Doreen's leg. She said she'd pray for them both. I'd put money on her smiling when she said it."

Devon gazed at the white roses he sent weekly to be placed on the grave.

"You lied to me, Alessandra. And I judged you for it. I was terribly hurt. But I've come to understand that I was the one who betrayed people with a lie. I ambled through a life divested of meaning...as a father, a husband, even as a writer, waiting for the perfect moment, that perfect moment of validation of my manhood and talent. You never held back. You gave life everything you had. Gave your all for the people you loved. I guess there's such a thing as a virtuous lie. Yours was virtuous anyway; my lies were just cowardly."

Devon's eyes wandered aimlessly, stopping abruptly at the top of Alessandra's headstone. He hadn't put a pebble on top! As he reached forward to place the pebble, he took a closer look at the inscription. Apparently, the Hispanic community of Los Angeles had decided to make sure everyone understood this was no ordinary Anglo grave. This was the grave of a person of great significance, and they requested in their own subtle way that all in its presence show proper respect.

ALESSANDRA ANGELINA ASENCIO
MATREONI GITTLEMAN
AUGUST 12, 1936 - JULY 25, 2010
BELOVED WIFE OF JACOB GITTLEMAN
BELOVED DEFENDER OF HISPANIC WOMEN
La Virgen de Guadalupe vea sobre ti, como ha visto sobre nosotros.
Estarás en nuestros corazones para siempre. Siempre estaremos
agradecidos.

Devon didn't understand all the words, but his heart understood. He thought about the little nonprofit Alessandra's spirit still animated.

"I was just at CASE. The place is jumping. They have a young director. The women of CASE selected her. I talked to Mr. Aruba, the security guard. He said she was a real firecracker. Apparently, she doesn't take crap from anybody. That should make you happy."

Devon put the pebble atop the headstone.

"*Walden* had more reaction to your story than to any in its history, Alessandra. Pledges flooded in for CASE. You'd be amazed at the people who wanted to be seen as having been your champion. Politicians, prosecutors, judges, ministers, heads of granting agencies that never gave you a dime – all of them claim you as their personal heroine."

Devon chuckled. "Your obit ran all over the country. It was great. I think they got all their information from my article. If you had remained tight with the Church, I think you could've pulled off sainthood. Pretty good for a tough old broad from Bensonhurst, huh?"

Devon felt another crying jag coming on and quit speaking. He breathed deeply and gathered himself. As he stood in front of the headstone, the quiet of the peaceful place made him aware of the closeness he still felt for Alessandra, a closeness he knew would never leave him.

"You taught me something so valuable, Alessandra. It's not enough just to go through life. You have to be willing to fight for the people you love and the things that matter to you. You have to be willing to sacrifice not only your time and energy, but the comforts that come from society's approval. I miss you, Alessandra. I always will."

He stood silently for a moment, almost hating to leave. He heard the chimes of a clock tower in the distance and checked his watch.

"Finally," he said, looking back at Jake's headstone. "You're finally on the hour."

He patted the top of the pink monument and turned to leave.

"Shalom, Alessandra."

The End

CPSIA information can be obtained
at www.ICGtesting.com
Printed in the USA
FSHW01n1617231018
53091FS